SECR
MY
FATHER
KEPT

Rachel Givney is a writer and filmmaker originally from Sydney, Australia and currently based in Melbourne. She has worked on *Offspring*, *The Warriors*, *McLeod's Daughters*, *Rescue: Special Ops* and *All Saints*. Her films have been official selections at the Sydney Film Festival, Flickerfest and many other festivals. Her first novel, *Jane in Love*, was published in 2020.

Also by the author

Jane in Love

RACHEL GIVNEY

SECRETS MY FATHER KEPT

MICHAEL JOSEPH
an imprint of
PENGUIN BOOKS

MICHAEL JOSEPH

UK | USA | Canada | Ireland | Australia
India | New Zealand | South Africa | China

Michael Joseph is part of the Penguin Random House group of companies
whose addresses can be found at global.penguinrandomhouse.com.

Penguin
Random House
Australia

First published by Michael Joseph, 2021

Cover design by Louisa Maggio © Penguin Random House Australia Pty Ltd
Cover photography: woman by Mark Owen/Trevillion; planes by Travel_Master/Shutterstock
Author photo by Tegan Louise
Typeset in Sabon by Midland Typesetters, Australia

Printed and bound in Australia by Griffin Press, part of Ovato, an accredited
ISO AS/NZS 14001 Environmental Management Systems printer

A catalogue record for this
book is available from the
National Library of Australia

NATIONAL
LIBRARY
OF AUSTRALIA

ISBN 978 0 14379 410 3

penguin.com.au

MIX
Paper from
responsible sources
FSC® C009448

To all the mothers and all the doctors that I know.

1
FLOORBOARDS

Krakow, Poland, February 1939

As Marie prepared to break into her father's bedroom, she felt a little pool of guilt well up inside her for betraying him. Her patriarch was a respected man in town who kept to himself and attended church eight times a week (every morning and twice on Sundays). He possessed no interests beyond the rapture of the Blessed Sacrament, and studying the reproductive habits of bacteria. He did not deserve such disrespect from his only daughter. But unfortunately, the burning desire to find something – anything – about her mother had become irrepressible for Marie, and that Wednesday afternoon, as the rain made lovely fat spatters on the cobblestones outside, was as good a time as any to betray him.

People only see what they want to see. That's what Marie's father always told her. He rarely gave out fatherly advice; this was his one dabble with cliché. If you only acknowledged the narrowest purpose of a person or object, the world was a far smaller and less interesting place.

She wasn't exactly sure what her father meant or why he liked to say it, but she would make use of this phrase now to break into his bedroom. She retrieved a hairpin from her blonde hair. She had no experience as a cat burglar, but Olaf, a local delinquent who caught the same tram as Marie on the days he chose to attend school, had bragged to her earlier that week that one could pick a lock with a piece of thin metal. 'Stick it in and jiggle,' he'd boasted as he coughed on a cigarillo. Marie held up her strip of brass and smiled. Most people who owned a hairpin saw only an object for holding back their tresses. Marie saw something else. A key.

She had little expectation of what she might find inside her papa's chamber, but she knew there had to be *something*. Letters, or a forwarding address for her mother? Her father locked no other rooms in the house, not even his study, where his important research notes lay. Nobody locked a door with nothing valuable inside.

As she climbed the stairs to her father's quarters, she heard the familiar sound of what could only be described as thwacking beginning outside. Mrs Nowak, who lived next door, was stacking sandbags again, one on top of the other. The portly woman, whose height did not reach a metre and a half, maintained an obsession that Mr Hitler would invade in the next day or two. She had warned her neighbours, her friends and whoever else would listen about this imminent visit from *Der Führer* for the past three years. Everyone shook their heads, proclaiming her insane, but she continued her task. She was building a wall of sandbags around her front door, to barricade herself inside for the night – along with the other tenants of the building, whether they wanted it or not. She performed this ceremony daily, adding more bags to the pile as she located more sand. Today's rain did not stop her; neither would a hurricane. But although the sandbags slapping outside unnerved her, Marie had other tasks to attend to right now. She arrived at her father's bedroom and bent down to inspect the door.

The lock sat within the doorknob itself, a modern contraption. No other doorknob in the house contained a lock, so her father had likely installed this one himself. She removed a second pin from her hair; according to Olaf, the aspiring criminal, lock picking required two. A piece of hair, set free by the pin's removal, fell into her face, covering her left eye and fuzzing her vision. She blew it away, then tucked it behind her ear. She inserted the pins – one into the base of the lock, then the second directly above it – and commenced with Olaf's instruction to jiggle them.

She jiggled and jiggled again. She jiggled so much it made her elbow hurt. Nothing happened. The doorknob felt looser as she did it, but the lock itself did not budge. What to do? She glanced at the clock at the end of the hall. The hands read almost six o'clock. Her father would arrive home soon. She would have to abandon her mission. She cursed herself and cursed the hairpins, which had promised her the world; she cursed Olaf for his defective advice; and she cursed Mrs Nowak too, who kept stacking her sandbag wall outside. She'd try again another time, when she had more than minutes to complete her task. She withdrew her hand to remove the pins from the lock. One pin fell into her hand. The other, however, didn't release itself from the door. Marie pulled again, but the lock had ensnared the metal in its jaws.

She planted her feet, gripped the pin and wrenched it with all her strength. She flew backwards onto the floor with the effort, and the pin came free. Unfortunately, so did the doorknob. The entire structure, with the hairpin still wedged in the lock, now lay in Marie's hand. A jagged hole yawned in the door where the knob had once stood.

She glanced at the hallway clock: the hands read two minutes past six. She expected her father home at 6.14, and his nature did not accommodate lateness.

Marie considered the possibility that her father wouldn't notice what she'd done. He worked as a surgeon at the city hospital and his pastimes included studying minuscule organisms under a microscope. The chances of him noticing a ten-centimetre hole in his bedroom door neared one hundred per cent.

She was perched to position the knob back in its place when the door creaked open, and she caught a glimpse of the interior of her father's quarters. A shard of afternoon light shone into the room through a window on the far side. She'd imagined her father's chamber many times. Sometimes the floorboards creaked as she lay in bed at night, and she'd imagine what he did in there. Did he write secret letters to her mother, begging her to return? She checked her watch. Before she could talk herself out of it, Marie darted inside. She'd snatch a quick glance, then repair the door.

Marie gazed upon the room. Spotless wooden boards covered the floor. A perfume of carbolic soap rose from the linens and a pound of starch seemed to imprison the sheets. A pillow rested uneasily at the bed's head; from its texture it seemed her father had stuffed it with stones. No dust besmirched the windowsills, no dirt befouled the floorboards: 'a hospital room dressed by a vindictive matron' best described the space. She felt disappointed, but also relieved. She'd secretly wondered if she might discover a den of iniquity in her father's bedchamber; that he actually concealed an altar for devil worship in there, or hoarded files from his missions as a double agent for Stalin. Instead she found that her father behaved in his private spaces as he did in the public ones; as a man of few pleasures, who darned Marie's school blouses and baked her bread, as conventional behind closed doors as he appeared to the world, a steadying presence who it would not be unjust to call boring. His propriety blazed in contrast to the apparently wanton behaviour of her mother, who, from the evidence presented, had left them for some selfish and lascivious reason of her own.

Her father slept in a single bed. A solitary photograph graced the bedside table, Marie as a six-year-old smiling from a brown leather frame. If she possessed any reserves in her body where more guilt could nest, it did so now. Marie appeared to be the only woman in her father's life, and now she'd broken into his bedroom.

A dresser stood in dull redwood. She opened the top drawer and sifted through the socks and underwear that sat in two straight lines. Marie felt funny viewing her father's socks rolled up; she'd only ever seen them on his feet. The wardrobe yielded more stiffly starched clothing and a spare back brace, which he wore to correct a childhood scoliosis. Two pairs of leather shoes sat in the footlocker, polished to a modest shine.

She replaced all the items she'd moved. The task presented little difficulty as the mathematical neatness of the previous positioning encouraged proper placement. She left everything as she'd found it. Marie wondered why her father bothered locking his door. Nothing existed there worth hiding.

But then her foot struck a floorboard it had not trodden on before and an irksome creak rang out across the room. She stopped. She struck the floorboard again with her foot. The wooden plank felt loose.

She dashed downstairs to retrieve a butter knife to prise up the wood. The board lifted. She placed it to one side, then squinted into the floor cavity. An extended space lay below her. Darkness obscured her view. Her breath increased. She plunged her hand down into the space, where warm dry air prickled her skin. She grappled around, her head and body above, her limb submerged in the hole.

She reached her arm around in a circle, patting the ground. Her fingers recoiled as she touched the cotton sponginess of a spider's web. She retracted her arm in horror to see her hand covered in white threads.

She wiped her hand clean on her skirt, gritted her teeth and plunged it under the floor once more. She winced, convinced the web's owner lurked somewhere down there, and was about to pull her hand back again when it landed on a square object. She tapped it several times, convinced herself of its status as inanimate and pulled it up into the room.

She inspected it from all sides. A small jewellery box of faded maroon velvet sat in her hand. Her heart thumped in her chest: a woman owned this box.

She went to open it, then hesitated. Did she want to know what lay inside? The floorboard, the lock – everything meant more now. Then a new sound rang out downstairs, one that terrified her with its familiarity. A key, a real one, entered a different lock. She heard her father open the front door and step inside their house.

'Marie?' he called.

Marie felt her blood chill. She replaced the floorboard and darted from the room, placing the maroon box in her pocket.

The doorknob still lay on the floor. She gasped in horror. It consisted of two pieces actually, which she'd not noticed before. The first piece was the doorknob that faced outwards, the second was the corresponding knob from the inside of the door.

'Marie?' her father called again. She needed to say something.

'Coming, Papa,' she declared in a bright voice.

'I want to show you something.' The sound of a clanging pot rose up the stairs; he was doing something in the kitchen. Marie silently begged him to stay there.

'I will be down in a fraction, Papa,' she assured him. The odds didn't appear in her favour that she'd emerge from this unscathed. A hole gaped in her father's bedroom door. No reasonable explanation existed for its presence other than the true one.

Marie imagined what would follow when her father discovered she'd broken into his private quarters. She enjoyed a warmth of relationship with her father that few girls in town boasted. Dominik Karski cared for and nurtured his daughter. He obsessed himself with her nutrition and fitness to a degree that went beyond professional pride and bordered on irrational concern. Whenever she complained of a headache or feigned an illness, he would fetch his stethoscope and analyse her breath sounds and heart rhythm for countless minutes until even Marie grew bored. He would pronounce the diagnosis, as always, that she was in full health, and he kept the record of her pristine vital signs in a binder. She imagined

6

the look on his face if he discovered her breaking into his bedroom. Her gentle and generous father. He would not show anger, but something far worse. He would look disappointed. She shuddered at the thought of it; she could not let that happen.

She collected the pieces of doorknob and examined them. Two screws hung loosely from one. She had not undone the lock; instead she'd removed the entire structure from the door. She repositioned the two knobs back in place as best she could and began to screw them together with the butter knife.

'They finished St Bartholomew. At long last,' her father called again from downstairs. Marie started and dropped the knife. The pots downstairs stopped clanging. She swallowed. As he continued talking about the church, his soft voice grew louder, the soundwaves shortened. Her father was coming up the stairs. Marie's hands sweated and she cursed; she had only managed one screw. She collected the knife and began twisting the second into place, but then her father arrived at the top of the stairs. Marie pocketed the screw instead and jumped up.

Her father wasn't looking at her, only at the pamphlet in his hand. He offered it to her. 'Here.' The flyer declared the completion of a window in the church she and her father attended. A photograph showed St Bartholomew being flayed alive in stained-glass glory, his executioner peeling strips from his body with a knife. Despite his skin coming away from him in bloody scrolls, like bark curling from a tree, St Bartholomew's face remained serene, looking upwards to God with a beatific smile. Marie strived to emulate such composure now.

'Hallelujah,' she said, stifling her puffed breathing. 'They took enough time,' she added.

'It might have taken even longer,' her father replied. He had sat on the committee to ensure the window's completion, attending summits with bureaucrats and priests. She studied his face for any recognition of her crime, but his gaze ran solely across the picture of his flayed saint. His voice remained at its usual soft, calm pitch. 'What is that?' he asked, pointing at Marie's side. Her stomach churned. The moment had arrived; he had caught her. But he was reaching higher than her pocket to lift her sleeve.

'Strawberry jam,' Marie answered, concealing her relief. She had wiped her mouth on her shirt cuff earlier. 'I'm sorry, Papa.'

Her father told her dinner would be served at seven o'clock, like every night, and as he expressed a desire to soak the blouse with the strawberry stain overnight, she returned to her bedroom to change.

Her heart pounded in her chest. How she had got away with it, she didn't know. She waited for her father to stroll inside and accuse her of breaking and entering. He would notice the screw still missing. Or something else she hadn't put back in its correct place. But her father never returned. She sighed and undressed.

She retrieved the maroon box, which had been burning a hole in her pocket the whole time her father had spoken to her. She'd find a way to return it to her papa's room at some point. But for now, she cared only what lay inside it. She studied the box once more, turning it in her hand, then tried to open it. The lid was sealed shut, not with glue, but something else. She pulled again, firmer this time, and the lid came free.

Inside lay a length of hair.

She lifted it out. It resembled her own yellow-blonde hair, but felt too long and thick to have come from her own head; her hair had never reached such lengths. The hair came from no child's head at all; it bore no gentle little strands like a parent might save from a baby's first haircut. Instead it consisted of a thick bunch of blonde, which the owner had plaited into a heavy braid, like rope, and someone had rolled it into a coil and stuffed it in the box. This hair came from a grown woman's head.

Her stomach turned at finding a piece of someone secreted under her father's floorboards. Hair disembodied from the head, even a baby's, had something disgusting about it, and although she felt this revulsion now, she couldn't help but touch and smell it. She revelled in her horror, likening it to the desire to roll in mud or smell milk that looked rancid, just to feel it, to possess knowledge of things previously unknown. She rubbed the hair between her fingers. The strands surrendered to her touch and separated; dust and grit fell to her lap. A glorious whiff of rosewater blessed the air. The sweet, fresh-petal smell took her back to the last time she'd seen her mother – she remembered now, her mother had smelled of rosewater! One of the only details Marie possessed of her matriarch. She gasped as she forged the connection.

This hair belonged to her mother.

It felt as though her mother sat alive in her hands. If Marie smelled the hair again, she might hear her laugh. She suddenly felt unformed, a half-person, with a chunk of herself cleaved from her body. Marie wrote with her left hand, her father with his right. Who was this left-handed person who had given half their genes to Marie, who had created fifty per cent of her? Marie's fingers were shaped differently to her father's; her nails ran to oblongs and elegant half-moons, while her father's sat square and right-angled in the nail bed. Did she have her mother's fingers? And there were other, deeper things than fingernails and handedness. Plainly Marie did not resemble her father, in looks or character. Where Dominik never raised his voice, Marie took pleasure in shouting. Marie loved to laugh, while her good and joyless father never smiled. Dominik existed as a deep pool of water, a thousand-year-old lake whose surface was never disturbed. Marie lived like a fire, burning its way through a forest. Sometimes she looked at Dominik and wondered if she knew him at all. She longed to meet the person who had given her their fire.

Marie had not yet spent two years on the earth when her mother went away. Her father had maintained the story for sixteen years that her mother had left for reasons unknown. He never said anything more on the topic, and any type of prodding shut him down further. Why had her father kept her mother's hair all these years? She had never considered him a romantic. Did he pine for her mother quietly, privately? Did he still love her?

She wiped the little wetness that had formed in one eye and forced herself to fold the hair back in the box. She pushed the lid down to reseal it as best as she could. She'd open the box again three times that night to smell and fondle the strands. The next morning, she returned the hair to its place under her father's floorboards while he worked, properly fixing the door she'd damaged as she locked it again behind her.

Marie had gone into her father's bedroom hoping for some morsel of information that would have allowed her to say to the neighbours that her mother left for a virtuous reason, that they could remove the stain from Marie's character that her mother's absence had made. But now, faced with this real piece of her mother, instead of satisfying the craving to gain propriety in front of the townsfolk, she had created a new one a hundred times worse. A cave of longing had opened up in her; she'd set a monster loose. The discovery of the hair – so macabre and strange, so unexpected – changed things. She could never go back to the way things were. She now put aside her concern for finding the reason her mother had left and focused on actually locating her instead.

If Marie Karska knew then how much she would come to learn over that year of 1939, she might have wished for something different. But for now, she felt confident of one thing only: she would not stop until she learned what had happened to her mother.

2

BACTERICIDE

Dominik Karski hadn't lost a patient in almost six months, which likely rivalled a record at the hospital where he worked. Krakow, where he lived, garnered fame and notoriety for its high death toll, infested as it was with all the common plagues and maladies, as well as several of the exotic ones. Not to mention that a proportion of the population comprised farmers who seemed determined to fight with their harvesting equipment. Yet Dr Karski had gone 174 days without witnessing the loss of a single soul in his care. It was an extraordinary run of good luck; the nurses even ran a pool, placing bets on how long his winning streak would last. But as he looked down at the child in the bed and the panicking mother beside him, he decided someone would collect that jackpot soon.

The boy wilted into the hospital bed. His mother mopped his brow with a flannel cloth, hand shaking. Nurse Emilia had summoned Dominik from his rounds and dragged him to the children's ward. 'We supposed you might take a look, Doctor,' she muttered. She didn't meet his eye, embarrassed perhaps to end his champion's run.

Dominik had arrived at the boy's bedside and pushed his spectacles back up the bridge of his nose. As the child remained supine in the bed, Dominik crouched down so their eyes were level. 'What is your name, young man?'

The boy's head lolled as he turned to face him. 'Daniel,' he replied in a lugubrious voice, his trachea wall thickened with mucus. A foul odour rose from the child's lips as he spoke. Dominik didn't recoil at the stench; instead he leaned closer and inhaled, to catalogue the exact nature of the infection.

'May I listen to your lungs, Daniel?' The child nodded. Dominik retrieved his stethoscope from around his neck, drew open the child's gown and stole a glimpse at the boy's torso. A giant distended stomach ballooned outwards from a bird-like frame. The collarbones jutted out under a layer of tissue-thin skin, the clavicles stabbing upwards like the spikes of a tent. Their shapes reminded Dominik of an earlier time in his life, which he felt grateful to have departed.

Dominik warmed the stethoscope's bell with his breath, then placed it under the child's shirt and asked him to inhale. Daniel did so with ease but winced as he breathed out again. Dominik listened to the sounds. The breath of a healthy human echoes and whooshes, displaying a clear passage of air through the lungs. This child's breath made no such sound; it crackled, like tyres rolling over an unsealed road. One never appreciates the joy of an easy breath until it's taken away. Each lungful for this boy would feel like breathing through a wet cloth.

Every clinician braces themselves for signs of dying, always the same. The breath quickens and grows shallow, the limbs flop. The bowels loosen. And one more sign, something less tangible, unique to mammals: the eyes gaze at nothing, signalling a general surrendering of the flesh, a mood change, an agreement that life is prepared to leave. Contrary to popular belief, most dying people go easily; they express no rage, just acceptance. But in this child, each item in the shopping list of death was accounted for except one. Instead of gazing upon nothing, awaiting the end happily, this child seemed to refuse to go. The little boy stared back at Dominik with eyes not soft and accepting, but intense and rebellious, like a pair of navy marbles, their colour as rich as bluebirds' feathers. They darted back and forth over Dominik's face, staring at him wildly, desperately. He showed no willingness to go to the other side. The boy looked past Dominik, over his shoulder, as though Death itself stood there, with its hooded cloak, waving its scythe, and the boy stared back defiantly: *You won't take me today.* The child then turned back to Dominik and stared at him madly again, as if making a deal. *Help me*, he was saying. *Try anything.* This look in the child's eyes, so rare in these situations, so unnerving, made such an impression on Dominik that he found himself forced to act.

'Show me how you sit up, young man,' Dominik commanded.

Daniel looked at him, unsure. 'He is tired, Doctor,' his mother said.

Dominik knew it seemed a paradoxical request, to ask a dying person to sit up. 'I know the effort is large, but you are a strong boy. I guess you run fast and jump high?'

The boy agreed in earnest at the assertion of his athleticism and attempted to pull himself up to a sitting position. His skinny arms wobbled and shook, he sweated at the exertion, and failed. He poked his tongue out of the side of his mouth and tried again. He locked his elbows with determination and finally lifted himself up. He turned to Dominik for his approval.

'Good man,' Dominik said. The child's breathing improved in an instant; a cleaner, drier breath sound replaced the heavy wet one. 'Nurse. Fowler's position.' Nurse Emilia rushed over and cranked the bedhead to 45 degrees, to enable the boy to remain upright.

The boy's mother, whom he'd heard Nurse Emilia call Ruth, smiled with joy. Dominik allowed himself a small nod at this progress but then turned back to the patient, for this solution would expire. The infectious fluid that now pooled at the base of his lungs would continue to grow and, left untreated, overwhelm the organ. This patient would drown from the inside.

'There is no point, the case is terminal,' a man announced behind them. Dominik recognised the voice and resisted the urge to sigh. Dr Igor Wolanski strolled towards him wearing a look of outrage, a vein in his forehead throbbing. 'He has influenza, advanced,' he said. Daniel's mother shuddered at the word, as though he'd sworn or blasphemed. A Polish generation had succumbed to this plague. 'It's killing him,' Dr Wolanski added, unnecessarily. 'There is nothing to be done. Why do you sit him up? He needs to lie down so he may die in peace. This is my ward, and my patient. Go back to your own department, Dominik.'

Dominik worked as a surgeon, but increasingly, his help was sought with infections. A sutured wound could become septic in hours if not managed properly; as such, he had become something of an expert in the field, and nurses from the infections ward – any ward, really – frequently asked him to look at their patients. He often found himself inspecting the staphylococcus- and streptococcus-riddled patients in the ward for venereal diseases, the pulmonary ward and, occasionally, the children's ward.

Dr Wolanski was the alleged expert here – he was a paediatrician – and so Dominik was walking on his turf. Another doctor might have expressed gratitude for the help. Not Dr Wolanski. This would end in a fight.

'What has been administered?' Dominik asked, ignoring Dr Wolanski and addressing the nurse.

'Tincture of laudanum. Four drops,' she replied.

Dominik said nothing. Such a quantity of opium would fell a grown man.

'The laudanum stopped his coughing,' Dr Wolanski said, his voice strident. 'And his agony. No child should be in pain. I refuse to justify my decisions, Dominik,' he added, doing exactly that.

'Pain is helpful,' Dominik replied with a nod and a calmer tone. 'It tells us something is wrong. Coughing is important, too. It evacuates toxins from the body.' He spoke in the soft tone he always adopted with Dr Wolanski, keen not to inflame him. 'I agree with your former statement, but with respect, not the latter ones.'

Dr Wolanski glared at Dominik.

'Perhaps we could have this conversation in private.' Dominik flicked his gaze to the boy's mother, Ruth, who watched the discussion eagerly.

'Absolutely not,' Dr Wolanski replied. 'My diagnosis and treatment are correct. If you lack knowledge on this subject, that's your concern.'

'Very well.' Dominik pushed his glasses up and continued the conversation at the child's bedside. 'Your patient has influenza, advanced. But the influenza isn't what's killing him. And there is something to be done.'

The other doctor laughed. 'You say influenza is not deadly? That the disease that felled a quarter of our young soldiers, our strongest and bravest in the Great War, does not kill?' He often made speeches like this, aligning himself with statistics and historical events, as though he were not a doctor but a politician, addressing a crowd, auditioning for public office.

'Influenza is rarely deadly,' Dominik replied. This statement usually provoked scoffs and today proved no exception. Dr Wolanski hooted and tutted while the boy's mother looked at Dominik as though he were mad. Even Daniel raised an eyebrow at him from the sick bed. 'This boy will not die of influenza. But he is dying.'

Dr Wolanski crossed his arms. 'What will he die of, then?'

'Pneumonia.' Dominik looked around. No one said anything, so he continued. 'The influenza virus has attacked and weakened his immune system. Opportunistic bacteria have seized their chance and established a small village in his lungs.'

Dr Wolanski waved his hand. 'Very well, then, he has pneumonia, too. Who cares, pneumonia kills as much as flu. No pharmacological treatment exists for it. He will soon be *tot*.'

Dominik bristled at the German word, which Dr Wolanski had a habit of peppering into arguments. The man admired current German policies on medicine, some of which one might describe as antisocial. 'I have a treatment for pneumonia,' Dominik replied.

'I beg your pardon?' Dr Wolanski said.

'A new medicine.' Dominik gazed at the floor. 'I made it.'

Dr Wolanski now bellowed with laughter. 'There's your saviour, madam!' he said, turning to Ruth. 'A mad scientist making potions in his privy. Don't listen to him, there's nothing we can do. Don't let your boy go through unnecessary pain.'

Dominik shook his head. 'Forgive me, Doctor, but if we continue along the current course, the child will die.'

Dr Wolanski continued to address the child's mother. 'The choice is yours, my dear woman. Continue the treatment prescribed by your doctor, which is the same palliation every respectable man has performed for decades. Or let this madman inflict more pain with his tonic.'

Dominik watched her as she looked back and forth between the two doctors, trying to choose. Based on looks alone, the decision was obvious. Dominik would never make it as a paediatrician; he knew no jokes and could sour milk with his face. His frame ran to the small and forceful; he wore cumbersome glasses with heavy frames. He also never, ever smiled. He might be a man mothers actually warned their offspring about, a fairytale villain, a child snatcher.

His colleague, on the other hand, possessed a superficial jolliness; if you didn't know him well, you would take him for a children's saviour. Dr Wolanski's cheeks bloomed with a merry rosiness, and his face made the shape of an almost perfect circle. His arms and frame explored only pleasant, roly-poly dimensions, and fluffy blond hair blessed his head. If he grew out his beard, he'd make an excellent Saint Nicholas. Based purely on looks, it came down to a choice between the child snatcher or Santa Claus, and Dominik wouldn't blame anyone for selecting the latter. Unfortunately for the boy's mother, Santa was also euthanising her child with opium, while the child snatcher would at least try to save his life.

Daniel's mother looked to Dr Wolanski, then to Dominik and back again. 'Thank you, Doctor,' she said, turning to Dr Wolanski. She spoke faintly and humbly. 'We can never repay you for the service you have done.' Dominik recognised the voice, the expedient tone of a woman. 'I am but a cobbler's daughter,' she said. 'I'd like to try the magic potion.'

A beetroot shade enveloped Dr Wolanski's face. He inhaled, exhaled, then nodded, as though a tempest had surged through him, then subsided as quickly as it came. He acted like this often, with a distracted mind, growing obsessed with something, then moving onto the next thing as though it was nothing. 'You poor woman. Still, you know not what you do. I pray for your child's soul.' Dr Wolanski turned to mutter to Dominik in a terse voice, 'So be it. The child's death will be on your hands.' He then spoke to the nurse. 'Sister, note that I have washed my hands of this case, that under cause of death on the child's certificate, it should be marked: murder, courtesy of Dr Karski.'

Dominik considered mentioning no space was normally provided for the murderer's name on a death certificate, but he held his tongue. Dr Wolanski left them, blundering down the corridor, tripping on a steel cart containing medical instruments on his way past, letting out a metallic crash that echoed through the ward.

Dominik, in all fairness, had two advantages over Dr Wolanski in treating the child. First, he'd seen many similar cases before, long ago. Second, for the past eleven years, Dominik had conducted a secret love affair with bacteria, the new animals that were smaller than a pin's head but could fell an elephant. He admired their power, and he studied their curious movements across walls and tissues, down arteries and into veins. He even spoke to them sometimes in his laboratory, when the nurses had gone home. 'You're a clever one,' he'd say to a gram-positive staphylococcus cell.

The nurse leaned in. 'What are you going to do, Dr Karski?'

'I will give him some medicine,' Dominik replied shakily.

'That you made yourself?'

Dominik nodded.

'From what did you make it?'

'Mould.' He cleared his throat.

'Mould?' the nurse repeated, as if by mere repetition it could become untrue. 'You are going to inject the child with *mould*?' She continued to stare at him.

'Fetch the vial with the yellow label from the cool chest. Draw up six grains.' He looked at the child's size and paused. 'Eight grains. Twenty-six gauge.'

Nurse Emilia sighed and headed down the corridor.

Dominik had read the Scotsman Alexander Fleming's paper on how to kill bacteria using mould, along with surely every other doctor in Europe. Most had tossed it aside, but the paper had transfixed him. An old-fashioned scientist, who believed in *nulls verba* – 'take no one's word for it' – he'd tried the concept Fleming proposed. The first thing he discovered was that Fleming lacked skill in organic chemistry. The mould, when placed in the petri dish, hadn't killed the bacteria cell as the physician predicted. In some cases, it had even improved the bacteria's life expectancy. However, where Fleming may have fallen short with his counting of carbon molecules, Dominik had not. He'd remixed the solution and, on his twelfth attempt, his penicillium mould had killed the bacteria. Less an achievement of advanced science and more one of simple engineering: the mould had penetrated the cell wall, weakening it, and the cell had folded in on itself and died.

Dominik looked down at the boy's mother. No stockings covered her legs. She had a black space in her mouth where her left incisor should have been. 'I make no guarantee this will work, madam,' he said to her. 'This may very well kill your son.'

The missing tooth gave her a brittle quality, a hardness, like a battle-weary soldier who had seen one too many of their friends die. 'Will he die anyway?' she asked.

'Yes,' he replied.

The woman paused and wrapped her coat tighter. Its fabric appeared too thin for February. It was almost spring, but the ground had frosted overnight. Had she gone through winter in just this threadbare mantle? He heard her teeth chatter and imagined the sensation of feeling cold for months, of never getting warm. She met Dominik's gaze and seemed to interrogate him with her eyes the same way her son had, reaching inside him. Dominik pictured his own child then – he was a parent too. He understood what the woman would be going through in that moment; she was confronting the very real idea that she was about to lose her son and anticipating the pointlessness that might encompass her life afterwards. She would be a mother no longer. Dominik swallowed, feeling the burden of holding someone else's life in his hands. 'Do it,' she said finally, nodding. 'Give him the potion.'

Sister Emilia returned with the syringe. She waited towards the end of the hallway so that Dominik had to walk to her, leaving the mother and the boy in the bed. 'Have you seen this done before?' she asked him.

He looked at her. 'I have tried it. On a pig.'

'What was the result?'

He coughed. 'The animal passed away.' The nurse made a face as though she regretted her decision to refer the patient to Dominik. 'Though I couldn't say for certain the mould was the cause,' he added in a bright voice, attempting to reassure her. 'I draw no scientific conclusion from a study size of one hog.'

'Don't you think you should try it on a person before you give it to a child?'

Dominik sighed. 'A clinical trial would take months, Sister. The boy will die this afternoon, whether I give him the shot or not.' The nurse said nothing. He stared at her for a time, then sighed.

He took the syringe and walked around the corner into a treatment room, exposed a buttock, and inserted the needle into his own flesh. He depressed the plunger and his concoction dispersed itself under the subcutaneous layer, where the blood vessels would swallow it, then return it via the veins to his heart, which then would pump the noxious mould around his body, into every organ and cell. He returned to the nurse.

'What did you do?' she said, staring at the empty syringe.

'As commanded, I tried it on a person first before giving it to the child.'

She stared at him with wide eyes. 'What happens now?'

'Wait half an hour?' Dominik checked his watch. 'If it doesn't kill me in that time, administer half that dose to the boy.'

Sister Emilia checked her own watch, which hung from a chain at her breast. 'Give it an hour. You're larger than he.' She smiled. 'It might need longer to kill you than him.'

Dominik nodded and left the children's ward to resume his rounds. He checked in on a patient whose spleen he'd removed the day before, and a woman carrying a baby in the breech presentation who might require a caesarean section. As he examined her to see if the baby had turned, he imagined the mould he'd injected into himself moving through his body, entering every cell. He pictured the kind of mould one scrapes off bread, those rings of grey and green blooming outwards in fluffy clouds, now undulating through his bloodstream. After an hour he hadn't died, so he returned to the children's ward. Sister Emilia administered four grains of the penicillium mould to the boy under his instruction.

'And now?' the nurse asked.

'Now we wait,' Dominik replied. They both turned to watch the boy.

The child jerked upwards in a fit of coughing.

'What's happening?' screeched the child's mother. 'He's choking!'

'Doctor?' asked Sister Emilia accusingly. She looked at him like he'd killed the child already. 'Has the mould produced an adverse effect in the boy, but not in you?' The child took great anguished chokes of breath, his face turned red and he clawed at his throat, as though fighting off a ghost who strangled him.

Dominik shook his head. 'I don't think so.' He exposed the child's chest and listened once more with the stethoscope. 'It's not the penicillium. The laudanum has worn off – it suppressed his chest spasms, but his cough is returning. This is good.' The child spluttered. 'We must break up the sputum before he drowns in it.'

Sister Emilia knew what to do: she grabbed a basin. 'Spit!' she commanded. The child roused and looked at her as if to double-check the naughty order. The nurse nodded and childish impulse overrode pain. He spat into the bowl, a large, brown globule of phlegm. He ogled the slimy ball and grinned.

'Good man!' Dominik cried. The child puffed out his feeble, pleuritic chest with pride. 'Continue until you've coughed it all out.'

'Another one, then!' the nurse ordered the boy, as though she were a general dispensing an order to her toughest corporal. She patted him on the back firmly, in a rhythmical fashion, a marching beat.

The child gripped the basin. He hacked his lungs once more, longer and deeper this time. Another globule plopped into the basin. The child produced another ten spheres of green mingled with reddish, rust-coated brown over the hour.

Dominic went home to prepare dinner for his daughter, then returned to the hospital once she'd gone to bed. He arrived to find the child sleeping peacefully, his temperature reduced. When the first injection didn't kill him, Dominik ordered a second one, double the grains of last time, to be given at midnight. Dominik fetched the leather armchair from his office and slept at the nurses' station. The day matron woke him at seven.

'You'd better go see your patient, Doctor,' she told him, a hand on his shoulder. Dominik swallowed as he jogged neatly in small hurried steps, keen not to show panic to anyone. If the child was dead, work would need to be done, measurements altered; he'd need to retrace his steps. He arrived at the end of the corridor and rounded the corner. His speed made him skid across the floor as he landed at the end of the child's bed. The boy was sitting up drinking a cup of broth. His cheeks were flushed pink. Dominik sent up a small prayer of thanks.

The child skipped from the hospital four days later. He clasped a candied apple that Sister Emilia had given him, licking it with glee. One doctor in ten thousand had tried Fleming's technique across Europe. The American army was apparently developing something, as was the Wehrmacht. Over centuries, this bacteria had killed a billion people. Now, in his one-man laboratory, Dominik had created a way to stop it, using kitchen mould. *Antibiotics*, the Americans were calling them.

As they departed, the boy's mother had got up and walked to Dominik, then knelt before him on the floor, like a knight before a king. Patients turned in their beds to whisper at the indecorous sight.

'Please stand, madam,' Dominik said to her.

She shook her head and stayed on the floor, then removed a trinket fashioned from tin from around her neck and pressed it into his
hand. Two triangles, one upright, the other inverted, sat one on top
of the other, forming the Star of David. 'Whoever saves a single life is
considered to have saved the whole world,' she said to him. Dominik
recognised the quote from the Talmud; he had heard this said before.

Dominik cradled the star and brushed his thumb across the surface. Its cheap sheen glinted in the morning sun that shone through
the lead-framed windows of the ward. He tried to give it back to her,
but the woman refused with vehemence. 'My payment,' she said.
It would not cover a tenth of the child's medical bill.

Dominik nodded in reply, then helped the woman from the floor.
From her softly lined face, she looked about thirty, though she likely
was far younger. Her elbow stabbed him like a needle as he lifted her
arm; she probably weighed just 40 kilograms. 'I will work off the
rest of the debt,' she said.

'All is paid for, madam. Take your son home.'

Dominik accepted handshakes from staff for the life saved, and
congratulations from the nurses for retaining his winning streak,
then he retired to his office to quietly celebrate alone his having
saved a human life. He sank into his chair and savoured the feeling for a time, but then he found that in the quiet, his thoughts
turned to his own child, Marie, as they always seemed to do. He
had ended up in this place because of his daughter; he did all of
this for her. And then it crept in, the reminiscence of the act he'd
performed, the removal of Marie's mother from her child's life, all
those years ago. A familiar black feeling gripped him, so he adjusted
his glasses and turned to the window to shoo it away. He hated that
the memory of this event had found him now. On days like these,
when he returned one soul to the balance, he should be allowed to
say what he'd done fifteen years ago, that questionable deed he'd
committed, had been worth it.

3

MY TRAVELS IN GERMANY

Two weeks earlier, the Chief of Medicine – a fancy way to say the hospital's chief cutter and sewer – had revealed to Dominik that he was retiring at the end of the summer. It was a well-deserved departure; Professor Jerzy Maklewski was seventy-five and couldn't have served the city better. A gentleman surgeon of the old guard, the professor had a mind still unencumbered by dullness and his hands remained unafflicted by shakes, but he was tired and wanted to go home to read and be with his wife, who was quite a nice woman once you got to know her. Dominik had witnessed the professor repairing an aorta with only three stitches and performing a caesarean section in under seven minutes; he possessed no qualms in proclaiming the man an exceptional physician.

The old man had found Dominik in his office to tell him the news. Dominik expressed his sadness at the decision but also his pleasure at having worked under the outstanding surgeon. He wished him a well-spent and well-earned retirement. Afterwards, the professor lingered in Dominik's office, as though he had more to say. He perused Dominik's bookshelf without selecting anything to read, stared out the window at nothing in particular, and glanced over some patient files, which he couldn't have been reading all that thoroughly for they were upside down. Dominik offered him tea, but he declined. Finally, he cleared his throat and delivered a speech.

'You are like a son to me, Dominik,' he began.

Dominik raised an eyebrow. 'That doesn't mean much, Professor. You have only daughters.'

The professor shrugged. 'Well, yes. But it's still true. And I think you like that I say it.' He smiled. 'I'd like you to replace me when I am gone. Chief of Medicine.'

'I am flattered,' Dominik replied, dumbfounded. He took a moment to savour the honour, then promptly turned the old man down. 'Of course, I can't accept. It violates protocol.'

Dominik ranked number three at the hospital: ahead of him stood Dr Wolanski, the Santa Claus–resembling, laudanum-peddling paediatrician. Dr Wolanski had recently celebrated his fifty-fifth birthday. If you checked Dominik's personnel file, it would state his age as forty-four. Dr Wolanski had also served at the hospital for over ten years before Dominik arrived. A scandal would result – or at the very least, a grand embarrassment – if the younger doctor leapfrogged his superior in both age and experience.

'I do not want the job, anyway,' Dominik said to the professor. 'It requires filing and attendance at meetings. I would prefer to spend those hours treating patients. It would delight me for a colleague to take on the burden. I shall offer Dr Wolanski my full support.'

The old man nodded. Dominik expected he would accept the answer and felt surprised when the professor persevered with the request. 'I assure you, you'd lose no patient time. We'd provide you with a secretary for your administrative duties.'

Dominik scowled. Why was his mentor insisting on such an illogical course? 'This surely is more Dr Wolanski's game, sir,' Dominik said bluntly. 'I would feel ridiculous trying to usurp him for a job I don't want.'

Finally, the old man arrived at the point. 'We think you'd make a better fit for the hospital,' he said. He gazed down at his coat and attempted to scratch a yellowish stain from the lapel, quark perhaps. The professor ate it daily and insisted that its gut-preserving qualities held the key to a long life. Considering his age and spryness, Dominik found no cause to disagree with him.

'Tell me, have you ever attended one of Dr Wolanski's lectures?' the older man asked. 'He conducts talks on medical matters once a week. They're free to attend, in the Piłsudski theatre.'

'I've never had the pleasure,' Dominik replied. The idea of listening to Dr Wolanski educating people on medicine sent a shiver up his spine.

The professor smiled. 'I have been to one or two.'

'Am I missing out?'

'Yes. But do not worry, for you are about to witness one. I'll make a deal with you, son. Attend this lecture with me, and afterwards you tell me if you think Dr Wolanski is the man for the chief's position. If you agree he fits the job, I shall never mention it again. If you disagree that he should run this hospital, you will assent to apply for the position yourself. Do we have a deal?'

Dominik paused, feeling intrigued. 'Very well.'

The professor held out his hand. 'Let's shake on it.' Dominik hesitated; the handshake bestowed a formality on the matter he hadn't expected. He reached out and shook. The professor's palm had the tissue-soft skin of a beloved grandparent, but his grip remained firm. 'Come. The lecture's beginning now.'

Dominik followed the professor to the Piłsudski room. A handwritten sign greeted them at the door: *My Travels in Germany*.

'Oh dear,' Dominik said. 'Are we to be treated to Dr Wolanski's holiday slides? Will he assault us with photographs of him posing with the flamingos in the *Tiergarten*?'

'Something like that,' the senior doctor replied, ushering him inside. The Piłsudski room had a space at the front for surgeries and autopsies, with a tiered theatre from where nurses and doctors could observe. But no patient lay on the slab, and no trays lay prepared with surgical tools. The stage sat bare, except for Dr Wolanski and an easel covered dramatically with a cotton hospital blanket, enshrouding whatever lay within.

Dr Wolanski beamed when he saw them walk in. 'Welcome! I am so pleased you have come. Finally, my research will receive the recognition it deserves. Professor, there's a seat for you here, down the front. I suppose you may join him too, Dominik.'

Other people filled about a third of the seats already. Several hospital janitors sat in a row by the door. 'I saw Dr Wolanski instructing them to attend earlier,' the professor said, nodding at the cleaners. Dr Wolanski's secretary and some nurses took up another row – seemingly, from the looks on their faces, against their will.

Everyone settled themselves, and Dr Wolanski shut the door and began. 'I present to you my travels to a recent showcase in Munich,' he told his audience, walking to his easel. 'Last autumn I had the fortune to attend an exhibit that opened my eyes to a grand tragedy. I attended as the special guest of the Reich culture chamber – a friend is a member.' He puffed out his chest and smiled proudly. 'We met at a conference last year and I have kept up the acquaintance. He presented me with fascinating documents. Behold.' He drew back the hospital blanket with great theatre.

A poster lay underneath.

It depicted a buffoonish man cloaked in a black kaftan. His straggly beard sprouted from his face in long tufts of black. He held three gold coins in his right hand and a whip in his left. He wore a small black cap, like they did in the east, towards Russia. Greasy locks of hair framed his round face, and his nose protruded in a hooked and bulbous mound of flesh. The figure was an anti-Semite's nightmare, a sweating tax collector with sweets in his pocket to lure young ladies, a demon who ground up blond babies to make his matzo. It was a ludicrous cartoon which had found a willing audience in Dr Wolanski. The right edge of the poster featured a hand-drawn map of Germany, stamped furiously with a hammer and sickle painted in red, the ink dripping down the image like blood.

'Look upon this man,' Dr Wolanski said to the small crowd. 'Does he not horrify you?' Some of the audience nodded in earnest. The professor raised one eyebrow and turned his head to Dominik. Dominik shifted in his seat.

Dr Wolanski strolled to his slide projector and turned it on. A photograph of a small child emblazoned the screen. The child squatted in a gutter below a row of soot-stained tenements. He wore torn shorts, a thin shirt and no shoes. Downy fuzz christened his head; someone had shaved it recently, and whoever had done the job had cut his head at the crown, and it had healed in a bloody scab. Children normally delighted at having their picture taken; now that cameras could take photographs quickly, with no standing still required, children clamoured to pose with giant smiles. But this boy didn't smile. He didn't look down the lens at all, but rather past the camera, to the photographer behind it, and he held out his hand, begging for help.

Dominik had seen such children in the famines after the Great War and knew something himself of what it felt like to starve. The child's knees were like saucers compared to his stick-thin shins. Dominik wouldn't be surprised if the child had died shortly after he'd featured in the picture, perhaps that afternoon as the photographer returned to his pension to take supper.

'Behold the pathetic sight,' Dr Wolanski said to the crowd. 'This child works as a scavenger and bears the marks of typhus. Do not waste your pity on him – this boy trades in thievery, and his mother would have done the world a favour by smothering him at birth.'

'Dr Wolanski can't expect that we'll take him seriously with this,' Dominik whispered to the professor. The old man made no reply.

'I was witness to shocking examples of disease and degeneracy,' Dr Wolanski declared in a horrified tone. The slide presentation continued with pictures of Russian villages with no plumbing, close-ups of open-air latrines, and more children, thin and barefoot, ignoring the camera, begging the photographer for food and money.

'I wish you all could have seen it,' Dr Wolanski said earnestly as he inserted the next slide. 'These pictures do not do the exhibition justice. I shook my head at the depravity! Such neglect of hygiene in these Jewish villages. We must keep such forces out of our hospital. I would have better outcomes treating plague on a ship filled with rats.'

The slides continued through a presentation of pornography, a tableau of human suffering. Starved bodies lay in gutters; toothless men begged for food and looked forlorn. The lecture concluded and Dominik grimaced, muttering, 'What a curious sight.'

Dr Wolanski walked up to them afterwards. 'So, what did you think?'

'A thorough presentation, Dr Wolanski. I had no idea you had such . . . passions,' Dominik said.

Dr Wolanski nodded, unsure, then seemed to accept the words as a compliment. 'Thank you. And you, professor?'

'Yes, Dr Wolanski. Good for you,' the professor replied.

'I rushed it in the middle – some I displayed weren't even my best pictures. If I had known you were coming, I would have arranged an even longer show. Please come back to my office – I want to show you my pamphlet.'

Dominik didn't think he could suffer much more. 'I wish we could, Dr Wolanski, but we've another engagement,' he said, and began walking off.

'Those can wait, Dominik,' the old professor said, tugging his arm. 'Let Dr Wolanski show us his project.'

Dominik followed them to Dr Wolanski's office. As the doctor showed them inside, Dominik stifled a gasp. He'd never entered Dr Wolanski's quarters before, and they looked as though someone had ransacked them. Papers lay on every surface and most of the floor. A typewriter remained loaded with a half-written page; ink leaked from somewhere onto the desk. More piles of typed pages covered the windowsill. Half-empty teacups sat on bookshelves and in between the stacks of papers, growing mould. Dominik peered into one cup with horror, but also interest; some half-decent penicillium might have been growing inside. A smell of rotting food permeated the room. The space presented not as the office of a physician but rather the hovel of a madman, who'd boarded himself away to write his manifesto. Dominik wondered how he had time to see any patients.

Dr Wolanski offered them tea, which they accepted out of politeness, and he handed them two dirty cups filled with a lukewarm black liquid, then continued rummaging around, employing excited and agitated movements. 'Yes! Finally, here they are. My secretary hid them, stupid cow,' he said. 'Here, please, enjoy.' He bestowed on each of them a pamphlet printed on office paper.

'Please, sit, read,' he said. He removed a stack of papers from a chair and offered it to the professor. He made no such arrangement for Dominik. The professor took the seat and Dominik stood next to him. They opened their reading materials and perused in silence. Dominik shifted his feet from left to right.

'I don't understand, Dr Wolanski. This pamphlet seems to say that we refuse to treat Jewish patients at the hospital,' the professor said.

'Exactly!' Dr Wolanski replied with a beatific smile. 'Well, this is not policy yet, but it's one of the positive changes I will make, when, ahem, the day comes.'

'That is absurd, Dr Wolanski,' Dominik said. 'We don't treat that many anyway. Most go to the Jewish hospitals.'

'We do! You haven't noticed, because you don't observe these things like I do. Twenty per cent of those we treat are Jews. Sometimes thirty. It's a disgrace.'

'What does it matter how many Jewish people, or people of any other religion, we treat?' the professor asked.

'Jews spread disease. The topic of my presentation. They make us look bad, when they come in half dead and die on us. They bring our numbers down.'

'I have not witnessed any greater communication of disease,' Dominik insisted.

'Of course, but you didn't see the exhibition,' Dr Wolanski replied, annoyed.

Dominik thought back over his recent patients. 'But this city is probably thirty per cent Jewish citizens. It's no surprise. It is also fifty per cent farmer. If you want to reduce disease, stop treating agriculturalists. Every exotic rash or boil that comes through here is from a sharecropper's behind.' He buried his head in the pamphlet once more. 'Send your Jewish patients to me, Dr Wolanski,' he said softly. 'I will be happy to treat them.'

'Thank you, Dr Wolanski. We feel illuminated,' the professor said, struggling to stand. Dr Wolanski rushed to help him, grabbing his arm and pulling him up roughly, too coarsely for a doctor, who should know how to handle elderly muscles and bones. The old man winced at the wrenching movement.

Dominik and the professor exited the ramshackle office and retired to the professor's rooms, where Dominik made them a second cup of tea. He left the leaves to brew for two minutes, the way the professor liked.

'Now do you see why I worry?' the professor said. 'Thank you,' he added as Dominik poured the tea.

'He can't mean this.' Dominik pointed to Dr Wolanski's Jew-banning flyer, which now lay discarded on a card table. 'It's a mishmash. He misspelled "hygiene". Both in the German and the Polish. Who was his typist? Who was his printer?'

'Evidently not the Mandelbaums.' The professor chuckled.

'Yes. Moshe Mandelbaum binds books so beautifully. Dr Wolanski went somewhere low-rent. Terrible typesetting.'

The professor sipped his tea and nodded. He looked anguished.

Dominik did his best to reassure him. 'I'm sure Dr Wolanski will be too busy with the business of doctoring to implement any policies,' he said. 'This is all just fluff that he thinks you want to hear in order to appoint him. Once he is in the job, he will be too caught up with the prestige of the title to start excluding patients from the hospital. It really is a stupid idea.'

'On the contrary: he will not do much doctoring at all, as I think you well know,' the professor said. 'I think he'd prefer to never lift a stethoscope again. He is the worst type of doctor. A misanthrope and a dreamer and a lazy brain. No tenacity, no stamina. I have witnessed him give a child a double dose of laudanum to shut her up. He turns up late for rounds, and whenever he gets something wrong, it's always someone else's fault. He would make a terrible window cleaner – the dirt would always be on the other side. If he succeeds in ascending to my position, he will enact these policies.' The professor pointed to the flyer.

'But he won't have the authority.'

The professor shook his head. 'He's only a doctor here because we can't get rid of him. His family donate money to the hospital. He knows every person in town. Mark my words, he will stack the board with his cronies and his father's business associates, and they will vote for whatever policies he suggests. His ideas are not objectionable to everyone. There are many in this town looking for someone to blame for their problems.'

'I know many people in town also.' Dominik bristled. 'I am not friendless. I have good standing.'

'Exactly,' said the old man. 'You are the only man with enough power, who garners enough respect, to take him on. No one else would be able to defeat him.'

'I am not an ambitious man,' Dominik said, scratching his head.

The professor smiled. 'You are the most ambitious man I've ever met.' He straightened his bowtie. 'It's all right, Dominik, I mean that as a compliment. You are ambitious, you must know this. A fire burns within you to be the best. Lucky for you, you *are* the best. You wait and think before speaking. You listen to patients. You consider both sides. You possess stamina and operate with grace. Now it is time to put these gifts to good use. You must put a stop to Dr Wolanski's plans.'

Dominik sighed, feeling exhausted already. 'I do not want to get involved in politics. I just want to be a doctor,' he said.

The professor touched his arm. 'I wouldn't ask if my only concern was that he'd behave like a despot to the nursing staff and take extended lunchbreaks. He will do real damage. If he succeeds in gaining this position, he will turn patients away, and they will die. Will you apply?'

Dominik walked to the window and weighed up the matter, and came to the unhappy conclusion that no way existed to turn the professor down. 'Very well,' he said, heavy-hearted. 'You may put me forward for the position.'

'Excellent,' the professor said. 'There will be a meeting in the summer. All candidates will deliver a presentation to the current board and me. Don't worry, Dr Wolanski will act upset for a while after he loses the position to you, but he will recover.'

Dominik nodded and said no more. Any awkwardness with his colleague was the least of his worries. He could handle Dr Wolanski's angry stares and passing him uncomfortably in the tearoom.

A far worse outcome gnawed at him. To justify their choosing him as the chief, due diligence would require the board of directors to scrutinise Dominik's past – they'd want to know what kind of doctor they were getting to run their hospital – and fairly so. They'd ask, at a minimum, to see his university transcripts, his birth certificate. His military record. They would ask questions about his daughter, Marie's mother, about what happened to her. A question to which Dominik had no good answer.

He acquainted himself with the concept that he now walked the halls as a dead man.

4

THE SCARIEST ROOM
IN THE LIBRARY

Marie hurried across the park. The fat rain continued today, soaking her boots through, but she didn't mind. The path to her mother had been shortened; Marie would find the woman herself. The population of the world had exceeded two billion people and, if necessary, she'd ask every one of them. She'd start at the library.

'Good morning, Lolek,' she said to the librarian as she entered the cavernous Gothic building that loomed over the edge of the park. The young man behind the counter was reading a newspaper and Marie glanced at the front page. 'What is Mr Hitler up to today?'

'This is the problem with him, you see,' Lolek replied. He pointed at the picture under the headline. The moustachioed leader was shouting from a verandah, at someone or something. 'I blame architecture. The way they built the Potsdam palace, the balcony faces full east. Every time der Führer makes a speech, he looks directly this way. If his terrace faced north, we wouldn't be in this mess. Only the ocean would be in trouble – the poor fishes of the Baltic would have to arm themselves, wear little helmets.'

'Perhaps you could give him some Blessed Sacrament, Lolek,' Marie offered.

Lolek nodded. With his ruby cheeks and golden-fleece hair, Lolek had the look of an altar boy. He put this to good use assisting

Father Wiktor at St Peter & Paul's every morning. Marie favoured him above all the other acolytes, not for his innocent looks or proficiency with incense, but for the proportion of wine he mixed in the Blessed Sacrament. Father Wiktor was a fire and brimstone priest who liked to spit as he thundered away, wishing everyone a week filled with guilt and shame. But after Lolek took over sacrament preparation, Father Wiktor emerged from communion rites rosy-cheeked, smiled off into the middle distance and bid his flock a good day. He once even took a nap during reflection.

'Unfortunately for us, Mr Hitler does not drink,' Lolek replied. 'Interesting language, German.' He pointed to his newspaper again, written in that tongue.

'How many languages do you speak now, Lolek? Eleven? Twelve?'

'Goodness, no,' he replied. 'Ten.'

'Do you know every book in this library?'

'I wish that were so,' he said. 'A shelf of geometry sits on the fourth floor, on which I couldn't name three books. It's always been my weakness, mathematics. Pythagoras had far more patience with triangles than me.'

'You know the storybooks, though? The myths and legends? Children's tales?'

'Those I know.'

'An easy task for you then. I'm looking for a fairytale. A children's book.'

'*Aesop's Fables*? Brothers Grimm?'

'It's one fairytale in particular. About a man. He climbs up . . . something.' She scowled. That was all Marie could remember.

'Jack and the Beanstalk?' Lolek suggested. 'As indicated by the title, the protagonist scales one. Far-fetched, but then it is a fairytale.'

'No. It concerns a grown man, on a quest.'

'Where does he go?'

'I don't know.'

'What is he looking for?'

'I'm not sure.'

'What colour is his hair?'

'I couldn't say.' Marie bit her lip. She possessed less information to go on than she'd first thought. She bowed her head.

'Never mind. Jesus had no map, and he still made it back from the desert.' He smiled happily and ushered her towards the rear of the building. 'I warn you now, Marie, though this is the children's area, this is in fact the scariest place in the library.' They reached the back and Lolek waved his arm across the room. 'Behold. The collected unconscious of the Western world. And most of the East, too. Every nightmare and moral and hope sits on these shelves.'

Marie peered around. A toy box lay in the corner, with trains and dolls stacked neatly inside. 'This is the children's room. Where are the children?'

Lolek chuckled. 'They never come in here. If we have storytime, we hold it up the front.' Marie scowled. 'The young ones think this room is haunted, and I'm inclined to agree with them.' He pointed again. Marie gasped. Some well-meaning but misguided volunteer had decorated the back wall with a collage of fairytale characters. At one corner, the wolf chased Little Red Riding Hood through a forest, its yellow fangs bared and gleaming. At another, the witch from 'Hansel and Gretel' baked children in the oven of her candy house. In the middle stood Shaggy Peter. The boy's fingernails had grown to the ground, appearing sharp as knives as the boy swiped one hand up, one down, as though trying to decapitate a child. Marie was unsurprised that children refused to enter the room; such images would scare a fully grown person. They were scaring her now, in fact.

The shelves held stacks of dusty books of varying sizes with cracked leather spines. 'I'd begin here,' Lolek said. He retrieved

Grimm's Fairy Tales from the shelf, handed it to her and left, wishing her luck.

Marie's hunt for this fairytale had a purpose. Until yesterday, her entire experience of her mother had consisted of a singular memory: of being read to when she was a baby. She couldn't remember the story she was being told, the characters or the plot. She'd never heard the story again. The fairytale itself was not the important part, but rather what her mother said to her afterwards, right before she departed her life forever.

Marie's mother had told her where she was going, and why.

Marie had clung to that moment ever since. She'd spent sixteen years trying to remember what her mother had said. Now the discovery of the rosewater and its connection to her mother's memory had inspired her. If she could find the fairytale, maybe she could reconstruct the day in her mind.

Marie tried to squeeze herself back into her younger body, to see the scene through that baby's eyes. The details Marie had so far of that day involved fuzzy images of furniture and sensations. A fire burned low. Embers glowed from a single lump of coal. She couldn't give her mother a face, nor clothes, but now, after her discovery under her father's floorboards, she could adorn her head with blonde hair. The vision sat there on the edge of her brain, teasing her; when she reached out to grab it, it jumped off and ran away. But if she could recall the fairytale, perhaps she could add more details to the frame and retrieve the full memory once and for all – including the words her mother had told her.

Marie took a deep breath and opened the book. The spine cracked. She flinched with excitement; she felt like she'd swallowed a firecracker. Was this the very book her mother had read to her? She glanced at the first page and took a moment to smirk at the puzzling register of borrowers pasted on the inside cover. Several caught her eye as people she knew from town. Dr Igor Wolanski, a clinician from her father's hospital whom she suspected Papa didn't like very much, had borrowed this book twice, for a month each time. The other names in the register raised equal puzzlement. A member of the city council took up a line, as did several priests and three members of the Unity Party. A curious assortment of town dignitaries possessed an interest in German folktales. Shaking her head, she turned the page and began scanning the contents for any tales that might involve a man climbing a mountain.

Marie read the book from front cover to back. Every fairy, demon and ghoul had their say. Men lured children with pipe music, then locked them in black rooms. Monsters munched on babies, giants ground bones into flour. She had to force herself to read each appalling tale; she wouldn't sleep for a month after this.

As a child, she'd been afraid of the dark. The city in which she lived still scared her. The kings of Europe had all taken their turn with Krakow, moved in, built castles and houses, then departed, leaving the people nothing but ruins, spoiled waterways and a decrepit castle. Dragon gargoyles from five different empires hung from every disintegrating turret and snarled as you passed underneath in the languages of their masters: German, Swedish, Russian. Now the soot from a thousand coal fireplaces stained the buildings black, forming ghouls that danced across them. The smell from the hot sewers wafted up, blowing one's hair back with its stench. Fog lingered, always. As though aware of the evil lurking, there was a church on every corner. But Catholicism only horrified Marie more, with its flayed saints and nuns boiled alive in vats of oil, its dried bones and relics. A book in the very library in which she sat was made of human skin, fashioned by the skilled hands of some heretic or other.

For a long time, Marie had thought the general sense of unease that gripped her – her nightmares and anxieties, her day terrors and disquiets – stemmed from these horrors, from the spooky place in which she lived. Now, she decided another culprit deserved the blame. Her mother's disappearance, and her father's reluctance to talk about it were the true reasons her ground felt so unstable. The gargoyles on the roofs and the books made of skin just enhanced a feeling that already lurked. It was for this reason she forced herself to keep reading. No horror that she unearthed in those pages could rival the dreadfulness of a missing mother, and a father who had hidden her hair under the floorboards of their house.

At six o'clock, Lolek returned to find her on the floor, bereft, surrounded by a pile of strewn books. Marie had read every fairytale in the library. Among the canon of villains and heroes, she found not a single account of a man climbing a mountain.

He gave her some bread and a pot of tea. 'Do you recall the book cover? Was it coloured, with cloth or leather?'

Marie shook her head. 'I do not know.' She closed her eyes. 'Perhaps I imagined it.'

The library was closing. Lolek was happy to let her stay as long as she liked, but the caretaker would turn off the fire for the boiler in fifteen minutes, which would plunge the building into regular Polish temperatures. Even close to springtime, this posed a problem; Lolek had once left his soup on the table and returned in the morning to find it frozen.

Marie got up from the floor. She helped Lolek lock up, and then he accompanied her home across the park. The rain continued; it now felt like a cold shower. Her nose stung in the frigid air and she wrapped her coat around herself more tightly. As they walked down the winding path, snaking their way through the birch trees, she waited for one of the ghouls she'd just read about to jump out and throttle her. The afternoon had begun so well. She'd strolled along this same path with such purpose earlier, but the idea that had appeared so clever now seemed facile.

'What was the reason for your search?' Lolek asked her as they arrived at her house.

'Someone read it to me as a child.' Her voice cracked as she spoke.

'Was it very important?' he said.

'It was to me,' she said, attempting a smile. 'Stupid, really.'

Lolek nodded and kissed her hand goodbye. He turned towards the road, then seemed to hesitate.

'What is it?' she asked.

'Perhaps you could ask Benjamin Rosen.'

Marie froze. 'Who?' She needed to catch her breath. She knew exactly who he meant, though she hadn't heard the name in years. A ball formed inside her throat; she swallowed twice but it didn't go away. She blinked and her heart raced.

'Ben Rosen,' Lolek said. 'Do you not know him?'

'Oh, I . . .' Marie said, her voice stumbling, 'I suppose I know him.' This was a lie; she knew him well.

'His degree was in Polish literature. He was required to complete a study of folktales. Perhaps he will know your story.'

'I didn't know he went to university.' Marie felt stupid as she said it, as though his life would have stopped once she no longer interacted with him.

Lolek looked up from his gloved hands, perhaps watching her reaction. 'He graduated a couple of years ago.'

Marie waved her hand. 'I do not know on what number to reach him, or his address to send a letter. He moved away, many years ago.'

'He's back.'

Marie's heart pounded in her chest. He was back? Ben Rosen, the companion to the warmest days of her childhood, who had left one day without saying goodbye. 'I don't think so, Lolek. If you can't help me, surely all is lost. I wouldn't want to bother him. He will be busy.' She adjusted her hat.

'Only a suggestion.' Lolek shrugged. 'Anyway, he lives on St Joseph Street now.'

5

OLD FRIENDS

The next day, Marie walked towards Kazimierz, the Jewish quarter, on the outskirts of Old Town. Her mouth felt so dry it almost burned, thinking of meeting him after all this time. She passed Mrs Goldfarb sweeping her porch with a straw brush. 'Look at this plague,' she ordered Marie, holding up her arm where a two-centimetre patch of impetigo blemished the old woman's skin. 'What say you?'

'Good afternoon, Mrs Goldfarb. I am unsure.'

'I say it progresses. It was once contained to my forearm. Now it approaches my head. Well, it has only reached my elbow so far, but it inches ever closer. You agree?'

'I suppose.' Marie squinted at the little blotch. People accosted Marie like this often; her father's serenity and proficiency with patients enamoured every hypochondriac in town. They assumed Marie held as much knowledge of medicine as her father did. She did not, but she wanted to one day, so while these interludes with patients always annoyed her, they flattered her somewhat too, and her aggravation was always interspersed with a small swelling of pride.

'Memorise this shape and describe it to your father. Ask him what I should do.'

'I don't believe you should fear, Mrs Goldfarb. The rash seems benign. But my father needs to see it for a proper diagnosis,' Marie said.

The skin of Mrs Goldfarb's face wrinkled like a prune. 'Tell him anyway,' the old woman said. 'I'm unsatisfied with the plague's progression. Tell him this, will you?'

Marie promised to tell her father about the rash and hurried down the street. She turned a corner and entered the main part of Kazimierz.

These houses wore a cloak of soot, different to those in the centre of town where she lived, which were scrubbed clean every Wednesday. A faint whiff of sewage blessed her nostrils. The dwellings sat lower on Krakow's plane and water and filth flowed downward, so they copped the stench. It had rained again earlier; sludge caked her boots from walking a road consisting primarily of dirt. She scraped her heels on a jagged cobblestone and an inch of mud came free.

Marie had first met Ben Rosen two days after she and her father had moved into the house they lived in now. Marie was eight at the time. As she had carried her doll inside, a neighbour had whispered that Marie had no mother. She'd turned to scowl at the old woman and seen a boy of around fourteen peering from the next-door window. He had waved at her. Marie had buried her head in her doll's face and not waved back.

A few weeks later, Janina Polaczuk invited Marie to play marbles, then declared her a boy. The other girls in the street had joined in and the discussion had culminated in Janina throwing one of the marbles at Marie's head. The stone globe had connected with a crack, and the hot blood that had poured out had stung Marie's eye. The boy who'd waved at her emerged from somewhere and carried Marie to her father, who sewed the wound closed with three stitches. She still carried the scar above her eyebrow.

'I have no mother,' Marie told Ben as he carried her away.

'Good. I have no father,' he said. He smiled and whistled as he walked.

Turning another corner, Marie arrived at Józefa Street. When he'd lived next door, Ben's townhouse had stood grand and large, with four storeys of prime Old Town real estate expanding towards the sky. Ben's mother, Rachel, was the daughter of Otto Blumfeld, the owner of the Blumfeld Toy Corporation in Berlin. Ben's father had run imports and exports of textiles from the Cloth Hall in the market square, a lucrative trade. They had been one of the richest families in town. His new place was a single apartment in a block of twenty dusty tenements. The address Lolek had given her required a journey to the second floor, so she located the external staircase of chipped concrete and climbed it.

She knocked on the apartment door and waited. Someone dropped a saucepan with a clang in the apartment next door and cursed. An old woman emerged from the communal outhouse downstairs, shaking her petticoat back into place. Marie had erred in coming here. She was turning to leave when the door opened behind her.

'Where are you going?'

Marie recognised that voice, though it was deeper now. She turned around. Its owner stood in the doorway, leaning on the door-frame, arms crossed. It was the strangest thing. A man's body held up the face of the boy she once knew. His hair fell in brown waves like it always had, but the frame underneath it had grown. She wondered if he recognised her.

'Hello, Professor Challenger,' he said. No one had called her that in almost ten years.

The day after he'd rescued her from the marble attack by Janina Polaczuk, eight-year-old Marie had knocked on Ben's door. She'd handed him a shovel and ordered him to her back garden.

She'd stayed up all night with a candle reading *The Lost World*, newly translated into Polish. Her father had bought it for her, a present for being so brave while he'd stitched her head. She devoured the daring tales of Professor Challenger finding dinosaurs and monsters in the Americas, and she wanted to do the same. A *Tyrannosaurus rex* had been dug up in Colorado, the *National Geographic* announced. If there was one in America, there would be one in her back garden. She pointed at the grass and ordered the palaeontological dig to commence. Ben protested concern at digging up her father's yard. No problem, she assured him. He'd replace all the soil before her father returned home.

They dug up half the yard and found no dinosaurs. Ben pleaded with her to put the soil back; her father was expected home within the hour. She cried, but he couldn't console her. She refused to accept that they wouldn't find bones there.

Marie had never forgotten the look on his face as he had put all the soil back. This young man, six years older than she, who likely had friends his own age to consort with and more exciting things to do. His face crumpled, his shoulders slumped. He looked in pain to see her so sad, as though the child he'd carried so carefully back to her father's house now occupied a little piece of him. A motherless girl for this fatherless boy. 'Please don't cry. What can I do?'

The next day, Ben showed her to the back garden. 'Let's start on the other half,' he said. Marie protested, her taste for the mission gone, but Ben began digging and she joined him. He dug down deeper and his shovel clunked on something. Marie scrambled with her hands and pulled up fistfuls of dirt. She brushed the dirt away and uncovered a bone. It was huge, larger than any dog or cat bone. Golden afternoon sun dusted the air; the white bone dazzled. She clawed at it until she unearthed the find.

'Professor Challenger,' he called her. She beamed.

45

Later, she presented the bone to her father. 'Look, Papa,' she said, puffing out her chest. '*Tyrannosaurus rex!*'

'*Equus ferus caballus!*' her father replied. 'Horse femur. Not only do I know the species, I suspect I know the exact horse. Old Kary – she was the Ginsberg's mare. She broke her leg three weeks ago and they knackered her. See the fracture line,' he said, pointing to a crack in the bone.

'It was not Kary! The bone was in our yard. Kary never went in our garden, and she certainly didn't die there.' She paused, then, realising what had happened.

Marie never let on she knew Ben had put the bone there. He never said anything more of it either. They reburied it in the back-yard, giving it a dinosaur's funeral. They fashioned a gravestone from a wooden plank off a milk crate. *Here lies Tyrannosaurus*, it read.

When Marie returned to school that September, a craze swept the classroom with the students' graduation from pencil to fountain pen. All the girls practised their signatures. They wrote their names in their books with glamorous calligraphy and curlicues. Janina Polaczuk, the girl who'd thrown the marble at Marie, signed *Janina Fairbanks* into her mathematics book, for she was to marry Douglas Fairbanks, the film star. Instead of a dot, a love heart marked each of the two i's. They were engaged, Janina and him, though Douglas didn't know it yet.

Weronika Katura signed *Weronika Wozniak*, for she was betrothed to her brother's maths professor. She drew no love hearts though, expressing a more subdued style.

The girls commanded Marie to write her signature. Marie could think of only one name and signed in neat black ink *Marie Rosen*, for she'd marry Ben.

They laughed at her. 'Marie Rosen!' they cried. 'You can't marry a dirty Jew!'

That night, Marie asked her father why the Jew was dirty.

He looked up from his newspaper and frowned. 'Perhaps they forgot to wash their hands before eating? No matter. I'm sure they will remember soon,' he replied with a satisfied nod.

Marie could see no issue with marrying someone with messy hands; she often forgot to wash her own before eating. She continued signing her name Marie Rosen in secret. She told Ben she did this, once. He said nothing, just smiled a sad smile and went home.

Their final summer together had been one of the hottest on record, and she'd passed the time in a dream. Linden tree blossoms perfumed the air; more apples fell from the trees than people had time to pick. They swam every morning in the Vistula, Marie in her woollen swimsuit that dragged her to the bottom with every breaststroke, Ben in his shorts. They picked apricots from the trees in giant bundles and ate them until their stomachs swelled. They spoke about dinosaurs, films and baseball. Ben wanted to see Babe Ruth hit a curve ball one day – what a swing! As the summer drew to a close, Marie begged for it not to end.

One particular day they had organised to swim in the river. Marie was going to tell Ben she loved him. School began the next week; it was now or never. She'd prepared a speech, which she'd written on a card. She waited for three hours, her heart thumping, clutching her card.

He never appeared.

She felt sick. Perhaps he'd got wind of her impending declaration and was avoiding her. She walked home feeling bereft, crossing the river at the bridge under which they'd planned to swim. She'd got the location right, yes? A ferocious wind blew, the water swirling in whirls of dark green, and creamy white foam chopped across the swell. Upon arriving home, she discovered her father painting the Rosens' house.

'Papa, why are you doing that?'

'I thought perhaps they would like a new colour.'

'May I help?'

He nodded, and Marie quickly returned with her own small paintbrush from her pencil box.

'You picked the wrong colour, Papa,' Marie said to him as she began her brushstrokes.

'I know,' he replied.

'We shall have to paint the entire wall.'

Mrs Polaczuk, mother of Janina, the marble hurler, walked past and spoke to her father. 'Don't bother with that paint – the job is done.'

Marie laughed at the comment. It was poor advice, for the job was only half done: the other paint still showed underneath. Mrs Polaczuk was clearly no painter.

'I shall fetch Ben to help us,' Marie said. 'It will be quicker.'

Her father replied that Ben was not home.

As she brushed over the surface, she painted over the outline of some letters. She squinted to read them but couldn't make the words out. She covered more, broken-hearted and annoyed that Ben hadn't showed up yet. She slowed her brushstrokes; she didn't want to do it all herself. She demanded that they find him, but Papa said he didn't know where Ben had gone.

She never saw him again. Until now.

As he'd carried her inside that first day, she'd felt the strength in his arms and chest; he was only fourteen but felt like a man to her. She recalled making excuses to go outside when he'd lived next door, offering to walk to the market for milk or run other errands – just to pass his house and perhaps see him studying at his desk by the window. She had once tipped half a litre of milk down the sink to necessitate its replenishment just so she could walk by, only to discover he was not home and fall into desperate sadness. She would conjure quests they might be sent on together. She had known the pain and ecstasy of love in her little heart at eight years old. She had never had a crush before or since. No one else had felt so like home to her.

Marie realised she must have been staring into space for some time.

'Can I help you?' Ben asked.

Marie shook her head, as if to release the memory. 'You studied fairytales?'

'What a strange question after all this time!' he said, laughing. 'You always did get straight to the point.'

Their eyes met. She wanted to know everything, where he'd been. She cursed herself for opening with such a question.

'I studied fairytales,' he replied. 'Although I was asleep 94.2 per cent of the time. Dull as ditch water. A stupid course – I took it as a requirement. We all study it now, like the Germans. The government takes an interest in national folklore. Still, I suppose I should be grateful I learned it while I could. They might not even take me now.'

Marie bristled at the bitter tone and felt confused. Ben had always been a good student. Perhaps he'd neglected his studies. She wished to move off this topic; they had other, nicer things to talk about.

'Why do you ask?' he said.

'I'm looking for a fairytale,' she replied.

'What for?'

Marie shrugged; she didn't want to answer that question, so she chose a different one. 'It's about a man who climbs something.'

Ben nodded. 'What's it called, the fairytale?'

'I don't know.' Marie suddenly felt annoyed. 'That's why I'm asking you. I didn't even want to ask you. I only did because Lolek the librarian suggested it. I'm humouring him.'

He nodded again. A breeze blew the hair from his face. A cloud moved from its place covering the sun, bathing the street in light.

It caught the stubble on his jaw, the short bristly hairs glinting along his cheek.

'You left without telling me where you were going,' Marie said.

'I'm sorry. We moved away.'

'Why? You had a nice house.'

'Yes. That street is the most fashionable address in the city. All the best people live there.' He smiled, but Marie was unsure if there was some aggression in his voice, or if it was just that he was older now.

'You are back,' she said.

'Evidently.' He swallowed. Marie squinted at him. 'Look, it's bad luck to talk in the doorway,' he said with a nervous laugh. 'Won't you come inside?' Marie's heart leapt at the invitation, to enter this grown man's house alone. But something felt so strange and disappointing about the situation that she couldn't bring herself to accept it.

'I'm fine to stay right here, thank you,' she said, aware she sounded ridiculous. She also silently counted the years of bad luck she was consigning herself to for talking in a doorway – one of the many Polish superstitions she sneered at on the one hand and took very seriously on the other.

'Why didn't you tell me you were back?' she said. 'Why didn't you come and see me?'

He stared at her, then turned and picked a splinter from the doorframe. 'I've been busy.'

'How long have you been back?'

'I returned in March 1936.'

Marie's mouth dropped open. 'That was three years ago.'

'You always were good at calculations.'

'You have been back for three years! Why did you not come and see me?'

'As mentioned, I was busy,' he said, shrugging.

'But I thought . . . we were friends.'

'That was a long time ago.' He sniffed. 'What do you want to know about fairytales?'

His coldness made her heart ache. She felt relieved not to have accepted his invitation to come inside, despite the apparent bad luck that remaining in the doorway would bring her. 'I'm trying to find one. I doubt you would know it,' she said, attempting to sound unhurt. 'Lolek didn't know it, and he knows everything.'

'He does. But maybe tell me the fairytale first, before you start deciding all the things I don't know.'

Maria stiffened at the tone. He seemed to attempt a look of anger towards her, but his face wouldn't comply: he smiled the whole time. He shifted his feet, the same way he used to when talking excitedly about the New York Yankees.

'What do you do now? Do you have a job?' she asked.

'I'm a schoolteacher,' he said. 'What do you do?'

'I'm still at school,' she replied. 'I matriculate in May. Do I look different?'

'Your smile is the same,' he said. 'Other parts are different.' As he said the words, she caught his eyes moving down her, then looking away sheepishly. She blinked. 'Why do you want to know this fairytale?'

'Never mind.'

'Are you looking for your mother?'

Marie stared at him. Anger coursed through her; how dare he act so cold, then bring such things up? 'Maybe you don't know the fairytale. You studied all that time and still don't know it.' She placed her hands on her hips, which seemed to amuse him.

'You have given me very little to go on, Marie. I wouldn't blame someone for not knowing what you are talking about.'

'I've given you plenty,' she said, raising her voice. 'A man climbs something. It's not a beanstalk, it's a quest.' She listed the items by

51

raising her fingers, one, two, three. 'He's looking for something. Not a goose. Something happens to him, but he gets there in the end. All right? Plenty of information. You wasted your whole studies on learning fairytales, and you don't remember them. You're right, they shouldn't have let you in. They wasted a space on you.'

Ben stared at her again. 'Forget asking me. If you want to find your mother, just go to the records office. They will help you much better than I can.'

'I can't do that.'

'Sure you can. It's easy. They're right up on the street behind the market square. Just give them your mother's name and say, "Please show me everything you have on her."'

'I can't do that!' Marie said again. 'I don't *know* her name.'

Ben laughed. Then, seeing her horrified look, his voice softened. 'Are you joking?'

'No. I don't know my mother's name.'

'First or last?'

'Both.' She bowed her head. 'I don't know her Christian name. I don't know her family name. I'm seventeen years old and I've never heard my mother's name.' Her cheeks burned.

Ben leaned on the doorway again. 'Oh, Marie,' he said. He held up his hand to her, as if to touch her shoulder, then hesitated. She wanted him to; he'd touched her this way often as a child, causing her to shiver each time and yearn for him to do it again. She wondered if it would feel the same now. But then she reminded herself of the frostiness of the present reunion, and she moved away instead. He dropped his hand and she felt regret for it, but it was done now.

'Do not pity me,' she said.

'I wouldn't dare. You'd beat me up.'

'All I wanted was some help to find my mother. Do you know what it's like to live without a parent?'

52

'I do,' he replied.

'Then you should be more helpful.' She turned and began walking off.

'Marie, wait. I'm sorry.'

She didn't wait. In fact, she walked away from her first meeting with him in eight years without even saying goodbye.

Marie had only realised adults had Christian names when she was about seven and heard another man address her father as Dominik. Before that, he was just Papa; she'd never conceived that he had a first name like the children in her class and Ben. A few days later, she'd asked Papa, 'Do all adults have first names?'

'Yes,' he'd told her. 'Your teacher Mrs Sobieski's name is Klaudia. Mrs Sezlack's name is Paulina.'

Marie had interrupted him then, excited. 'Does Mama have a name?'

He'd gone quiet for some time. They reached the end of the street and still he'd given no answer. They boarded a tram and Father spoke to Mr Powolski – Paweł was his first name – about his club foot, which had stiffened in the cold weather, giving him grief. They alighted the tram and walked home. Still he gave no answer.

'Never ask me that again,' he said, finally, as they reached their front door.

'But . . .' Marie inhaled to ask why not again.

'Your mother left you,' he said in a short voice, which stopped her. 'Why speak of things that will only bring you pain? Forget her.'

He turned the key and walked inside.

Those few sentences were the most words he'd ever spoken about her mother. Marie spent the afternoon and the better part of the next week turning those words over in her head, examining the phrases and tone her father had used, extracting combinations of meaning. She emphasised a different word each time, trying to remember how he had said it. Was it 'your mother left *you*' or 'your mother *left* you'? She'd stopped trying to decipher these words now, whether her father meant Marie's mother had abandoned her because she hated her, or simply left for some nefarious reason of her own. There was a quicker way to decode what her father meant: she would find her mother and ask her. She put Ben from her mind and resolved to find another way to do so.

6

A DANCE FOR HEALTHY YOUNG PEOPLE

'This looks interesting,' Marie's father said some nights later as they ate dinner. He placed a flyer beside her plate of beef stew and potato pancake.

Marie swallowed a mouthful and read the flyer's title aloud: 'St Mary's Dance for Healthy Young People'. She laughed. 'Papa, you can't be serious.'

The flyer advertised a dance hosted by the church they attended. Underneath the auspicious title, an illustration depicted a young man and woman, both dressed in highland costume, waltzing across a room in a sterile embrace. Both stared straight ahead, not at each other. A crucifix loomed above their heads on the wall behind them. Jesus Christ had his head bowed – due to the fatiguing nature of his crucifixion – but the angle also allowed the son of God to look down on the couple from his cross, as though he was supervising and perhaps approving of their chaste dance steps.

'What's wrong with it?' her father said, pointing at the flyer with his fork. 'It says here, "a fun evening for young Polish men and women". You are a young Polish woman.'

'What's wrong?' Marie replied. 'Allow me to pick an item at random.' She surveyed the page again. 'To begin, I am commanded to appear in highland dress. "Come dressed as lords and ladies of the highland," it says. Those are folk clothes. Woollen skirts, moccasins. A blouse with flowers on it.'

'What's the problem?'

'Why must I dress up like a farmer?'

'It means you are proud to be Polish. It's harmless fun.' Her father endeavoured to grin to show how fun it could be. The corners of his mouth rose up in a strange way, as though they had never attempted the mission. He held the expression for three seconds, then his mouth relaxed to its normal position, a perfectly straight line in precise parallel to the floor.

Marie laughed. 'I can't go. I have no highland clothes.'

'There is a fine shop on Bracka Street,' he answered quickly, as though he'd predicted this objection. 'The top seamstress in the city will sew you an exquisite costume from the best fabrics and leathers.'

Marie shook her head. 'Highland clothes must be handmade! By the family. Even I know that. I can't go. My mother should be making these clothes!'

She swallowed as the word 'mother' hung in the air. She hadn't spoken that forbidden noun to him in years. Her discovery of the hair had brought out a brazenness in her. Whereas before she had performed the role of dutiful, timid daughter, never questioning her father's version of events, finding that braid under the floorboards had torn something open inside, releasing a boldness which shocked and delighted her. She shot a glance at her father to gauge his reaction to what she'd said. To her dismay, her father made no grand response; instead he shook his head and spoke softly.

'Tradition dictates the dress must be handmade, yes. And it must be made by family. But nowhere does it say it must be the mother. Any family member can make the dress.'

She felt annoyed at his easy, unperturbed response. 'Yes, but I have no grandmother, either. No kindly aunt or older married sister who knows how to sew. I have no family whatsoever except for you, do I?'

She waited for her father to flinch or to betray some guilt with an anguished swallow, but again, he made no reaction to show she'd rankled him. His gaze remained calm; he looked straight at her. He was either a greater deceiver than the devil, or her mention of her mother truly didn't bother him. Either way, the conversation continued, and Marie was left stumbling around the infinite mystery of her father.

'I can make the dress,' he said then.

'Papa. That is not what I meant.'

He shook his head. 'You deserve handmade clothes – that is what you will get. I will make them.'

'You don't know how to sew!' Marie scoffed.

'I do indeed,' he said. 'I put twenty-five stitches in Jan Borowski's flank this morning. Sister Emilia declared them the smallest sutures of her nursing career. There will be minimal scarring.'

'Sewing skin and sewing fabric are not the same!'

'I beg to differ.'

'You will embarrass me. I refuse to look like a repaired tendon.'

'A deal, then. I will sew you a costume. If you resemble a maiden of the highland, you will attend the dance. If you resemble a repaired tendon, you may stay at home.'

Marie had run out of reasons to oppose him. 'Fine,' she said. Her father attempted another smile and failed again. Marie squinted at him and returned to her meal. He'd cooked the meat to perfection, as always; it was soft and falling off the bone. He folded a piece of meat neatly into his mouth and chewed.

'Why do you wish for me to attend this dance?' Marie asked.

'All of the town will be there,' he replied. 'People your own age, from similar families. You will enjoy it.'

'I doubt that,' Marie replied with a snort. She tore a piece of bread from her side plate and buttered it.

57

'Perhaps you will find a husband there,' he offered. He coughed and looked away.

'I knew it.' Marie glared at him. 'I'm seventeen years old!'

'You will be eighteen this year. I was wed at twenty.' He swallowed a mouthful of cabbage. 'And I'm a man. Women marry younger.'

'What's the rush?' Marie said. 'I have not finished school yet.'

'You will soon, and then what will you do? You've already stayed at that school an eternity compared to most girls. Your chums are getting married. There must be fewer than half the girls in your class now than when you began. You look strange in your convent clothes, a grown woman in a school uniform. Soon you will be done and then you will sit idle. Far better to be married.'

Marie inhaled. 'I don't want to marry. I want to study. I want to attend university.' She could feel her heart thumping as she announced the plan she'd never breathed to anyone.

Her father scowled. 'To what purpose?'

'I want to study medicine,' she said, a note of panic rising in her voice. She suddenly felt like an injustice was being done to her.

He chuckled. 'What for?'

Marie grew furious. How did he not know this? Yes, she had kept the plan to herself, embarrassed to say it out loud, but she had expected her father to have an inkling as to what she was about to say. 'I want to become a doctor.'

'Oh.' He gazed at the floor and appeared to think. He looked at her again. 'Do you believe you possess the intelligence for such things?'

She felt as though someone had knocked the wind out of her. She'd never expected her father to say that to her. She always thought her father approved of her intelligence, that he regarded her as a person of cleverness and acumen, reasoning and common sense. She felt as though her core had ruptured. 'I achieve the highest mark in everything at school. Have always done,' she said, hearing a whine of protest in her voice.

'Yes, but you attend a girls' school,' he said. 'That is no great achievement.'

Marie pushed her chair back from the table, dumbfounded. Who was this man, whom she'd thought of as her friend, her champion? Finally, she spoke in a shrill voice for which she hated herself afterwards. 'Do you not think I possess the mind to become a doctor, to do what you do?'

He sighed. 'I don't know.'

Marie nodded once and stared out the window.

'It is not that I think you don't have the intelligence.' Her father shrugged. 'Only that I have never observed it. This comes as news to me, your intention to study further. You must give me time to adjust.'

Marie grew enraged again. This she must take issue with. 'What did you think when I asked to attend the hospital with you during my holidays? When I borrowed your *Merck Manual*?' She couldn't tell if he was feigning this ignorance or if it was genuine. 'Do you not know me at all, Papa?' She was on the verge of tears and willed herself not to cry, unless the tears would help her case, in which case she'd call them forth. Her heart broke at the idea that her father didn't know her.

'Come now, Marie, there's no need for histrionics,' he said.

Marie crossed her arms over her chest. 'I insist you tell me what you think of me.'

Her father met her eyes. 'I do not believe you lack intelligence,' he said after a time.

'Allow me to study, then.'

'I don't see why. Even if you possess the requisite cleverness to pass the course, this is not even the central issue. There stands a roadblock far greater than the question of your cognitive abilities.'

'There does?' she said. 'Astonish me.'

He collected the dinner plates and moved to the sink. 'When I studied at university, among my class of around one hundred men, I also had the pleasure of knowing three lady students. One of these ladies dropped out to marry in second year, and the other two graduated to become lady doctors. Of the two who graduated, both married and started families within two years. Neither of them practise medicine now, they both have multiple children requiring their care and attention. Once those children are grown, these women will not work either, for a new generation of doctors will have come up behind them and taken their positions. Even if by some miracle they manage to convince their husbands they could begin working as forty-year-old lady interns, no one would give them a job. Women simply don't achieve employment as doctors.' He filled the sink with water and began washing the dishes. 'I did not make these rules.'

Marie gasped at the arguments, knowing she had no answer for them. She scratched the tablecloth. 'You could give me a job,' she said.

He shook his head. 'Not my decision. That lies with the hospital board. They won't employ a woman. Not if there's a man who can perform the job, of which there are plenty. Men who need to support a family.'

Marie felt herself choke on her own breath. She'd never heard her father's views on such matters. Though they horrified her, she also felt grateful. This was the most adult conversation they had ever had.

'I don't say this to be cruel, Marie, only to put you on your guard. I don't want to see you heartbroken.'

'It will break my heart if I can't study.'

Her father nodded. 'I'm sorry. I don't want you to study. I want you to marry.'

60

'Why are you in such a rush to see me married?' she asked. Her father stared out the window and remained silent for some time.

'Papa?' Marie said at last, when he didn't answer.

'I may not be around forever,' he said finally.

'Where are you going?' she demanded.

'Nowhere.' He shrugged. 'If something happened to me . . .'

'What's going to happen? You don't leave the house.' She laughed.

'I do,' he insisted.

'When? Apart from reasons of employment, when do you leave the house?'

'I leave to play tennis,' he said.

'I hardly expect tennis to cause your demise.'

'Other things are coming,' he said.

'Germany has threatened to invade for years now,' Marie scoffed. 'They will never dare.'

Her father adjusted his glasses and seemed to ignore her comment. 'When the war comes, I may not be able to protect you as I do now. Therefore you must marry.' He placed the last of the dishes in the drying rack and sat back down.

'I could become a doctor and help on the battlefield with injured soldiers,' Marie said, sitting as well.

'Do not speak to me of war, child, like you know what it is. Imagine the most wretched misery you can,' he spat. 'This equals one hundredth of one per cent of war.' Marie startled at the bitterness of his tone, but also yearned to hear more. It was the most her father had ever spoken of the Great War. Of anything about himself, really. She studied his face. It comprised such a peculiar mixture of features, soft where it should be hard and hard where it should be soft.

'What are you looking at?' her father asked without glancing up.

'Nothing,' she replied, though she kept staring.

'You are staring at me.'

'You have such an odd face,' she said.

He went to move from the table, but then seemed to think better of it and instead turned to look straight at her. His eyes bored into hers, two green orbs peering. 'Take a good look for as long as you like.'

Her heart thumped in her chest, unnerved by the weirdness of the invitation. This was not their usual dinner conversation. Marie liked to challenge herself with how much discomfort her body could stand. Could she go without sleep for two days? Could she sit in freezing water for ten minutes? Her father's offer to look directly at his face would trump both of these. 'No, thank you,' she replied, looking away, trying to sound casual. The beef stew in her stomach churned and suddenly tasted old and bloody. She stood and walked to the window.

Her father cleared away the salt and pickles and wiped down the table. 'If you marry, you can study,' he said finally.

Marie turned back to him.

'A second deal,' he continued. 'If you marry, I will permit you to attend university.'

'Do you mean it?'

He nodded. 'I will even pay your tuition.'

'So I must marry? What if I can't find anyone who wants me?'

'You won't have trouble,' he said. Marie nodded. She knew the looks men gave her on the tram, in the square. 'Do we have a deal?' He held out his hand. 'We can shake on it, like adults.'

'This is silly, Papa.'

'Shake or nothing,' he replied. 'I will allow you to pursue medical studies and in exchange you will marry. We will both get what we want.'

Marie finally, with reluctance, raised her hand in silence. Her father took it and shook her hand. She'd never shaken her father's hand before. His fingers felt strong and fine-boned. A surgeon's hands.

'Deal,' he replied in a strong, soft voice. Her father's voice always combined those two elements.

7
NEW FRIENDS

A new internist was to begin his career at the hospital the next morning and Dominik had arranged to greet him at the nurses' station. His name was Dr Jan Gruener.

Dominik felt an urgency to gain a new pair of hands. With the professor moving to emeritus status, he was now the only physician on staff able to remove an appendix or repair an aorta. It was madness to have only a single person capable of these surgeries in a city where people seemed to enjoy destroying their bodies with ploughs and by crashing into things. And if the Germans ever visited, the need for hands that could repair torn flesh would only grow.

He moved towards the nurses' station in quick but controlled steps, careful not to show his eagerness. A fishhook in Paweł Radikova's thumb had delayed him; he'd spent thirty minutes extracting it. Dominik squinted as he turned the corner and took off his glasses to wipe them. No doctor waited at the nurses' station. Instead, Errol Flynn leaned over the counter.

Not in the literal sense. The film star hadn't given up his Hollywood career and become a general surgeon in a Polish clinic. But the man in the white coat chatting to a nurse looked disturbingly like the actor who solved crimes and wooed dames at the city's twin cinema every matinee. Dominik made a vow. He would not hold this

64

man's appearance against him, so long as he could resect a bowel with minimal complications. He strode forwards to meet him.

'Dr Gruener.' Dominik held out his hand. 'I am Dr Dominik Karski, surgical consultant. I apologise for the delay. I look forward to working with you. Where would you like to start?'

The man gripped Dominik's hand with a large warm palm. He shook it twice, then released. 'Good to know you, Doc. Call me Johnny.'

Dominik shuddered. Johnny! He would never address a physician he'd just met by his first name, let alone this ridiculous foreign moniker. He decided to politely pretend he'd not heard the suggestion. 'May I assist you with your first patient, Dr Gruener? I could show you around at the same time.'

'Already seen her,' the new doctor replied. 'Mrs Hat-flowers. Breast examination. She left happy.' Dominik couldn't tell if the man was being serious or not. Dr Gruener leaned on the high counter of the nurses' station and smiled. Dominik felt absurd.

'Mrs who?' he asked.

'The lady with the flowery hat.' Dr Gruener pointed to his head.

'Mrs Katura,' Matron Skorupska said, sitting behind the nurses' station. She tapped a patient chart in front of her.

'What are you doing, Matron?' Dominik squinted. 'What do you write there? Is that Mrs Katura's record?'

Matron Skorupska nodded.

'Why are you writing in the section called "physician's notes"?'

'I am helping Johnny out, Dr Karski. It's his first day.' She looked at Dr Gruener and blushed.

'Call him Dr Gruener, Matron.'

'I told her to call me Johnny,' the doctor said cheerfully. 'I prefer it. You should call me it too.'

Dominik tried to remain calm, but he could feel a vein bulging in his temple. He peered at the papers again to confirm he wasn't hallucinating. He wasn't. 'Matron. Are you doing Dr Gruener's paperwork for him?'

Dr Gruener grinned. 'Easy, Doc. She knows Mrs Hat-Flowers and she offered to do it. It will be quicker if she does it. She likes doing it.' He wore a self-satisfied grin.

Dominik glowered at him. He studied him, carefully this time. The new doctor wore his white physician's jacket like a frock-coat. He'd turned the collar up, as though shielding his neck from a wind that, since they stood inside, was non-existent. A signet ring of smooth gold on his little finger announced ancestry of Prussian nobility. He was probably the middle son of a penniless duke who lived in a decaying castle somewhere. He reeked of privilege and idleness. Dominik tried to contain his anger. He'd asked for a physician and they'd sent him a buccaneer.

'This is preposterous.' Dominik turned to his new colleague. 'Nurses do not perform your administration, Doctor. You are a physician – you took an oath – and paperwork is part of that. I'm sorry if you expected something more glamorous, but there you are!'

'Doctor. Johnny wants to buy you dinner,' the matron said.

The new doctor nodded. 'That's right, old chap. To thank you for letting me join your outfit. I'm honoured. I've heard you're a genius.'

Dominik bristled. He had no problem with being called a genius, but coming from an individual who'd already conscripted the nursing staff to complete his patient notes, the compliment rang somewhat hollow.

'No, thank you,' Dominik said, turning away to leave.

'But Dr Karski, you haven't heard where he wants to take you.' Dominik turned back to Matron Skorupska. 'To Kamiński's.' She said it with reverence, as though uttering a saint's name. The new doctor puffed out his chest and grinned. He seemed to expect that Dominik would be impressed.

Dominik grimaced. Kamiński's was a lavish restaurant a block back from the square that all the beautiful people in Krakow attended. It served blackbird pie and chocolate soup, and for the price of a small automobile, one could dine on a whole roasted peacock, complete with feathers. The clientele smoked opium-laced cigars and rearranged Europe over their card tables as they watched the dancing girls. The evening would likely end with some light chandelier-swinging and an orgy. 'I cannot, with deepest regret,' Dominik said flatly. 'I must get home to prepare dinner for my daughter.'

'Bring her along. I shall treat both of you.'

Matron Skorupska gasped, as impressed as if the new doctor had offered a flying carpet ride instead of offering to pay for three dinners at an overpriced restaurant. 'You and Marie. You can't argue with that, Dr Karski!'

Dominik glanced at Dr Gruener. He was watching him, running his eyes over Dominik's face and grinning in a manner Dominik found insufferable. The man seemed to think he had Dominik's character pinned; that offers of lavish dinners would impress him.

'Thank you for the offer, Dr Gruener, but I'm afraid I must decline. I did not ask you to come work here so I would be treated to free meals. I asked for another surgeon because one of our own is retiring – a superb physician, I might add – and we need the help. If, instead of inviting me to dinners, you would kindly do your job, including your own paperwork, that would make me very happy. Do you think you can manage such a thing?'

Dr Gruener's face fell; he looked genuinely hurt. Dominik smarted. He was sure it was an act. 'Good idea, Dr Karski,' Dr Gruener said to Dominik. 'I shall do just that. Sorry for bothering you – I'm sure you are very busy.'

'I am.'

'Thank you for introducing yourself.' Dr Gruener smiled professionally, the playfulness of his prior expression gone. 'Looking forward to working with you.'

'And you, Dr Gruener,' Dominik replied, though he didn't mean it. 'If you will excuse me, I have patients to see.'

Dominik walked off. He caught sight of his reflection in a window as he walked by and made the idle indulgence of comparing it to Dr Gruener's. His coat, instead of hanging soft and carefree, was starched within an inch of its life – it could have stood up on its own. He'd parted his hair with the precision of a Swiss watchmaker, exposing a perfectly straight route of white scalp, starting in line with his right eyeball and running back to his crown. Dominik nodded, pleased. In contrast with the new doctor, who seemed to style himself as a foppish scoundrel, Dominik appeared neat and tidy and the picture of professionalism: all that was required in a doctor. He returned to his patients.

As Dominik walked to the tram that evening, he found Dr Gruener in the parking area for automobiles, behind the hospital. He cut a curious figure as he sat on a fallen log, alone. Dominik rolled his eyes and contemplated ignoring him, but instead walked over to him.

'What are you doing? Do you need directions to Kamiński's? The number four tram will take you straight to the restaurant.' He winced before making the next offer, which he didn't want to do. 'I'm going to the tram stop myself. I could take you there.'

'I've changed my mind about the restaurant,' Dr Gruener replied. 'Stupid idea. I'm not going to sit in that place all by myself.'

'Surely your wife must be waiting for you.' Dominik checked his watch. He needed to get home; Marie would be expecting her dinner.

'I don't have a wife anymore.'

Dominik grimaced. 'You are going home to no one then?' A pitiable look seemed to engulf Dr Gruener's face, as though great pain flowed through him. Dominik rolled his eyes. The man performed an admirable show; perhaps he really was an actor.

'It's true. I'm alone, old chap. I arrived in the city yesterday. I don't know anyone.' He offered a clownish smile.

'I'm sure you will make friends quickly.' He believed this; Dr Gruener possessed enough easy manners and superficial charm to fool many into liking him.

The Prussian nobleman nodded and lit a cigarette. 'See you tomorrow.'

Dominik turned and began walking towards the tram stop. An anguished cry rang out behind him. He turned back to Dr Gruener, who was rubbing his shoe. 'What happened? Are you all right?'

'I dropped ash on my loafer. I just got these.'

Dominik sighed. He watched the other doctor sit on the log and rub his expensive-looking, impractical shoe. Twilight was ending; darkness would soon enshroud the parking lot. Outside the hospital, with his flamboyantly styled white coat removed, Dr Gruener took up far less space than he'd first appeared to. Dominik saw now that the doctor's trousers hung loose around his middle, the top of them gathered like a scrunched paper bag; he'd started using a new hole on his belt to keep them up, the previously employed notch sitting slack and worn, three markers up from the one now in use. He must have lost significant weight.

Dominik made the mistake then of imagining what Dr Gruener's evening would be like, returning home to a cold rented apartment with no furniture, eating nothing and staring at the wall until it came time to turn the lights out. He closed his eyes, already regretting what he was about to say. 'I suppose if you will be sitting at home alone, you might as well come to my place for dinner. I cannot attend Kamiński's – as I said, I must cook for my daughter. We shall eat something very boring, sausages and cabbage likely. Though better than you starving, I'd imagine.'

Dr Gruener's face lit up; he was already getting up from the log. 'Do you mean it?'

Dominik gritted his teeth. He did not mean it, but he found some words. 'You're no use to me as a surgeon if you do not have the strength to lift a scalpel.'

'Truly? Yes, I shall come.' Dr Gruener beamed and started walking in the wrong direction for the tram; he did not know where he was going.

'Good, then. This way.' Dominik ushered him the other way.

'Why don't you call me Johnny?' the doctor asked as they began walking. 'It's what everyone calls me.'

Dominik glared. 'Are you aware that in England, Johnny is slang for prophylactics?'

'Yes, they named them after me,' Dr Gruener replied with a grin. The crumpled figure from the log evaporated as he adopted his earlier swagger. 'I bet you will call me Johnny one day.'

'I highly doubt it,' Dominik replied with a loud huff. He was already regretting his decision. The broken-wing act of pitiable log-sitting and weight loss had tricked him. Now he would have to suffer through an evening with this person. The tram arrived. 'This is the number five,' Dominik said, 'if you still wish to come to dinner.'

'Of course!' Dr Gruener replied. He leapt onto the tram, greeting the driver warmly as though he were an old friend and beaming at all of the passengers. He found an empty seat and motioned for Dominik to join him, patting the seat merrily. Dominik sighed and sat down. The tram pulled out from the stop and began its journey through the broken cobblestoned streets, past decrepit tenements and broken buildings, towards Old Town.

'I'm sorry about earlier,' Dr Gruener said. 'I don't always have the nurses do my paperwork.'

'You could have fooled me,' Dominik replied, looking out the opposite window.

'It's true. Sometimes I get an intern to do it. Or the janitor.'

Dominik could feel the corner of his mouth rising up – what was that? A smile. He felt horrified. He forced his mouth back down to a position of non-amusement.

'So you have a daughter? Tell me about her,' Dr Gruener said.

'Her name is Marie. She wants to become a doctor,' he scoffed. He cursed himself for revealing the information, a thoughtless outburst; he did not want to talk to anyone about Marie.

Dr Gruener laughed. 'Preposterous. Women have emotions and no killer instinct. A woman doing a man's work is obscene.'

'I agree,' Dominik replied. The tram rounded the bend, approaching the small patch of open country between the hospital and Old Town. 'Although Marie Curie is a woman.'

Dr Gruener looked over to him. 'Her Nobel was all Pierre, the husband,' he replied. 'He was the puppetmaster.'

'Right. Though most of her discoveries were made after Pierre died.'

'That's not the point,' Dr Gruener said. 'Women are unable to compute. They have smaller brains. They are not as strong.'

Dominik scowled. 'Of course. Though my daughter's lack of heft with a coal shovel does not equate to lack of skill with a scalpel.' Dominik recognised the absurdity of the situation. He was now making the very arguments his daughter had put to him. 'To value a person's workforce contribution solely based on brute strength offends all concerned.'

'Very true. All people who must use their bodies to earn a living are wrecked before their time,' Dr Gruener replied. 'The trick is to use one's brain to make a living. But that's my point. Your daughter doesn't have the brain. I've never met a woman who's as clever as us. Women are softer, too.'

Dominik smarted. He agreed wholeheartedly in principle, of course he did. But Dr Gruener had never met Marie. The tram made a stop. Dominik could hear his voice rising but found himself unable to stop talking. 'Perhaps softness is a good thing,' Dominik suggested, ignoring Dr Gruener's laugh. 'Some would say medicine is the perfect union of male and female brains.' He wanted to kick himself for the looniness of his words, aware of how lumpy and soft he sounded. 'The deduction of the male with the humanity of the female. To heal sickness, one must both attack and nurture. Coleridge the poet said the greatest minds are androgynous.'

'Coleridge. I heard he had gonorrhoea, quite a virulent strain.' Dr Gruener lit cigarette, inhaled and flicked the ash out of the tram window. 'Women can't do men's work.'

'Women in the rural villages of Albania often live as men,' Dominik offered. 'For economic reasons. When a family is burdened only with daughters, one daughter may apply to the elders of the village to live as a man. Daughters can't inherit land there, so she assumes the male gender and takes over the family farm. The only stipulation is that she must never marry.' He coughed self-consciously, aware he sounded like an anthropologist.

'Exactly,' Dr Gruener replied with a satisfied grin. 'Albanians,' he snorted. 'Obscene.'

'But what if a woman is capable of some breakthrough we've been waiting for? What if she possesses within her the ability to cure polio, or cancer? Wouldn't it be better for everyone?'

Dr Gruener looked at him thoughtfully. 'If she is, then surely a man is too.'

Dominik couldn't argue with that. 'Our stop is next,' he said, and rang the bell.

8

I TOOK HERMANN
GÖRING TO SEVEN SETS

'Marie? Are you home?' Dominik called nervously as he entered the house. He had never invited another doctor to dinner, nor anyone. Marie might scream at seeing another person in the house, the sight was so rare.

His daughter came down the stairs wearing her convent school uniform. She looked past Dominik at Dr Gruener who stood behind him in the doorway.

'This is Dr Gruener,' Dominik said.

'Call me Johnny.'

'Johnny.' She raised an eyebrow and looked at Dominik.

'Dr Gruener will be staying for dinner, Marie. I can take him to a restaurant if this inconveniences you?'

Marie laughed and turned to Dr Gruener. 'Would you like a drink, Johnny?'

'Water, thank you.'

She nodded and went to the kitchen, returning with a glass. Dominik harrumphed under his breath at her ease and friendliness, providing such hospitality to his charity case.

Dr Gruener gestured to the newspaper on the table. 'I played tennis against him once,' he said, pointing at the rotund man pictured on the front page.

Dominik squinted at the picture. 'Who, Hermann Göring?'

Dr Gruener nodded keenly.

Dominik closed his eyes. He'd brought home not only an aristocrat but a Nazi.

'We had a tournament at my father's country estate,' Dr Gruener said. 'Mr Göring was there.'

Dominik pictured the scene; juleps on the Juncker lawn, barons shooting the waitstaff, opium and swastikas.

'Who won?' Marie asked.

'Göring did.' Dr Gruener sighed. 'For a fat person he was unexpectedly spry. But I gave him a run for his deutschmarks, took him to seven sets.'

Marie laughed, appearing unshocked. In fact, she looked thoroughly entertained. Before Dr Gruener could continue with his next anecdote, about walking Hitler's dog, perhaps, or charming Eva Braun, Dominik showed him to the sitting room, offered him a chair, and asked Marie to help him in the kitchen.

'I had a wonderful nursemaid,' Dr Gruener said, depositing another crescent pillow of dough in his mouth and chewing. He was onto his second plate of dumplings, consuming the first in less than a minute. Dominik, bemused, had offered him more and Dr Gruener had vigorously accepted. 'Her name was Dorota. She had gigantic bosoms.'

Marie laughed. Dominik rolled his eyes.

'She'd bundle me up in those two glorious mounds until I fell asleep. I never saw my father. Or my mother.' A sudden flash of sadness moved over his face, then he smiled. 'But Dorota raised me. She made such wonderful food, just this way. How do you get the pastry so thin? Dominik, you *are* a genius.'

'You mix the flour with hot water instead of cold to make the dough,' Dominik explained. Dr Gruener turned to him, surprised and interested. He seemed to wait for him to continue. Dominik pushed his glasses up his nose. 'It's chemistry,' he said with a shrug. 'Heat softens the flour, allowing the dough to stretch further, thinner—'

'But you have done something more than chemistry,' Dr Gruener interrupted, beaming. 'You have performed alchemy! These dumplings have a golden-brown hue. They are not stodgy like others. What else have you done?'

'I finished them in the frypan with a little butter.' Dominik spoke quickly, then regretted it instantly, feeling like he had offered a simple secret that was not so wondrous. He commanded himself to stop talking.

'They are like little parcels of heaven,' Dr Gruener exclaimed. 'Little pillows of joy! Have you met Dorota?'

'What else did she make?' Marie asked. 'I'll wager Papa makes it too.' Dominik shot a look at her and wished her to stop talking as well.

Dr Gruener gasped. 'Do you know how to make potato pancake?'

'Of course,' Dominik replied with a nod.

'Dorota was from somewhere . . . the town escapes me.'

'From the cuisine you describe, she came from the east.'

'She did! How about the little swirly things?' he said excitedly. Dr Gruener scratched his chin. 'There's pastry in them, and they're savoury, but also sweet. Black seeds whirl through them in a glorious wheel.'

'Poppy seed swirl cake,' Dominik said swiftly, then ordered himself to calm down.

'Yes!' Dr Gruener cried.

'Papa can make those,' Marie said. 'You must come every Wednesday, Johnny. Each week, Papa will make one dish from your childhood.' Dr Gruener's face lit up; he looked as happy as a boy on the last day of school.

Dominik shot another look at his daughter. 'Marie, no,' he said, shaking his head. 'Let's not monopolise Dr Gruener's free time.'

'Of course, sorry, Johnny,' Marie said.

'It sounds a fine plan to me,' Dr Gruener replied. 'But only if your father agrees, dear girl. He's the one doing all the cooking and will be put out.'

'I won't be put out,' Dominik said. 'I will be making supper for Marie and myself in any case.' He couldn't believe what he was saying.

'It's settled then!' Marie said and Dominik shuddered.

After dessert and tea, Dominik showed Dr Gruener out. 'I am sorry if the night was rather boring, compared to Kamiński's. Though better than sitting at home alone, eating nothing and staring at the wall.' He shuffled a stone on the front porch between his feet and snuck a glance at Dr Gruener's face.

'Yes, it differed from that,' Dr Gruener replied. He stepped out onto the porch. The night air chilled Dominik and he crossed his arms over his chest.

Dr Gruener retrieved his cigarette case from his pocket and pointed it at Dominik. 'I know your secret. I'm onto you,' he said, smiling broadly.

Dominik swallowed and looked at Dr Gruener sharply. The man placed the cigarette in his mouth. He flicked the match out and seduced the vapour into his lungs, then sent the smoke from his mouth in a ring.

'You like to grumble and look stern,' Dr Gruener said finally. 'But you know what I think?'

'I feel like I'm about to,' Dominik said nervously.

'I think you're not that angry at all. I think underneath that grizzly exterior, you have a warm heart.'

'You're wrong.' Dominik rolled his eyes.

'Am I?' Dr Gruener wore a giant smile on his face. He blew more smoke out of the side of his mouth, away from Dominik. 'So I shall come again next week?'

Dominik scoffed. 'You might as well come every Wednesday, if you'll be sitting at home otherwise.'

'Staring at the wall, yes. Very well.' And Dr Gruener walked off into the night.

Dominik watched him go, but when he reached the road Dr Gruener turned back. 'I almost forgot,' he said. 'Your daughter.'

Dominik frowned. 'What about her?'

'I was wrong before, on the tram. I spouted some wisdom about how she couldn't be a doctor. I spoke before I knew her.'

'And now that you know her?'

'I stand thoroughly corrected. She'd make an outstanding physician. Like her father. Goodnight, Domek,' he said, shortening his name into the affectionate diminutive. Dominik bristled; he wouldn't have the gall to bestow a nickname on a person.

Dominik raised his hand to wave. 'Goodnight, Dr Gruener.'

Dr Gruener nodded and twirled back around. He flicked his cigarette into a bush and vanished; the black night engulfed him. The council had ordered all streetlamps to be extinguished: someone had decided that if Germany elected to invade, they might be unable to find the city if they switched off all the lights.

Dominik returned to the house to find Marie smiling at him. 'Papa, you didn't tell me you were inviting someone to dinner.'

'Dr Gruener is a person I've taken pity on. I asked him because he was sitting on a log, with nowhere to go.'

'Either way, I am pleased.'

'Pleased why?'

'Pleased you've made a friend,' she said.

He struggled to decipher her expression. 'He's not a friend. He's a charity case. Besides, I don't need to make friends. I have many,' Dominik protested.

She spoke teasingly. 'You have one friend, and he is seventy-five years old. You have no friends your own age. Everyone likes you and respects you, but no one is your friend. Why not? You don't possess foul breath or a lunatic's temperament. You talk about the church way too much for my liking, but there are many people in this town with whom you could converse on those subjects. You are a prime candidate for someone who should have friends. Yet you decline invitations all the time and never socialise. This man could be your friend. Therefore, I am pleased. Life doesn't have to be miserable. You can have a little pleasure now and then.'

'You talk nonsense sometimes. May I go to bed now?' he asked his daughter.

'Go, go,' she said, smiling again, and Dominik walked up the stairs.

It was not that he didn't want friends, just that he didn't want anyone to enter those private spaces of brain and heart where he might slip, and the friend might discover the truth or see him a little too clearly. He would find a way to cancel the planned Wednesday dinners. They would do only harm. He kicked himself for his foolishness in inviting someone into his home. He would make certain to avoid Dr Gruener as much as possible, to maintain a distance so he could only be viewed from far away, never allowing a man like that to see him too well.

9

I HAD A HORSE
LIKE YOU ONCE

Every Friday, Dominik baked trout for dinner, one of the dishes permitted by the church on that day of the week and Marie's favourite. On this particular Friday, as he fried off cabbage and onion in the griddle pan, the doorbell chimed. Piotr Strawiński, a patient, was standing on his porch, rain soaking his trench coat. As cancer ran in the man's family, Dominik guessed he was there to tell him of blood in his stool or some other detail that bore enough threat to warrant not waiting until Monday.

'Good evening, Dr Karski. I hope I am not disturbing you?' He pointed to Dominik's apron, which he'd wrapped over his beige suit, and chuckled.

'Come in, Mr Strawiński. To what do I owe the honour?' Dominik said, knowing full well he'd be offering his medical services.

'The honour is all mine. When I heard your child was to start medicine in the autumn at our little school, I had to stop by. Hanna, my office girl, told me.'

Dominik forged the connection; he knew Mr Strawiński primarily as a potential harbourer of bowel tumours, but the man also worked as admissions officer at Krakow's tertiary institution. 'Not at all. Please sit down.' The man did so, sitting in Dominik's chair at the dinner table. 'Would you like to stay for dinner? Have you eaten?'

'I'd be delighted. It smells wonderful. Forgive me, Dr Karski, I didn't know you had children. You always struck me as an old bachelor.'

'You are forgiven. You're not expected to know everyone in town.'

'In any case, I feel elated. One of our most spectacular alumni, and the cleverest man in the city! Any child of yours is most welcome at our university.'

'Would you like a drink?'

'Absolutely! Vodka if you have it. Or beer.'

Dominik retrieved a small flask of vodka from the cupboard that he kept for such occasions, when the pretence of social lubrication was required. He did not drink himself – a scandal for a Polish man; he had colleagues who nipped vodka for breakfast. He revealed his sobriety to no one; he didn't want them thinking he suffered mental illness. Whenever asked, he proclaimed himself a standard-litre-of-vodka-a-week man. He poured Mr Strawiński and himself both a drink; he'd have one sip to appear social. He never drank more, not for not liking the taste; the loss of control from over-imbibing, no matter how slight, the looseness of tongue or sideways glance that might come, posed too much of a risk in his situation.

The front door opened and Marie walked in. 'Good evening, Papa. Oh, good evening, sir,' she said, nodding politely to the man sitting in her father's chair.

Mr Strawiński sprang up and brushed some hair off his face with his hand. 'Good evening, mademoiselle,' he said. He straightened his jacket. His breath grew hoarse; this often happened to men when Marie walked in the room.

'Mr Strawiński, this is my daughter, Marie.'

Mr Strawiński ran his eyes all over her. 'You are a beauty. I had a horse like you once. I know that sounds strange, but I really did. A magnificent creature. Coat the colour of honey. Her name was Magda.' He spoke in a hushed, reverent tone, and then he was gone for a minute, staring into space.

Marie clenched her teeth in a smile and looked at Dominik.

'Mr Strawiński works at the university,' Dominik said, giving her the name of the institution he himself had attended. He'd telephoned them during the week. 'He runs the admissions office.'

'Oh,' Marie said. She smiled and released her shoulders, which had been hunched towards the sky. 'Can I get you a drink? Will you stay for dinner?'

Mr Strawiński laughed. 'I have one already, but I shall take another. And your father has already invited me, thank you! What hospitality. What are you cooking?' he asked her.

'I don't know,' Marie replied. 'Smells like trout.'

Mr Strawiński grimaced. 'Does your father always do the cooking? I guess it wouldn't be fair to get those pretty hands of yours covered in grease. How did you get to be so beautiful?'

Marie glanced sideways, as if stumped. 'I don't know. From my mother, I guess? Not from my father!' She shot a look at Dominik but he did not react.

There was a silence, then Mr Strawiński bellowed with laughter. 'Too true, my dear! No offence, Dominik, but she tells the truth!'

'None taken,' Dominik replied. He stirred the onions.

'And what do men need looks for anyway?' Mr Strawiński cried. 'They would be wasted on Dominik, a physician and a genius. He needs to appear serious, not a fop! No one wants to receive treatment from a dandy. They wouldn't trust him! Come and sit by me,' Mr Strawiński said to Marie, taking a seat again and patting the chair next to him. Marie nodded and sat down.

Dominik was both curious and repulsed to witness the actions of the portly man. Flirting always appeared grim, especially when one was neither the recipient nor the deliverer, only a witness to it. Dominik felt concern for his daughter as she moved within grasping reach of Mr Strawiński. Could she handle herself against lechery? How much did she know of things? The years of Marie's life that American advertisers were now calling teenagehood had shocked and saddened him. The little girl had vanished, and a creature with a mind of its own had replaced her.

'How lucky to have such children!' Mr Strawiński declared. 'So where is this prodigy of yours, Dominik? I am dying to meet this young genius.'

'They sit beside you,' Dominik said. Only the spitting of fat in the onion pan pierced the silence in the kitchen that followed.

Finally Mr Strawiński spoke. 'What a good joke! No, I mean, where is your son, Dominik? The one who will study medicine?'

'I have no son. I only have one child, sir. A daughter.' He pointed to Marie.

'Yes, but . . .' He trailed off, mouth open, looking confused and angry.

Dominik coughed. 'It is my daughter who wishes to study medicine.'

Marie smiled eagerly at the bureaucrat. Where earlier he'd rejoiced in moving his eyes down her body, now he seemed unable to look at her.

'We all wish for many things,' he said. 'That doesn't mean they'll happen.' The man turned back to Dominik.

'You said any child of mine is welcome to study.'

'Yes, but that was before.' Mr Strawiński chuckled.

'Before what, sir?' Marie asked, smiling sweetly.

'Nothing,' Mr Strawiński replied, a curious look crossing his face. The expression contained pure anguish, as if the pull between lust and principles tore the man in two. Dominik would have laughed, if laughing was something he did. But he never indulged in the pastime – that might reveal too much – so he kept his countenance serene.

'I am welcome, then?' Marie said.

Again Mr Strawiński looked at Dominik, who said nothing. He passed his glass from one hand to the other, then stared into it, as though the answer lay there. 'Yes. Of course,' he said. 'You will need to pass the entrance exam, naturally.'

Marie scowled. 'The entrance exam?' Dominik lifted his head; it was news to him too.

Mr Strawiński waved his hand. 'A short assessment,' he said. 'To see where you are at. If you pass, you may enrol.'

'There was no entrance examination when I attended,' Dominik said.

'Things are different now.' Mr Strawiński shrugged. 'You received a scholarship, as a returned serviceman.'

Dominik felt Marie's eyes on him. 'Yes, I did,' he said.

Mr Strawiński smiled and drained his glass. 'Anyway, must be going.' He stood.

'Oh, you can't stay for dinner?' Marie took the glass from him.

'No, I have an appointment. I forgot,' he added.

'Let me get your coat.' Marie fetched it from the hook in the hallway. She held it up and Mr Strawiński threaded his arms through, nodding his thanks without looking at her. It was as though something now repulsed him about the lovely young body and smooth-skinned face; there previously for his consumption, it now wanted something of its own.

'When should I come to the university, Mr Strawiński?' Marie asked sweetly.

'What for?' he said, giving her a puzzled look.

'To sit the examination?'

'Oh,' he grumbled, buttoning his coat. Mr Strawiński met Dominik's eye, looking uncomfortable. Dominik stared back at him and nodded; Marie continued smiling at him. He turned from one face to the other, caught between them. 'Tuesday,' he said finally.

'This Tuesday?' Marie pressed him.

He sighed. 'Not this one . . . Tuesday next,' he replied. Then, scurrying to the door like a rat from a sinking ship, he muttered a farewell and darted into the night.

'I didn't know you fought in the Great War, Father,' she said.

Dominik nodded.

'I should like to hear about it.'

'Nothing to tell.' He retrieved the trout from the oven and the hot, briny odour wafted through the room.

'What did my mother do while you were away fighting?' she asked in her most innocent tone.

Dominik stirred the onions; he'd neglected them during the conversation and action was required before they burned. 'Don't know, wasn't there.'

'How long was my labour?' she said, a touch of daring appearing on her face.

'Why do you talk of such nonsense? Have you gone mad?' he said. He trained his eyes on the onions.

'Not mad,' she replied in a calm voice. 'Curious.'

'Preposterous,' he muttered. He moved to the pantry for additional butter and deposited a small knob into the onion pan, where it bubbled and hissed, as though on command. She said nothing, just waited. He grimaced. 'As I said, I wasn't there. I never saw you until you were one year old.'

Marie seemed to study him.

'There's an exam to sit,' Dominik said, hoping to change the subject.

'I heard,' Marie said. 'I will study.'

'Very well then, and we shall see if you pass.'

The butter dissolved into golden brown and the onions appeared salvaged. He asked Marie to go to the garden to cut some more dill for the trout. She rolled her eyes, complaining that he had more than enough herbs already and stood still, not moving from the kitchen. She clearly wanted to talk more, but Dominik turned back to the stove and said nothing else, praying she would leave. Finally she sighed and disappeared into the backyard with some scissors and an oil lamp.

Dominik waited until she had gone, then let out his own sigh. She had never asked him such questions about her mother before; each day her impatience and impertinence on this topic seemed to grow. He did not know how much longer things could stay as they were. She was too old now, too intelligent, to stay in the dark. This only confirmed his belief that the best solution was to get her married, and soon. That way, once he was discovered and the truth about what had happened to Marie's mother came to light, his daughter would be ensconced in the safety and security of her husband's home and family, and she would remain as unscathed as possible by the scandal and ruin that would follow.

That wasn't to say that disgrace would not touch her at all. No way existed for her to come away truly untainted by his shameful story, but at least if she was married into a good family with high standing in the city, people would still speak to her and her new family would defend her, if only to protect themselves and their own interests. Even better, if she bore them a son and heir, they would envelop her into their bosom, quickly forgetting her maiden name and any connection she had once had to Dominik Karski.

The difficult part would be finding someone of this ilk willing to marry her. His daughter's beauty could stop automobile traffic, but she also possessed a spectacular streak of stubbornness that she had inherited from her mother. She would refuse to play any part in a courting game with someone she did not love. This was where the trouble would lie. How would he convince her to play, to recline, to submit, to be gracious and listen, even if the conversation partner was an imbecile? Rich men – or their sons, anyway – tended towards fecklessness, and Marie would need to charm one of them. But she gave no indication that she'd cooperate with this scheme. He would have to do what he could to encourage her, and throw as many rich men as he could into her path.

10

THE SOLUBILITY
PRODUCT EXPRESSION

Marie arrived at the university admissions office to sit her entrance exam the following Tuesday as scheduled. She applied her most polite yet authoritative smile, saying, 'Good day' as she entered.

A secretary looked up from the counter. She appeared unmoved by Marie's greeting, seeming annoyed instead to have been diverted from her magazine. The woman, who the nameplate on her desk announced as one Hanna Sadka, peered at Marie with irritation from behind a pair of small-framed spectacles. 'What do you want?' she asked.

'My name is Karska,' Marie replied. 'I come on the invitation of Mr Piotr Strawiński.'

Secretary Sadka studied her for some seconds. She moved her glasses down her nose and peered intently at Marie with a look of apparent bemusement. Finally, she shrugged and told Marie to wait there. She left her counter and disappeared through a door, which she closed behind her.

Marie stood in the room alone. She looked down at her clothes, wondering if they had been the source of Secretary Sadka's scepticism. She hoped she wore the correct ones, that she bore the appearance of a doctor. Her father always wore a white shirt and beige trousers, which he covered with a white physician's coat, his name and title embroidered on the breast pocket. Marie didn't own any trousers, nor a white coat. She had contemplated borrowing a set from her father, but that would have appeared comical. So she'd elected to dress like a lady doctor instead, only she didn't know what lady doctors wore, for such people didn't seem to exist. She'd settled on her plainest suit, a teal jacket and skirt. She'd covered up the edelweiss that lay on the blouse's collar; this made her look un-doctorly. Female. With the flower banished underneath her jacket, the outfit held the title of her most unfeminine ensemble.

Secretary Sadka returned with Mr Strawiński behind her. His face bore a look of annoyance but it changed to delight when he saw Marie. 'Good morning, mademoiselle, do we know each other?' he said. Polite but not unwelcome confusion moved across his face.

She adjusted her hat. 'I am Marie Karska, Mr Strawiński. Dominik Karski's daughter.'

His face fell. 'Oh. What do you want?'

'Sir, I'm here to take the entrance exam.' She smiled.

He studied her, then smiled back. 'What's a dolly like you want with an examination?' he said in a teasing tone.

Marie stepped back. She caught her reflection in the window glass of the office; the red of her lipstick gleamed in the portrait. She felt stupid. She should not have worn make-up: she had done it to appear grown-up, but it sent the wrong message of adulthood: not of male command, but feminine submission. She had taken such pains to hide the flower on her shirt and now she blatantly adver-tised her woman-ness with her lips.

'How about we forget this whole thing?' he said. 'That's what you want, yes? You look nervous, I know you don't want to take this exam. I won't tell your father, I promise.' He placed a finger to his lips: *this could be our secret.*

Marie's heart sank. 'I *do* want to take it. I admit I am nervous, but I have studied. I am prepared.'

He tilted his head and spoke as though he was comforting a child. 'This is a big, serious institution. You won't like it here. You have much finer things to do with your time.' He laughed. 'I say this for your benefit.' He emerged from behind the counter and squeezed her shoulder.

Marie tried not to wince at the touch. 'I promise I'll work hard,' she said.

He shook his head with irritation. He checked his watch and took a different tack, moving from soothing tones to infuriated ones. 'You are wasting my time now.'

Marie felt like running away. She gritted her teeth and exhaled. 'My father didn't send me, sir. I am here of my own volition. You said there was an exam to take. Let me sit it and I will be out of your hair.'

Secretary Sadka, attending to some papers on her desk, shot a glance sideways at Mr Strawiński. The man took a breath. 'Very well, the exam. Yes. Please take a seat.' He disappeared behind the door again. Marie sat in a chair by the window. She wished she'd brought her study notes to look over.

It took thirty minutes for the man to return, so long that Marie asked Secretary Sadka to check if he'd fallen ill. But finally he ushered Marie inside, telling her she could take the examination. He escorted Marie to a small office that appeared to be still in use by someone, perhaps away that day. She sat at the desk. A plant in a brass pot sat by the window; black spots covered its leaves. She raised an eyebrow. Why did she not sit in a hall, like they did at her convent school for end-of-year examinations?

'Am I the only student sitting this exam?' she asked.

He wiped sweat from his brow with a handkerchief. 'Of course,' he said. 'The others come on different days.'

'I see,' Marie said in an apologetic tone, though she felt suspicious. She vowed not to ask anything else, however, lest he change his mind and remove her from the university.

He placed a booklet in front of her and gave her a pen. Marie stared down at the page and squinted, as though if she stared hard enough, she might see what lay inside.

'Someone has torn off the front cover,' she said, pointing to the jagged edge of paper at the side of the book.

He opened his mouth to speak, then seemed to think better of it and waved his hand instead. 'Don't worry about that.' He sounded annoyed. 'That's how we do it.'

As she picked up the pen, he opened the door to leave. 'Wait!' she said. He turned to stare at her. 'How long do I have?'

'Oh.' He checked his watch and shrugged. 'Until twelve-thirty?'

Marie nodded. 'Thank you.'

He nodded back and exited, pulling the door shut behind him.

Marie took a deep breath and opened the booklet. She scanned the page and read the first question.

Her blood ran cold.

She'd asked Lolek about the test as soon as she found out she was required to take one. He was a student at the same university; perhaps he'd retained some past papers she could prepare with.

Lolek had said that he never took an exam to gain entry. Though he studied philosophy, ethics, literature, he told her: 'different to medicine.' He investigated the entrance process for his brother, who'd attended some years earlier, only to find he never sat an entrance exam either. Marie had panicked, thinking she'd have nothing to study, but then Lolek had returned two days later and presented her with a set of past papers from a university in Warsaw, on logic and general knowledge. 'An intelligence test,' he'd explained. 'Perhaps this is the assessment they will use. I think you will do fine,' he'd added with a smile.

Marie had breathed a sigh of relief; now she possessed the means to practise. She'd taken to the past papers with compulsion, like she did with most things. She completed the questions so many times, she knew them off by heart. 'Select the odd tile in the pattern' was one, and 'How many triangles do you see?' was another. Logic questions, assessments of general aptitude; she'd sat up with them every night for nine days. And the questions that sat in front of her now bore not even the slightest resemblance to them.

Q1. What is the correct solubility product expression for Ag_3PO_4?

A. $K_{sp} = [3Ag^+]^3 [PO_4^{3-}]$

B. $K_{sp} = [Ag^+]^3 [PO_4^{3-}]$

C. $K_{sp} = [Ag^+] [PO_4^{3-}]$

D. $K_{sp} = 3[Ag^+]^3 [PO_4^{3-}]$

E. $K_{sp} = [Ag^+] [PO_4^{3-}]^3$

The letters and numbers swirled before her. The paper could have been upside down for all she understood of it. It was a science exam – that she could tell – requiring prior knowledge of what she believed was organic chemistry. She commanded herself to remain calm, not to panic yet. She flipped through the other pages of the booklet. The exam comprised forty questions, all multiple choice, repeating the format of the first question. Now she panicked. Every question was the same, a series of random letters and numbers she couldn't decipher. This was not an intelligence test; it required the memorisation of formulae and knowledge of theory.

She left the room to fetch Secretary Sadka. 'I've received the wrong paper,' she told her.

The woman glanced up from her magazine. 'He's gone to lunch.'

'What time will he be back?'

'Tomorrow? Next week?' The woman laughed. 'Who knows with him?'

Marie's voice caught in her throat. 'He won't be back before the time is up? What do I do?'

'Do your best.' Secretary Sadka shrugged. 'Answer as many as you can.'

'That's impossible,' Marie cried. She felt like screaming. 'I don't know the theory. I will fail.'

Secretary Sadka stared at her, then shook her head. 'Look, I'm sorry, all right? There is no exam for entrance to medicine at this university.'

Marie swallowed. 'I don't understand,' she said, out of politeness more than anything else, for she understood fully.

Secretary Sadka sighed. 'He grabbed that exam from a pile – I saw him do it. He gave it to you to shut you up. Medical students do not need to pass an examination to study here. We grant entrance based on the candidate's high school results and an interview.'

'What shall I do then?' Marie said in horror. 'Shall we call him back?'

'And say what to him?'

'Confront him!' Marie replied. 'About what he has done. Denounce his behaviour.' She crossed her arms.

'And will that get you what you want?' Secretary Sadka asked, peering over her spectacles.

'Perhaps he'd see reason.'

'Oh, yes.' The woman laughed. 'He is a reasonable man.'

Marie looked at the paper, with its preposterous questions, written in gibberish. 'This exam looks like it's for students studying first-year organic chemistry.'

'Second year,' Secretary Sadka replied. 'This is an honours paper. Students complete this exam before graduating the year. Three weeks later, if they pass, they will be refining petrochemicals as a summer intern at IG Farben.'

'What should I do, then?' Marie asked, growing desperate.

'Leave. Running away is probably for the best.'

Marie fought back tears and stared out the window. A stone gargoyle sat perched on the roof across the courtyard. It stared at her, its giant mouth contorted into a clownish grin, laughing at her. She turned back to the woman. 'I don't want to do that.'

'There exists another option.' The woman smiled and raised both eyebrows, a look of respect and challenge. She paused. Marie waited for her to speak. 'You could ace the test,' she said. She returned to her magazine and did not look up again.

Marie heard herself sigh. She returned to the stranger's office and sat.

Q1. What is the correct solubility product expression for
Ag_3PO_4?
A. $K_{sp} = [3Ag^+]^3 [PO_4^{3-}]$
B. $K_{sp} = [Ag^+]^3 [PO_4^{3-}]$
C. $K_{sp} = [Ag^+] [PO_4^{3-}]$
D. $K_{sp} = 3[Ag^+]^3 [PO_4^{3-}]$
E. $K_{sp} = [Ag^+] [PO_4^{3-}]^3$

She scoured every memory she had of open textbooks on her father's desk, every chemistry equation she'd ever glanced at. She looked at her watch. The hands read eleven am. Ninety minutes remained until she would return her paper, possibly with nothing written on it. She wanted to panic, die, defenestrate herself. If she failed this exam, Papa would never let her try anywhere else.

She looked again at the question. Ag_3PO_4. What did those letters stand for? Ag was silver; it came from the periodic table. Very well, she knew that part. Ag_3 – well, that meant three molecules of silver. PO_4 . . . what was this mysterious thing? Not mysterious at all! It was phosphorus, P, and oxygen, O – four of them, 4 – making phosphate. Yes. Then she pictured three pieces of silver and one piece of phosphate in her mind. Phosphate was a mineral, she knew that.

Important for strong, healthy bones, among other things. Her father had told her that.

She tried to recall everything her father had ever mentioned about chemistry. *Chemistry is the transport and movement of particles*, Dominik had told her. *Everything is connected.* And his favourite, *The periodic table is the universe. Everything in the cosmos is contained within it.*

She flipped to the back of the exam book. A periodic table stared at her. She gasped with joy, having not realised it was there before, and read the question again. It asked for a solubility product expression. Solubility – she knew that one. It meant how much water was required to dissolve something completely. The question asked how to dissolve silver and phosphate. How much did three molecules of silver weigh? The periodic table listed it! She looked at the multiple-choice answers. The coefficient, the number denoting the number of molecules, appeared at the top of the letters as well as a power. The coefficient was written again, for some reason. Why?

Because that was the rule. Ah. She'd never learnt this rule before, but she was learning it now. Could she teach herself a chemistry concept while sitting the exam for it? Of course not. Impossible. But she was there anyway, with the paper and pen in her hand, so she selected answer B. It looked correct, with what she knew about solubility and how coefficients worked, and from the new things she'd learned while taking this exam.

As she worked her way through the paper using this inelegant but utilitarian method, she began to notice something. The multiple-choice answers for each question were all similar, with the same letters and numbers rearranged in different combinations.

The examination's author had employed laziness when setting it; they'd utilised the same structure for each question so one could gain the answer by a process of elimination. Two wildly inappropriate

94

answer choices always presented themselves in the set of four, to be discarded quickly, leaving two similar ones with a small but crucial difference between them. All she had to do was decipher the difference. And now that she actually understood the questions' contents, it made them twice as easy to answer.

But then she looked at the clock: an hour and ten minutes remained. She'd spent twenty minutes on the first page! She'd have to do better. She rushed forward. Some of the questions required only mathematics to answer, addition and subtraction, although they too used chemical compounds. This was lazy questioning as well, and to her advantage. She pressed on.

When the time was up, Marie put down the pen. She waited for the secretary to come to fetch her and collect the paper, but she didn't. Marie waited another five minutes; still no one came. She opened the paper to check her answers, to make use of the extra time. She turned a few pages and decided that everything was complete, no more time was necessary. She walked out of the office and handed the paper to Secretary Sadka, who remained seated at her desk, stamping folders.

'Oh. Thank you,' the woman said. She didn't appear surprised, as though she'd forgotten to fetch Marie when the time was up. It seemed instead that she'd have left Marie there as long as she liked.

'You've answered every question?' she asked, flipping through the paper.

'I have,' Marie replied, suddenly feeling the urge to snatch the paper back to check her answers one more time. She realised she could have stayed inside another hour, double-checking and perhaps locating her errors and correcting them, and the woman would never have fetched her. But then the secretary took the paper to her desk and placed it in an envelope.

'I'll see he gets it,' she said, sounding impressed. 'Best of luck.'

Marie left the building. Whatever the result, it was done now. There was nothing more to fret about, so she returned home. She didn't tell her father what had happened; she didn't want him to know. It would just be another reason for him to say no. Why insist on studying somewhere that people don't want you? he'd say.

11
THE TRI-STITCH

A week later, Marie walked home from school to the sight of people wearing gas masks in Main Square. Hitler had occupied Czechoslovakia, the newspapers announced, the country that sat below Poland on the map. The men who ran France and Britain had presented him with the Sudetenland, the ring of land that sat across the top of that country, as though it was theirs to give. They'd thought it would satisfy him. He'd replied his thanks by taking the whole grand Slavic nation and tearing it up. A panic ripped through Krakow; he might come for Poland next.

As Marie walked across the broken pavers of the market square, people sat before their coffees and cakes in their flannel suits and workday attire, with those eerie covers on their heads. One woman peered up at Marie through the two black circles of her mask, breathing through the muzzle: the sight made Marie shiver. As she walked through her front door, Marie had to force herself to jettison the image from her mind; she had more frivolous concerns to grapple with.

'Well. It's the week before the dance for wholesome young people, Papa,' she said when she found her father reading in the sunroom. 'But I've not seen any highland clothes. You have upheld your end of the bargain by allowing me to pursue my studies.

Now it's time for me to return the favour, to attend your husband-finding dance. But, alas, I find myself unable to complete the request through no fault of my own.'

Her father peered up from his journal to look at her over his glasses, saying nothing. A soft dusk light shone through the curtains, making his face appear blue.

'If you recall,' she continued, 'the custom is for a woman's highland costume to be handmade by a relative. As no handmade clothes have come my way, I shall not be fit to be seen. Thus, I shall decline my invitation to the event with the deepest regret and satisfy myself with a good book for the evening. I guess the clothes were too hard to sew. I overheard two silly girls from my class today – their mothers complained at the difficulty they experienced constructing these garments. The stitches required are so small! And the embroidery is so delicate! Do not trouble yourself at your failure to sew them – who knew of the sophisticated work required to make someone look like a farmer?'

Her father got up and left the room. Marie grinned, satisfied. She sat in the chair he'd vacated and began reading his book on advanced surgical techniques.

'Don't be too hard on yourself, Papa,' she shouted down the hall. She flipped through the pages; her father was reading about tri-stitching. 'You can't be expected to fashion such garments if two seamstresses couldn't—'

She halted mid-sentence as her father re-entered the room, carrying a woman's highland costume over his arm. 'I need you to try these on first, so I may make any necessary alterations.'

'Oh,' Marie said, her mouth falling open. She put down the book.

'Will you put them on, please?'

Marie studied the clothes in silence. They lay flat on a hanger, so she couldn't tell their shape, but their beauty already transfixed her. Tiny stitches lined the cuffs. A brilliant cherry-red drenched the percale cotton skirt like blood. Soft white silk comprised the blouse.

'You sewed these?' she asked in a quiet voice.

He nodded proudly. 'I will leave you to change,' he said, laying the clothes over a chair.

Marie removed her school clothes and placed them over a Chinese screen. She pulled the blouse over her silk slip, donned the skirt and slipped the black corset over the shirt. She entered the front room where a large mirror hung on the wall. She stood in front of it and gasped.

She could have passed for a folk doll. A full skirt of thick red percale bloomed from her middle. Cotton roses festooned the black tape that decorated the skirt's hem; her father had embroidered them in the folk style with thick petals of orange and yellow.

'There. Will I embarrass you?' her father asked, popping his head round the door.

'No,' Marie said softly. It was less a sewing effort than a feat of engineering, a thousand tiny stitches blended together.

'The stitches look small enough for you?'

'They do, Papa,' she replied.

He nodded and gestured to the skirt. 'This here? I used a fine cotton, very similar to our six-O catgut sutures.' He pointed at her arm. 'I used a triangular stitch here to attach the sleeve to the blouse's shoulder. It copies the formation I use when repairing the aorta.'

'What is this?' She ran her fingers over the small letters stitched into the blouse: *MK.*

'Your initials. It's the tradition,' he replied. He motioned to the costume. 'Will it do?'

'It will, Papa.'

'So you will go to the dance, then?'

Marie nodded. Considering the beauteous, perfectly constructed outfit, she had no choice but to uphold her side of the bargain.

Her father adjusted his glasses. 'If you will hold still, I should like to mark a few alterations before you change clothes.' Marie watched her father as he inserted pins into the impeccably sewn outfit at errors visible only to him. His deft hands pinned tiny folds of fabric to enclose one extra millimetre at her waist. His mouth twitched with the precise effort, as if he were a servant who stitched clothes for a vindictive queen, whose life depended on the garment being the most beautiful in the land.

Walking through the market square the next day, Marie came across Ben Rosen in front of a café. He wore a grey suit and carried his satchel for work. She hesitated when she saw him, recalling the awkwardness of their prior exchange, and ducked behind a pylon, hoping he hadn't seen her, but he came up beside her and said hello. She nodded a perfunctory greeting but said nothing. She reached a compromise with herself that she would not run away from him, but that she would not talk to him either.

A minute passed in silence. Marie felt foolish but refused to relent by talking. He had hurt her at their last meeting; his abrupt tone had shocked her and she couldn't understand why he'd acted so coolly, considering the ease and friendliness with which they'd once related to each other. Compounding this, he'd spoken casually about her mother. The bells in St Mary's Basilica rang out in a series of deep clangs, announcing that it was four o'clock. People stopped walking and peered up to watch.

'Look,' Ben said, pointing to the clock tower. Marie lifted her head begrudgingly to look up. A trumpeter dressed in a fawn suit and hat stood at the top and exhaled into his bugle. A five-note military dirge rang out across the square, the song consisting of tones one should only hear at a funeral.

'Why do they always play such dreary tunes?' Ben said, scratching his chin. 'That trumpeter is a friend of mine.'

Marie rolled her eyes; she did not believe him.

'It's true,' Ben said. 'His name's Marcin. He has a spectacular view of the city from up there – you'd think he'd play something sprightlier, a mazurka perhaps.' Marie glared at Ben and willed him to stop talking. The trumpeter halted playing his song suddenly, halfway through a bar. The tune cut out mid-note, a strangled cry.

'Why do they always stop playing halfway?' Ben said. 'It's very Polish, don't you think? We always quit before the finish—'

Marie snapped. 'They are not dreary tunes, plural, it is one dreary tune – the same one, every day, on the hour, every hour. It cuts out halfway in memory of the trumpeter who was shot through the throat while sounding the alarm when the Mongols invaded in the thirteenth century.' She crossed her arms, exasperated.

Ben smiled. 'I knew I could get you talking.' Marie glared at him, and kicked herself for falling for the trick. She decided that the cool and impressive action would be to confidently walk away. She began to do so, when Ben gently grabbed her arm. 'Please don't go. I came here looking for you, to apologise,' he said. 'I know you walk through here sometimes.'

'You do?' She searched his face. She had no idea why he'd know that.

'You spoke of your mother last time and I acted thoughtlessly. Seeing you again . . . it disarmed me a little. I hate myself for acting how I did. It must be awful to not know where your mother went. Forgive me?'

Marie studied him and said nothing. He wore a genuine look of pleading on his face, the curls of his brown hair waving in the gentle wind of the square.

'I almost forgot,' he added. 'The fairytale you seek, the one your mother read to you – it concerns a man who climbs something?'

'It does.' Marie waited for him to continue.

'He climbs a mountain. Made of glass,' Ben said.

Marie inhaled, remembering. 'Yes, that's correct.'

'In fact, it's not a man who climbs the mountain in the fairytale, it's a boy. Many men attempt to scale this mountain made of glass – strong men, powerful warriors. They all fail. Finally, a boy from the village tries. He uses his brains instead of brawn. He tricks a giant eagle into flying him to the summit and he succeeds. He scales the mountain.'

Marie jumped on the spot. 'That's the one! That is the fairytale! I remember now!' More details of her mother added to the vignette in her head as Ben spoke. She saw herself on her mother's lap. A straw broom now sat in the corner of the room. A floor made from wood appeared underneath her. 'What's it called, the fairy-tale?' she asked.

'"The Glass Mountain",' he replied. In these words she heard her mother's voice. She had said those words to Marie; now she could hear the sound that had always existed somewhere inside her. Whenever she wanted to visit her now, Marie would say the name of that fairytale in her head and her mother would appear to her, in voice only, but it was better than nothing. She would utter the name of that fairytale a thousand times each day, every day, for the next month or so. A feeling of ecstatic warmth flowed through her and she turned to Ben to smile, but he wore a look of pain on his face.

'What's the matter?' she asked.

'You look so happy,' he replied. 'What else can I say to make you smile like that?'

That was easy. 'Help me find my mother,' Marie said.

'Done,' he replied.

The air seemed to ease around them; a new feeling hung.

'I'm going to a dance this Saturday night,' Marie said finally. 'It will be awful. You should come.'

Ben shifted his feet, seeming nervous. 'Oh. Where does it take place?'

'At the church hall, up the block from here.'

He laughed. 'The church? I don't think that's a good idea.'

She scowled. 'Are you afraid? Do you not know how to dance?'

'Of course. I jitterbug. I charleston. I know the Lambeth Walk, the Lindy Hop.' He moved his arms back and forth, dancing a little on the spot, as if to demonstrate his qualifications right there.

She chuckled. 'But do you know the Polish dances? The mazurkas and polkas?'

'I suppose,' he said, chuckling more, nervous again. He studied her, his eyes darting back and forth over her face.

'Then you must come,' she said. 'We are friends now.'

He gazed at her with a look she didn't recognise. 'Are you sure?'

She felt disarmed by the way he looked at her. 'Absolutely. I insist you attend.'

'Very well,' he said, swallowing. She gave him the details and they agreed to meet there at six pm. Marie farewelled him – 'See you Saturday' – and felt his gaze on her as she walked away.

12
A HIGHLAND FLING

That Saturday night, three hundred young parishioners descended upon the church hall of St Peter & Paul's in the centre of Krakow. Truly, it was a sight to behold. Almost every young person in town had crammed themselves inside the building, each dressed like a highlander, their bodies forming a heaving sea of broadcloth trousers, moccasins and red skirts.

Marie entered the hall with Lolek, whom Dominik had arranged as her chaperone. They had walked together from the park around Wawel Castle and arrived a little late to find the dance in full swing. Young men threw young women around the dance floor to the sounds of a folk band, which played one boisterous highland jig after another. Some of the men had begun to sweat and had rolled their shirtsleeves up, exposing giant forearms and elbows the size of pork knuckles. The larger the men got in this part of Poland, the smaller the women seemed to grow. Priests and nuns stalked the room, their mouths fixed in warm welcoming smiles but their eyes darting left and right, quietly watching the dancing bodies, passing comment if anyone stepped too close, if any hands crept too far down.

As they came in, Marie saw Father Marek patting down Paweł Skorupski at the hall's entrance with moves that would have impressed the Gestapo. The padre located a flask inside the young man's left sock that appeared to Marie like homemade cherry vodka. Paweł, a young semi-delinquent who lived in a shack by the Vistula, had made a name for himself producing litres of this liquid with a concentration of eighty per cent alcohol. The priest accused him of planning to dump the bottle in the punch bowl. Father Marek bundled him from the room, the crowd laughing and applauding as they left. Paweł Skorupski needn't have bothered. Though Mrs Pacek at the refreshments table served only fruit punch, the room reeked of beer, and a stain of pre-consumed cherry vodka blessed the young men's mouths like lipstick. From the bopping and the jumping and the flinging of young women about the room, a week's worth of liquor had been consumed by each attendant prior to their arrival at the hall.

Lolek went to hang up their coats and Marie moved to the corner of the room, watching the dancing. A young man approached before she'd even sat down. 'Marie Karska? I am Jozef Kowalski,' he announced.

'Yes, I know you, Jozef,' Marie said. He lived a few blocks west of her in a lavish and gaudy house decorated with gables and rococo scrolls. His father held contracts with IG Farben and they skied each winter in the alps south of Krakow. The son owned a coupé, inherited from his father, in which he ran laps around the market square every night with his buddies, harassing dog walkers, café customers, and anyone who possessed the audacity to look their way. Marie avoided talking to him as much as she could.

'Do you know how to dance?' he asked.

Marie laughed at the question. 'I do. Do you?'

'I think so. Let's go.' He took her hand and pulled her towards the dance floor.

Marie resisted. 'I beg your pardon,' she said, withdrawing her hand.

'You have to dance with me. My father arranged it.'

'I didn't know about this.' She saw his confused face and realised her own father must have struck a deal on her behalf. Marie scowled. 'Thank you for the charming offer, but I respectfully decline.'

He ignored her, looking instead towards the band, which was beginning its next tune. He had slicked his hair back in the fashionable style; she saw the oily sheen of his blond strands as he turned his head. A small paunch protruded through his shirt and hung over the leather of his highlander belt. 'No, actually,' he said, 'this is the polonaise. I don't know this one. No bother. We'll wait for the next.' He collected a chair and motioned for her to sit down.

'Lucky me,' Marie said. She sat, not wanting to make a scene, and he sat next to her, shifting his chair closer. She looked for the exit, silently fuming. So this was how the night would go. She'd spend it dancing with brutes her father had arranged for her. She willed Lolek to return and rescue her.

Against the opposite wall, a sea of burly blond youths tussled and watched the dance floor. Among them a head of brown curls scanned left and right. The crowd parted to reveal Ben Rosen, who stood in the corner politely cradling a glass of fruit punch in his hand.

Marie let out a laugh of joy at the sight of him. He wore the peasant costume of the highland. Trousers of cream broadcloth encased his legs and the fabric bloused over brown moccasins. A shirt of homespun flaxen cloth enshrouded his chest. Roses embroidered in white thread traced across his shirtsleeves and moved down the centre of his shirtfront. A brass clasp shaped into a pagan sun held his collar together. He resembled a strapping farmer from Zakopane attending a wedding or a military parade, attempting to impress and intimidate a neighbouring Slovakian village. His cuffs remained at his wrists, polite and respectful of the costume. He didn't sweat or puff like the others; he'd not danced yet. Instead he sipped his virgin punch and shifted his feet. He looked adorable. The more uncomfortable he appeared, the more tenderness she felt for him, she realised; he was here at her invitation, and he'd put on these absurd clothes for her.

When she stood, her dance partner protested. 'Where are you going?' Jozef Kowalski asked, his greasy hair continuing to glisten as he shook his head in protest.

'The ladies' toilet,' she replied brightly, and walked over to Ben. His face lit up as he saw her. 'You came,' she said. She motioned to his folk costume. 'Where did you get the outfit from?'

'A friend with a sense of humour,' Ben said. She smiled. 'I feel silly. Do I look like a yokel?'

'Not at all. You look handsome.'

'You look beautiful.' He stared at her. His face seemed to be fighting between smiling and frowning. His brow furrowed and then relaxed. 'Would you like to dance?' he asked.

'Yes,' she replied.

Ben lifted his hand to take hers. Marie took a breath to calm herself. They'd held hands many times, but as boy and girl. They were man and woman now. Their hands were just about to touch when a voice interrupted them.

'Good evening, Ben Rosen,' said Patryk Kowalski, the father of Jozef, Marie's erstwhile dance partner. The older man wore a fancier costume than the others, a similar shirt and trousers to the younger men, but he'd added a cream suede jacket adorned with tassels and a leather belt festooned with brass moons, as though the costumes meant something and he'd assigned himself a position of highland chieftain that outranked all others in the room. His son stood behind him and stared at the floor. The father held out his hand.

'Good evening, Mr Kowalski,' Ben replied, shaking it.

'You look ridiculous,' the father said. A menacing tone filled his voice.

'Thank you,' Ben replied. 'Am I wearing it wrong?'

Marie stifled a laugh.

'No,' the man replied. 'But what I mean is, you're not from here.' He waved his hands, as though expecting Ben to understand. Some people from the crowd ceased watching the dancing and turned to listen.

'I was born in Senacka Street,' Ben replied, 'about three blocks from here.' He spoke with an easy and agreeable tone that made Marie smile.

Mr Kowalski sighed. 'Yes, but your family—'

'My family moved here in 1456,' Ben said. 'Krakow was still the capital of Poland back then. Aren't you from Lithuania?'

Mr Kowalski scoffed. 'No.' He shrugged. 'I mean, I was born there, yes. But then I moved here.'

'Well then.'

'But that's not the point,' the older man said, his voice growing louder. 'The point is, you're not really Polish.' More people looked over. Marie felt her eyes sting as she watched in stunned silence.

'Not really Polish? I think my costume begs to differ,' Ben said, maintaining a cheerful tone. He pointed to his outfit.

'Yes, but you're not a patriot,' Mr Kowalski said. 'You're not Polish first.'

Ben raised an eyebrow. 'My great-grandfather and his brother both fought in the January uprising of 1863. Moshe lost a leg – we've never heard the end of it. He's still alive, Moshe. Ninety-four years old. Lives in Białystok. If having ancestors who vainly fought in a doomed uprising isn't the most Polish thing on earth, I don't know what is.'

Some of the crowd laughed. Mr Kowalski gritted his teeth and leaned in. 'Very well,' he muttered. 'We all like you, Ben. I'm only saying, you can wear all the broadcloth you like – it doesn't change the fact that you're a Jew.'

Someone gasped. Ben blinked. 'I don't see the problem.'

'Of course!' Mr Kowalski said. 'The problem? There's nothing for you here.'

Ben went quiet.

'Why waste everyone's time?' Mr Kowalski continued. 'This is a dance for young Catholics to meet – it's serious business. You're Jewish. It's fine to chat and laugh with her,' he pointed to Marie, 'but where can this go? Why lead her up the garden path?'

Ben nodded. The old man seemed to soften, placing a collegial hand on Ben's shoulder. 'I know you're not one of those ones with the curls and the hat, who won't look me in the eye,' he said cheerfully, 'but you're still a Jew.'

Marie bristled. She watched the outrageous conversation in a kind of stupefied horror.

Ben glared at him, a flash of anger now crossing his face. 'I don't wear the clothes. I don't observe as they do. But I am just as Jewish as them.'

'Exactly!' Mr Kowalski said. 'So you agree with me. There's nothing for you here.' He nodded triumphantly.

Ben opened his mouth to say something more but then seemed to decide against it. He turned to Marie with a defeated look. 'Good evening,' he said with a smile. 'Thank you for the kind invitation. If you will excuse me.'

In a way she'd feel ashamed of afterwards, Marie let him go. 'All right, Ben. Goodbye,' she said, feeling rooted to the floor.

Ben walked over to the table and handed back his punch glass. He thanked Mrs Pacek and headed to collect his coat.

Lolek found Marie; he'd seen the discussion. 'I'm sorry you had to witness that, Marie. Old man Kowalski should feel mortified, though I doubt he will.'

'Ben is Jewish?' Marie asked.

Lolek laughed. 'Yes, young Ben is of the Hebrew persuasion. You didn't know?'

'Um, well, yes. I suppose I did.'

It sounded ridiculous to say it. Of course he was Jewish, though she had never acknowledged it. She had never seen him at Christmas. He'd never painted Easter eggs with the other children in her street. He taught at a Jewish high school and lived in Kazimierz. Her eyes had collected these indicators of Jewishness, yet her brain had elected not to process the data. And then there was the last name Rosen, which she had added to her name as a child; it was as Jewish as keeping the Shabbat, yet she had never noted this, only how it looked on the page next to her own. Her blindness to all of this came not from some idealistic standpoint; she didn't harbour some philosophical ideal in never seeing people's religion or nationhood. No, her failure of consciousness towards his different faith stemmed simply from complete, childish, entitled ignorance. It had never occurred to her, because it had never affected her. His Jewishness likely affected *him*, if this altercation was anything to go by, in numerous and varying situations. But as the event she'd just witnessed was the first of its kind for her, Ben's faith had never been something of interest to her.

She looked again at Patryk Kowalski, a person of standing and wealth in the town, who, with his comfortable house and holidays in the alps, had not the graciousness to let two young people, to whom he had no real connection, dance together. That their affairs concerned him seem pitiful to Marie. He suddenly looked ridiculous in his chieftain's clothes; she saw him as a little boy who had been humiliated by his father for wetting the bed, later hitting a smaller boy at school. How the fear of otherness crept up and strangled some people! Those who had not the strength nor the upbringing to embrace difference. How much sadder the world was when sameness won. She watched Ben waiting at the coat check and felt utterly ashamed.

'Don't worry, girl,' Mr Kowalski said to her. 'You're due to dance with my son next. This is for the best. It would be a tragedy to waste such a beautiful woman on a dirty Jew.'

The words had the opposite effect to what the old man had intended. Marie now recalled how her schoolfriends had called Ben the same when they wrote their married names into their ledgers, and Ben's reluctance to attend the dance. He had shown up anyway, knowing a scene like this might occur. Marie awoke from her spineless slumber and elected to reward his bravery with a small dose of her own. It was less valour in her case, more plain stubbornness. She'd always possessed a healthy insolence, a desire to stir things up, to provoke. She must have inherited these qualities from her mother; they did not come from Dominik. He made no noises and defied no one.

Mr Kowalski's son walked towards Marie, threatening to dance with her once more. She could see Jozef counting to himself as he walked, as though rehearsing the steps in his head.

'Oh dear. Say goodbye to your poor little toes, Marie,' Lolek said, pointing at the young man. But Marie walked in the opposite direction, towards the door, and caught up with Ben as he collected his coat.

'I thought you asked me to dance,' she said.

Ben turned. His eyes darted across her face as if to check she was serious. 'Marie. I think you know I must go.'

'You promised to dance with me,' Marie replied. 'If you leave now, it will be a scandal. One dance and then you may depart.'

The music quietened; Marie looked around the room. Six hundred pale-green Catholic eyeballs now watched them. Five hundred and ninety-nine, actually, as Tadeusz Nowak had lost one eye to an angry birch branch. The one working eyeball he had left, however, was now trained on them.

Lolek appeared beside Marie again. 'Stay, Ben,' the acolyte said loudly, with a smile. 'You bragged of your dancing prowess. I should like to see it.'

Marie thanked Lolek silently. Ben looked around the room once more, and sighed. He returned his coat to the confused woman behind the counter who had just given it to him, then strolled towards the dance floor. He stayed on the edge of it; Marie figured he thought they would be better concealed there. Still rumbling with indignation and stubbornness, she instead nudged his shoulder towards the centre of the room. 'We'd best go into the middle,' she said. 'We'll get squashed here in the corner.'

He nodded again. She placed her hand on his back and gently pushed him forward. The muscles between his shoulder blades tensed and Marie caught her breath at their hardness, remembering once more that he was now a grown man. Marie waited for someone to stop them. Father Marek looked over, but then a nun asked him a question and he turned to listen. Everyone else looked too shocked to intervene. Mr Kowalski did nothing also, just watched with beady eyes from the corner of the dance floor and remained mute. While the self-proclaimed chieftain appeared happy to intimidate a Jew, an outsider, he would not stand up to Marie, the daughter of Dr Karski. Here she learned another thing about humans; she was learning so much tonight. People didn't stick their neck out to put a stop to something if no one else did. Humans went with the crowd, and as no one seemed willing enough to impede them, they retook their places and prepared to dance.

Ben turned to face her and held out his hands. He put one arm on her back and took her hand with the other. At the touch, their eyes met.

The band began playing a languid waltz. Marie gasped quietly under her breath. It was the Kujawiak, the most romantic of all dances, or at least of this highland fiddle band's repertoire. This slow, sad dance piped and fluted in triple time, *one-two-three, one-two three*, resembling more a waltz of France or Spain, the melody weighted with pauses and notes of longing. It provided the perfect opportunity for holding one's partner closely, for smelling what perfume they might be wearing, for learning what shampoo they used. The program listed speeches and a blessing from the parish priest as the culmination of the soiree, but for the young people, this dance made for the true climax of the evening. Mutters rippled through the crowd at the sound of the first bars and new couples assembled eagerly.

'Do you know this dance?' Marie asked Ben. She was unsure what she meant by the question: did she mean whether he knew the stories and the romantic meaning behind it, or simply whether he knew the steps.

'I do,' he replied, and she felt unsure of which meaning he'd meant. Perhaps both.

As his hand rested on the middle of her back, his fingers had no choice but to meet the fine boning of her corset. Marie's cheeks had burned when she first beheld the garment, aware that her father had sewn the boned structure intended to lift and shape the soft flesh of her upper torso. Marie wondered if Ben knew what he was touching, if he knew its purpose. She studied his face. He smiled and looked away quickly, shifting his fingers but not removing them from the boning. He knew. This whole time Marie had been aware of Ben's transition from child to adult; surely by now he must have come to the same conclusions about her.

They moved back and forth to the music, with Ben saying nothing. He was close enough now for her to realise he was wearing cologne. It smelled not of the heavy spiciness that the other young men liked to wear, but of something lighter and fresher – sandalwood perhaps. She found herself nervous, so she began to chatter. 'You're very quiet,' she remarked. He nodded and still made no sound. He seemed to be concentrating. 'Are you counting under your breath?' she asked. He wasn't, but she found it funny anyway.

He twirled her in a circle. He was a good dancer, moving her gently in perfect time.

'Not bad,' Marie said.

'Be quiet,' he said, in an annoyed tone that made her laugh.

'You never get angry, do you? Even when truly agitated,' she said. 'I remember, even when we were children. I bossed you around, every day. You never protested, you never got angry. Why?'

Again, he didn't reply.

The music continued its sad, urgent melody. They danced around the room smoothly, his large hand on her waist, guiding her gently. She became aware that everyone was watching them once more, but this time it was not because a gentile had stood up with a Jew. Something else held their gaze; they were watching the dancing now, the way the pair moved together. Ben turned his head and their eyes met, and she saw in his face a look of what she could only describe as desire. She realised then why he was silent. Talking wasn't necessary at this point in time.

'I will stop talking now,' she said.

'Good,' he replied.

They danced a few more steps. She spoke again. 'Just one more thing. I must say, you dance well.'

'Thank you.'

'I apologise if my steps do not make the grade. I've had only a few days to grow used to the shape of you now. It is such a surprise to see you grown. I assume it's the same for you.'

'I have had a little longer.'

She screwed up her nose. 'What do you mean?'

He shook his head and she somehow knew not to keep asking. They continued to dance. The music rose to its climax, and Ben reached up to take the back of her head in his hand: the famous conclusion to this dance, difficult to master. She tipped her head backwards, so the whole weight of her body lay in his hand. He cradled her head gently and she saw him swallow. Their eyes met again. They spoke no more for the rest of the dance.

The evening passed in a daze. Marie danced more dances with Ben, jigs and polkas, and several marches with Lolek. The only thing that occupied her brain, however, was the way Ben had held her, the look on his face as they'd danced that first time. Everything had changed now. She'd glanced at his distracted face throughout the evening and sensed he felt this too.

The night drew to a close and the band began packing up. Marie found herself on a chair, with Ben sitting next to her. Lolek went to fetch her coat to take her home.

'Will you walk me home?' she asked Ben quickly as Lolek returned with the coats.

Ben swallowed. 'I don't think so. It wouldn't look good.' He gazed at the floor. 'I would like to.'

Marie's heart sank. She liked Lolek, but she couldn't think of anything more terrible than the idea of him walking her home instead of Ben.

'I want you to,' she said, touching his hand. He shot a look at her.

'Ready, Marie?' Lolek asked as he arrived beside her.

'I will do it, Lolek,' Ben said. 'I'll take her home.'

Excitement and nervousness rumbled together inside her.

'Are you sure, Rosen? Isn't it out of your way?' Lolek looked at Marie. 'I promised your father,' he added.

'You have my word, I will take her straight home,' Ben said. Marie smiled at Lolek to assure him this was all right. Lolek agreed, shook Ben's hand and bade them farewell. Ben held out Marie's coat for her and she slipped her arms inside. He rested his hands on her shoulders as he adjusted it. Marie shivered.

They said goodbye to some others, laughing about Paweł, the would-be punch-spiker, and the other events of the dance. Then they made their way out into the street and found themselves alone at last, walking down the cobblestones in the cool night air. Most streetlamps were out, and a handful of house lights and the moon guided their path down the laneway. They walked without talking, their breath the only sound. Finally, Marie spoke. 'You said earlier, you've had longer to get used to me. What did you mean?'

Ben shrugged. 'Did I? I was joking.'

'I don't think so,' Marie replied.

He adjusted his coat. 'It doesn't matter now.'

'It does. Tell me what you meant.'

'Forget I said anything.'

They walked along in silence and rounded a corner. 'I will scream if you don't tell me.'

'Don't you dare, Marie.'

'Yes!' she said, warming to her theme. 'I will scream the national anthem.' She took a breath and began. '*Poland has not yet died!*' she sang down the street in her loudest voice. '*So long as we still live!*' A dog howled. A man in a tenement building beside them exited onto his balcony and joined in.

'*What the foreign power has seized from us,*' the man bellowed into the night air in a drunken baritone. He wore only a dressing gown.

'Thank you, sir!' Marie called up to him.

'*We shall recapture with a sabre!*' he sang. He pushed his hips out in a lascivious fashion.

Marie inhaled to continue singing, but before she could release another note, Ben placed his hand over her mouth. 'All right, I will tell you. Please, stop singing.'

Marie nodded in muted agreement and he removed his hand. They walked on a few steps more before he spoke.

'Every afternoon, on my way home from work, I stop at the Schwarzwald Café. It's a Viennese coffee house on the corner of the market square.'

'I know it,' Marie said.

'One day, about three years ago, in the springtime, I was order-ing my drink and sat down in the courtyard. It was a lovely Krakow day, one of those strange ones in spring when the sun has come out. The air smelled of primroses. I had arrived back in the city about two weeks before and had just begun my job at the high school. I had always gone to that coffee house as a child with my mother. I came back to Krakow, but my mother refused to; she stayed in Berlin. It was my twenty-first birthday. It was a pathetic thing, to visit that café. But I sat at the table outside where my mother and I always used to sit, feeling sorry for myself, and I saw a young woman walk across the square. She wore a blue jacket and skirt, and she moved with such elegance and grace, I had figured her for a woman of twenty-five or thirty. Perhaps she was a German woman, off to a job at the diplomat's office, or an actress going to rehearsals at the playhouse. As she came closer, I saw she was far younger than I'd first assumed. There was something about the walk that stuck with me. The way she threw her hand out. She knew exactly where she was going. But it unsettled me as well – I couldn't place it. By the time she was fifty metres away, I knew. It was you. I watched you walk across the square and felt unbearably sad.'

'Why did you not say hello?' Marie cried. 'It was your birthday. I would have bought you a slice of cherry cake and sung to you. We could have caught up.'

Ben gazed at the ground. The brass pagan sun that clasped his collar together glinted in the moonlight. 'I told myself I would never go to that café again.'

Marie scowled. 'Why?'

He didn't answer that. 'But the next day, I went to the square. I ordered coffee and sat at the same table.'

'I walk across the square every day.'

'I know. I have sat there every day for three years and every day you have walked past.'

'Why didn't you say hello?' she said again. 'You watched me for three years? Ben? Why?'

His face hosted the most extraordinary look; now she could feel her heart thumping. He stood there silently and looked up at the moon. Marie waited. He turned back to her and choked the words out. 'Because I like you.'

Marie swallowed. 'I like you too.'

The man went away and the boy of fourteen replaced him. Months later, she would still recall the look he gave her as he said it, his eyes wide and hot. And from this person with whom she had enjoyed a collegial, loving but brotherly partnership in her childhood. She already knew he loved her as a person, as a sister or friend, but now he *liked* her, too.

But then a look of great anguish crept across his face, replacing the other one. 'But I'm Jewish, and you're Catholic, and nothing can happen, so why pursue it?'

'This will sound juvenile, forgive me. This whole time, I never thought of you as Jewish.'

He chuckled. 'I know.'

'You don't look Jewish,' she protested. 'I mean, you don't wear the clothes.'

'I assume you practise polygamy?' he asked.

She scowled at him. 'Huh? Of course not.'

'But you are a Christian, and Christians practise polygamy.'

'They do not.'

'The Mormon Christians do.'

She grimaced. 'Point taken.'

'Just as there are many types of Christianity, there are many types of Judaism.'

She felt embarrassed. 'Which type are you, then?'

'Which type of Jew? The worst kind. I only do the fun stuff. I observe Shabbat when I remember. I light candles, share bread, play songs.' She watched him as he listed these parts of himself she'd never seen and felt stunned. 'I guess you could say I am a Reform Jew. I accept gifts on Hanukkah. I eat apple with honey on New Year. I fast on Yom Kippur; I feast on Passover. I eat a multitude of delicious beige foods.'

'Beige foods?' she repeated, laughing.

'Indeed. Cholent, knishes, kugel, latkes. All very beige. All very warming and scrumptious. I will feed you them some time.'

'I would love that,' she said.

He coughed nervously. 'Yes. Well. I even went to Palestine to work the land. I curled my bare toes in the earth, milked cows.'

'You did?' She'd had no idea.

He nodded. 'When I was twenty. You see? I'm afraid I am very much a Jew. God is present, of course, but more important is man. I'm a humanist Jew. My Judaism is about love.' He looked at her.

She felt elated. His face had grown so animated; she loved to see him speak this way, with light inside him.

'My favourite thing is to sing, actually,' he continued.

'You sing? The national anthem like me?' she joked. 'Though likely not as well.'

'No. Not as well as that. I sing zemirot, Jewish hymns. I sound like my father. When I sing on Shabbat, people say it's like my father is there. I get to have him back for a few minutes.'

'Sing one for me.'

'What? No.'

'Yes. I want to hear your voice.'

He nodded shyly, then cleared his throat, and to her astonishment, began singing the first bars of a song in Hebrew. '*Adon olam, asher malach*.' The ancient words fell from his mouth in a deep, gentle voice, a little shaky at first, and he looked at her nervously. But she smiled her encouragement and he continued. '*B'terem kol yetzir niv'ra*,' he sang. The words rang out, hitting the cobblestones and echoing softly. The song followed a strange melody in a minor key, contradicting the exultant choruses she knew from her Catholic songbook. At first it sounded quite ugly to her, but as he reached the end, she realised the lingering, melancholy song was the most beautiful thing she had ever heard. As he finished his tune, she did not want it to end. She still could not believe he had sung for her.

'Would you like to kiss me?' she said.

The request made him stop walking. He laughed outrageously, then a serious expression crossed his face, and then he scratched at his chin nervously. 'Would you like to kiss me?' he asked back. She swallowed and privately cheered his audacity. She ached for what she'd suggested to happen. She nodded. His blue irises shone at her. He seemed to hesitate, and Marie despaired and silently begged him to continue. Perhaps he sensed this and it emboldened him, for he bowed his head and pressed his lips to hers.

Wetness filled her mouth. It surprised her. She'd never kissed anyone; she'd never wanted to before. While all the other girls had necked with boys behind the toilet block, she'd never followed them. No boy had interested her. She saw now that there had never been anyone but Ben. And this wasn't necking.

How strange a kiss was! Two beings pressing together the same devices they used for eating, speaking, vomiting, screaming – now using them to show affection and desire. But then, why should it not be this organ, used for some of the basest of all human functions, that showed love. For what was more intimate and special than to put one's mouth on that of another, saying, *This is where I breathe from, talk from, sing from, this is who I truly am, and now I show it to you.* She put her tongue in his mouth and he groaned. She felt glad she had never kissed anyone else; she didn't want another person to know this part of her. It was all for him.

13

CAST DOWN FROM THE PACK

A strangeness came over Marie the next day.

She had lain awake in bed for hours, staring at the ceiling, her mind emptied of all thought except the kiss. He had taken her home and kissed her hand at the door, unable to look at her. She had taken herself to bed, thankful to have not seen her father; he must have been at the hospital or already asleep. She noticed a faint smell of rankness or mustiness out the window as she'd lain in bed, cut grass perhaps, and a strange excitement overtook her. She stared at the ceiling for some minutes, then checked her clock to find she had been doing it in fact for five hours.

At almost six am, she must have fallen into a restless slumber, then she woke again at seven, as wide-eyed and agitated and as full of energy as though she'd slept for a week. She woke to find everything had now come alive for her; she placed her head out the window and stared, smelling the fragrances of the street below, the rudimentary and the exquisite. The honeyed smell of fresh bread that wafted up from someone's kitchen, the sweet and bitter tang of a newly tarred road, the fragrant soap flakes from nearby laundry – she smelled it all. It was as if the world had turned on its senses for her suddenly; she had stepped into another plane, a sweeter, warmer one.

All because of him. He had brought this change in her. She found herself dressing slowly, taking time with her negligee, letting her fingers hang here and there, every touch savoured, imagining him doing the same to her. How she wanted him. A sickness had come over her; the only cure was to kiss him again.

Finally, after hours of this, she got a hold of herself, dressed for church and managed to make it downstairs. There she found a little mound of lemons waiting chopped on the breadboard; her father was preparing curd. She secreted a half moon from the bench, placed it in her mouth and began sucking. The tartness blasted her lips and made her tongue sizzle. Her father entered the room and asked her what she was doing; she jumped and mumbled something, then excused herself to her bedroom, claiming a need to change her coat. She ascended the stairs, running her hands over the wooden banister and letting them linger, just to feel the cool bumps of wood underneath the pads of her fingers.

They were running late for church and there was no time to discuss the dance with her father. Her dawdling and nonsense had made sure of it. She was glad; she did not want to share this just yet. They went to church and the normality and banality of the day was allowed to return, helped along heartily by the sermons and benedictions of mass, the homily and the reflection, in which talk of the Lamb of God and the Sins of the World beat the sensuality out of her, banishing the lemon sucking and the banister grazing.

They arrived home from church and finally she knew she had to tell her father what had happened. She felt sad to have to reveal this to someone else; she would quite happily have experienced this on her own for a few more days or at least hours. Unfortunately, her father had asked several times now, and putting him off again would be impossible unless she ran away.

'How was the dance?' her father asked again as they hung up their coats. His voice was tentative, as though he expected bad news, as though her complaints and reluctance about the whole enterprise beforehand would now take themselves to their natural conclusion. He sat.

She decided to tease him, to draw things out before delivering the good news. 'I received compliments on my dress,' she replied. 'Many events occurred.'

'Good,' her father said, sitting up. 'What events?'

'Someone tried to spike the punch, for example. And several other hilarious occurrences.'

He slumped back down in the chair; his face bore a disappointed look. 'And you? Did you have a nice time?'

Marie smiled at her ability to annoy him so easily. 'I suppose. The band could have done with a second flute. No one's costume rivalled mine. And I guess I also fell in love.'

Her father had been staring out the window with a grim expression on his face but now he snapped his head to her and stood up.

'Yes! Why did you not tell me sooner? Marie, this has made my year. I confess this is what I was hoping you would say. May I ask who the lucky man is? Did you dance with Jozef Kowalski, by any chance?'

Marie grinned and shook her head. 'I didn't fall for the industrialist's son.'

'Oh.' Her father sat back down. 'I suppose someone else turned your head. Never mind, you must have found someone better.'

'I did.'

'Well, now. And does he deserve you?'

Marie sat in the armchair opposite. 'He does, Papa. He's a wonderful man. He is handsome and kind and clever.'

'What is his profession?'

'Teacher.'

'A schoolteacher? He won't possess the wealth of an industrialist, Marie. Still, he will have secure work. We will always need schoolteachers. Very well, as long as you understand. You will never have a lavish house, no holidays abroad.'

'I do not want a lavish house, Papa. But you needn't worry, in any case. He is a schoolteacher, yes, but he comes from a wealthy family.'

'Splendid. He stands to inherit a fortune, then. Now I am casting my mind over all the schoolteachers we have in our town.' He stood up again and paced the room.

Marie scoffed. 'You can't know every teacher in Krakow, Papa.'

'I would get close. Please give me a clue – his age perhaps?'

'Twenty-four.'

'Twenty-four? A good age. He must be two or three years into the profession, then. Excellent. He shall be earning more than a recent graduate. Let me see, what teachers do we have? There is Jan Pilsudski – he is the mathematics professor at Damascus. No, he is too old, he must be twenty-seven at least. Someone younger.' He rolled his eyes upwards as though physically searching through the contents of his head. Her father's skull was likely not large enough for all the things he knew, so perhaps he was not looking through his head but up to the sky; perhaps he stored some of his excess thoughts there.

'I have it!' He pointed at Marie. 'Michał Dobry, from St Aloysius? I thought he was away in Warsaw visiting his aunts.'

'It is not Michał Dobry, Papa.'

'Aleksander Slamanski? Janusz Sadowski?'

'No and no.'

'Forgive me, Marie, I require another clue. What school does he teach at? St Aloysius? St Thomas? Star of the Sea?'

'The Hebrew Lower Secondary School.'

He blinked.

'It's a Jewish high school.'

'I know what it is.'

'Their literature and history teacher is Ben Rosen.'

A horse and cart trundled over the cobblestones on the road outside. The mare puffed and hoofed, making unmistakable sounds of pain, of knee and hip problems from walking all day over the uneven cobblestones of Krakow. Every empire in Europe had invaded the city at one time or another, erecting palaces, opera houses and pleasure domes for their nobles, then left again. No one had ever repaired the roads, the locals' problem.

'You are surprised, Papa?'

'Not really, no. You always loved that little boy.'

'He's not little anymore, Father. Did you know he'd returned to town? He has been back for three years.'

'Yes. I was aware.'

Marie gasped. 'And you never told me?' He didn't answer. 'Do you not like Ben?'

'On the contrary,' he replied.

'Papa, you could show a little more excitement. I have fallen in love.'

'I won't allow you to see him again.'

Marie almost laughed at the absurdity of the words. Her father had never not allowed her to do anything. 'I thought you wanted me to find someone!'

'I do. Still, I can't permit this. You know why.'

She'd never known why. She'd never discussed these things with her father – she'd never even known that her father was aware of such whys – but as soon as he said the words, she knew what he meant. 'Papa. I would not have taken you for a bigot.'

'I am not one. But this is your life – it's different. I know something of being cast down from the pack. You don't want a life like that, Marie. I don't want it for you.'

Marie wondered for a moment what he meant by 'being cast down', then her lip quivered, and her father looked pained. She hoped her tears would make him reconsider, but he said nothing, and made no move to comfort her. 'Papa, I love him.'

He scoffed. 'Don't torture yourself, Marie, I will not change my mind. I'm sorry. If you are wise, you will never see him again. Take comfort – I'm sure the industrialist's son will still have you.'

She felt tugged to the ground where she had soared just moments before. She left the room.

She ran to Ben's house. She knocked on the door of his apartment, and when he answered his face lit up with delight at the sight of her. 'Come in.' He looked left and right, then showed her inside. Excitement flowed through her as she walked down his hallway. She had never been inside his house before. 'May I offer you a drink? Something to eat?' he asked, showing her to a living room.

'No, thank you.' They both went quiet, an excited awkwardness coming over them. They were alone together. Marie wished he'd kiss her again.

He seemed to consider it, leaning forward, and her heart leapt into her throat. But then he sat back. 'What are you doing here?'

Marie had to remind herself of that. 'Escaping my father. You won't believe what he's told me. He said I couldn't see you anymore.'

Ben's face fell; he grew still. 'He's right.'

She blinked. Him too? The words sounded like clanging; Marie's ears struggled to accept them. The man who had kissed her was siding with her father? She felt reckless and desperate; this wasn't happening. She could think of nothing to say, so she stood and left the room.

He caught up with her as she reached the front door and grabbed her arm. 'Please, Marie, please don't cry.'

She slapped his shoulder. 'Why did you watch me walk across that square for three years if you knew nothing could ever happen?'

'I tortured myself with the sight of you, but preferred that to the alternative – not seeing you at all. I would rather a tiny piece of you than nothing. I am a realist. Being with me would destroy you. I couldn't live with myself.'

'A realist?' she said, angry. 'You are a coward.'

He bowed his head. 'What old man Kowalski said last night? Every word is true. We can dance and kiss all we like, but I can't be with a Catholic, and you can't be with a Jew. I have an uncle, Samuel. He married a Catholic woman. At first, everyone tried with them – on both sides, Jewish and Catholic. But then they raised their children Catholic because they thought this would be easier. A boy and a girl. The Catholic school wouldn't accept the children, pronouncing them Jewish, as their father was. Samuel had to bribe a priest to let them in. After that, the Jewish side stopped accepting his wife: so much so that she remained Catholic, and the Jewish women never invited her on their outings, fearing she would feel uncomfortable. Eventually, she stopped trying. Every Easter and Hanukkah became a trial, with some portion of the family always feeling unwelcome. Soon, they stopped coming altogether, to avoid the fights.

'Family is everything. But their poor children did not belong anywhere – not with the Catholics and not with the Jews. My grandparents missed them dearly and speak of them now in hushed voices only. I assume the same occurs on the other side.

'A fish may love a bird, but where would they live? If we did the same, it would feel daring for a while, but eventually you would grow tired of people spitting at us. Your father would disown you, my mother me. Every Christmas, every Passover, we would have nowhere to go. Our children would grow up as bastards, belonging to nothing, existing nowhere.'

'It would not be like that with us. My father would always welcome you.'

'Are you sure about that? Did he not forbid you to see me?'

She went quiet. She could not argue with that. It seemed a hopeless situation, but then she had an idea. She smiled. 'Did your uncle remain a Jew?'

'Who, Samuel?'

'Yes. When he married his Catholic wife.'

'He did. Of course.'

'Perhaps it was because your uncle remained a Jew,' she said. 'If he'd become a Catholic, if he'd been baptised with his children, then at least he would have belonged somewhere!' She beamed, warming to her theme. 'Is that not the solution for us?'

He scowled.

'No, listen,' she said, talking faster. 'If you became a Catholic, yes, your family might be angry, they might even disown you for a time, but at least you would fully belong somewhere. You would belong to *my* family. You could start anew.'

'Do you suggest I renounce Judaism to be with you?' He blinked at her, looking pained.

'Oh goodness, Ben. Have I said the wrong thing?'

'Being Jewish defines me. If I left behind the culture, the thousands of years of history, the hymns, the language, my family, my job, what would remain of me?'

She had hurt him; she felt terrible. 'No, I'm sorry. I don't want that. I ...'

'Judaism is hard to get into, but impossible to leave. Even if I renounced my faith and disowned my family, as you want me to do, I would still be Jewish. People would always insist on my Jewishness. They would never let me forget. Once a Jew, always a Jew.'

An automobile beeped its horn outside, making Marie jump.

Ben held her arm to steady her. She moved close enough to him that she could hear him breathing. She exhaled.

'Now, please, go find another,' he continued. 'We must never see each other again. Don't knock on my door – I won't answer. Don't call my telephone – you will only hurt yourself. You must forget me. Take care.' He opened the front door and walked back down the hallway, leaving her standing there.

'Ben!' she cried.

He didn't turn, ignoring her and entering some other room of the apartment she'd not seen. She considered following him but then decided, her heart breaking, that no purpose existed for doing that, so she left the apartment, closing the door gently behind her.

As she walked down the stairs of the tenement block, she glanced back at his apartment and saw he'd come to the window and now watched her as she walked away. She would find a way to heal this. She began to realise what she would have to do.

14
SMALL STITCHES

Some days in the hospital lasted the requisite hours, with patients maiming and infecting themselves in only low numbers and arriving through the main doors at politely staggered intervals. Other days went on and simply refused to end, like a stroll through the outer circles of hell, with every person in Krakow deciding to come down with some catastrophic injury or biblical plague and being wheeled through the doors all at once. On this occasion, Dominik was experiencing the latter; he had not slept in thirty-eight hours. The marathon had started the previous day, which had endured long enough itself. He'd extracted three inguinal hernias (the farmers in the town needed to stop lifting their weight in grain), removed two benign tumours, visited forty-four patients on the ward, and attended to a man who required counselling over the death of a beloved dog more than he did treatment for a lacerated leg.

Dominik had reached the end of this already long fourteen-hour shift, exhausted, only to be met with an outbreak of food poisoning from a nearby restaurant, which had seen twenty-three waiters, diners and chefs moaning on gurneys, each requiring fluid therapy and salts, and two needing cardiac monitoring. After lecturing everyone on the importance of hand hygiene and the dangers of bacterial contamination of food, Dominik checked his watch and discovered it was now nine o'clock in the evening. Of the next day. He'd been awake all day and all night, only leaving the hospital to prepare a meal for Marie, scream silently, and then return again.

All he desired now was to collapse into a chair by his fireplace and stare at the flames longingly in a grateful stupor. He hadn't the energy to run a bath, but he could position himself next to the fire and pretend its warmth was hot water; that would have to do. So it was with great reluctance that, as he stumbled towards the tram, he turned his head when Matron Skorupska called after him. 'Dr Karski, you must come back inside! You're needed.'

He pretended to have sudden-onset acute deafness and kept walking towards his stop. Unfortunately, the sound of her wooden clogs clacking on the footpath behind him indicated she'd followed him out of the hospital.

'Let Dr Wolanski handle this one, Matron,' he said, still walking.

'He won't do,' she replied, following him.

'I really must insist, Matron. I've not slept since last week. I must beg you, find someone else. The janitor will have better success diagnosing patients – or seeing out of both eyes – at this point.'

'That's the thing,' she said, grasping his arm as she caught up to him. He slumped, defeated, looking down at the jagged cobblestones. They appeared as soft as clouds to him; he might have lain down on them and slept for a hundred years.

'It's not a patient we need you to see,' she said. 'It's Johnny.' Dominik looked at her. 'He's gone missing.'

'Missing where?'

'Somewhere in the woods. He was drinking in the staffroom at the end of his shift.'

Dominik rolled his eyes. 'Best we leave him to it. Let him sleep it off by a birch tree.'

The matron shook her head. 'He was saying sad things.'

'People tend to do so when they've consumed large quantities of alcohol. If you are so worried, then why have you not gone to find him yourself?'

'That would be improper. I am a woman! Find him, talk to him. You're his friend. He speaks of you all the time. Dr Karski this, Dr Karski that. "Let's ask Dr Karski what to do," he says about patients.'

'I would call that professional admiration, and possibly a desire not to kill a patient, rather than friendship.' Dominik peered wistfully at the jagged cobblestones once more.

'Please, Dr Karski. We're worried.'

Dominik grimaced. 'If I die from exhaustion or aggravation, Matron, it shall be on your head.'

'Yes, yes,' she replied with a smile, already urging him back towards the hospital. Once there, Nurse Emilia met them with a bottle of cherry vodka. 'Take this,' she said to him.

Dominik stared at the flask; a lurid red liquid sloshed inside it. 'Has the man not consumed a significant amount already?'

'It's not for him, Dr Karski, it's for you,' Matron Skorupska said.

Dominik harrumphed. 'What do I say to him?'

'You're a man. He's a man,' the matron said. 'Pour some vodka and figure it out.'

Dominik let out one large, sustained groan as the nurse handed him the vodka and a torch and directed him to the woods where Dr Gruener was last seen. He walked up the embankment, across the small square and into the forest.

The month was April. The weather, aggravatingly, was cold enough to keep him awake, but not cold enough to kill him. He couldn't decide which outcome he'd prefer at this point. Death won slightly as an option; at least it would allow him to sleep. He wandered through the woods, directing the torch at random trees and shrubs, hoping that by shining it harshly the battery would run down quicker and he could go home. These hopes were dashed when he turned his torch left to find the man he was looking for walking towards him.

'Go away,' Dr Gruener said. 'Leave me alone.'

'If you want me to go away, stop walking towards me!'

'Domek! I am done for!' Dr Gruener declared, sounding hysterical. 'I'm so warm,' he cried. 'Why?'

'Hard to say without a physical examination, though I suspect the litres of alcohol you've consumed might have something to do with it.'

Dr Gruener ignored him, flinging his coat from his body with great ceremony, then catapulting it onto a nearby rock. He slammed his back against a tree and sank down until he sat in the dirt, resting against the trunk.

Dominik tried to think of something to say, recalling Matron Skorupska's instruction to provide manly advice. He considered what wisdom he could give. 'You should soak those trousers in cold water, to remove the grass stains,' he said with a nod.

'Thank you, washerwoman,' Dr Gruener replied.

Dominik shrugged and started to leave. 'Look after yourself, Dr Gruener.'

'Why do you not call me Johnny?' the doctor called after him.

Dominik stopped walking and turned. 'You are my professional colleague. It's a mark of respect to call you by your title.'

'I consider it *dis*respectful. I asked to be called Johnny. I don't like my surname. Everyone calls me Johnny, except you.'

Dominik found himself rapidly losing patience and moved to leave again. Dr Gruener looked upwards. 'Domek, all this time we've been talking, I have not noticed. I am sitting under the most magnificent tree. Point your light, if you don't believe me.'

Dominik sighed and pointed his torch upwards. 'Hardly magnificent. A little larger than most, I grant you.'

'It is the most spectacular tree that ever grew on the earth,' Dr Gruener declared. 'I'm going to climb it.'

'No, Dr Gruener. That's not a good idea.' But he had already grasped a second branch and pulled himself upwards. 'Dr Gruener, you are drunk and upset. There's a good chance you will fall and die,' Dominik implored him.

'Nonsense. I'm an excellent climber. Better than Tarzan.' He had reached halfway up the tree. 'I'm going to get to the top.' His voice slurred, unsettling Dominik.

'Please come down, Dr Gruener. The nurses will kill me if you die.'

'But you won't care,' he said. 'Look, I've reached the top.'

'Yes, you have,' Dominik called. 'Goodness.' He shone the torch at the oak again. Now he truly had to agree with Dr Gruener. The tree deserved to be called magnificent. The hospital had three storeys; this tree stood taller. Dr Gruener was balancing on the second highest branch. Dominik swallowed. 'Dr Gruener, I beg you, climb down. Carefully.'

'Not until you call me Johnny.'

Dominik stiffened. 'Don't be ridiculous. No.' Dr Gruener lifted one foot off the branch and moved forward. The trunk swung and creaked. 'Good God! Johnny!' Dominik exclaimed.

The doctor replaced his leg on the branch and smiled. 'No need to shout.' He retrieved a cigarette from his pocket and lit it, grinning.

'You foolish man,' Dominik shouted. A branch cracked. 'What was that?'

'I heard nothing,' Dr Gruener declared. 'Wait, oh.' He barely had time to complete the words before the branch gave way and he fell.

'Heaven preserve us,' Dominik whispered. The doctor fell from one branch to the next, each breaking his fall for a moment before it broke too and gave way. He fell to the next branch, dangling there for a time, then fell again. He bounced off the next branch and then found some clean air; there appeared to be no more branches to stop him, so he fell to the earth instead.

Dominik ran to where he lay on the ground, unmoving. 'Dr Gruener? Johnny. Please say something.' He placed a hand on his neck and felt for a pulse. His skin felt wet and warm. A pulse rippled under Dominik's fingers. He groaned. His face now bore a disfigurement: a gash ran under his left eyebrow. 'Johnny, please say something.'

'I think I'm blind,' he said.

'You have blood in your eyes.' Dominik sighed. 'Your head wound needs repairing.' He helped him to his feet, and they walked back through the forest and returned to the hospital.

The clock struck ten. Moonlight shone through the window, bathing the ward in blue as patients slept in rows. Matron Skorupska was completing paperwork at the nurses' station, her pen and page illuminated by a little lamp. The wireless played low beside her; Radio Krakow performed a Brahms concerto. She smiled at them as they walked in, saying nothing, before returning to her papers. They made their way to Dominik's office.

'I've never been inside your office, Domek,' Dr Gruener said. 'It's as I expected.'

'Cold and impersonal?' Dominik asked in a jeering tone.

'Warm and clever. I like your plant.' Dr Gruener pointed to the Spathiphyllum that sat beside Dominik's desk.

'Sit down, please,' Dominik said, offering his desk chair. Dr Gruener sat in it. Dominik arranged the suture equipment on his desk. He fetched a magnifying glass and secured it to a laboratory arm, positioning it over Dr Gruener's eye. He'd read textbooks on plastic surgery, a new craft developed during the Great War to treat disfigured soldiers. The smaller the stitches the better. He injected a local anaesthetic into Dr Gruener's head and began work.

'I wasn't always so drunk, you know,' Dr Gruener said.

Dominik tied off the first stitch and cut the loose thread. 'I'll take your word for it.'

'I keep having a silly dream,' Dr Gruener said. 'I can't for the life of me work out what it means. Please tell me you've had it also.'

'Very well,' Dominik replied, wincing. He had never rejoiced in hearing of other people's dreams and couldn't understand those who did.

'In the dream, I'm standing four metres down at the bottom of an outhouse,' Dr Gruener said, laughing. 'It's one of those sturdy long-drop toilets at the back of the servants' quarters, dug into the earth. A pool of urine and faeces swirls around me, bathing me up to my neck. People keep going to the toilet up there, not seeing me, sending their excrement down onto me. I call up to them but my voice doesn't work. The level rises, and I try to climb out. I claw my way upwards, tearing my fingernails, banging my kneecaps, but the walls are too slippery, slimed with brown mess.'

Dominik winced again at the terrible description. He had expected Dr Gruener to relate some vision of being chased by a giant snake, or attending a dinner party that dissolved into an orgy. But the dream he spoke of contained no such clichés, and Dominik found himself thinking of it, and feeling sad, for some time after. 'I have not had this dream,' he said.

'I continue to claw upwards,' Dr Gruener said, 'screaming, trying to climb out. Then I look around at the pool of excrement that surrounds me, and the walls that glisten with brown, and I think – and here's the worst of it – how about I just lie down instead, under the surface, and breathe in.'

Dominik put down the needle. A look of desperate sadness had overtaken Dr Gruener's face. 'Do you lie down?' Dominik asked. 'In the dream?'

'I don't know.' Dr Gruener shrugged. 'I wake up before I see what I do.' He grimaced. 'I had a wife, once. And a child – a son.'

Dominik recalled Dr Gruener's lamenting display about the wife who'd left him. 'I see. Though your wife is gone, your child is still somewhere. You should try to see him.'

'The child is nowhere. My son loved cars, like me. Always pestered me to take him driving. Drove me mad with his demands.'

'What is your son's name?'

'Julian. He was better-looking than me. Charmed every grandmother in town. He returned from school every afternoon with three to four little old ladies walking him home, his pockets stuffed with sweets.'

Dominik smiled. 'You should take him driving. You can use my car. I'm sure your wife wouldn't mind, you taking your son for an afternoon.'

'I took him driving. My wife too. I was quarrelling with her, didn't look. A lorry ran a traffic signal; he didn't see us. I didn't see him. He ran into the side of the car, destroyed the paintwork, ruined the entire chassis. That car cost a fortune.'

'I'm sorry. Is that why your wife left you?'

'She didn't leave me. She died in the accident. The boy too.'

Dominik stepped back. 'My God.'

Dr Gruener took a deep breath and forced a grand smile. 'I became something of an alcoholic after that.'

Dominik sat down. 'My dear man.' He touched his arm.

'Don't look so bereft – you'll make me cry.'

Dominik felt helpless and ashamed; he'd misjudged this man. 'I don't know what to say.'

'There's nothing to say, see,' Dr Gruener replied. 'That's the boring part. So you have to forgive me sometimes, when I drink a touch.'

'When was the accident?'

'It was a year ago today. Hence my little escapade. My father – a hard man, a military man; has a bigger moustache than Otto von Bismarck – tells me to get a hold of myself, to stop embarrassing the Gruener name with my memories and tears.'

'But it has only been twelve months. These things take time.'

'That's long enough for my father. He's disowned me. He's a Nazi, did you know?'

'I had an inkling, after you mentioned you played tennis with Hermann Göring,' Dominik replied.

'Indeed, my patriarch is a Nazi. A zealous one, too. I've grown to be quite the disappointment to him. They don't go in for sentimentality in the party, mourning dead wives and children. I've tried to get over losing them, but I seem to be falling deeper into that outhouse.' He laughed. 'I don't really want to be here, see.'

'At this hospital?'

'On this earth.'

Dominik grimaced. With his face wracked with anguish and guilt, Dr Gruener reminded him so much of someone he'd known long ago who was now gone. He had to say something. Dominik touched his shoulder. 'Please keep swimming. Please keep breathing. You are only halfway through this life. If you go now, you will never find out what happens to you.'

Dr Gruener stared at him.

'On a practical note, I would advise you to reduce your drinking. If you can.'

'Are you insane, man?'

'It can make the sadness worse, especially the next day.'

'Yes, but I get around that by never stopping. There's no morning after for me; I'm already drinking again. You don't drink at all, do you?'

'No,' Dominik said.

'That's very un-Polish of you. Are you well?'

Dominik realised he would reveal something else of himself here. Too late now – the man was thinking of killing himself. He chose his words carefully. 'I endured a dark time in my youth. I bore witness to cruel and regretful acts, coaxed from their perpetrator with vodka. I swore after that I would never drink to excess again. I will have a sip to appear social.'

Dr Gruener chuckled. 'You surprise me constantly, old chap. Every day I see another side to you. How many have I seen now – seven, eight? Most people struggle to have one.'

Dominik cleared his throat and changed the subject. 'What can I do to help you?'

'Stitch me poorly, give me a big scar. The ladies love scars.'

'I'm afraid I will let you down there.' He pointed to a mirror.

Dr Gruener checked his face in the reflection. 'Damn you, Domek, those are the smallest stitches I've ever seen. There will barely be a scar at all.'

'I am sorry.' Dominik brushed the area with antiseptic. He washed his hands at a small basin by the window. Outside, a rough breeze made the fallen leaves spin in a whorl. 'I can cut your other eye, perhaps, or remove an ear to help with the ladies?'

'I shall be in touch if it's required.'

'Very well.'

Dr Gruener gathered his coat. 'Thank you, Dominik. For the good-terrible stitches.'

'You're welcome . . . Johnny.'

He would have to keep calling him that now. Dominik always insisted on addressing people by their titles and surnames for as long as possible. It helped to keep an arm's length between him and them. But it would be rude and cruel to return to calling this man Dr Gruener after hearing of his lost family, after stitching his head. The pleasure of making a friend might have brought joy, had the circumstances been different. But in the current situation, this spelled nothing but danger. Dominik saw this man clearly; it was but a matter of time before his colleague began seeing Dominik clearly in return.

15
THE LIZARD BRAIN

'He wouldn't dare invade,' Matron Skorupska insisted. 'England and France would declare war; Germany would be destroyed.' She bit into her bread and chewed. 'Poland has too many friends.'

They sat around the tearoom, Dominik, Johnny and the nurses. Dr Wolanski was there too. The past days had brought warm weather to Krakow, and newspapers announced that a German tank had been spotted strolling along the northern borders. Hitler had made a speech expressing his great concern for the plight of the ethnic Germans living in Poland and, as the saviour of his race, his intention to come in and rescue them. People spoke of nothing else, and Dominik had grown tired of the topic. When a meeting had been arranged at three o'clock to discuss the matter in the tearoom, Dominik declined the invitation with the deepest regret, for he began his afternoon rounds at three. He had expected them to go on with the meeting without him – his presence at the discussion was hardly imperative – yet to his dismay, he discovered that they'd arranged to meet on his lunchbreak instead, to accommodate him, only minutes after he'd sent his regrets.

No one responded to Matron Skorupska's confidence that Hitler would be reticent to invade their exposed country; they consumed their food in silence. 'How does one surrender properly?'

Nurse Emilia asked finally. 'To avoid being killed. Do you hold up white handkerchiefs?'

'That's only in books, Sister,' Dominik replied. He checked his watch; he should return to the ward soon, because a patient who had earlier exhibited signs of puerperal fever needed attending to.

'Did you fight in the Great War, Dr Karski?' Emilia asked. Everyone turned to him.

Dominik shifted in his seat, unsure of what to say. He could feel a drop of sweat on the back of his neck and he hoped none showed on his forehead. He really should get back to his patient. 'I'll wager every man in this room fought in that catastrophe,' he said finally, with a shrug.

'I did,' Dr Wolanski said, tucking in to a plate of dumplings and potato pancake that his wife had delivered to the hospital, steaming hot. 'I fought for the Austrian Empire with valour. Don't worry about surrendering, Nurse,' he added, stabbing his fork in the woman's direction. 'You won't need to. The Germans will love Krakow. It is the height of Polish refinement, a testament to culture. Our style and architecture will appeal to their noble sensibilities.'

Sister Emilia pulled a face. 'Our town is a ruin of every nation that has come in here and tried to overrun us. An Italian opera house, an Austrian square, a Swedish tower. It looks more like Vienna than a Polish city. You cannot, because there are none.'

'Either way.' Dr Wolanski shrugged. 'I'm telling you, the Germans will like this place. So if we be good to them, and make sure they know we're aligned with their policies, they will be happy to keep us alive. They might even clean this place up a little.'

'Easy, old chap,' Johnny said.

Dr Wolanski turned to Johnny excitedly. 'Do you speak German? You look like you do.'

Johnny nodded. 'Yes, badly.'

'You are being modest.' Dr Wolanski chuckled. 'I'll bet your German is as good as the *Führer*'s.'

'That would not be difficult,' Johnny replied. 'That man speaks terrible German. He achieves a grand feat: using every word in the dictionary to say absolutely nothing. He tells his people of the epic struggle they face. There is no struggle. He got rejected from painters' school and now the world is going to pay. It would be funny were it not so tragic.'

Dr Wolanski blinked and seemed to ignore the content of Johnny's speech by pure will. 'You sly thing, you do speak excellent German then! We must go to the club and speak politics. Most people around this place are so provincial, I do apologise. Dominik is not political at all,' he added.

Dominik nodded. 'He's right. I don't care for those matters.'

Dr Wolanski sighed. 'See, but I keep myself up to date. I shall have my secretary book a day for us to luncheon.'

Johnny raised an eyebrow at Dominik.

Nurse Emilia changed the subject. 'Will you fight, Dr Karski?' she asked.

'I hope they have the sense to use me as a doctor,' Dominik replied. 'The others, too. But I will go wherever I am put.' He swallowed.

'Did you fight in the Great War, Johnny?' Matron Skorupska asked.

'Yes,' Johnny replied. 'I killed Rasputin, then seduced the Empress. Mother Russia was so demoralised, she surrendered the next day.'

Everyone laughed. The conversation turned to what each would do if war came, where people would go. Dominik checked his watch again and mentally composed some excuses to leave.

'I suppose I will return to my hometown,' Matron Skorupska said. 'My son is there, with his wife. It is only twenty minutes on the

143

train from here, but out of the city, so it will be safer. Those beasts will raze Krakow.'

'Where are you from, Johnny?' another nurse asked.

'Up north, Old Prussia.'

'How dashing,' Emilia noted. 'Will you go back?'

'I don't think so.'

'He is needed here,' Dominik replied with a nod.

'And where are you from, Dr Karski? Will you go home?'

'I'm from up north too,' he said. 'I will stay here.'

Dr Wolanski interjected in an obstructive voice. 'You don't sound like you are from the north.' Dominik shifted in his seat. He waited for the subject to change. It didn't. Dr Wolanski stopped eating for the first time in twenty minutes. 'You sound like you are from the east,' he said, grinning. 'From Lwów or even further. The way you roll the letter r with your tongue.'

Dominik laughed and shook his head, the sweat on his neck growing thicker. He commanded himself to breathe evenly, not to inhale raggedly, or gasp, or stutter. 'I don't roll my r's any particular way.'

'I am sure of it – you are from Lwów!' Dr Wolanski picked up his fork again and stabbed it in the air at Dominik.

Emelia laughed. 'And how would you know, Dr Wolanski?'

'Because I lived in Lwów.' The room fell silent. Dr Wolanski looked at them all, now his captive audience, and beamed. He spoke confidently. 'My father was a diplomat and we moved often, but we lived in that city for two years when I was a teenager. I never noticed before, because you try to hide it, and you conceal it very well. You speak in clipped fancy Polish most of the time. But when you're fatigued, you drop down into the dirty peasant growl of the east. Hurrah, I knew there was something odd about you!'

'There's something odd about someone, old chap, and it isn't Dominik,' Johnny said. But Dr Wolanski wouldn't be deterred. He could not sit still in his seat, like a gloating child who had finally beaten his little brother at chess. He said everything laughing, half joking, but he continued to stab his fork as he spoke each sentence, pointing the utensil at Dominik.

'Families from the east lived in the stinking tenement next to us when I was a boy. I had no problem with some of the natives of Lwów – lovely, cultured folk. It was the immigrants who offended me – you sound like them. I recall one family in particular . . . the father was a half-gypsy and a drunk, and the mother kneeled before every tradesman in town for spare pennies. Dreadful, dirty gutter people. They should have gone back to where they came from. There was no place for them in my town! Sometimes you roll your r's the way the father did, the way only a bumpkin can.' He pointed his fork again and laughed uproariously. 'I knew it.'

The group seemed to laugh nervously, not knowing what to say, and they all turned to Dominik, waiting for his reaction. Dominik felt frozen.

'I think you've had too much vodka for breakfast, old chap,' Johnny said to Dr Wolanski, thankfully breaking the silence. 'I am from the north, and I can tell you that Domek sounds exactly like a man from my hometown. Everybody sounds like Dr Karski where I come from.'

The group all nodded and went back to their food, the only person not in agreement being Dr Wolanski. He continued to stare at Dominik with a knowing grin. 'I see. My mistake.'

As they left the tearoom, Johnny caught up with Dominik and walked with him down the corridor. 'If you want to sound like you're from the north, you must flatten your r's more.' Dominik stopped walking and stared at him, shocked. He felt the sweat returning to his neck. 'I don't recall the damn word,' Johnny said, scratching his chin. 'Guttural! That's the chap – yes, make them sound more *German*. You pull it off most days, but our friend

Dr Wolanski is wrong about a thousand things and right about one: sometimes when you relax your guard, when you rush, the r rolls.' He nodded to Dominik kindly.

'Oh.' Dominik swallowed.

Johnny gave him a strange look, not unfriendly but it bore through him. He felt sick at being caught out by Dr Wolanski, but more so at being discovered by Johnny.

Johnny seemed to detect his discomfort. He smiled and tapped Dominik's arm. 'Not to worry, old friend. No one would notice but me, and that's only as I'm from there.'

'Thank you, Johnny.' Dominik excused himself hurriedly, mentioning the infected patient who required his immediate attention, and left his friend standing in the corridor.

Later that afternoon, Dominik retired to his laboratory and found Dr Wolanski waiting in the doorway. 'May I enter my office, Dr Wolanski?' Dominik asked. He stepped to the side to walk around the large man, but Dr Wolanski blocked his entry. He put his hand on the doorframe, his giant elbow forming a boom gate of flesh that Dominik couldn't pass through, unless he bent to walk under it.

'Shall we play limbo, Dr Wolanski?' Dominik said, attempting a joke. 'I am busy, but I suppose I could play one game.' He bent backwards in jest, but Dr Wolanski moved his arm down and blocked the path again. Dominik studied Dr Wolanski's face. 'May I help you with something, Doctor?' he asked. 'Because really I have much work to do.' Dr Wolanski opened his mouth, then closed it again. 'Would you like to tell me something?' Dominik asked. 'You seem lost for words. Is it about a patient? Or perhaps you have a rash on your person you secretly wish me to inspect?' Dominik tried to move past him once more but the arm boom gate, which had slumped briefly, now sat rigid again across the doorway.

'I know you have a secret,' Dr Wolanski said.

Dominik laughed. 'Yes, the secret is I have work to do. I've seen thirty-four patients today and I need to write up their reports. May I pass now?'

Dr Wolanski straightened; his eyes darted. Dominik had given a wrong answer here. He'd either laughed a little too hard or spoken a little too hurriedly. 'Why do you never talk about where you are from?' the other doctor said.

'It's a boring story.' Dominik shrugged. 'You'd be asleep in two minutes.'

'I doubt that.' Dr Wolanski's gold molar glinted in the fluorescent light. Despite indicating thousands of zlotys worth of dental work, the tooth clung to his gum like a greased pebble, nestled between a row of yellowed cinder blocks lacquered with tobacco and red wine. 'You come from the east, whether you say so or not.' He waited for Dominik to answer. 'Why do you not want to tell me where you are from?'

Dominik searched the man's face. 'Where I am from is my business.'

'It's my business now. The only reason a man refuses to talk of his past is when he is ashamed of it.'

'We are all ashamed of our past – some of the clothes I used to wear in my youth, goodness!'

'Allow me to rephrase. Not when ashamed of his past. When he has something to hide.'

'I have nothing to hide about my clothes, though they're embarrassing. I shall bring you some photographs next week.'

Dr Wolanski grinned again. 'I don't think the board would be pleased to hear about your past.'

So that was his angle, then. Dominik tried not to react, to give nothing away, but before he knew he'd done it, he made a crucial error. He blinked, and Dr Wolanski saw.

Dr Wolanski pounced on the reaction. 'You are no good at lying, Dominik. You are not well versed in it. But do you know what the biggest indication is that you are lying to me, that you do have something to hide?'

'Enlighten me.'

'I have been standing in your doorway for several minutes now. If you had nothing to hide, you would have told me to shove off.'

Dominik chewed his lip and looked down the corridor. No one else was around. 'Piss off, Igor.' It was the first time in ten years of working together that he'd cursed in front of him.

Dr Wolanski laughed and straightened his back, more relaxed now. He seemed convinced he'd landed on some prized intelligence. 'You are happy for me to go digging around in your past, then? I still have old school chums in Lwów. All I would need to do is telephone. I have one particular friend, quite an obnoxious fellow – he knows everyone. He now works in the war office there.'

'Sure. Go ahead and call him,' Dominik said.

'Very well.' Dr Wolanski dropped his arm from the doorway and Dominik walked into his office. The nausea returned to him and his heart thumped as the man walked away.

He rushed back to the doorway. 'Dr Wolanski!'

The man turned around.

'All right. What do you want?'

Elation and smugness danced across Dr Wolanski's face. 'Ha! I was mostly bluffing. But now I see I have truly rankled you, I am curious to find out what you did.'

Dominik felt his heart sink.

'What did you do, Dominik?' Dr Wolanski walked back to him slowly. 'Did you have an affair with the daughter of some nobleman? No, that is not your style. Women are not your weakness. What is your flaw, I wonder? Everyone has one. You are a sanctimonious fellow, never getting into any trouble. No embezzlement, then.' He scratched his face and peered at Dominik, beady-eyed. 'You are one of those quiet ones. But why are you *so quiet*? It's the discreet men who always end up surprising you. You must have done something terrible. It must bother you every day. What did you do, Dominik, did you kill someone?'

'I said, what do you want, Dr Wolanski?'

Dr Wolanski crossed his arms. 'I want you to withdraw from the running for hospital chief.'

Dominik straightened. 'I can't do that.'

'I shall be off to telephone my friend, then.'

'Fine.' Dominik shut his eyes. 'I'll withdraw.'

'Good, then! I shall let the hospital board know.'

'And your friend in Lwów? From the war office?' Dominik asked nervously.

Dr Wolanski shrugged. 'What friend? Can't remember his name, anyway.' He turned and left. For a heavy-set individual, he danced down the hallway like a child on their way to a name-day party.

When taking neurology at university, Dominik had studied the limbic system, which some fellow students had called the lizard brain, the most primitive parts of the mind in charge of the most basic impulses: fight, flight, feeding, fornication and fear. The limbic system possessed no knowledge of empathy, compassion, humour, love, friendship or selflessness, or any of the other qualities that went into constructing a human being. Dr Wolanski's behaviour and motivation for everything was led by self-preservation. Dominik didn't blame Dr Wolanski for this; everyone survived differently, and prior to this, the brutishness of his colleague hadn't bothered him. They had existed purely as co-workers, uneasy at times, but largely separated, with very little to do with one another. From today, however, they were connected forever by Dominik's secret and the power Dr Wolanski held over him. Now that Dominik lay at the mercy of a man who was led by his lizard brain, he found it difficult to see how he could ever relax again.

16
A COUSIN IN DRESDEN

'I hope you are happy, Papa,' Marie said to her father as she entered the house. She had not seen him in two days. 'All your dreams have come true. Ben Rosen won't answer his door to me and he won't pick up the telephone.'

'You failed the entrance exam,' Dominik said in response. He was sitting in the old leather armchair, the one in which he always sat when reading letters.

Marie froze. 'What?'

Her father read from a letter he held in his hand. '*We regret to inform you that your daughter Marie Karska has not attained the required entrance mark—*'

Marie snatched the letter from him. She read the words. Among other things, they revealed she'd scored forty-two per cent in the examination. She sat down in the chair opposite. 'Impossible,' she said, though, remembering the exam, her heart sank.

'My dear. If you were not up to this standard, why did you take the test?'

'I was up to the standard! I can be a doctor, Papa!'

'Not anymore,' he said.

Marie felt a well of shame open up inside her. 'I tell you, Papa, that exam was unreasonably difficult. Meant for very advanced students.'

'Or difficult for you.' It was the most horrible thing he'd ever said to her. He walked into the kitchen; she followed him and watched him fill the kettle and set it on the stove.

She gritted her teeth. 'You didn't let me finish,' she said. 'The exam was a fake. He set me up to fail, gave me a paper meant for students already at university. The first question asked for the product solubility expression of silver! A preposterous question to ask in an entrance exam.'

'I understand why you failed, then. Do not be too hard on yourself.'

'That's just it. I don't believe I failed. I believe I answered that question, and a great many others, correctly.'

'Your self-belief warms me, daughter. I am pleased you think you performed so well; it shows great confidence. The fact of the matter is, though, you failed. The questions you thought you answered correctly you did not.' He poured the boiling water into a teapot. 'Would you like some?' he asked. Marie scoffed and didn't answer. 'I am sad for you, Marie. You must have studied incorrectly for the exam. I know you are not stupid. But do you know that a part of me is relieved, too?' He collected a cup and saucer from the cupboard. The bitter smell of tea leaves wafted through the room. She felt like hitting him. 'Your studies might turn a prospective husband off. The best thing for you now is to marry.' He looked up. 'Someone Catholic, that is. Preferably wealthy. I learned this lesson twenty years ago and nothing I've seen since convinces me otherwise.'

She watched him pour his tea and sensed a scream rising in her throat. Her father took a sip from his cup and adjusted his glasses, and Marie became aware that she would now do something reckless.

*

She boarded a tram to take her south of Old Town. She didn't go to Ben's house; she went instead to the door of a man she'd never met. This man attended her father's rooms as a patient for his sarcoma – that's how she knew of him – but that was the sum of their connection. She knocked on the door. A scrawny old man answered. 'Yes?' he said, squinting through thick wire-framed spectacles.

'Rabbi Katz? I am Marie Karska. Dr Karski's daughter.'

His eyes widened. 'My skin test. All is not in order? Tell me now, dear girl, what's my prognosis?'

Marie scratched her head; she hadn't expected this. 'Oh, I am unsure.'

'Your father relieved me of some epidermis yesterday. Said he needed to inspect it under his microscope. A small brown piece of my flesh. He said he'd call me tomorrow with the news! It is too terrible to be told over the telephone line, so he has sent a messenger to deliver the blow in person. Abigail, do you hear? Abigail?'

Light hurried footsteps tumbled down the hallway. 'What? What!' A shrill voice attached itself to the footsteps.

'I'm not here about that,' Marie protested to no avail.

A tiny woman no taller than a metre and a half arrived at the doorway. Her hair was bundled on top of her head like she'd attached a ball of black wool there. She pushed the rabbi across and stood next to him in the doorway. She looked Marie up and down. 'What's the prognosis?' she demanded. 'Tell us, we can take it. I knew you were doomed, Sol! Why do you go on with all the prunes?'

'Prunes are good for the digestion, Abi. The doctor said.'

'But you eat too many!' she cried. 'You are the only man in Krakow who goes too far the other way – you'll wear your bowels out.'

They both turned back to Marie. 'So what's the prognosis? Tell us. I've made my peace with it,' the wife said.

'I have no news about your husband's health status. I do apologise. I come on another matter.' She cleared her throat. 'Rabbi Katz. I wish to convert to your faith.'

Silence fell. They both stared at her. Mrs Katz removed the spectacles from her husband's face and placed them on her own. She looked Marie up and down again. Her eyeballs were magnified by the glass of the bifocals into two giant black orbs, which peered at Marie and blinked.

'Are you crazy?' she asked Marie. She lifted Marie's right arm and then released it, as if inspecting for madness and hoping to find it there.

'But why?' Rabbi Katz said.

Marie shrugged. 'Do I need a reason?'

'Yes,' the couple said in unison.

The answer was obvious to her. She had insulted Ben by callously ordering him to renounce his faith like it was nothing. If she was prepared to accept this as a solution, she had to be prepared to do it herself. One of them needed to convert, so it might as well be her. She tried not to think about what her father would say.

But she could not give this reason now to the rabbi. It would sound juvenile and mercenary, to say you wanted to change your faith for a matter of love.

Marie pushed her shoulders back and searched for another explanation to give them. 'It's a lovely religion,' she said.

'No, it's not,' the rabbi said. 'People throw things at you in the street if you possess this faith. It is strong, and grand, and full of fire. But it is not lovely.'

'Do you know the bakery on Grodzka Street, just before the market square?' Mrs Katz said. Marie nodded. It made the best doughnuts in Krakow.

'They refuse to serve me.' She jutted out her chin with steely pride. 'Or any Jew.'

Marie blinked, feeling ashamed. She hadn't known such things occurred, but after witnessing what had happened to Ben at the dance, she was beginning to see they happened often.

'I don't agree Judaism is lovely,' Mrs Katz said.

The rabbi nodded. 'Not lovely. Lovely is a superficial thing. Go deeper.'

Two children in kippahs and tasselled shirts played marbles on the road in front of the house. She hadn't predicted she would come up against such opposition to her joining their faith. She thought they would have simply accepted her request to convert, perhaps with open arms. They stared at her. Marie searched for another answer. 'Um, the Jewish food! It's delicious,' she said, trying to sound as complimentary as possible.

'Delicious, ha!' Mrs Katz said. She tutted and shook her head, as though Marie had offended her greatly. 'I'll make you a challah right now. You can take it with you back to Old Town. You don't need to convert to eat the food.' She turned to her husband.

'Wife, may I have a moment with Dr Karski's daughter?'

The rabbi's wife sighed and retreated back into the house.

'How did you get here?' Rabbi Katz asked Marie once they were alone.

'The number four tram,' Marie said.

He grabbed his coat from somewhere just inside and placed it round his shoulders. Marie smelled cedar as he swung his arms through it. It reached his ankles. He shut his front door and motioned for her to walk down the street with him.

'You are a good girl. From a good home,' he said as they began walking.

'Thank you, Rabbi.' The Kazimierz residents watched them as they went by. Every house in the street had coughed out one or two of its residents, who now pottered about on their respective porches, pretending to sweep, or check the mailbox, all the while keeping one eye on Marie and her companion. One woman whispered to another as she swept her front doorstep. The sight of the rabbi walking with a girl whose hair was as blonde as his was black, whose height exceeded his own by a quarter-metre, was not the most common of sights.

'My wife likes to act hysterical, but she makes a good point,' Rabbi Katz said. 'We are flattered that you find our faith interesting enough to want to join. Truly, some would say we are foolish to knock back such a well-connected girl – we have great respect for your father in this neighbourhood. You seem like an intelligent, thoughtful young person. You are lost, yes? Asking questions of this confusing life? I tell you, Judaism is not the answer. For you, anyway. As flattered as we are, this simply won't happen.' They had arrived at the tram stop, where a number four tram approached. 'Ah, good timing.' The rabbi signalled the driver and before Marie knew what he was doing, he was helping her onto the tram, taking her by the elbow, like one did a child. 'Goodbye, miss. Tell your father to call me when he finishes watching my skin in the little dish.'

'Goodbye, Rabbi,' she replied on instinct, out of politeness.

The tram pulled out from the stop. The rabbi waved to her once from the street, then turned and walked back to his house.

A week or so later, on a Saturday, Marie found Rabbi Katz. She accosted him as he exited a temple in the centre of Kazimierz. 'Rabbi, please listen,' she said.

'Miss Karska, you have some nerve, invading my space and interrupting me on the holy day.' He proceeded to walk down the street, away from her.

She followed him. 'I had no choice, Rabbi – you've stopped answering your front door when I knock.' She had visited his house a further two times and each time she had been politely denied entry.

'I am sorry, I won't change my mind. You don't look Jewish, don't sound Jewish, you will never *be* Jewish.'

Marie inhaled. Her tactic of flattery would not work. She would now resort to honesty. 'I don't want to convert because I like the food. The cuisine is nice, yes, but that is not the reason.'

'I'll admit you did not have me fooled with your professed love of gefilte fish. Very well. What is it, then?'

'I am in love with a Jewish man.'

The rabbi stopped walking. 'Who?'

'Does it matter?'

He crossed his arms. 'It does. Tell me who.'

She opened her mouth to speak but then didn't have to, for the man in question exited the building and almost ran into the back of the rabbi.

'Oh, it's you,' she said. Her heart leapt into her mouth; she had not seen Ben since she was inside his apartment.

His face lit up too, then returned to a frown, as if waking from a happy dream and then remembering some sadder reality.

'Good morning, Marie,' Ben said. He coughed. 'Rabbi.'

The rabbi looked at Ben, then looked at Marie. People around them began to stare. The rabbi walked towards a laneway and motioned for them both to follow.

'This is why you want to become a Jew,' he said to Marie. 'Why didn't you say?'

'What's going on?' Ben asked.

'This young lady has come to me, multiple times, to ask me to convert her to Judaism. She told me she loves the religion. I laughed at her. Now I see the truth. She's in love with you. The question is, do you love her back?'

'Leave, Miss Karska,' Ben said, a desperate tone creeping into his voice. 'This is not the answer.' Marie noticed he did not say please and the lack of courtesy excited her; in the hierarchy of emotion, she took anger over politeness.

The rabbi seemed to observe the exchange with interest. He turned to Ben. 'Why did you come back to Krakow, Benjamin Rosen?'

He shrugged. 'To teach Polish literature and history, Rabbi.'

'Yes, you are a fine educator. I have known you since you were a boy. Do you know what I always thought of you? Here is a kind young chap, who everybody loves. And look how he dotes on that goy doctor's daughter, the one with the green eyes and blonde hair, who commands him to collect dried berries to make her a necklace, to pull posies from the grass to build her a crown? Benjamin Rosen, heir to the Blumfeld toy fortune, who could have his pick from the debutantes of his own faith. Why does he do that?'

Marie waited for Ben's reply but he made none.

Rabbi Katz cleared his throat. 'Benjamin Rosen. Do you love this girl? I advise you to think carefully. Because if you say you love her, beware of the scandal and pain that will follow.'

'I know the scandal and pain,' Ben said. 'Why do you think I say nothing?' He shot a glance at Marie.

'My,' the rabbi said, clutching his chest. 'You do love her.'

'I have never loved anything as much as I love her.' He looked up resolutely and stared at Marie.

Marie felt a fire bloom in her chest.

'I must go,' Ben said. 'I will leave Krakow tonight. This is all my fault; I should never have come back.' He started walking away, as if his departure would begin directly, straight to the main station.

'No,' Marie cried.

'Steady. Where will you go?' the rabbi asked.

'Back to Berlin.'

The rabbi scoffed. 'Oh, sure. You'll be safer there.'

Marie touched his arm. 'Make me Jewish, Rabbi.'

Ben threw his hands up. 'No, Marie.' Then he paused. 'You would do that for me?'

'I would do anything for you. I love you too,' she said.

He sighed, and straightened his shoulders, as though imbued with the strength of the world.

'You said yourself, you will always be a Jew. You can never leave this faith. But that doesn't mean I can't join you. It's different for me. So that's what we shall do. If the rabbi converts me, will you marry me?' She watched his face to see his reaction, and she received the look she'd expected, one of shock and astonishment. But she'd asked now, and he had to answer, so she waited for him to do so.

'Rabbi Katz, you cannot seriously consider this' was his reply. Her heart leapt: it was not a no, then.

The rabbi looked at him. 'Ben, if you were a foolish sort of person, a gambler, we would not be having this conversation. But you are not a fool, you are a man of sense and dignity. And she is no fool either. Before your father died, he made me promise I would look out for you. If this will make you happy, I will do it. I'm inclined to convert her just so she leaves me alone,' he joked. But then his tone grew serious again. 'If she converts, will you marry her?'

Ben turned to Marie. 'Do you understand the danger this could put you in? I won't ruin your life like this.'

She smiled. 'I am the only one who can ruin my life. And marrying someone I love won't be how I do it.'

The rabbi looked at him. 'You had better decide quickly, Ben, for I like you, but I am a proud man, and if you continue to bellyache like this when I make you this grand offer, you will find I will quickly retract it. Think now, for I will ask once more, and then never again. If I convert this woman to Judaism, will you marry her?'

Marie held her breath.

'Of course I will,' he said.

'That settles it, then. I hope you both know what you're doing.'

Marie kissed the rabbi's cheek. He blushed and waved her away. She walked over to Ben and kissed his cheek too, a chaste kiss in front of the elder, but still, she heard him inhale as she pressed her face to his. He turned his head, as if his lips tried to catch hers, having a mind of their own, and although he quickly corrected and turned back to the front, the damage was done: Marie had seen the excitement in him, and the rabbi, no dimwit, surely had too.

'You must not see each other now, until it is done,' he said. 'We must study in secret. No one must know. Only once I've converted you shall we tell people. I don't want my own kind coming at me with pitchforks. We are not missionaries; we don't solicit. It is frowned upon, you know, for us to attract new members.'

'I came to you, Rabbi, not the other way around,' Marie replied.

He sighed. 'Make sure you tell people that when they try to hang me in the square.'

The rabbi met Marie on Monday in the synagogue to prepare her for conversion. She had never stepped inside a Jewish temple before.

'There is another thing,' the rabbi said to her as she entered, marvelling at the plain walls, the scrolls, the candelabras arranged in straight lines of seven, so different to the church of her birth. 'You must prepare yourself that when the truth of this comes out, your family may shun you.'

'I have no family, only my father,' Marie replied.

'That's even worse. If you only have your father, you will lose your whole family in one go. Your father may never speak to you again. Are you willing still?'

Marie looked at him. She wondered what her father was doing in that moment – arriving at work, probably, helping someone with their aching chest, or looking at cells under his microscope. Her only family. 'Yes,' she replied.

And so they began. He initiated her into the world of the ark of the covenant, the Torah and the Talmud. The Bible stories of her youth were all wrong; they championed the wrong man. It was the older minor characters who were the stars: Abraham, Moses, David. The prophets she had always known as ancient and inconsequential were the big hitters, closer to God than Jesus.

Early in their study, Rabbi Katz had expressed dismay – he still wanted to do things properly. Just because she was converting for love, that didn't mean she shouldn't study. But he needn't have worried. Marie took to her new religion with passion and gusto, and she found herself revelling in this strange and wonderful ancient faith. It appealed to the two contrasting parts of her nature, the mystical and the pedantic. She adored the tales of Abraham and Isaac, of ritual sacrifices, of Job with his perpetual bad luck, of Jonah and his consumption by whale, of Lot's wife turning into a pillar of salt. These odd and horrific tales of ancient magic and mystic wonder stirred her. And while the spiritual part of her loved the chants and prayers, the scrolls and ram's horns and the cloaked ritual, the meticulous part of her revelled in the rules. There were six hundred and thirteen! Do not eat creatures that live in water other than fish. Do not mix beef with dairy. Never take revenge, never bear a grudge! Men must not wear women's clothing. Women must not wear men's clothing.

It delighted her how these rules were all found within her own Old Testament. All this time they had been hiding in places like Genesis, Exodus, Leviticus. She had studied them before, under duress at her convent school, with a Catholic, intellectual eye. Now they came alive in her hands; they were not cold texts to be examined, they were guidebooks for living life, a set of rules to live in the service of something greater. The rabbi had told Marie that Judaism was not lovely. But now she had experienced it she found cause to disagree with him. She loved it all.

'Do not fear, Rabbi. I am taking this seriously,' she said one rainy dawn, and as if to prove it, she began reciting those six hundred and thirteen commandments, one by one. '*To know there is a God,*' she began, '*To not entertain thoughts of other gods besides him.*' Rabbi Katz stopped her after she'd recited the twentieth rule, looking shocked. 'Did you commit the entire six hundred and thirteen mitzvot to memory?'

'Only the first hundred so far,' Marie replied. 'Was I not supposed to?'

A look of admiration, then worry, crossed his face.

'What is it, Rabbi? Have I not satisfied you?'

'On the contrary,' he said. 'You may know the Torah better than I do,' he quipped. 'You will make a fine Jew. You have mastered in a few weeks what it takes most months to achieve.'

Marie's heart leapt. 'What is it, then?'

He clasped his hands behind his back and paced the room. 'Remember how my wife and I warned you about people not serving you when you are a Jew?'

'I do.'

'If you convert to Judaism, being humiliated by a fellow Pole once in a while is the least of your worries. You need to know this.' He paused.

Marie put down her pen.

'I had a cousin in Dresden, Walter. Nice man, nice family, minded his own business. Something of a train enthusiast, Walter had a wonderful toy set. He'd lay tracks in every room of his house and when you went to visit, little trains would speed along from the kitchen to the dining room. You could attach a note to a carriage, asking for a vodka. On November ninth of last year, a date they are now calling the Night of Broken Glass, men in brown shirts woke Walter at gunpoint at two am and marched him downstairs. They forced him and his wife to strip naked, and made them stand outside in the street, where all the neighbours could see. They smashed the front of their jewellery store and relieved it of its contents, then they set the store and their house above it on fire. They stole a year's worth of earnings that night, putting a hundred-year-old company out of business. Not that Walter would be needing money anymore. Before they moved on, they pushed him to the ground. His wife, a dignified woman of fifty, stood naked in the street, screaming, as they stomped Walter's head with their boots until his brains came out.'

Marie swallowed and looked at the ground. 'I'm so dreadfully sorry, Rabbi.'

'They say they killed ninety-one Jews that night.'

'But that was in Germany,' Marie declared. 'That would never happen here.'

'I hope not. But are you willing to take that risk?'

'The chance of dying sometime in the future at the hands of a racist mob? Rabbi, if I cannot live with love, there's no point in living at all. Haven't you ever been in love?'

'Don't bring love into this.' He sighed. 'I have. You met her.'

'And what would your life have been like if you'd never known your wife?'

The rabbi raised his eyebrows, seeming to take her question seriously, for he stared into space. A look flashed across his face of thoughtfulness, then genuine sadness.

Marie smiled sadly. 'That look you just made? That's what you will be condemning me to. A lifetime of it. Rabbi, I know you want to keep me from danger. I thank you for that. But please know the danger you will put my soul in if you *don't* help me. I won't live without love. I am a grown woman; I know what I'm doing.'

It began to rain outside. The rabbi walked to the window and shut it. He returned to her and sighed. 'I suppose you do.'

The only thing left now was to attend a *mikvah,* a ritual bath.

Marie arrived at the bathhouse in the early evening and was greeted by Mrs Katz, surprised and pleased to see her there. The rabbi's wife waited at the front with her small hands folded in her lap, her black hair in a ball on her head again.

'I will inspect you and be your attendant,' she said, standing. 'Look at me, I come up only to your armpit.' They went inside into the darkened bathhouse. The floor tiles felt cool against Marie's bare feet. In the corner lay a pool, steam rising from the water. 'The water has been drained since the last person used it,' Mrs Katz said.

'Oh, thank you,' Marie replied, not even considering that to be an issue.

'Marriage is like handwashing,' Mrs Katz said. 'You are one hand, he is the other. A hand can't wash itself. One hand must wash the other and, in turn, become washed. Some days you wash his hand, the other days he washes yours. See? Like this.' She rubbed her small hands together. 'You are a team now. Hand washes hand.'

Marie smiled at the tender notion; she had not thought the rabbi's wife a sentimental woman. 'Thank you for coming, Mrs Katz. I intend to be a good wife.' She meant it.

'Now you remove your robe, and I inspect you.' Marie did as ordered and Mrs Katz checked her body, making sure all jewellery, make-up, nail varnish and dirt had been removed, explaining that she was to ensure that no barriers existed between Marie's flesh and the consecrated water. 'Now I shall watch to ensure all your hair is submerged.'

Marie stepped into the giant bath, the water warm on her toes and thighs. She moved to the centre of the little pool and bobbed down, so her hair went completely under the surface. She revelled in every detail of the ritual, the inspection, the submersion, the cleansing in the sacred liquid. She stayed under the water for a moment, looking up to see Mrs Katz holding her towel at the side of the pool, her shape watery and refracted as she peered at her through the surface.

As Marie emerged from the water, now officially a Jew, she thought of Sarah and Rebecca, the Jewish wives she had read about. Hand washes hand. She smiled. Then her thoughts turned to another Jewish wife, the wife of Rabbi Katz's cousin Walter. Marie pictured Walter's wife standing in the street in Dresden, naked and screaming, and wondered just what she'd done.

17

THE BEST MOMENTS
ARE UNEXPECTED

Marie endeavoured to shake that image from her mind as she met Ben a few days later for the first time since converting. She had blessed her food before leaving and had said a morning prayer, wanting to do everything to embrace her new faith. She dressed carefully, wearing her blue suit, the one she knew he liked. She had spent over an hour clumsily letting the hem of her skirt down, making sure it covered well past her knees. It might have seemed a prudish task, concealing more of herself, but she found it quite the opposite. Shrouding her body for him did not diminish the excitement; rather, it increased it. The more of herself she hid from him, the more he would want to view. Even her knees would become exciting, because he couldn't see them. She felt trembles and fluttering all over, which doubled as she saw him waiting for her in the square. Ben looked nervous and handsome in a grey suit. He gave her roses.

She accepted them with a shaky delight, not knowing what to do with them; no one had ever given her flowers before. She wondered if they should embrace or kiss. Perhaps he wouldn't want to until they were married? She told herself to stop: she was getting ahead of herself.

'Hello,' she said to him. He nodded a hello back. She scoured her mind for something else to say. He leaned towards her and Marie offered up her cheek, then realised with mortification that he had reached out his arm to kiss her hand. They met in a sort of crash-embrace; she felt idiotic as she banged her head on his arm a little. She wanted to die.

'I have something to show you,' he said. She nodded and said nothing, trying to recover. He led her to St Mary's Cathedral in the middle of the square. He took her hand and led her inside the door-way of the bell tower.

Marie looked up. A spiral staircase twisted above them. 'Where are we going?' They climbed the stairs, two hundred or more. Marie's lungs burned as they reached the top. 'Why are we here?' she asked through puffs of strained breath.

'You didn't believe me about the trumpeter, that he's a friend of mine. Well, here he is. Marcin, Marie. Marie, Marcin.'

Marie scowled at Ben. The mortification of their cumbersome greeting still gripped her and she felt confused. The trumpeter smiled at Marie and held out his hand for her to shake. She shook it, feel-ing awkward.

'Excuse me for a minute,' Marcin said. He walked around the curved, narrow hallway and stood before a glassless window. He raised the trumpet to his lips and blew.

The sad, mournful tune rang out, the noise almost deafening her, a tinny, blaring din. Marie slapped her hands to her ears; Ben did the same. The notes continued as the trumpeter walked his instrument slowly through its pitiful dirge, the solemn hymn to Poland's mili-tary failures.

'Not the happiest of tunes,' Marie shouted over the cacophony.

'What?' Ben called back.

Marie shook her head. 'Never mind.' She stared at the wall. The trumpet's wailing continued for several more bars. 'When is this over?' she asked no one in particular, aware Ben couldn't hear her.

'Pardon?' he mouthed to her.

She inhaled a giant breath. 'WHEN IS THIS,' she bellowed, throat burning with the effort, 'OVER?!', finishing the sentence just as the song ceased, mid-bar.

Her bloodcurdling screech, no longer masked by the trumpeter's tune, echoed across the square. People down below peered up. A woman dropped her groceries, apples rolling along the cobblestones. Marie crept back to avoid their bemused glares. Ben laughed. The trumpeter replaced his instrument in a velvet case and shook his head. Marie offered him an apology and a shrug. He collected his case and walked down the stairs, leaving her and Ben alone. Ben laughed again and Marie hit him. The afternoon, which had held such promise, had degenerated into embarrassment and discomfort; this was not how she had pictured their reunion would go.

'Do you believe me now? About Marcin the trumpeter?'

'Did I need to be rendered deaf to have this truth shown to me?'

'It was the only way, I'm afraid.'

'Can we go back down now?' She felt defeated and wanted to go home.

'I thought it would be nice to look at the view first,' Ben replied. 'You don't want to?'

'I'd prefer to push nails into my ears to stop them from ringing.'

'Just for a minute.' He stepped towards the window and beckoned her to follow.

'What am I supposed to be looking at?'

He pointed. 'There is the café where I used to sit. I sat and watched you walk across the square every day for three years.' She peered down. The people of Krakow were making their way home for the day. Men carried their briefcases across the square, while the woman collected her spilled apples from the ground. 'The sun is setting. Is it not pretty?'

'It would look prettier with some lights on. We might actually see something.' The sun had dropped below the horizon, plunging the square into grey dusk. A mist hung in the air and all the colourful buildings painted in pinks, greens and yellows now took on the same muted grey.

'And we came all this way,' Ben said. 'But wait,' he added softly. Marie looked down to where he was pointing. A small yellow light bloomed in a shop window. Another one appeared next to it. A shopkeeper walked out of his café and lit a brazier by his door. One after the other, small flames bloomed from windowsills until almost every window in every building shone with a little fire. A thousand tiny flames twinkled and blinked as the sun truly set, making the flames shine brighter against the darkness.

'Everyone is lighting candles,' Marie said. 'Why?'

'They may have turned the streetlights off to protect us, but people still need to eat, work. So everyone's lit a candle. It's beautiful.'

'It's medieval,' Marie remarked. Though, as she stared at the thousand little flames dancing in the windows, she smiled to herself. 'We light candles in our house. But it doesn't look like this.'

'Yes. You have to be up high to appreciate the effect.' He lifted his arm and placed it around her shoulder. Marie inhaled. He said nothing, just kept his arm there. He had never done this, not even as a child. She could smell soap on his shirt, and something else. Cologne? Yes, she'd smelled the same fresh scent on him at the dance.

She'd reflect later on how the nicest moments in life were the ones that take you by surprise. Planning, wishing, wanting was helpful; striving and hoping or expecting all possessed grandness and ambition; and, when the thing you had planned and hoped for finally came to fruition, one tended to feel great satisfaction. But one also felt emptiness, as though with the anticipation now over, the nervous energy gone, there was nothing left to do but find the next thing to strive and struggle for. So when an event took one by surprise, and was another person's doing, there was no nervous anticipation to spend, no energy to dissolve; in fact, energy came with it, a new energy you hadn't expected.

That was why when Ben told her that her conversion to Judaism was the most beautiful thing anyone had ever done for him, then knelt down on one knee, retrieved a ring from his pocket and asked her to marry him, it felt far sweeter than any scenario she could have concocted in her head. For all her planning, her wishing and hoping, she'd never entertained a thought that when walking up those stairs that afternoon, she'd walk back down them wearing his grandmother's ring.

They descended the tower and Marie caught Ben gazing at her with a brazen but still somehow shy face. She wondered what he was thinking.

'We shouldn't touch,' he said.

Her heart sank. 'No. Not until we are married.' So that was the rule. Ben's face fell; he looked forlorn. She laughed. 'And once we're married? Will we touch then?'

He swallowed. A silent agreement had forged itself between them; neither spoke but both knew what was coming, both were lost in their own thoughts. People walked past them, left and right.

'I want to touch you everywhere,' he said.

Her mouth suddenly felt dry. She shivered. She could not believe he'd said the words. When she finally looked at him, a magnificent pink flushed his cheeks.

They parted, making a plan to meet the next day, and Marie walked home smiling and biting her lip. She'd reached the edge of the square when he ran back to her. 'I almost forgot. While we were apart, I had an idea. There's a way you could find out your mother's name, you know.'

'Oh.' Marie drew in a breath, the change of topic momentarily throwing her, but then she trained her ears to listen and waited for him to speak.

'Your father surely knows your mother's name. You could always just ask him.' He said it cheekily, knowing how obvious it was, but unlikely to happen at the same time.

Marie had to step backwards. The suggestion seemed so reasonable, yet the idea of broaching such a question with her father made a lump form in her throat. She laughed. 'I can't do that.' She was barely able to fathom how she would break the news to her father of her conversion to Judaism and her engagement, let alone ask him the name of the parent he'd refused to speak of for seventeen years.

'Only a suggestion,' he said with a shrug. She thanked him and tried to put it from her mind as she walked from the square.

18
A NEW NAME

A few weeks later, Dominik rode the last tram home. He'd returned to the hospital after his evening meal to visit a patient who'd experienced a bowel obstruction earlier in the day. He'd left the hospital again, exhausted but satisfied the man would make it to morning, boarding the tram just before midnight and nodding to the only other occupant, a woman in her early thirties who sat at the opposite end of the carriage. The woman nodded a hello back and returned to her book.

At the next stop, a group of five young men, perhaps in their early twenties, boarded the tram and took it upon themselves to converse with the woman. They began by requesting things of her – 'Would you like to go to bed with me?' for example – following each question with snickers and grunts. The woman did her best to ignore them, keeping her nose in her book, but found herself unable to continue this tactic when they began touching her. 'What do you have on underneath? Nothing?' the ringleader asked, flipping the bottom of her skirt up, revealing a hint of underwear and garter belt. 'I thought Jews weren't allowed on this tram.'

Dominik winced at the word, which echoed through Krakow increasingly often now, delivered as a slur rather than a descriptor of one's religion. The youth said it in a stabbing tone as though bestowing an insult, the same way you would call someone a dog. 'Show me your dirty parts and I'll let you stay on. Otherwise I'll throw you off,' the young man added. Dominik sensed the bullying fun the boys were having might tip into something more terrible; from the way they swayed gently as the tram rocked, they had enough liquor and youth in them to do something regretful. He turned and peered through the windows at the end of the car, which allowed a view down the length of the mostly empty tram. He located the conductor, standing three carriages down and selling a ticket. The tram driver sat at the same end; both would take too long to reach. As the young gentlemen announced their intention to see the woman's breasts and began flicking her there, Dominik stood and walked to the other end of the carriage, where all the excitement was taking place. 'Hello, Mrs Borzdesga,' he said to the woman, making up the name for her. 'It's Dr Karski. I treated your husband last month – nice to see you again. May I sit down?'

The woman had the good sense, perhaps the weariness of experience as well, not to dispute the name Dominik had given her. She nodded and shuffled across the seat to allow him to sit. She looked slightly shocked, but not half as much as the drunken young men who surrounded her. 'Excuse me,' Dominik said to the ringleader. The boy opened his mouth to say something, but then moved to the side with a confused look on his face, and Dominik sat next to the woman. The other youths scratched their heads and seemed to pause, deciding what to do.

'Nice to see you too, Doctor,' the woman said, playing along. Dominik pointed to her book. '*The Manuscript Found in Saragossa*, any good? My daughter has read it, but I confess I have not.'

'I'm enjoying it so far,' she said, forcing a smile. The young men continued to stare. Dominik ignored them and encouraged the woman he'd christened Mrs Borzdesga to continue.

'What's it about?' he said.

'It's set in Spain, about a man who tries to unravel a family mystery,' she said. She glanced up at the young gentlemen furtively; they made no further moves, retaining their stunned faces only. She looked back at Dominik and continued with a summary of the characters and plot. Dominik kept his eyes trained on her, not acknowledging the young men's presence. As he inquired about the themes of the novel, and the woman indulged him, the conversation increasingly used two- and three-syllable words. One of the boys yawned. The youths moved away and sat down, chatting and laughing with each other. They alighted at the next stop.

Dominik wanted to sigh but didn't for fear of scaring the woman, of letting her see how flimsy his tactic had been. He'd had no weapons with which to fend off the youths; his only arsenal had been that he was a man. Purely through clothes and manner, Dominik had presented some modicum of power, someone not worth their hassle to maim. If he'd been a woman, he would not have managed it.

'Thank you, sir, you saved my life,' the woman said. She touched his arm in gratitude, her hand shaking. 'My name is Cybulska,' she added with a smile, 'Olga.' She offered him her hand and Dominik shook it.

Three nights later, Dominik boarded that same tram home, the last for the night. To his surprise, he saw the woman again. 'Miss Olga,' he said. 'Nice to see you again.'

She walked over to him. 'I wanted to give you this. I finished reading it.' She held out her copy of *The Manuscript Found in Saragossa*.

Dominik studied her. She was dressed nicely, in a fawn skirt and heeled shoes. She'd painted her lips and wore her hair out. She smiled at him. He accepted the book. 'Why are you on the tram tonight?'

The smile fell from her face and she bowed her head. 'I confess I was looking for you,' she said.

Dominik tilted his head. 'Why?'

She looked up and seemed to search his face. 'Oh. I guess I wanted to give you the book.'

Dominik shifted in his seat. The tram rolled over an uneven piece of road; the carriage shook. The woman, who was standing up, lost her balance and had to grab the overhead rail to avoid falling over.

'Are you all right?' he asked.

'Yes, thank you,' she replied, looking embarrassed.

Dominik's stop approached next. He smiled and gave her the book back.

She frowned. 'You don't want it?'

'Thank you for the offer, but as I said, my daughter already has a copy, which I can read when I like.' She took the book back and nodded. A look of desperate hurt took over her face. Dominik winced. He thought of saying more, but then they reached his stop. He touched her arm. 'Take care, Miss Cybulska,' he said, and alighted the tram.

When Marie was small, Dominik had kept a maid, a buxom older woman called Tereska, who possessed rosy cheeks and smelled of apple tart always. The woman would douse Marie in kisses and lather her with oil in winter. She'd follow the little girl everywhere, dressing her non-existent wounds and soothing her cries. One day when his daughter was about five, Marie had asked Dominik if he could marry Tereska so she could be her mother. Dominik had glared at her and, though he'd seen on her face the innocence of her question, the topic required shutting down permanently, so he'd chosen some words carefully and spoken in a low voice, which made her move her head closer to him to listen. 'Don't dare ever ask me that again,' he'd told her. 'I only ever loved one person, and I will never love that way again. I am happy to love that person for the rest of my life – I need no others. And you don't need a mother. You have me.' A look of pain had enshrouded Marie's face, as though she knew she'd said something terrible.

After this, he'd gone quiet for several days, the closest he came to rage, and she had seemed ashamed for months afterwards.

His reaction procured the desired effect: Marie had never asked for a new mother again.

The next night, Dominik returned home and prepared dinner for himself and Marie, frying sausages on the stovetop. The sausages cracked and spat in the little pool of fat on the griddle, filling the kitchen with a greasy fog. Marie entered and set the table in silence, then they ate without speaking; she seemed determined not to look at him.

Dominik tried to think of something to say, some topic that might pique her interest, but Marie seemed resolute in her intention to avoid him, staring away from him at nothing, and his mind ran blank. Soft rain blessed the kitchen window and drizzled down the glass. Dominik collected Marie's plate. She'd consumed only half the food he'd served her.

'Are you unwell?' he asked, pointing at her plate. The vegetables and bread had gone, while the sausages remained.

'I am well, Papa, thank you.'

'So why did you leave your sausages uneaten? Do you not like them?' He examined the unconsumed meat on her plate. 'Was the cut too fatty?'

'Not too fatty at all. I like fatty sausages.'

'Did you not approve of this recipe, then? Too many herbs?'

'An elegant sufficiency of herbs. But they contain pig flesh. I don't eat pork anymore.' Marie paused and took a deep breath. 'I'm Jewish now.'

Dominik stopped studying the sausages and put the plate down.

'I see,' he said. He picked up the plate once more and walked to the sink. He pushed the two sausages onto the spread of newspaper that lay there, already laden with food scraps. He fetched an extra two sausages, which he'd cooked to put between bread for her lunch tomorrow, and added them to the rubbish. He bundled last Tuesday's evening edition of the *Gazette* into a ball and tossed it on top of the meat, then returned to sit at the table.

'You didn't need to throw them out, Papa.'

'They won't get eaten. Best to throw them away before they spoil and stink up the house.' He inspected his sweater where a splodge of grease from the sausages had blemished his elbow while cooking. Stupid. He'd need to soak it; he may have already ruined it. 'Please continue. Actually, please start again, from the beginning, because I'd busied myself clearing the plates before, and I believe I misheard you.' He scratched the stain on his elbow. 'I heard you say that you were Jewish, which must signal a mistake on my part, a fault of hearing, because that is impossible. You would never do a stupid, irresponsible thing such as that.'

His daughter chewed her lip. 'There is no mistake, Papa. I'm Jewish.'

'You can't be, for you were baptised into the Catholic Church. I was there – I recall the moment with great clarity – and we stood at the front of the church where a priest poured water on your head and said a prayer. I distinctly recall it was a priest, not a rabbi, who performed the ceremony, and a statue of Mary watched over us – yes, not an icon of Moses. No Torah was—'

'I converted,' she said, interrupting him.

His heart raced; his throat felt dry. 'I see. And who converted you?'

'It doesn't matter.' Had she asked one of his patients? How many Jewish people did she know? This could not be happening – this was a catastrophe.

'We will go to the rabbi and cancel what you've done.'

Marie laughed. 'Even if that were possible, I wouldn't. I don't want to. I am marrying Ben Rosen in four weeks.'

Dominik felt his chest tighten and he wondered if he was about to have a heart attack. He loosened his tie and ordered his lungs to breathe. A biblical dread crept over him. He had observed the faces of many in this predicament, men and women clutching at their chests in the midst of myocardial infarction, begging for help with futile, voiceless cries as their hearts spasmed and convulsed, throttling them from beneath the breastbone. He now appreciated the panic in their eyes: this was what death must feel like.

'Four weeks? You don't mess about. You couldn't get any sooner?' He tried to sound calm, though he heard himself speaking in desperate, strangled tones. How could he have let this happen? His meticulous nurturing of her had given her security, and she had reacted by doing something reckless. Every parent, with the exception of sociopaths, spent the first few years of their child's life in anguish. Was the baby breathing? Was that porridge too hot, did it burn the oesophagus? When I fell asleep and did not hear their cry, did I damage their brain by leaving them too long? Dominik went far beyond these parental paranoias. He did not take a breath without thinking of how it would impact his daughter. He had kept her safe for nearly eighteen years. Now, in one deft, reckless move on her part, all his work would be undone.

'Ben called the community hall and they offered him two dates, one in ten months' time, the other in just under a month. A cancellation. I refused to wait ten months.'

'Good God. You are even stupider than I thought.'

Marie stared at him, her irises ringing out in that same shade of violent green they'd had since birth. His daughter's eyes haunted him every time he looked at them, for they bore the exact hue of her mother's. Marie appeared on the verge of tears but Dominik knew he must make her see reason. He worked to remain calm; anger wouldn't do in this situation. His daughter would flee, then all would be lost. Perhaps it was not too late.

'You must let me handle this now. I don't say these things to hurt you. It is only . . . you are so young, you know so little. This is my fault; I have sheltered you.' He tried a placatory tack. 'Tell me the rabbi who did this to you and we shall sort this out.'

'It is already done, Papa.' She stood and looked at the door, as though preparing to walk out of the house.

He wanted to grab her and stop her from leaving, but that was not in his nature, so instead he reached over to pick up a book he had been reading earlier, and pretended to read it, as though if he maintained his calm this might all go away.

'Did you hear me?' she said.

'Why are you telling me this? Do you seek my blessing?' He turned the page of his book, his hand shaking a little. His eyes ran over the words, absorbing nothing.

'No,' Marie replied, straightening. 'You wouldn't give it anyway.'

'So why bother telling me?' He kept his eyes on the book but saw Marie wince.

'Because I thought you might like to know,' she replied in a breathless voice. 'I am your daughter, your only child, and I am getting married. I thought you might like to know the date of my wedding day, so you can walk me down the aisle. I have spoken to the rabbi – it's a Christian tradition for the father to do this with his daughter, but he will allow it.'

Dominik put his book down and raised his eyes to her.

'Well? Do you want to?' He could see her holding her breath, waiting for his response.

'Is that what you want?' he said to her, holding his own breath. He imagined doing such a thing, accompanying his child on her wedding day and how lovely that might be.

'I'm not sure now,' she replied.

'If you decide, do let me know,' he said, and returned to his book.

Marie whimpered and gazed at the floor. 'Maybe it's for the best you don't,' she said, lifting her head. 'You will probably embarrass me.' She grimaced as the words left her mouth, as though aware of the sting they held.

He closed his eyes. 'I didn't raise you to act this way.'

'Act which way?'

'Like a bitch,' he replied. The instant he said it, he knew he'd gone too far. He understood the power of that word, its capacity to hurt. One only said it to grown women, to reduce them, to show contempt. Now he'd said it to his little girl.

His daughter stared at him. Her lip quivered.

If he'd known more pain than in that moment, he couldn't remember it. He saw the child in her woman's face now, holding his hand to jump across stones, sitting on his lap, her chubby little fingers, warm and sticky, the smell of her when she was a baby, that time he'd prayed to God for her, all gone, destroyed.

'Marie, forgive me. I was angry.'

Something cracked in her; he saw it in her face as she stood from her chair. 'Raise me? You barely open yourself to me. You won't even tell me her name.'

He didn't ask her whose name. 'Don't start with that again. We are talking of important things.'

'Don't start again? I've lived my whole life not knowing my own mother's name. Do you know what that feels like? Like I do not even deserve a reply. Every time you refuse to tell me her name, you show me your contempt. Not only do you think I am nothing, you also think me that word you just called me.' She ran out of the kitchen and up the stairs.

Two days passed in horrid silence. That word he'd used in anger had broken some spell. They were not friends like they used to be.

He had banished himself from that warm place. He made her dinner; they ate in silence. He asked her, 'How was the library today?' in a bright voice, knowing she'd gone there. 'What are you reading at the moment?'

He received no reply. He collected the dishes and delivered them to the sink. Marie drained her teacup and stared out the kitchen window.

Dominik often anguished about the story he'd told Marie about her mother. He'd claimed Marie's mother had left them, which he knew caused his daughter unending grief. No crueller story existed for a child than that of a mother's abandonment. It meant that her mother didn't love her, which in reality was a statement so far from the truth that one could only meet it with laughter.

He had run out of things to say, of ways to try to get her to talk. The fight over her impending marriage to a Jewish man seemed like nothing now when a grander problem had appeared: that his daughter might never talk to him again. He returned to the table and sat down and told her the only thing he could think of that might close the crevasse that had opened. He did not want to say it, but he had no choice. He turned to the young woman who was his universe, opened his mouth and spoke.

'Your mother's name is Helena Kolikov.'

19
THE RECORDS OFFICE

Six words, eleven syllables.

Your mo-ther's name is He-len-a Ko-li-kov.

Marie didn't know which word in this little sentence bewitched her most. Spoken together, the words already compelled her, but taken on their own, each presented a universe of possibility.

Your mother's.

The first two words were a rudimentary pronoun and noun, uttered by parents every day, but not by her father. Her father had said those words to her together – 'your mother' – only twice in her life.

Your mother's name.

'Name'. So much was wrapped up in this noun, too. It conjured an idea of a state of being: it referred to a person now, not some intangible thing.

Helena Kolikov.

Then the final two words, the name itself. She rolled the words around in her mouth, trundling the l in Kolikov over her tongue: *llllll*.

Her mother came from Russia then, or perhaps the Ukraine. The possibility startled her and she considered things anew. Her own slender face and high cheekbones: they came from tsarist ancestors then, not Nordic ones? Her mind tumbled. Did she come from the east?

But the middle word of the six bewitched her most of all, comprising two letters only.

Is

Your mother's name *is* Helena Kolikov.

Not 'was'. 'Is'.

She had always believed this, hoped this. Now it was confirmed.

Her mother lived.

Marie entered the civic records office on Sienna Street and asked a clerk who sat behind a dusty counter to see every record they had on Helena Kolikov. He was reading a *Tintin* comic intently and didn't look up, and she needed to repeat the question before he finally met eyes with her. Marie felt crestfallen that he didn't possess the same excitement for her endeavour as she – though, as she reminded herself, he didn't know that Marie hadn't known her mother's name until yesterday, that today was the first day of her life she possessed the ability to ask such a question.

'What information do you require?' he asked, clearly bored.

'Birth certificate, marriage certificate. Anything you have.'

The clerk sighed. 'Which? Pick one.' He wore wired spectacles that looked like they needed new lenses. He glanced at Marie with a cross-eyed look.

'Birth certificate,' she said.

'Are you a relative?'

'I am her daughter.'

He stared at her. 'So *that's* your mother's name.'

Marie looked at him more closely. She knew him. He had been in the year above her at school, attending the boys' college that partnered her convent. 'Matthias?'

She'd once defeated him in a regional debate. The topic had been 'We should milk the cows' and she had been on the affirmative team. She had argued with precision that the cows were there to be exploited. He had lost the thread of the argument halfway and had dropped his notes on the floor. It had been a resounding victory at the time but posed no good for Marie now. She hoped he wouldn't hold it against her.

He disappeared behind a partition. Marie bit her nail. Information on her mother lay within these walls, she could feel it. After all that. How easy it was to find someone when you knew their name. Fifteen minutes passed, and he didn't return. Marie decided she'd embarrassed him and now he was penalising her. He hadn't gone to look at all; he was smoking or had gone to the pictures. Finally he returned, but empty-handed.

'No record by that name,' he said.

'Are you punishing me for defeating you in the debate?' she asked.

He smirked. 'No.'

'I don't believe you,' she said. 'This is important. I'm trying to find my mother. It is more important than your petty problems with me and my debating skills. I can't be blamed for your poor definition of a debate topic. You were not the worst, in any case. It was your second speaker who really let you down. Everyone forgets the second speaker; he really has the most difficult job. It is easy to define and easy to round up. The middle is where the devil lies.'

'I promise! There is no birth certificate for Helena Kolikov.' He even spelled the name out for her to show he'd looked correctly. Marie bowed her head, crushed with disappointment.

Matthias glanced around. The room contained the two of them and no one else. 'We're not supposed to do this, but do you want to search yourself?' Marie nodded eagerly, and he showed her behind the partition. A gentle breeze blew through an open iron window.

The building hailed from the sixteen hundreds at the oldest, the walls made from bricks stacked one metre thick to withstand cannon balls. Steel filing cabinets sat back to back in lines of twenty, and another forty lined the rear wall. He showed her to one and pulled out a metal drawer.

'This is every birth certificate from the year of our Lord eighteen-seventy to nineteen-ten, of women, last name beginning J or K.' He patted the steel cabinet. It rattled, the sound echoing through the cavernous room. Dividers between the files denoted the different years with small letters. 'Be my guest.'

'Thank you,' Marie said. She flipped through the first section of folders.

Matthias stood there and watched her. He tilted his head. 'Is your mother dead?'

'Worse. Missing,' Marie replied. She scanned through the first dozen files.

'How is missing worse than dead?'

'Only those missing someone can answer that.'

He studied her face, offering a look of pity. 'I'll leave you to it.'

Marie smiled her thanks, not looking up. She walked her fingers across the tops of the files. Certificates sat one behind the other in alphabetical order, many bearing the creases and yellowing of time. The steel cabinet smelled of lignin and cellulose. It contained a thousand human beings inside, each possessing their own life, their dreams and failures. A Helena Jankowicz had sat there in that cabinet for twenty years; next to her birth certificate was that of her death, her life reduced to two pieces of paper. But it didn't contain Marie's mother. Helena Kolikov didn't live inside that cabinet.

Marie fetched Matthias. 'She's not here.'

'Told you,' he replied. 'I'm sorry.'

'Wait. These are not in order!' Marie showed him two files.

Between Helena Anna Jankowska and Hildegarda Maria Jarewska, there sat a death certificate for Hanna Rzankowicz.

'What? Oh. How did that get there?' He looked at her like she would know.

Her heart leapt a little. 'I shall go through all of them,' she said. The clerk stared at her, eyes bulging, and informed her that it would take a day at least for them to go through every birth certificate. Luckily, she was a pig-headed, stubborn sort of girl, very used to getting her own way. She assured him he didn't have to help her; he could leave her to it and she'd check the files. Once he'd been relieved from engaging in the insane task himself, he happily agreed to it going ahead. He left her to it, returning to his *Tintin*.

Over the next six hours, Marie read every birth certificate from K to Z, starting with the females' files and moving on to the males'. She felt fairly certain she'd ascertained the entire history of Krakow. Nineteen-sixteen had been a busy year at the records office. At least two thousand death certificates had entered the cabinets. The clerks would have exhausted themselves with the filing. The year 1917 lauded over 1916, with three thousand death certificates joining their counterparts proclaiming birth. These certificates bore the names of young men aged twenty, eighteen – quite a few were thirteen – she even found one young hero who'd joined the Almighty at twelve. The certificate listed Przemyśl as his place of death, a town situated a few hours' train ride east of Krakow. Marie pictured the young Polish lad in his Austrian uniform, fighting back the Russians to stop them from entering Krakow. The death certificate rested next to that of his father, who'd died the previous winter in southern Russia. The son would have been sent to defend his home when the father died. She considered the fluke of being born female, what it spared and excluded one from.

Thousands of death certificates from 1919 and 1920 sat there too, each bearing the name of a child, one or two years old. Cause of death: influenza. Ben's birth certificate was there; he was born in 1915. His father's death certificate sat next to it. The paper listed Moses Abram Rosen's death in 1929. Just before Marie had met Ben. He had torn his shirt. 'Why has no one repaired your collar?' Marie recalled saying to him. She knew now it was the custom to show one's grief by breaking something.

She went back the next day and the next, obsessively working and searching. She returned any certificate that sat in the wrong order to its correct home. Her mind worked this way. The cabinets, once peppered with months of dust, now gleamed and sparkled in the afternoon light that shone through the steel-framed windows. She hadn't wiped them down but the dust had removed itself, as though her furious activity had disturbed its restful slumber and it had departed for a quieter part of the room. Once complete, she ran her eyes over the reordering and smiled, pleased with her efforts.

When the clerk returned the next morning, he gasped. 'What have you done?' He rifled through a cabinet, his face bearing a panicked look. 'They will bust my ass for this!' He said 'ass' in the American way, like a gangster in a film.

'I'm sorry. All I did was reorder a few things.'

'A few things? You've completely changed my system.'

Marie tried not to laugh; the system had been non-existent. 'I didn't. I only cross-referenced. Everything can now be found by name or year, depending on what you know. That's all.'

He flipped through some files.

'It's all right?' she asked.

He nodded. 'I suppose. I'm not happy you changed my system!' He made a strange noise that Marie struggled to categorise, like the harrumphing of a villain from his comic book, perhaps. This failed to lift her mood though, which had descended into darkness as the days had ticked over. She'd catalogued and arranged the entire collection of birth certificates of Krakow, and her mother didn't exist within that group. She was ready to leave when she suddenly was struck by a thought. She hadn't found her own birth certificate either. She told the clerk as much.

He shrugged. 'So?'

'My father would have registered my birth. He's meticulous – he records everything.'

'I see the resemblance,' he replied. He scratched his head. 'If that was the case, you weren't born in Krakow.'

Marie shook her head; the idea was impossible. 'But I asked my father. He told me I was born in the hospital where he works.'

'He either didn't register your birth or he's lying.'

Marie stiffened. Neither concept sat well with her.

People often asked, what was the moment one became an adult? At what point did one switch from girl to woman, from boy to man? Some answered the question with physical milestones: menarche or marriage, or the first time you held your child – all worthy contenders. But Marie felt certain that this moment, when she discovered her parent had lied to her – not a white lie to spare her feelings, praising an ugly dress or celebrating a low mark in a school subject she did not enjoy, but a real lie about her life – was the moment that began her transition to adulthood. 'If I was not born in Krakow,' she asked the young man, 'then where was I born?'

Matthias shrugged. 'Somewhere else in the world. I need a smoke,' he said. 'Can't smoke in here, it makes the files brittle. Care to join me outside?'

Marie wondered at his selective dedication to document preservation: he let inches of desiccating, mould-harbouring dust gather, yet he worried about a few puffs of smoke. Nevertheless, she gathered her coat and followed him out.

'You father saved my thumb, you know,' he said as he lit his cigarette. He offered Marie one but she refused. The smell of jasmine hung in the air and Marie gratefully lifted her nose to breathe it in. 'I got into a fight with a saw blade. My thumb hung by a flap of skin – everyone said it was toast. They told me I should bury it next to my dear mama in the graveyard, pray it was a long time until I met it again and get on with my nine-fingered life. But Dr Karski took a look and asked me if he could try reattaching it. I said, "Sure, why not?" He took a chair and put on those big glasses, with the black frames?'

'I know the ones,' Marie said, picturing the magnifying bifocals her father wore when performing small surgery. They made him look like a fly. 'He built them himself.'

'Boy, he made me hold my arm still for seven hours. It was horrible. I really needed to pee. I had drunk two litres of beer. I thought he'd need to repair my bladder too. I explained this and Dr Karski got the nurse to bring a pan. She pulled my trousers down like I was a baby and I peed into it. I didn't care – I was glad for the relief. I apologised to your pop. He was good about it. Nothing he hadn't seen before. He kept right on working while I peed. I had my John Thomas right in front of him – sorry, my, you know, *thingy*.'

'Yes,' Marie said. 'Go on.'

'Your papa said every second counts when you're reattaching skin and muscle.'

'It's the nerves. The tissue dies very quickly. It's vascular, you see – you must work quickly before the blood and oxygen supply is depleted,' she said. 'Did it work?'

'You tell me.' He held up his left hand and wiggled his left thumb up and down and around. It bore a full range of movement. 'Good as new! Your father works miracles.' He stubbed out his cigarette, employing his reattached thumb to do so, and they walked back inside.

'I also couldn't find my father's birth certificate,' Marie said.

Matthias nodded. 'Then he wasn't born here either.' Marie knew this; her father had indicated he came from the north of Poland. 'We've other records on him, though. He's one of the men about town. Boy, he sure donates a ton, to charities and such.'

Marie's ears pricked; she hadn't known that. 'Can I see these records?'

'Oh, I don't think so. Those ones are private. It wouldn't be right.'

'But I am his daughter,' she said.

'Yes, but he's a grown man. A woman looking at his money, even his daughter – it's not right.'

'I am not interested in his finances,' she said. 'Only he is such a private person. You mentioned some charity work he has done? I should like to see it. He is so modest, he never tells me anything. It would be nice to know all the wonderful acts my father has committed in the name of charity.'

'I suppose a quick look,' he said. 'This way.'

He showed Marie upstairs to another room, located some files and handed them to her. 'Here's the deed to a house purchased in 1924.' Marie smirked. The clerk had but minutes before asserted his right to protect her father's privacy and now he was showing her house deeds.

Her father had purchased their house in Grodzka Street in 1928 for 24,000 zloty. A tidy sum even then. Her classmate Hanna, one of the richest at school, had bragged once that their house cost 16,000 zloty. She explored more pages, locating another three deeds for property in Krakow. Each bore the name Dominik Karski. Her father owned three more properties, and not just any old pile of bricks: one had cost 52,000 zloty. She'd passed this place every day, an elegant office building near Main Square. Her father owned three floors of it!

Yet while records of her father's wealth piqued her curiosity, they did not shock her. He was a doctor and treated most of the richest people in town. She even felt a little impressed at her father's financial prudence, investing in real estate. But the next set of records made the hairs on her neck stand up.

Her father had donated 30,000 zloty over the years to various charities. Repairs to the town hall in 1932 had been made with his money. The Catholic orphanage on Jerzy Street had its rent paid three years in advance by her father. She was stunned. The stained-glass window of St Bartholomew, for which her father had sat on the completion committee? Not only had he attended meetings to see the flayed saint finished, he'd also donated 10,000 zloty to make it happen. Ten thousand: a year's rent on a three-bedroom apartment. He would have had every priest and church bureaucrat worshipping him thereafter.

Marie recalled an article she'd read in the *Gazette* about a man whom authorities had caught embezzling extorted funds from Warsaw city coffers. For a roof repair that a builder had invoiced the city 20,000 zloty to complete, this accountant had altered the bill so it read 30,000 instead, pocketing the other ten himself. After a decade, he'd swindled the good taxpayers of Warsaw out of almost one million zloty. Neighbours and colleagues refused to believe the charges and had shaken their heads after he was arrested, begging for his release. 'But he was such a nice man,' they cried. 'He's not capable of these things. The police have got it wrong.' Injustice had in fact not been done; this man had committed every crime he was charged with. So how had he fooled everyone?

For every zloty he'd stolen, he'd given thirty per cent of it away.

He'd made handsome donations to local schools, a literacy program for veterans, hospitals, churches. Every charitable institution in town had benefited from his largesse. Like the illusionist who dazzled you by pulling colourful flowers from his sleeve while he swapped your card out of sight, this man had slipped money into their left pockets while removing double from their right.

As Marie scanned the pages of her father's own charitable payments, his exorbitant philanthropy to the churches, schools and municipal works of the town, she thought of the scoundrel in Warsaw and felt her blood chill. Was her father fooling Krakow in the same way? If so, what crime was he distracting its people from when he lined their pockets? Only one offence stood out to her that Dominik might feel keen to divert attention from. The thought of it made her shiver.

For sixteen years, Marie had believed her father when he'd told her that her mother had simply walked out one day of her own volition, abandoning them both. She'd taken Dominik's reticence to talk about the matter as resulting from his humiliation at being left, from his broken heart. Perhaps her father refused to talk about her mother's disappearance, not from grief, but because if he spoke, he might give too much away. For the first time, she began contemplating that her father might have had a hand in her mother's departure.

She took a moment to reflect on her mother and to imagine what her last moments within the family had been. Had she wanted to leave, or had fear gripped her? When she'd looked upon Marie for the final time, had resigned acceptance filled her, or joy, or terror? The closer Marie came to finding her mother, the more her heart ached. She would die to meet this woman, to touch her, to hear her speak, to know her story. She hoped she wasn't too late.

20
A TRIPLE DOSE

Lwów, October 1918

Helena Kolikov watched the girl's face and contemplated the unenviable task of saying something to her new employer. She'd worked at Karski's Apothecary for only three weeks, the first paid position of her life. Before this her only experience in the arena of work was to milk the skinny cows and till the barren earth on her father's godforsaken farm.

If she tried to help the girl sitting in the treatment chair, it would seem like a criticism, a rebuke of the management, and she'd lose the work and the four zloty she earned from it per week. There was no question: starvation would occur without this job. Anyway, who was she to speak up? She was but a hick child, seventeen years old, from a putrid, flea-bitten hovel, beyond the Pale of Settlement. She could not say with any authority that the younger girl was being poisoned.

But she'd seen Mr Karski, the pharmacist, give the girl the laudanum, carefully measured to a child's dose and titrated upwards to match the requirements of her body mass to the milligram, with instruments he'd sterilised in the precise manner Helena had already come to love. She'd witnessed him medicate the girl perfectly, in the way she'd read about in the textbook when she'd snuck a glance in there; the man followed each step to the letter. The only problem was he'd done it twice.

Helena's job was to clean the apothecary. She washed the floors, scrubbed the benchtops, collected the rubbish, burned the waste, emptied the chamber pots, cleaned the bandages and steamed the cloths. She was not permitted to touch the beakers and pipettes and glasses; the apothecary cleaned those himself. She loved to watch him do it, the tiny glasses glinting and sparkling in the light as he worked. He had a box of little bottle brushes, as slim as a needle with bristles like the hairs of a dormouse, which he'd use to clean the beakers. He worked expertly, deftly, with fingers that had done the same task for decades. It was a rare thing to witness, a master executing his skills, and she delighted in viewing it. But this morning, the young girl had arrived at twenty minutes past seven, received her dose of the brown syrup and waited on the corner with the other children for the trolley to take them to the schoolhouse. When the trolley hadn't showed up, one child had inquired up the lane and returned to say one of the trolley horses had thrown a shoe, delaying its arrival. The children had waited out the front of the apothecary, playing hopscotch, and then Helena had watched through the window with astonishment as Mr Karski walked outside and fetched the girl to give her the medicine again.

The girl had protested, saying she'd already taken her dose, but when Mr Karski insisted that she needed it, on the order of her parents, the child had submitted and swallowed the medicine. The girl returned to her hopscotch game looking decidedly sleepy but still upright, losing the next game and surrendering a marble to her friend. The girl suffered from something called asthma, a word Helena had never heard before, but she'd watched with fascination how the liquid eased the girl's cough. Now he'd given her two doses, however, and she felt curious to see what swallowing a double quantity might do.

Until recently Helena had never seen laudanum in real life, though she'd heard of it. There was no medicine in the town she came from except for a tea made from bark that was administered to put hairs on a man's chest. She'd spent the last three weeks viewing Mr Karski's potions with wonder; she thought he must be a sorcerer. But when the trolley had still not come a few minutes later, Mr Karski went outside again, and in almost an exact replication of before, ordered the schoolgirl to come inside and receive her medicine for what would be a third time. While he might have been a wizard, he was also a forgetful old man.

Helena knew nothing about medicines, but she did know that the bark tea, when one drunk too much of it, made one rather sick. And the farmers and wives in Helena's village had spoken of laudanum's power in hushed voices, weeping for the faraway, city-dwelling brothers and grandmothers it had killed when they'd acquired too much of a taste for it. Two doses and the girl might sleep very well tonight. Three doses and she might sleep forever.

Helena could see that someone had cleaned the girl's nails and polished them, and they'd placed a silk ribbon in her hair and dressed her in a jacket of fine wool. Her mother, who sometimes brought her to the apothecary, wore a coat of mink. Even the maid who brought her most times wore finer clothes than Helena. This girl came from a rich family. It would be a scandal if Mr Karski poisoned her.

Helena grimaced. What to do? As Mr Karski led the girl to the chair, she protested once more. He gave the same convincing arguments as previously: your parents have instructed me, et cetera. The girl sat in the chair dutifully, looking unsure but likely to comply with the order from a respectable man in a white coat all the same. Mr Karski prepared the dose as before, in as skilled and sure a manner as Helena had ever seen someone do. Helena, on the other hand, could read and count only from the instruction of her father; she'd left school at ten. Three weeks' wages, one pair of shoes and one set of clothes were her only possessions. She had acquired this job through a stroke of luck. No one would hire her again if it became known that she, a filthy orphan, had contravened the orders of a city pharmacist who wore shoes costing more than she'd earn in a year. She made one final rationalisation: if the girl died, perhaps no one would ever know why. They would assume it was the coughing, Mr Karski wouldn't be blamed and Helena could forget the need to say anything.

But as he raised the syringe to the girl's mouth, Helena could scarcely believe that her arms, seemingly under their own authority, grabbed the girl and pulled her outside. 'The trolley is here, miss, you had best not be late,' she said. She ignored Mr Karski, who shouted for her to come back. Once outside, she pulled the girl down the street and rounded the corner, out of his sight.

'Hey,' the girl said when they finally stopped. 'I needed my medicine. Mr Karski said to take more.' Helena watched her eyes, which were drooping shut, the drug's double dose now taking its proper hold, and made her keep walking. 'Where are we going?' she asked, slurring.

'This is our little secret, yes? Mr Karski made a mistake today,' Helena told her, leading her down the road by the arm. 'You need only a single dose. Promise me if he ever tries to give you more than one syringe again, you will run from the building.' The girl stared at her through one drooping eyelid, confused, the other one now shut.

Helena walked her all the way to school and to the infirmary, where she told the nurse the girl was unwell and instructed her to watch her breathing; if it slowed to nothing, to stand her up and force her to walk around the block. Helena couldn't tell what was going through the nurse's mind, being instructed what to do by a country girl with holes in her boots, but Helena's suspicions about the girl's wealth and her family's influence must have been correct, for the nurse took one look at the girl and bestowed a satisfactory amount of importance on her ongoing health, training her eyes on the child's chest, watching it rise and fall. Helena walked back to the pharmacy.

Mr Karski grabbed her as she walked inside. 'Where is the patient for this medicine?' he asked, the syringe still in his hand.

Helena searched his face for recognition. 'You already gave her the laudanum, Mr Karski,' she said. He stared at her. He was tall and wiry, handsome, but something was off. Unshaven, that was it. Small grey bristles emerged from his jaw, their removal missed in his toilette routine, giving him a dishevelled look like a tramp, an odd sight in his expensive clothes. His eyes flashed a hint of recognition and sadness. Helena saw that this had happened before. But then he grew angry.

He shouted at her, outraged and defiant. 'How dare you! Who do you think you are? Get out, you no longer work here.'

Helena nodded. At the door she paused, then opened her mouth. What did it matter, she'd lost her job anyway. 'You gave her the laudanum twice and would have given it to her a third time if I hadn't stopped you,' she said. 'You would have killed her.' She had an idea. 'Let me help you.'

He laughed cruelly. 'Help me? What do you know about pharmacy?'

'Nothing at all. But you could teach me enough. I could make note of the medicines and patients. I will tell no one, I will protect your secret.'

He stared at her with such fury she wondered if he might burn a hole through her.

She flinched; she should not have mentioned mistakes, secrets. 'You are a wonderful apothecary,' she added, speaking the truth.

'Get out,' he said. She did.

She walked the three kilometres home; she couldn't afford the tram fare. She reached the front door of her bedsit, more of a cupboard in dimensions, which felt wet with damp, only to realise she'd left her coat at Karski's Apothecary. She closed her eyes; how could she have been so stupid? She'd prefer to poke needles in her eye than return to that place, but she had only the one coat and the weather was cooling by the day; there would be frost soon and if it arrived and she had no outer covering, she could add freezing to death to the list of other methods ready to kill her, such as starvation, disease, random attack and loneliness. She walked the three kilometres back to the pharmacy, this time without her shoes. She had worn a hole in the sole of her left boot and couldn't afford to have it worsen, so she walked barefoot, arriving with her feet shrivelled and aching. She added trench foot to the possible causes of death that awaited her.

She prayed Mr Karski would be with a customer so she could slip inside and take her coat without having to speak to him, but when she stepped through the door, she found him standing behind the counter, staring at her, still holding her coat in his left hand. She nodded and took the coat from him. 'Thank you,' she said. She waited for him to say something, but he didn't, so she started to leave. He didn't speak until she reached the doorway.

'You saved that girl's life this morning,' he said. Helena turned around. He gazed at the floor. 'Thank you.'

'You're welcome,' she said.

He picked up a flask of camphor oil and inspected it. 'I forget things,' he said. 'No, that's not it exactly. I don't forget them, it's that I can't remember them. I can't make the memory.' She nodded. 'I remember everything from before – how to mix tinctures, how to titrate a dosage. I could recite you the periodic table.'

'I have seen you at work. You are a brilliant chemist.'

'But I can't make new memories. I don't know what's happening to me. I walk into a room and don't know why I'm there. It fills me with dread. If that girl had died, I would have lost my business. If I can't administer medicines anymore, I will have to sell this place.

My son was going to take over, but he is at the front. My wife's been deceased ten years. I have no one.'

'You can still administer medicines. Let me help you.'

'I don't see how it could work.'

'I will stand beside you and record every medicine you make, every dose you administer. You keep all your old memories; I will look after your new ones.'

He peered at her. 'No one could ever find out.'

'No one will. We shall make a secret system, just between us. I could pinch you if you are about to kill someone, for example.'

He smiled. 'But how will you know? That was a lucky guess last time. You know nothing of chemistry. Do you know the atomic number of helium?'

'No.'

'Exactly. You don't even know the basic things. This won't work.'

'So teach me.'

He laughed. 'Impossible.'

'Teach me for one week. Set me a test at the week's end. If I pass, I will be your assistant. If not, you may kick me out.'

He laughed again. 'You are a girl; you can't be my assistant.'

Helena couldn't argue with his assertion, but then she smiled. 'That's the best part,' she said. 'No one will suspect me. No one will see me coming.'

21

LET ME SHOW YOU
THE UNIVERSE

They began that afternoon. 'Lesson one,' Mr Karski said, rolling up his shirtsleeves. 'The first thing you must know about chemistry is: everything is connected. Would you like to see the universe?' He paused with portentious anticipation and stared at her, waiting for her answer.

Helena shrugged. 'Surely, yes.'

'Here it is.' He pointed to a wall chart containing the periodic table. A hundred or so boxes stared back at her, arranged in rows, each containing numbers and letters she did not recognise. 'Everything contained in the universe fits on this paper. Look at me. You see my whole person, my arms, legs, head, face? Wrong! I am not a whole being at all, I am simply millions – no, billions – of particles that have clung together. And every particle that makes up me is listed here.' He pointed at the table again.

Helena looked at the boxes and scratched her head.

'You are the same. And between you and me,' he continued, 'there's not *nothing* standing around us right now in this room – there are billions of other particles clinging together that make up the air. We can't see them, because they're tiny, but they're there. When you look at water you see a clear, wet liquid, but it's really billions of hydrogen and oxygen particles, two elements you see here

199

on the table,' he pointed, 'arranged in molecules of H_2O, two hydrogen, one oxygen. But move only a few elements and the substance changes completely. Add three oxygen and one sulphur, for example, and water now becomes sulphuric acid, vitriol. One gives you life, the other can kill you. You can break anything down, anything at all! Every substance on this planet consists of the same hundred-odd elements, just arranged and grouped in different ways. Do you see?

'You must consider the composition of everything from now on. You must learn to speak a new language.' He pointed at a biscuit. 'Sugar is no longer sugar. It is now twelve carbon molecules, twenty-two hydrogen, eleven oxygen, repeated over and over. Once you know what a thing is made of, then you ask yourself: how does it move? How can I make it move? We came from dust, from the stars. And the dust from the moon rocks, and the dust that makes up people? Both consist of the same ingredients! From the periodic table. Just in a different combination. We are all particles. We are all connected. Once you understand this, the world is yours. Do you understand it?'

Helena stared at the table, her mind whirring. If Mr Karski had blinked or taken a breath during his speech, she had not seen it. He'd asked her if she understood what he'd said; she felt like laughing, or vomiting. She paused, trying to recall his words to make sense of them. She did not understand, but she could feel an *inkling* of understanding – certainly an appreciation of what he was telling her. He looked at her, smiling expectantly, and waited for her to answer.

'I do understand,' she said, out of politeness more than anything, and hoped she'd understand it for real one day.

He beamed. 'Lesson two: repeat lesson one. Everything is connected. Do you have any questions?' He moved away and began polishing a beaker.

Helena swallowed. 'That's all you will teach me? One lesson?'

'I just told you how to master the universe in that one lesson! Yes, that is all. Perhaps I will also show you how to clean the beakers. That is very important as well.'

From the bench he fetched the pharmacy diary where all the appointments were listed, and flipped the pages forward one week. He wrote in the diary: *Girl, exam, 09:00.* He looked at her. 'So I don't *forget*,' he said.

She forced her smile away; she couldn't tell if he was joking.

The next day they invented a system for dealing with customers. A customer would hand over their prescription and Helena would write it into the ledger. She'd tell Mr Karski the order and he'd prepare it and hand it to her. Helena would deliver the medicine to the patient and mark it off in the ledger. When a customer was required to receive their medicine in the pharmacy, they added a step. She'd confirm the milligrams, grams or tablets required on the prescription and tell Mr Karski.

He required no help in measuring out the correct dose. She watched in awe as he placed the little piles of powder onto the scales and found them balanced perfectly each time. He could size up a gram of anything with his eyes and knew instinctively how much to place on the scales. Her assistance came later, after he had measured the correct dose precisely and administered it to the patient in textbook fashion. If the patient had the misfortune to hang around the store for whatever reason – to browse Mr Karski's tonics, or to wait for the rain to pass – Mr Karski would, without fail, try to give the person their medicine again. In these cases, Helena would inquire about a ledger entry she couldn't make out. He'd huff at her interruption but follow her to the book all the same, and she'd draw the local butcher or milkman away from being poisoned.

She began to learn the different uses for each substance, watching intently, snatching every morsel of information she could. Cocaine was for toothache; laudanum was for coughing spasms or asthma. Laudanum also arrested the digestive tract the same way as it did the lungs, thus it could treat cholera. Aniline dye not only transformed a grey dress into the deepest indigo blue, it could also lower fever when combined with the right liquids.

By the end of the fourth day, Helena's mind felt like it might explode as she flopped onto her bed in a euphoric, painful exhaustion. Methods for making tinctures, chemicals and their properties, ideas for reorganising the shelves filled her head. She felt ecstatic. No one had ever asked her to do anything beyond tending to animals or sweeping a floor. No one except her father, and he was dead now.

On a couple of days during the week, Mr Karski had remembered every customer who walked through the door, greeting them cheerfully and inquiring about newborn children, harvests, remarking on the weather. On those days he seemed annoyed at Helena's presence, of her standing beside him curiously, being in his way. Other days, he remembered no one and no current events, and he remained quiet, mixing eighty prescriptions in succession, saying nothing but greeting each client with a nod, and keeping Helena close.

Monday arrived and along with it, Helena's examination. She saw the entry written in the diary and wondered if Mr Karski would remember. He did; without looking at the note, he alerted her to the fact. 'Your examination, little girl.' He only ever called her that – little girl – never her name.

Helena nodded; it was all she could manage. She'd felt nervous since she walked in that morning; she'd lifted every beaker with a shaky hand. She swallowed.

'Make me a tincture for athlete's foot.'

Helena exhaled with relief and disappointment. Relief because she knew how to make it; the recipe and methods were easy. She'd combine a few ingredients to make an anti-inflammatory balm and the test would be over. Disappointment for the same reason; there was no risk, so if she made it incorrectly, no harm would come to the tincture's recipient. Clearly Mr Karski didn't trust her with complex mixtures; he didn't think she was intelligent enough to be presented with a challenging task. Still, she'd make this correctly and would retain her employment. She would satisfy herself with that.

As she prepared the ingredients and equipment, the telephone rang. It rang rarely; few people in town had telephones. The caller must have been wealthy. Mr Karski answered and spoke with them, then replaced the receiver in its holder and turned to her.

'That was the butler at Krajczuk House. Baron Krajczuk suffers a fever and needs aspirin. Change of plans – new examination. You will make the aspirin, then you will hand-deliver it and administer it to the man. If you do not kill him, you can stay.'

Helena blinked. 'You won't help me?'

He shook his head. 'You told me you knew what you were doing.'

'But aspirin? It contains many ingredients and requires reactions to make.'

'You had better get started, then. He needs it now.'

She knew that the active ingredient in aspirin was acetylsalicylic acid; this was the powerful compound that soothed the body's thermostat and reduced dangerous fevers. She looked for the substance on the shelves but couldn't locate it. She sighed as she ran her eyes up and down over the bottles, flasks and pots, finding nothing with that name.

'Are you looking for acetylsalicylic acid?' he asked with a smile.

She nodded. 'Where is it?' she asked, feeling out of breath.

'It's there,' he said, pointing his arm left and right, to multiple locations around the pharmacy. 'In parts. You have to make it.'

She felt her mouth go dry. She searched her brain, pilfering its memories of the past week. Had she witnessed Mr Karski making this acid? She had, partly. At least *this* was something she could do – from an early age, she'd become aware that she had a remarkable memory. She could look at a page of writing once and recall it later in her mind. Her father used to remark on it, and they were never cheated in the village because Helena remembered the orders the locals had placed with them to the penny, even from the year before.

This past week she had exploited this muscle to its fullest, watching Mr Karski like a hawk, recording in her brain as many of his actions as she could. She hadn't seen him make aspirin from start to finish, only some of the steps. She would have to rely on this now and make up the rest as she went along. He had combined salicylic acid with acetic anhydride. But how much? She recalled him measuring these out. Three grams of the former and six millilitres of the latter. Was this right?

She took a deep breath and guessed yes, placing the acid in the glass and adding the anhydride, trying not to panic. She knew something was needed to settle the concoction – sulphuric acid? She'd watched him add it to many things; she thought it sounded right. She drew some of the liquid into a dropper with a shaking hand and added it to the mixture. She added five drops, then one more for good measure. He watched her the whole time; she didn't see him blink. She took a deep breath and continued, swishing the glass around gently, careful not to splash, until the mixture was combined.

She tried not to dwell on the absurdity of the situation, the gargantuan errors she might already have committed. Acetic anhydride could burn a hole through an arm if it touched the skin. How could a man ingest it without it doing the same to his insides? She half-expected the beaker to explode. It did not, so once the mixture was combined, she placed the glass inside a flask of warm water and let it rest for ten minutes.

'Have I mixed it correctly?' she asked.

He shrugged. 'We shall soon find out.'

She added distilled water to the solution to dilute it and rested it in cold water. Crystals began forming. She smiled. She'd hoped this would happen. It meant she'd done something right. She couldn't confirm if they contained medicine or poison, but they were crystals.

She added some ethanol to increase the crystallisation and warmed and then cooled it to coax them out, all things she had witnessed him doing. Finally, she pushed the mixture through a funnel and set it on some paper to dry. She could barely watch, but slowly and surely, tiny yellowish crystals emerged on the paper. She blinked and looked at Mr Karski.

'Now administer the medication to Baron Krajczuk,' he said.

'Is it right?' she asked, exasperated.

'There's only one way to be sure,' he said. 'You must give it to him and see.'

She couldn't believe what she was hearing. She wanted to hit Mr Karski for his playful mocking. She stared at the crystals.

'Go now, there's little time. If you wait any longer, the patient might die before you've even had a chance to kill him with your medicine.'

Helena packed the crystals in a little china pot and walked to Krajczuk House. The building protruded from the earth in a grand mass of white walls and columns. She knocked on a black oak door and the butler answered. 'You are Karski's maid?' he asked.

'Yes, sir.'

'He telephoned to say you were on your way. Where is he? Why is he not here?'

Helena shuddered and searched for an answer. 'My legs are faster,' she offered. 'Mr Karski wanted the baron to have the medicine as soon as possible.'

He nodded and pulled her inside, showing her up a grand staircase. Crossed sabres and portraits of noble ancestors decorated the walls. Its dimensions exceeded Helena's entire living quarters tenfold. She'd never stood inside anywhere as grand or beautiful. She swallowed, realising the penalty for poisoning a nobleman was likely something worse than death; torture, probably. Did they still hang, draw and quarter people? They might reinstate the penalty just for her.

The baron lay on a chaise in the centre of the room. He still wore his riding boots, which were caked with dirt, and was reclined in a position both rigid and limp. His skin looked clammy and dull. Perspiration covered his face and soaked down his shirt in a half moon. He made little gasps and sighs, but didn't notice her standing there; he seemed not to notice anything. Helena had seen fever like this before, where she'd come from. It was always fatal.

'Where is the medicine?' the butler asked, gesturing to a doctor standing in the room. Helena retrieved the pot from her pocket. The butler snatched it from her and handed it to the doctor. Before she could say anything, the doctor gave it to the patient and he swallowed it in a shaky, delirious gulp, then washed it down with a glass of vodka. Helena gasped; he'd ingested it.

The doctor walked to the window and the butler stayed with his master. Helena crept over to a corner of the room and stood by a grandfather clock. She wanted to leave, to run away back to the countryside, but she couldn't bring herself to look away from the man's face as the fever and nausea gripped him. He was in a world of twilight horror, probably feeling no pain at all. She wondered how long it would take for the mixture to kill him, if she'd got it wrong. She could barely believe where the morning had taken her. She decided if the concoction did slay him, it would be instant, because the danger lay in the acetic anhydride, that volatile, angry liquid that could burn through an iron bar if it wanted to. If she hadn't mixed it correctly – in the wrong amount, for example – it would eat through his throat, his tongue, his stomach passage, and everything would be over.

She watched his delirious face for any sign of this happening. A minute passed and he hadn't clutched his throat or screamed in horror. Another minute passed with the same result. She exhaled a breath; she might have been holding it the entire time. She hadn't killed him.

How had she not killed him? She grimaced and scratched her head. She'd taken the carbon, hydrogen and oxygen from the salicylic acid, added it to the carbon, hydrogen and oxygen of the acetic anhydride. The two chemicals had rearranged their elements into different combinations, taking the poison of the acetic anhydride and turning it into something benign – no, something helpful. She'd put in two dangerous substances, they had rearranged themselves according to the laws of the cosmos, and medicine had come out.

And then she saw it, what Mr Karski had been talking about: everything was connected. There was no dog standing next to a boy, two separate beings. They were both the same elements, simply clinging together to make a dog standing there, a boy standing here. She saw the universe, the stars and the moon, the trees and the salicylic acid, each of them composed of the same ingredients, just in different combinations. The room appeared before her, no longer curtains, lounges and fireplace, but different combinations of carbon, hydrogen, oxygen and nitrogen. She had discovered a new language – the language of the universe! – and now she could speak it. She could alter any substance once she knew what it was made of and how it moved.

A trance of rumination and wonder enveloped her. She almost didn't notice when the doctor returned to his patient and placed a thermometer in his mouth. Twenty minutes must have passed while she'd stood there, dreaming of the universe. He waited, then retrieved the glass pen and inspected the mercury. He smiled.

Helena nodded and slipped out of the room. She walked back to the pharmacy, seeing the universe in the trees, the people, the rocks around her. Before he died, Helena's father had never pushed marriage on her. 'You will get by on your brains, daughter,' he'd said proudly. He'd made her count the rows of cabbages in the field: there were twenty-five. 'And how many cabbages in each row?' Helena had counted: there were fifteen. 'How many cabbages, total?' She'd shrugged and told him they would be pulling 375 from the earth. She had been five years old at the time. He shouldn't have been surprised; he was the one who had shown her how to multiply. They had studied each night of her life: mathematics, philosophy, literature. 'You are too clever to till the dirt,' he used to say. 'As soon as you get the opportunity, get out of here. Leave this place and never look back.' She always said nothing in reply, only nodded and smiled each time he said it, for where would she go, how could she leave him?

On her sixteenth birthday, he presented her with enough money to travel to the closest city – still six hours away – as well as an address for a place she might live when she arrived there, and two books. It had taken him six months to save the money.

'You want me to leave you, Papa?' she said, looking down and feeling desperately sad.

'As soon as you can,' he replied with a smile.

She put the money away and hoped he'd forget about it. Some months later she found him in bed, dying. She cried and asked him not to go. He turned to her and grabbed her arm. 'Get out of here as soon as you can. Go make a life for yourself. If you stay here, you will die.'

'But what about the farm, Papa?' she said. 'People need me here.' She mopped his brow with a cloth and wept.

He shivered with the fever that gripped him. His large, strapping frame had reduced itself to a bag of bones. 'People will need you wherever you go, Helena. You are that type of person. People will prey on your goodness and your conscientiousness. Do you know this word, "conscientious"?'

She shook her head.

He tutted. 'Leave here, so you can find out what it means. I'm sorry I didn't teach you to read more.'

She smiled. 'I read well, Papa.'

He gripped her with both arms then. 'Promise me you will get out of here. You must go and find out what the words mean.'

'Which words, Papa?' Helena scowled.

Her father looked up. The room contained no ceiling, just the rafters and beams that held up the thatched roof. It was raining. A drop came through a crack in the roof and hit Helena on the forehead.

'All the words,' he said. 'Find out what they all mean.'

'How is Baron Krajczuk?' Mr Karski asked. He was polishing a beaker and didn't look at her as she walked in.

'You knew I had made the aspirin correctly – you knew it would work?' Helena replied.

'Yes.'

She waited for him to congratulate her.

'Clean the glasses by the sink, then remove the dust from the front sills. Then we shall get to work.'

22
THE PERIWINKLE

A quiet moment occurred at eleven o'clock each morning, after the early rush and before the lunchtime customers. Mr Karski would retire upstairs to take a nap and Helena would prepare the ingredients for the afternoon's prescriptions, after which she'd clean and polish the glasses until they shone. She treasured these periods alone in the apothecary. She'd run her hands over the marble countertops that stretched the length of the room, polish the porcelain sinks until they gleamed in creamy white, and dust the oak shelves with their vials and ampoules, potions and elixirs. She would smell the herbs hanging from hooks, the chamomile, garlic and foxglove, as they gently swayed in the breeze that came through an open window. She loved the ruby bottles the best – Mr Karski had coloured them red to preserve the contents within from deterioration – and when the sunlight hit them, she'd watch as they cast pink and orange refractions on the glass display cases. The space was a sorcerer's hovel, a witch's lair. She'd never encountered such wonder. She opened the salicylic acid and measured out a portion to make aspirin. She hummed to herself.

'Who are you?' a male voice said.

Helena looked up. A young man who looked to be in his mid-twenties stood in the doorway. He wore a uniform of the

Austro-Hungarian army and was studying her in a way that made her nervous.

'I am Mr Karski's maid, sir. I clean the pharmacy,' she said. It was the line they had agreed she'd say.

'Why do you have the salicylic acid out? Are you making medicine?'

'No, sir,' she said quickly. Fear gripped her. He knew enough to identify the substance from its appearance only; the bottle carried no label. Lies would not go far with him.

'Are you stealing it? Salicylic acid costs a week's wages for a cleaner.'

Helena shook her head. 'I would never.'

'I don't believe you. You are stealing the acid while my father is upstairs. You are taking advantage of him.'

Helena protested again. So this was Mr Karski's son then, returned from the front. She couldn't tell him the truth and reveal Mr Karski's secret, for she didn't know what he knew of the situation already. So she persisted with the denial, futile as it was.

'What's going on here?' Mr Karski appeared in the doorway; he'd awoken from his nap.

'Nothing, Mr Karski,' Helena replied, trying to make peace.

His eyes went past her and rested on the man at the door. He gasped. 'Dominik,' he said. He gripped a bench, as though he might fall down otherwise.

'Hello, Father,' the man replied. He scratched his face and stared at the old man. Helena watched him carefully, studying his face. He resembled Mr Karski in appearance, standing slightly shorter, but he possessed the same eyes, a deep blue. 'Father, do you know your maid is robbing you? She's pilfering your acid.'

Mr Karski turned to Helena. She smiled at him and waited for him to speak, hoping he'd know what to say. 'I don't know this person,' he replied. Helena's heart sank.

'Oh my, even better,' Dominik said with a laugh. 'A thief and you don't even work here.'

Helena shut her eyes, trying once more. 'Mr Karski, I am your maid, Helena Kolikov. I help you in the shop.'

The older man shook his head violently. 'I don't know you.'

Helena looked at him hopefully, begging for him to remember. He had done this before, forgotten her in the middle of something, but after some prompts, he often replied angrily, *Of course I know who you are.* Sometimes he remembered her for days at a time; other times it took hours for him to come around.

'Please, Mr Karski, I am Helena,' she said.

He turned to his son with only confusion gracing his face.

'I think it's time you left,' Dominik said to her.

'No, sir, please. I promise you, I do work for your father.' She wanted to tell him, to explain the situation, but she'd promised Mr Karski never to breathe a word to anyone.

'Leave now or I will handle things myself.' He placed one hand on his hip, drawing his coat back, revealing his side-arm. The metal glinted in the sunlight. Helena felt bereft. She nodded and went, with no choice but to leave, the one small mercy being that she remembered to collect her coat this time.

She cried all the way home, desperately sad. She hadn't yet collected her wages for the month; she'd expected payment tomorrow. All the pennies she'd carefully saved over the preceding months wouldn't last long; she'd need a new job straight away. She knew no one, except those people she'd met through the pharmacy. She couldn't ask any of them to vouch for her, to tell the son who she was, as that would mean revealing the secret that she was Mr Karski's memory, not his cleaner, and the gossip would rip through the town in an afternoon.

On top of the grief of losing her employment, she also felt something else. In the months she'd worked there, she'd befriended

Mr Karski. He had taught her pharmacy, laughed with her, encouraged her. His was the only friendly face she'd encountered since her father's. Now he was gone, and she'd never felt so lonely. She lay in her bed and cried herself to sleep.

She woke to the sound of knocking at her front door. She grimaced; she knew no one in this city and it was likely a mistake, but she wiped her eyes and answered the door. It was Mr Karski's son, Dominik.

'What is wrong with my father?' he asked. His eyes seemed full of fear.

'I don't know, sir,' Helena said. She wouldn't reveal her ex-employer's secret.

'Stop calling me sir – I'm twenty-four years old. And how old are you?' He studied her again with squinted eyes.

Helena felt unnerved. 'Seventeen.'

'Something is wrong with him, and I think you know what it is. Are you sworn to secrecy?'

She said nothing.

'Tell me or I will shoot you.' She looked at his face and saw he was not serious. If anything, he looked scared. 'He forgets things, doesn't he?' the young soldier said, gazing at the floor.

'Yes,' Helena said.

'You are not a thief, but you are not a maid either. You have been helping him so he can continue his business.'

She nodded.

'You were preparing something with that acid, not stealing it.' He scratched his boot on the doorway. She nodded again; she'd been in the middle of making more aspirin, as supplies had run low. Word had got around about Mr Karski saving the baron and people flocked to the shop now wanting his potion. It seemed to help not only with fever, but heart problems, too. Helena had been struggling to keep up with the orders. 'How bad is he?' the son asked.

'Some days he fares very well,' Helena said.

'And others?'

Helena shrugged. 'I am sorry. I don't know what to tell you.'

'I think you have saved his business.'

She studied Dominik's face. Other soldiers of her acquaintance had been faceless brutes, men who shredded villages, starring in tales of rape and murder. Where she came from, they taught you to fear this breed; no good could come of them. But this young man wore sadness in his eyes, a cautious gaze. His bones were finer than she'd originally perceived. He possessed a gentleness, a softness, that ran at odds with his present occupation.

'Would you like a cigarette?' he asked, holding out a small gold case.

'No, thank you,' Helena said.

He took one for himself and placed it between his lips. Strong, long fingers operated the match; a thin line of dirt sat under the nails.

'You will come back, won't you,' he said. His voice didn't rise at the completion of the sentence; he intended a statement, not a question.

'I don't think I'm wanted,' Helena replied.

He smiled and puffed on his cigarette. 'Whatever made you think that? He's been asking for you all afternoon.' He turned and walked down the stairs of the tenement.

'Wait,' Helena called after him, leaning out the doorway. He paused on a step halfway down and turned back to her. 'What does he say about me?'

He grinned. 'He says, "Where's Helena?" over and over again.'

It was the first time she'd known Mr Karski to call her by her name, not 'little girl'.

The son ran a hand through his hair and looked up at her. 'See you tomorrow.'

A few weeks later, Dominik gave her a silver badge, with *Helena* engraved on it in cursive letters. He pinned it to her shirt. She watched him as he did so; his fingernails no longer hosted any dirt. He had discarded his army uniform now and wore civilian clothes every day, fawn trousers and a white shirt. As he pinned the badge over her right breast, she hoped he couldn't feel her heart thumping.

She felt like a great imposter if this was some romantic overture on his part. Her father had raised her to help him with the plough, and she'd grown up an oafish daughter, with a large body best suited to manual labour. Boys had teased her in the few short years she'd attended school, setting her rough, wiry hair on fire and putting excrement through her schoolbooks. She'd pined for men before, suffering grand and desperately pathetic crushes on the local farmhands and young tradesmen. She'd harboured a deep love for a kindly older fishmonger who one time gave her extra herring because he'd witnessed a boy trip her over in the marketplace. He must have been forty years her senior, yet she silently longed for this man and others. She conjured elaborate fantasies in her head of them embarking on quests together to save a local injured animal, or travelling over the Tatras to rescue a princess. She never uttered a word to these people in real life, their conversations and connections existing only in her mind.

As far as she could tell, she'd never inspired in any man that type of violent affection and declarations of love that other young women seemed to excite. The best regard she could hope to entice from men included praise for her ability with animal husbandry and appreciation for her well-ploughed fields. She reminded herself of this every time the pharmacist's son greeted her or smiled in her general direction – that she couldn't possibly be the subject of his, or any other man's, romantic affections – and tried instead to concentrate her energies on learning her new trade of pharmacy, using the extra blood pumping around her body from her excited, thumping heart to power her mind instead.

Three months passed in this manner. Winter came and went, and they slipped into an easy rhythm of Helena working at the apothecary alongside the pharmacist's son. Later, she would recall it being one of the happiest, giddiest times of her life, when every glancing touch, every look from him was savoured. Then one morning as the weather turned warmer, Helena arrived early, before seven o'clock, to check on some acid she'd refined with ethanol and left to crystallise overnight, and as she approached the building's rear entrance, she encountered Dominik sitting on the cobblestones in the laneway, slumped over. At first she thought he might be sleeping, but as she came closer she realised a better diagnosis was unconscious. She paused for a moment to watch his face, which was relaxed with eyes shut, only for her pining reverie to be broken when he began violently vomiting. She considered him horribly ill from some malady at first but as she got closer and had the misfortune to smell him, she realised he was drunk. He deposited the contents of his stomach onto himself, his military coat and the cobblestones, and as she reached out to stop him from falling onto the ground and breaking his head, he vomited on her also.

'Lieutenant Karski,' she said, 'try to stand up.' She received no reply, verbal or physical. The sickly sweet smell wafted upwards and assaulted her nostrils. She noted with interest that she didn't gag; the odour didn't affect her at all. Perhaps her affection for him blinded her nose to the offending stench, the way a mother does not retch while changing her baby, or perhaps she had simply encountered enough horrid smells in her lifetime already, rotting bovine and porcine carcasses, raw human waste, fermented crops and the like, to feel intimidated by the small problem of stomach contents and bile.

She managed to stand him semi-upright and placed herself between his right arm and his body, shouldering him inside. He ceased vomiting long enough for her to assist him up the stairs without leaving any mess on the floor of the hallway. They reached his bedroom door. She found herself absurdly knocking on it, a force of habit, which made him chuckle in his semi-conscious state. They entered and she pushed him onto the bed as gently as she could. He flopped onto the covers and seemed to settle into a contented sleep, so she moved to exit the room, planning to leave him there to sleep it off.

She allowed herself a few quick, furtive glances around his bedroom, having never been inside it before. Handsome oak furniture graced the room, a photograph of someone she supposed was his mother on the dresser. She found herself astonished at the cleanliness and orderliness of the place; he'd arranged his clothes and effects with precision. The experience of standing in his private space gripped her: being in the place where he dressed and undressed, washed himself, combed his hair.

She was about to shut the door behind her when the sound of him vomiting graced her ears once more. How could there be anything left at this point? He lay flat on his back, so now not only did he vomit, but he choked as well. He coughed a terrible gurgling cry and she rushed over, cursing herself for her thoughtlessness at leaving him so and thanking God his stomach had chosen to resume spasming at that moment, when she could still hear it and be alerted to the danger.

She grimaced and eased him onto his side to help the vomit drain, placing two fingers in his mouth to clean the airway of the deadly debris. This latest episode of retching subsided, and he collapsed with exhaustion. She moved the pillow under his head. She stayed beside him so he remained lying on his side, his body resting against her hip. She sat there quietly, and maybe fifteen minutes had passed where he appeared to fall asleep, when finally he said, 'You have to help me. What time is it?'

She checked the clock on the wall. 'It's eight in the morning.'

'I must report for duty at ten. I'm returning to the front today.'

'Oh. I thought the war had ended?' She had read as much in the newspapers; the Austro-Hungarian Empire had disintegrated, and Germany had surrendered in a French railway carriage.

'So did I.' He bowed his head. 'The War to End All Wars has finished. Another one has taken its place. I must fight for Poland now.' He spoke with a rueful smile.

Helena sat up, shocked. She felt her heart breaking; she'd come to enjoy every minute in his presence – except, perhaps, for the vomiting. 'I don't think you are capable in your present state. You must tell them you are ill.'

He shook his head, wincing as he did. 'It's not like reporting sick to a job in an insurance office. This is the army. If I don't show up at the assigned time, they'll charge me with desertion, then shoot me.'

Helena questioned the wisdom of him spending the night imbibing alcohol if such a responsibility awaited him the next morning, but she kept this to herself.

'You're wondering why I became drunk last night, aren't you, if I have to report this morning? You wouldn't think that if you'd seen what I've seen. You don't know what it's like out there.'

'What needs to be done?'

'I need to look like I haven't been out all night, disgracing our great and noble nation,' he said, in a tone so bitter that it shocked her.

Helena was not sure what that meant exactly, but while she couldn't help his attitude, she could improve his physical appearance.

'I've clean clothes over there,' he said, pointing to the wardrobe. Helena opened it and marvelled at the five pristine olive dress shirts that hung perfectly equidistant on the rail. Boots were neatly placed underneath and polished to a regulation shine. Everything was ordered with a mathematical precision.

At that moment, he vomited again, the spasms bringing up only water and bile this time; there was nothing left in his stomach, yet his body continued the contortions. His muscles would keep spasming in the misguided view that it was helping dispel poison, when really this would only end now with the young man cracking a rib or dying from dehydration.

She fetched a powder Mr Karski had extracted from the henbane plant, which calmed seizures of the digestive tract, and gave it to him dissolved in some water. He collapsed again from the exertion of sitting up to drink. 'My father can't see me like this,' he said. Mr Karski slept in the room at the end of the hall and would emerge for breakfast soon. She helped Dominik out of his clothes, leaving on his drawers but removing his shirt, trousers and undershirt, replacing them with cleaner versions from the wardrobe.

She watched him, and when, after twenty minutes, the solution she'd given him had not been brought back up, she gave him more, gently coaxing him to drink as much as he could. 'This is the only cure for drunkenness,' she told him, as he lay back down again, resting on her hand.

He looked up at her with wide eyes. 'One day I will stop drinking. I must, I want to. But I can't yet. The things I've done. Do you understand? I don't want to go back.'

Helena watched him, aware she cradled his head in her hands. He looked as though he might cry. He blinked twice.

'You go east, yes?' she asked him. He nodded. 'You must go, then. Because it's almost April, and the periwinkles are beginning to bloom, but only in the east. Have you ever seen a periwinkle before?'

He scowled at her and seemed unwilling to continue the absurd conversation. She felt unwilling to continue it herself. Nevertheless, for it was all she could think of, she said, 'Periwinkle was my father's favourite flower. He would pick them for me – they grow wild in the fields out there – and he'd put them in a vase by our kitchen window. He is dead now, and no periwinkles grow in this city – the conditions are not right – but if you go to the east, you will see fields and fields of these little blue flowers, and they will bring a tear to your eye with their beauty. You must go and tell me what it's like. I have not been east in so long and I doubt I will ever go back there. But these periwinkles are a sight to be seen.'

She swallowed and couldn't believe what she'd just said, revealing so much of herself to a stranger – such sentimental things, and speaking of her father. She felt silly making a show about periwinkles, truly nature's drabbest flower, which her father had plucked from the earth around their farmhouse because that was all that grew there. They were special to her because her father had done so. But she need not have worried, for almost as soon as she finished speaking, Dominik shut his eyes and began to gently snore.

At nine-thirty, she woke him. He'd been sleeping peacefully for about an hour. 'Lieutenant Karski, it's time to leave. You will need to go now to make it to the army office.' He woke with a start and gripped his head in what she presumed was post-drinking agony, then looked down at himself, observing the clean clothes with bemusement and disorientation.

'I've washed your other clothes and placed them in your duffel, along with your personal items. I dried the clothes as best as I could by the fire, but as I had less than an hour, they are still damp. Please hang them up again when you arrive at your barracks to dry them fully, else they may begin to smell.' He nodded as she said this; she felt confident from the immaculate state of his room that he would have carried out these laundry tasks even without her directions.

'I attended to your face and appearance as best as I could,' she continued. 'I removed the stains from your coat.' She checked the wall clock. 'Please go now or you shall be late.'

He stared at her with a bewildered look and opened his mouth to say something, but then shut it again. He grabbed his military duffel bag, put on his coat and ran out the door.

She waited until she was sure Mr Karski was inside the pharmacy proper and wouldn't see her exiting his son's bedroom, then walked out.

She didn't tell Dominik all the things she'd done for him. In fact, she'd combed his hair and placed pomade in it, shaved his face carefully with a razor, taking great pains not to scratch him, and she'd bathed him. She didn't mind that he hadn't said thank you for any of it, or even said goodbye; she didn't want to embarrass him. Expressing gratitude was to acknowledge that the event had taken place, that she'd seen him at this vulnerable moment, and she didn't want to cause him further pain.

Six weeks later, a letter for Helena arrived at the pharmacy. At first, she didn't know what to do with it, or what it was, really, for she'd never received a letter before. Her name and the pharmacy's address were written on the front in a large, neat hand.

She opened it; a piece of paper lay inside. No words were written on it; a single periwinkle looked up at her instead. Someone had carefully pressed and dried the flower. Though the petals now lay dry and dusty, they still bore the faintest hint of the deep blue they must have once been.

23
A PARENT'S LOVE IS
UNREQUITED

Krakow, June 1939

Four days after he'd revealed Marie's mother's name, Dominik
received an invitation to his daughter's wedding. It arrived with
the morning post, a thick card in creamy white that contained all the
standard information one expected from such notices: the time and
date of the ceremony at the Old Synagogue in Kazimierz, followed
by a reception at the community hall. Someone had handwritten
Dominik's name at the top of the card, on a line reserved for such
annotations. Dominik studied the handwriting and found it came
not from his daughter, but someone else – Ben, perhaps. His daughter hadn't invited him to her wedding.

Several days later, a patient with an inflamed appendix wished
Dominik congratulations on his daughter's upcoming nuptials.
'She's marrying a Jew, yes?' the woman asked, as Dominik palpated
her abdomen.

Dominik bowed his head. 'She is.' He braced for a stern remark
about the dangers of mixed marriage.

'Oh well, you can't have everything. So what does her dress look
like?' The woman had doubled over in pain by this point, as people with appendicitis tended to do, yet she still found the strength
to pat his arm and ask. She didn't seek any specifics about the cuts
of lace or fabric used, she merely requested an overview to help her

picture it – perhaps he'd seen something like it in a magazine once? Dominik replied that he'd not seen Marie's dress and didn't plan to, and sent the woman down the hall to Theatre Two. As he opened her up and inverted and stumped the inflamed vestigial organ, he asked Matron Skorupska, who was assisting him with the procedure, just how many people knew of his daughter's wedding.

'The whole town knows. Exciting, isn't it?' she replied. She had received an invitation also. Dominik stopped himself from asking to see it, to check if Marie's handwriting graced the card or if someone else's did. He grimaced instead and proceeded to suture the patient closed.

Dominik went home that night and threw the invitation in the bin. He prepared the dinner for himself and Marie, left Marie's serving on the kitchen table with directions on how to reheat it, then returned to the hospital. He had no patients to attend to but his paperwork could always do with a clear-out. He arrived home at midnight to find Marie's dinner eaten, her plate washed and put away and Marie herself in bed. In the morning he rose and left the house at six o'clock, before Marie had awoken. He maintained this routine for the next four weeks, coming home only to pre-pare meals, change clothes and sleep. He didn't see Marie once in that time.

On the day of the wedding, Dominik received a knock at his front door. He answered it to find Johnny there, dressed in a blue suit. He had combed his hair back and set it with pomade. He looked both debonair and debauched.

'Hello, Johnny,' Dominik said, offering his colleague a perfunc-tory nod.

'Are you ready? You're not dressed,' Johnny said.

'Dressed for what?' he asked, aware he sounded foolish.

'Your daughter's wedding, old friend! It begins in twenty minutes, as I'm sure you know.'

'Oh, that,' Dominik replied. He noticed a loose piece of timber peeling from the doorway. It could do with a repainting; perhaps he'd get to it that afternoon. 'I'm not going. Enjoy yourself.' He offered a tight half-smile that he felt contained the appropriate amount of politeness and dignity for the occasion. Johnny possibly possessed an alternative take on it, for he laughed. Dominik touched the doorframe: did he have any paint in Imperial Red left in the storage cupboard under the stairs, or would he need to venture to the hardware store to procure some? 'Are you going?' he asked Johnny, still inspecting the door.

'Of course!' Johnny replied, pushing his shoulders back, as if to bring attention to the formal outfit he wore and the lack of any other possible reason why he'd wear such an ensemble on a Sunday afternoon. 'I was invited, old chap.' He held up his invitation, and Dominik couldn't stop himself from inspecting it. The little card bore the same appearance and offered the same information as Dominik's, but it bore the small, neat letters of his daughter's hand. So there it was. Marie had invited Johnny to her nuptials, and likely Matron Skorupska, too. But someone else, not Marie, had invited Dominik, either out of pity, or as a sop of an olive branch.

'I'm not going,' Dominik said again, forcefully this time.

'But you must walk your daughter down the aisle!' Johnny said, gasping.

'I must not do anything, Johnny. Goodbye.' He went to shut the door on him. He had never attempted such a dramatic gesture in his life and he hoped he was pulling it off with the requisite composure of someone who performed it regularly. However, Johnny responded with an action of even greater drama and, Dominik had to admit, greater style. As Dominik pushed the door closed, Johnny stuck his foot in it.

Dominik rolled his eyes and reopened the door. He felt unjustly treated by this whole situation, but he was not about to break the metatarsals of a fellow surgeon to make his point. 'I didn't return any RSVP,' he said. 'I can't simply turn up. It will throw the numbers out. They will have already found someone else to accompany the bride down the aisle. Enjoy yourselves, you and the nurses. I have papers to attend to, and this conversation keeps me from my documents. Now I must beg you to leave me be.' He couldn't help himself, and gazed at the ground at that point.

Johnny patted his arm and spoke softly. 'I know you are upset, old chap. Your daughter marries a man you, *ahem*, weren't expecting. But she is a wonderful girl, and I know that if you don't see her on her wedding day, you will regret it forever. Come on, old friend. This is not like you. My wife was Jewish, did you know? My son too, by extension.'

Dominik shook his head. 'Is that why your father disowned you?'

'Ha! He disowned me because I let the master race down by having depression. But yes, he wasn't all that happy about my marrying Sarah, either.'

'I have nothing against the young man, nor his religion,' Dominik said.

'I know that.'

'She might lose her life over this. I can't condone it. She's making a terrible mistake,' he said quietly.

'She sure is.' Johnny lit a cigarette. 'People in love do funny things. If you let me come inside, perhaps I can help you choose a suit?'

Dominik sighed and collected a black suit from the hallway, still in its bag from the tailor's. 'I have one,' he admitted.

Johnny unzipped the bag and inspected the jacket, a black dinner coat fashioned from wool and silk, the appropriate cut and colour for the event held within his daughter's new culture. 'A smashing get-up,' he said, running the fabric of the lapel between his fingers.

Dominik nodded and stifled his delight with a shrug. 'Get dressed and we'll go.'

Dominik changed and they began walking to the synagogue. He checked his watch. 'It's already too late! The wedding started at three-fifteen. That was two minutes ago.'

Johnny checked his own watch. 'Dash it,' he cried. 'I'll run ahead and tell them to wait.' He darted off.

Dominik ran after him. Rabbi Katz was known for his punctuality; there was little chance he'd tolerate a wedding starting late. Old Synagogue stood just over a kilometre away. Even if Johnny sprinted, it would still take him five minutes to get there. The only chance he had was if Marie had asked them to delay proceedings, in the vain hope that her father was on his way. But for that to have happened, it would mean she actually wanted him to walk her down the aisle and, seeing as how they hadn't spoken since their fight, and how her handwriting hadn't even blessed his wedding invitation, he doubted this would've crossed her mind. He suddenly felt silly. Perhaps Marie didn't even know Ben had sent the invitation. Dominik would turn up at the synagogue, puffed and sweating, in an ostentatious black suit, not even really invited. He sat down on the ground.

Johnny turned around and ran back to him. 'Dominik, what are you doing?' His voice was strained with panic.

'Go without me – it's already too late. The wedding has already begun. Someone else has taken my place.'

'You don't know that,' Johnny said. He looked up and down the street, left and right, frantic, eyes darting.

Dominik thought about what Marie was doing right now. Had she looked to the door and hoped to find him walking through it? Or had she proceeded down the aisle on schedule, with some senior man of the synagogue, or an uncle of her fiancé?

Johnny sat down next to him in the gutter. 'What I'm going to say you won't like.' He cleared his throat. 'Today is not about you,

Dominik. It's about your daughter. Better to arrive late than not at all, to show at least you tried. A parent's love is unrequited – it's only when we become parents ourselves that we truly understand what love is. I would give anything to have another day with my son.' He smiled.

Dominik nodded. 'But we are so late. What should I say to her? What excuse should I make?'

'Make no excuse,' Johnny replied. 'If you are late, say you are sorry, then tell the truth. Tell her you didn't want to come because you were upset, tell her that she looks beautiful and that you are sorry for running late, but that you are so glad you got to see her on her wedding day.'

Dominik nodded again and they ran onwards. They would stand up the back and he'd apologise to Marie when he got the chance.

As they neared the building, his shined leather dress shoes chafing his ankles and the thin elegant soles clipping on the cobblestones, he found himself moving faster, sweat on his brow. He felt foolish now, hoping like an imbecile that she'd waited, that she'd refused to walk into the synagogue without her father. In a state of futile fantasy, he forged some telepathic connection in his head, silently begging for her to have waited. *Please, Marie*, he said to himself, *please*. He found himself overcome with the sadness of it all, how he'd ruined everything. He broke into a sprint, bounding across the cobblestones like a madman.

Arriving at the back of the building, he threw himself around the heavy oak door. The sound of Johnny still running up the laneway trailed behind him; Dominik had run well ahead with his sprinting. Inside he found a woman in white, a lithe, elegant figure, waiting at the back of the synagogue. Her back was turned as she spoke to a teenage boy in a black suit, who had the discomfited look of someone being sent on an errand he wanted no part of. 'Rabbi says we must begin. I am to take you down the aisle.'

Dominik waited in the doorway to hear what she said to him. 'He is coming. Just one more minute.' His heart leapt.

The boy saw Dominik and Johnny, who'd arrived behind him at the door. Marie, turning around, followed the boy's gaze, and the most beautiful vision Dominik had ever seen blessed his eyes.

She wore an ivory gown, the sleeves stretched to her wrists, and she'd pulled her hair back into a chignon. A white band crowned her head and flowed into a veil. No beads or jewels adorned her, except the necklace Dominik had given her on her sixteenth birthday.

Their eyes met. Dominik opened his mouth to speak but she'd already wrapped her arms around him. She hadn't embraced him since she was eight years old. Dominik remembered the moment so vividly: she'd broken her arm but not cried, and after he'd set the greenstick fracture in plaster, she'd leaned in and held him, the pain visible on her face. After that, she'd never embraced him again; she'd become a woman at eight, never needing him after that point. But she held him now, and Dominik could feel the fine strong bones of her spine.

In the end, nothing was said between them. She held him so tightly that he could feel her breath on his collar, and he felt her shudder and sob quietly. His heart wrenched with relief that he'd arrived, that Johnny had persuaded him to come, and that Marie had insisted to the rabbi that they wait.

'Can we start now?' the teenage boy asked, clearly wanting to move things along.

'Yes,' Marie replied. She held a bouquet of white roses and, as they brushed against her veil, the smell of honeyed nectar rose to Dominik's nose. Marie moved to the left side of him and looped her arm around his. He found himself throwing his shoulders back and straightening his spine.

Just as they were about to enter, Rabbi Katz shuffled towards them from the front of the synagogue and met them. 'Here, put this on,' he said to Dominik, handing him a kippah.

Dominik thanked him and placed the small circle of fabric on the back of his head. 'I am allowed to walk her down the aisle?' he asked. 'I'm not Jewish. I don't want to offend anyone.'

'Bah,' the rabbi replied, waving his hand. 'What do you think, God will see and smite you with a lightning bolt? He's got other concerns today. Walk her down the aisle – I said so. Now, let's get going. I've got another three of these this afternoon.' He ran back down the aisle, wiping his brow as he went.

A dirge played from a fiddle somewhere, sending haunting notes into the room. Dominik escorted Marie towards the front. The hall and the congregation within it made for a humorous sight. Guests for the groom numbered into the hundreds, while those for the bride made less than twenty. But though the bride's guests were small in number, they made up for it with their importance to Marie. Johnny and Lolek stood towards the front, Professor Maklewski and his wife next to them. Matron Skorupska and Nurse Emilia were both there, dabbing their eyes and smiling, as well as several other nurses from the hospital. Some schoolfriends of Marie's sat in the next row. Everybody wore their best clothes and beamed and waved at Dominik and Marie as they walked past. Dominik felt his chest swell with pride, and he breathed with giant relief, thanking God he'd showed up.

'I didn't know Ben knew so many people,' Dominik whispered to Marie as they continued to walk.

She chuckled. 'He doesn't. People have travelled from Warsaw just to catch the spectacle. A gentile converting to marry a Jewish man. Some might call it a reckless move, considering what might be coming.'

'I'd be inclined to agree with those people,' Dominik said. He walked Marie to the end of the aisle and deposited her in front of a white silk canopy. They stopped there and waited.

The rabbi addressed the congregation. 'Who gives this woman away?'

'I do,' Dominik stammered. He took in the sight of Marie's future husband, who walked out from under the canopy. Ben wore a suit similar to his own, cut from black wool and tailored well; he'd likely purchased it from the same store. He looked handsome. He'd been good-looking in his youth and this continued. He had adored Marie as a child, saved her from bullies, listened to her stories with patience and care. The look on his face now showed that he worshipped her. He would make an excellent husband. Dominik would never approve of this marriage; his daughter had done an irresponsible and rash thing. But he could not fault her choice of partner.

He had been determined not to make eye contact with the man who wanted to take his daughter from him, but as he found himself standing next to him now, his heart wasn't in it. Instead, he looked the young man in the face and held out his hand. Ben hesitated, likely from shock, then reached out with graciousness and shook it. Pleased little gasps rose from the crowd. Ben took the veil, which hung from its hairpins at the back of Marie's head, placed it over her face and led her under the canopy to begin.

24
THE MOTHER-IN-LAW

Ben hailed from the Reform tradition of Judaism, practising a kind both assimilated and secular; he did not belong to the Orthodox faith. Still, the wedding had included many of the beautiful traditions: they were married under a canopy held up by four men, they broke a glass, the husband served his new wife wine. Dominik had stared in awe at his daughter throughout. She looked so poised and grown; she knew exactly where to stand and what to say.

They had all moved to the community hall afterwards and the reception was now in full swing. Twenty-four circular tables had been laid with white tablecloths to host a four-course dinner of smoked salmon and capers, followed by the finest brisket and goose. 'Ben's family would have paid in blood for this,' Johnny had quipped as they walked into the reception hall, decorated magnificently with silks and candles. Dominik had nodded and said nothing. The bride and groom had broken up a giant challah and placed a portion on every table. Dessert was doughnuts filled with pâté and dusted with sugar, and a resplendent wedding cake. The finest chef in Poland had prepared the feast and no expense had been spared. The cake had been served on china plates with silver cutlery. Now the dancing began.

Dominik had enjoyed the meal and now sat on his own, belly full, watching the dancers. He was almost relaxed, maybe even enjoying himself a little, with one small speck of uneasiness making him sit crookedly.

A small woman traced the edges of the dance floor. She wore a dress of pink silk that reached the floor, the fashionable, feminine silhouette at odds with the stern and implacable look she wore on her face. Her frame was rail-thin but she looked elegant – as elegant as a skeleton could appear, anyway. She didn't walk, but rather stalked the edge of the dance floor, sucking on a cigarette in a holder fashioned from ivory. Dominik kept track of her out of the corner of his eye and strained to avoid making contact. He wondered if he might survive the whole wedding without talking to her.

The woman's name was Rachel Rosen, and she was Ben's mother. Dominik had last spoken to her eleven years ago, when they lived next door. He had been afraid of her then, and was terrified of her now. She looked over at Dominik, boring into him with her steel-blue eyes, and he swallowed.

Dominik recalled once peering through his kitchen window, which looked directly across the way into the Rosens' study, to find Mrs Rosen furiously stabbing her fingers onto the keys of a gigantic typewriter. She'd tied her lustrous black hair into a horribly chic, tight chignon, and a cigarette had sat in the corner of her mouth, as it did now, bobbing obediently between her lips, up and down in time with the rhythm with which she'd struck the keys. Dominik had felt sorry for the typewriter. He couldn't tell what she was writing – a love poem perhaps, or a termination letter to a supplier – for her demeanour never changed; it could have been either. She had looked up from her typewriter briefly, and as their eyes met, she had scowled at him with a look so demonic Dominik had gasped and hidden behind his kitchen curtain. She'd never said anything about it afterwards, but she'd glared at him from that day onwards. He had feared her ever since.

Dominik tried to shake the traumatic memory as Johnny sat down next to him. 'Why do you sit here, Domek? Get up and dance!' He had removed his jacket and tie, his shirtsleeves now rolled up to the elbows. He'd been dancing manically with the male guests all night, spinning around in circles for three hours. They'd welcomed him into their fold, rebirthed him as Yohan and made him an honorary brother.

Dominik shook his head. 'No, thank you.'

'Are you avoiding someone?' Johnny asked.

Dominik stated it plainly. 'I am afraid of Ben's mother.' He motioned in the direction of Rachel Rosen, who continued prowling the dance floor like a jaguar.

'Jeepers.' Johnny's eyes bulged. 'I bet she likes to smack men around. Be still my beating heart! Why is her hair pulled back so tightly? Perhaps she's one of those naughty schoolmistress types – starched suit, leather underpants.'

'I find her quite an urbane woman, Johnny. Highly educated. A thinker.'

He grunted. 'Yes. The thinkers love a little Johnny. She keeps looking over here like she knows you.'

'The Rosens used to live next door. Ben's father came from an old Krakow family. He died from pancreatic cancer when the boy was about thirteen. Ben's mother hails from Berlin – she's German.'

'She looks it.' Johnny smirked.

'Oh dear, she's coming towards us.' Dominik's heart was gripped with fear.

'I'll handle this,' Johnny said.

Dominik cried no, but it was too late. Johnny had stood from the table and advanced in a direct line towards Rachel. Dominik winced and prepared himself for that least desired event at a wedding: a scene.

'Mrs Rosen, I am Dr Jan Gruener. Will you make me the happiest man in this room?'

The woman stopped walking and stiffened, staring at Johnny. Dominik felt sorry for him, though also a little pleased, for he'd warned Johnny, and the man had ignored him.

She inhaled on her cigarette. 'I beg your pardon?'

'I must dance with you,' Johnny cried, 'or my heart shall break.'

Dominik watched the woman's face as she took Johnny in with her terrifying azure eyes. Dominik paused. The eyes looked familiar; where else had he seen those eyes, like two rock pools of deep, cold blue water?

'Do you know who I am?' she spluttered.

'The mother of the groom. I see where he gets his looks from.'

She glowered at him, then did something very strange. She nodded. Johnny bowed and held out his arm, and she took it. He led her to the dance floor.

The band struck up the opening bars of a charleston. Johnny moved through his steps, suave and able; Mrs Rosen stood stiff as a board, but kept time, striding back and forth, bopping and jumping, the expression on her face never changing from its usual squint. She seemed to be concentrating intently. Was she enjoying herself? It was hard to tell. But when the next tune began – the Lindy Hop, of all things – Johnny held out his hands again and, to Dominik's surprise and joy, she took them. Next they danced the tango. The accordion and the violin played the stormy melody and they moved through the intense romantic dance with fanatical precision.

They danced another five dances. Each time a new tune began, she waited patiently for Johnny to take her hand again, even though she showed no outward sign of enjoying herself. They only stopped dancing when the band took their scheduled break. Johnny escorted her from the dance floor. He looked exhausted, beads of sweat assembled on his brow.

Dominik was still smiling to himself, oblivious, when Rachel Rosen sat down next to him.

'What did you know of this, Dominik?' she asked him – no greeting, no congratulations, despite having not spoken in eleven years. She spoke in the delicate lilt of *Hochdeutsch*, the High German accent.

'Nothing, I assure you, madam,' he replied, adjusting his glasses.

'Nonsense. You are a smart man; you tell me you knew nothing?'

Dominik frowned. 'I had an inkling.'

Her blue eyes pierced him. 'How long have you possessed this inkling?'

'About ten years.' He braced for some sort of beating.

She sucked on her cigarette. 'I too,' she said. 'I worried when he came back to this soot-stained city. I knew why he did it. He loved your girl from the first second he laid eyes on her. A hopeless love. He always was such a sensitive boy.'

'Consider, madam. I have lost a daughter,' Dominik replied.

'And you have gained a son. When we left in 1930, someone painted some helpful advice on our building. Do you recall what it said?'

Dominik swallowed. 'It said, "Fuck off, Jews".'

She stubbed out the cigarette, lit another and dragged a lengthy, considered inhalation. 'I heard from friends that you and your daughter painted over this writing.' Dominik nodded. 'That was stupid. What was the point? We were already gone. If we had come back, they would have written more advice.'

Dominik looked over at his new son-in-law as he held Marie's hand and introduced her to some guests. 'And I would have painted over it again,' he replied. 'How are things in Berlin?'

She flicked some ash. 'Do you refer to business? My health and leisure activities? Or do you mean, how are things living with ninety per cent of the people in my building now members of the

National Social German Workers' Party? Which things do you refer to?'

'Madam, I apologise.' Dominik swallowed. 'I didn't mean to pry or give offence.'

'Hush. You are curious and it's in my nature to tell you. My six-year-old neighbour, a sweet girl with blonde pigtails, called me a filthy Jew to my face last week, and I can no longer buy apples and oranges from my favourite grocer. They won't permit me entry to the store, despite me spending thousands of marks over the years there.'

'Did you suffer any losses last November?' He recalled the images in the newspaper of men smashing windows, looting Jewish businesses.

'No need to be coy, Dominik. I take it you refer to that orgy of violence the newspapers now call *Kristallnacht*, where one set of Germans in brown shirts pulled another set of Germans from their beds and stomped on their heads in the street until their skulls fell in?'

Dominik cleared his throat uncomfortably. 'Yes. That.'

She laughed bitterly. 'They burned down one of our toy factories that night. We didn't own the building – we rented it, from an Aryan partner. The same poor man owned all the machinery inside. They burned their own buildings, destroyed their own stock. The interior ministry paid our partner reparations for his lost income, twice what he was owed. We had the last laugh, for now.' She stubbed out another cigarette. Was that her second, or third, in the few minutes they'd been speaking?

'Ironically, the business my father started is enjoying some of the biggest months it's ever had. The English and the Americans love Blumfeld toys – we shipped twenty thousand rocking horses to New York last month. Every child in Britain wants our "Nikki" bear, with its floppy ears. These clients will only trust the contract with my father's name on it. Even if that name, according to some nineteen thirty-three laws, is – shall we say – *non-Aryan*. It's the only reason the government won't touch us. We make up a bigger part of their GDP than Krupp.' She looked around the room. 'I never thought I would come back to Krakow but the non-Aryans here still put on a good spread.' She sat back in her chair. 'But this is not their spread, is it?'

Dominik made no reply.

'You paid for this wedding, didn't you?'

'I confess I did.'

'But I heard you didn't approve?'

'Nothing against your son,' he replied. 'Or your faith.'

'Don't explain yourself to me, Dominik. I don't approve of this marriage either. But they are in love and were always going to do it, so why fight it and make yourself a stranger to your children, yes?'

Dominik again said nothing.

She smiled, for the first time ever, perhaps. 'Does your daughter know that you paid for all this?'

'I don't believe she does.' He had been careful to keep it a secret.

'My. You are a good man,' she replied. She tapped her mouth. 'Please, let me pay my share.'

'Thank you, but I cannot,' he said. 'The bride's family should pay for the wedding.'

'You did your research.'

He shrugged. 'It's the same in Catholic circles. The woman's family pays.'

'Yes, but I think you checked this all the same. So you should know also, the man's family may contribute a few things. Please allow me to do so.'

'No. Please, madam, I can't accept,' he protested.

'Oh hush, Dominik. I am not poor. You heard me about the rocking horses? I probably have more money than you. We wanted Ben to go into the toy business. He refused; he wanted to be a teacher. Then he said he'd return to Krakow for a year or two. We thought he was crazy. I knew why, of course. And I look at him now and I say in the twenty-four years I've known him, I have never seen him this happy. So please, send me a bill for my share.'

'Very well.'

'And if for some reason you forget to send me my total, I will confirm with the caterers and deliver a suitable amount to your rooms. No more about it.'

When Rachel replaced her cigarette and stood, Dominik thought their conversation had ended, and she would relieve him of her company, but then she stopped moving, lit the cigarette and sat back down. Dominik raised one eyebrow, then the second one joined its twin, high on his face, when Mrs Rosen opened her mouth once more and made an inquiry Dominik hadn't expected. 'Do you know my family name?'

'Rosen?' Dominik replied, nodding at the obvious.

'That is my married name. I mean my maiden name.' Dominik shook his head. 'It's Blumfeld,' she said, exhaling a streak of smoke from the corner of her mouth.

'Oh, yes, of course,' Dominik said. 'Blumfeld Toys.' He scoured his head for where else he'd heard the name before, other than on the side of a rocking horse. It took him a moment before he located it in the filing cabinet of his brain. Confidentiality prevented him from speaking further, but the woman offered the information herself.

'Earlier this year, you treated Daniel Blumfeld in your hospital. For pneumonia.'

'If you say so.'

'Does he look like me?'

Dominik turned to her. 'I beg your pardon?'

She repeated the words and stared at him. Fine bones and

tanned skin framed her blue eyes. She made no further remark, and Dominik didn't answer her question, so it hung in the air like the cigarette smoke that seeped from her mouth in threads.

Dominik tried not to cough and failed. 'I can offer no opinion on that,' he replied between the coughs.

'Why? Do you forget what the boy looked like?' she asked.

Dominik had once calculated the number of patients he'd seen in his almost twenty years of practising medicine. Even if he had treated only six patients per day, which he never did, but for the sake of argument, six per diem, for two hundred and forty days per year, for twenty years, was 288,000 people. If he allowed for seeing the same patient twice, thrice, even four times, which happened rarely for he operated primarily as a surgeon and internist, seeing most patients only once, by dividing by four, that brought the number down to 7200. Did he remember every face in those 7200? He wouldn't like to stake his life on the claim, but he prided himself that he probably could. And of those 7000-odd faces, none had stared at him like the face of Daniel Blumfeld, none had reached in and clawed his soul like the gaze of that child, the little boy who had refused to die, though the Reaper had already come to claim him. He remembered every eyelash on that boy's face, every hair on his head, and especially those deep blue eyes.

'You can offer no opinion, because of confidentiality?' Mrs Rosen asked.

Dominik nodded but said nothing.

'I respect your scruples, Doctor. Well done for having them in these exciting times.'

'You have maintained yours also, Mrs Rosen.'

'Call me Rachel. We are family now.'

'Very well.'

'I'll tell you why I ask about this child. We'll see if you maintain your opinion of my high principles. I have a brother. Had one, anyway. His name was Jakob Blumfeld. Jakob and I are the heirs to my father's little toy business.'

Dominik sipped from his glass of water as Rachel paused to look around the room. He followed her gaze. The band played a klezmer jig while the men and women danced in circles. No flesh touched flesh; the dancers had relieved the tables of their linen napkins and the small white cloths linked each person in the circle, hands connecting hands this way. Johnny stood in the centre, cheering and hollering and flailing his legs about. Dominik frowned; he couldn't see Marie.

'The women have taken her,' Rachel said, as if reading his mind. 'They will bring her back.' She motioned with her head to a door, indicating where his daughter might have gone. 'I shall continue my story. My brother, Jakob Blumfeld, visited Krakow once a month to meet with our suppliers here. He cheated on his wife, had an affair with a local woman.' Dominik tilted an ear to Rachel, his eyes trained once again on the dancers. 'A scandal for my parents. They hoped it would be hushed up, as these things usually are, but the woman in question, the seductress, wouldn't keep quiet. A sneaky piece of cunning and bile if ever I saw one. But then, I believe you have met this woman and could give me your own opinion.'

Dominik stopped watching the dancers and turned to her. He remembered the pitiable creature in the torn jacket.

'Do you recall her surname?' Rachel asked.

'I do not,' Dominik said. 'I never asked it. I assumed at the time, considering her son's patient file, that her name was Blumfeld.'

'A fair assumption, based on the facts made available to you, though incorrect. Her name is Ruth Landau. She bedded my brother in an illicit affair. Then she claimed she'd fallen pregnant with my brother's child, and he'd given her a son.'

'I see. That's Daniel?'

'The boy you treated for pneumonia.'

'That would make him your nephew.'

'It would, only Ruth is a known fantasist and harlot who made trouble wherever she went. My brother's age surpassed hers by twenty years. From sixteen she'd give her body to anyone who smiled at her.' Rachel pointed her cigarette in the air as she spoke. 'Krakow never beheld a greater slut or witch. She seduced the butcher, farmhands, every man in a five-kilometre radius.'

Dominik stared as bile poured forth from Rachel's lips. Her words shocked him, one woman judging another for choices made in desperation. He felt he must defend the woman whose child he'd saved, who'd given him the tin charm shaped like a hand, though he sensed something unusual in Rachel's demeanour that showed she perhaps did not believe half the vitriol she spouted. 'That was not my impression of her. Though I guess you know her better than I do.'

She blinked. 'I do not. But others assured me she is a succubus. So now that you know my opinion on the matter, how deeply I condemn the whorish behaviour, I must ask you. My brother died two winters past. Without my brother to protect her, Ruth and her bastard slipped down the rungs of society so that even the Jewish grocer wouldn't serve her. You would think she'd learn her lesson. But no, she didn't – she screamed even louder after my brother's death of their special love and their beautiful son. *Can't you see the resemblance?* she'd crow to people in the street. *My son and his father, they have the same eyes.* No one believed her, of course; she'd had it off with every man in town, and my brother, the golden son and heir to the Blumfeld Toy Corporation, would never have possessed the carelessness and stupidity to put a son in any woman other than his wife.'

Dominik tried not to look up to study Rachel's eyes lest she catch him. He scoured his mind instead for memories of them – of Ben's as well – and any passing resemblance to the skinny, decrepit boy he had saved from Dr Wolanski's and pneumonia's clutches.

'What did you make of him, of his character?' Rachel asked, inhaling on another cigarette.

'His character, madam?'

'Did he strike you as a strong boy, of good moral fibre, of talent or intelligence, of stamina? Likely not, I assume.'

Dominik gazed back at the dancers as they twirled in a blur on the dance floor. The klezmer rose to a moody crescendo, a haunting pipe melody in a minor key, some ancient tune from the Carpathian Mountains. He conjured in his head the face of Daniel Blumfeld as he lay in the hospital bed, moments from death. He tried to recall the boy's character. Did he contain cunning and deceitfulness, like his mother? Hard to say. He had witnessed the boy in no situations to recommend much of his disposition; Dominik hadn't dropped a zloty on the ground to see if the boy would pocket it rather than turn it in; he hadn't caught the boy telling any lies. He had sent the boy on no errands but one – he had asked the boy not to die, and the boy had fulfilled his request. Most people went quietly, happily, even; for all their raging in life, the majority of patients accepted death willingly. But this boy had refused, and Dominik now saw why. He had refused to leave his mother because he cared for her so. *He* looked after *her*, not the reverse. The whole time in the bed, while on death's door, he'd begged her to eat, to cover herself with the spare blanket. He had offered her the food from his own tray and would only take a bite himself when she had eaten some. He had stayed alive to look after her. Dominik couldn't speak for the boy's honesty or strength of character, but he could say he loved living, and he loved his mother.

'I found him an extraordinary little boy, Rachel,' Dominik said. 'I didn't expect him to survive, but he did.'

Rachel seemed to consider him, to assess his truthfulness. 'A tribute to your genius, Dominik. I have heard many tales of your daring acts in that hospital. You injected the child with mould, I am told, and saved his life.'

'I helped, that is all. His will performed the majority of the heroic act.'

'Now tell me, in your honest medical opinion: was I right to spurn this child, never opening the letters his mother sent me, refusing all requests to see the boy, knowing they were a grab at the handsome inheritance or support that would have come her way if I'd acknowledged the child? Please confirm for me I did the correct thing in snubbing her. Tell me Daniel Blumfeld is not my nephew.'

The band's tune reached its conclusion and the players halted for a break. Clapping and excited chatter resumed as people returned to their tables for vodka and cake. A waiter placed a plate in front of Dominik and one in front of Rachel. She refused. Dominik eyed the dessert and felt his mouth water.

'Please,' Rachel said, 'don't let me stop you. Enjoy your cake – you half-paid for it, after all.'

Dominik picked up a fork and carved a triangle from the slice's tip. He deposited the cake in his mouth and a honeyed, buttery sponginess spread across his tongue and worked its way over his teeth and gums. He chewed and swallowed the morsel, blinking from the sweetness.

'Good, isn't it?' She nodded at the cake. 'You used Mendel's, did you not?'

'I used whomever Rabbi Katz told me to.'

'He would have said Mendel's. The best patisserie in town.'

'I am glad.' And he was pleased. Rabbi Katz seemed to have organised everything perfectly. When he'd asked Dominik for a blank cheque, Dominik had naturally baulked in horror, but seeing now the band, the food, the table settings, the decorations, the number of guests who'd shaken his hand and, most importantly, the smile on his daughter's face, he was glad he'd done so.

Rachel turned to him. 'Did you hear me? Is he my nephew?' Her cigarette continued to burn but she hadn't inhaled, so a cylinder of ash had formed at the end where the paper once stood, burning down like a fuse.

Her stare allowed him to look directly into her eyes without censure, to satisfy his curiosity. He'd seen irises of that unmistakable bluebird hue twice before in his life: once in the young man who was now his son-in-law, and the other in the skinny boy whom he'd injected with penicillium mould and saved from the clutches of pneumonia.

'Madam, with the certainty of a doctor, I say that boy is your nephew.'

Rachel Rosen sighed and looked down at her cigarette. 'I see.' She took a long drag. 'Will you do something for me?' she asked. 'Will you visit the boy and tell me how he is doing?'

'I couldn't do that; that would breach confidentiality. If what you have said is true, if Daniel's mother is maligned by all, I do not want to molest the poor woman further by showing up at her house.'

'On the contrary. Your saving the boy rehabilitated her image somewhat. Condescension by the great gentile Dominik Karski, saver of bastards and host of the best non-Aryan wedding this century. You can do no wrong.'

'I'll try to see him. I make no promises.'

'Thank you,' she said.

'What shall I look for? What would you like to know about them?'

Rachel shrugged. 'I should like to know how they're doing.' She frowned. 'Ruth is known as a terrible mother, vindictive and neglectful. I should like you to seek the truth. Perhaps you could also tell the boy that his aunt says hello.' She chewed her lip.

The band members returned to their instruments and struck up another tune. The guests, now with bellies full of vodka and the best cake in town, returned to the dance floor with vigour. Men converged in two circles and, with much rumbling, arguing and discussions, they piled on top of one another, shouting and issuing orders. Dominik squinted to see what they were doing but could make out nothing specific in the pile of bodies, except to see that Johnny was one of them, pointing and shouting at the others. But then one dancer sang out, 'One, two, lift!' and four of the men lifted Dominik's new son-in-law, seated in a chair, high above their heads, and turned him in a laughing circle, to cheers from the crowd. Not a moment later, another quartet of men hoisted a second chair aloft. Atop it sat his own daughter, her face painted with a look of trepidation at first but also joy. He knew every face she made, from a little girl to now, and this expression was something different, one he'd not seen before. She looked over at her husband, who offered her one end of a white napkin. She took it while he held the other, and the men underneath them lifted the chairs up and down, in time with the music, as a hundred people aged eight to eighty danced around them in circles, clapping and cheering and singing in time.

He allowed himself to indulge in the faintest hint of a smile and turned back to Rachel, only to find she had left empty the chair next to him. The only sign of her former presence was a discarded cigarette, sitting stubbed and smouldering in the ashtray beside him.

25
A MISSED BREAKFAST

Seven hours had passed in moments. Marie felt like she'd shaken hands with every person in Krakow. She'd danced, and they'd hoisted her to the sky. She'd barely eaten anything except some chicken soup, after fasting for twenty-four hours prior, as per Jewish tradition. The women had grabbed her – not the young ladies her age, no, they eyed her suspiciously. What business had she being there, stealing one of theirs, and a rich one from a good family at that? Ben should have married one of the girls of his own kind. But the grandmothers and mothers seemed more forgiving, and they had welcomed her, complimented her dress, stroked her blonde hair, admired her tiny waist and given her advice for the wedding night, which they laughed at, making her blush.

And then it was over. The women had taken her to a room to change, and she now emerged in her honeymoon clothes, a silk skirt and jacket in cream with a red corsage. The women all clucked and tutted. 'He won't keep his hands off you! He's a lucky man,' they said.

Marie swallowed and saw Ben smiling nervously by the door; a car waited for them. The band struck up again and played a farewell song while the crowd clapped and pushed her towards her husband. Marie looked around but couldn't see her father. She hadn't spoken to him since the beginning of the ceremony, and for the past four weeks they had lived under the same roof but had not seen each other once. Quite a feat, considering their bedrooms stood opposite one another and they ate from the same kitchen, but they had managed it.

They had exchanged brief words earlier that day as he'd walked her down the aisle, but they had been in front of the whole congregation and could discuss nothing of importance. She wanted to confront her father, to ask him about those documents listing his charitable donations she'd found at the records office, his strange and suspicious financial affairs, to see his reaction, yet on the other hand she wanted to avoid him completely, for she felt unsure she wanted to hear what he might say. She found herself hoping she would leave the reception without seeing him; by the time she returned from the honeymoon, the urge to ask him about his double life as the benefactor of Krakow might have passed.

Marie scanned the room once more and, when she didn't see her father, she felt grateful for it. She made no overt efforts to locate him. Instead she found Ben, who was now standing next to his mother. Mrs Rosen reached out her hand and Marie placed a dutiful kiss on her cheek. 'Let me look at the woman who has ensnared my only son,' Ben's mother said. They hadn't spoken the whole night, either.

'You have looked at me before, Mrs Rosen,' Marie said, lifting her chin.

'Yes and, if it's possible, you have grown even more beautiful. You must call me Rachel now. My boy didn't stand a chance, did he?'

Marie blushed and said nothing.

'The car is waiting,' Ben said, motioning her outside. Marie nodded and turned once more to the crowd, secretly scanning the room's faces, checking for her father's. She couldn't see him. Ben took her arm and she allowed herself to be led outside. The guests followed them, cheering and dancing as the newlyweds climbed into the car and it drove off. Marie breathed a sigh of relief.

The car delivered them to the station, where they boarded the train to Zakopane. They reached the mountains at half-past one in the morning and found their hotel.

As Ben spoke to the concierge to check in, Marie touched his bare forearm and felt him shudder. It gratified her she could extract such a response from this grown man who could grow a beard and push an automobile down the road. She could see he knew she'd seen the shudder, and he smiled a half-smile at her.

As they entered their hotel room, Marie excused herself to the bathroom, where she bathed, redid her hair, touched up her lipstick, powdered her armpits and groin, and changed into a new silk night-dress and gown that she'd purchased especially for this. The fabric slipped over her body softly, making her shiver. She'd never worn such adult clothes before, and she wondered what Ben would think of them. She heard her new husband moving about in the hotel room. He'd nervously dropped a book at one point, and she heard him open the window, then close it, and then he seemed to return to his original decision for he opened it once more. She smiled to herself, imagining the tortured look on his face, the restless anticipation, and continued her powdering. When she finally emerged from the room, however, she found Ben seated in a chair, fast asleep.

She stared at him for a time, disbelieving. Then she glanced at the clock. It was past three; she had been in the bathroom for more than an hour. Surely, though, his excitement would have kept him awake? But his eyes indeed remained shut, his face stayed relaxed, his body sunk deep into the chair. She scratched her head. After all her efforts to beautify her exterior, he was rewarding her with this? She considered throwing something at his head – a book or an ornament, perhaps – or bashing the door loudly to wake him, but once he'd awoken, what then? If he slumbered so easily, perhaps he didn't find her attractive, for how could he, if he had fallen asleep on their wedding night? If she woke him and he muttered some excuse then escaped to bed, she would crumble into a puddle of embarrassment. So instead, she left him sleeping in the armchair, covering him with a blanket. She didn't kiss his forehead, but instead patted his shoulder in a manner one might use for a work colleague, then climbed into bed herself and cried.

'Marie,' he said softly, walking to her. She dried her tears furiously, hoping he wouldn't see.

'I'm well, thank you. Goodnight.'

He placed a hand on her shoulder. 'Oh, Marie,' he said, and sat on the bed. He seemed to wait for her to say something, but when she didn't, he walked back to the armchair and sat down.

'You fell asleep!' she said. 'How could you?'

'It's three am. I rose at six yesterday, stood all day, had little to eat or drink, shook hands with every person in Krakow. I couldn't keep my eyes open.'

'It's our wedding night!'

'You went to the bathroom and didn't emerge for an hour and twenty-three minutes.' He laughed.

She wanted to hit him. 'One moment. How did you know I stayed in the bathroom for an hour and twenty-three minutes?'

He looked at her and made no immediate remark. She waited for one. 'I picked a number from my head, to make a point.'

'No, you said it as though you had timed it, as though you had checked the clock. It sounds accurate too.'

He spat out a laugh, as though she'd said something ludicrous. 'No,' he protested but still wouldn't look at her.

She knew she'd caught him in a lie; she'd known him ten years, despite the gap when they'd spent years apart. What had arrested her most was not what had changed about him, but what had stayed the same from boy to man. He still moved hair from his face the same way, with a puff of breath upwards from out the side of his mouth. He still laughed the same way, silently exhaling, a stab of air outwards, without vocalising, his shoulders rising like they had when he was a child. Laughing and brushing back hair were superficial mannerisms (or were they? Perhaps they signalled everything?), yet he still performed the deeper actions the same as well: he still couldn't look at her when he was lying. He still went quiet when wounded.

'I pretended to sleep.'

Marie sat up in the bed. 'Why?'

He screwed his face into some contortion of sadness, shutting his eyes and seeming to wince. She thought he might collapse with the effort. She'd never seen him make this face, not as a child, nor as an adult. 'Have you ever been with a man?' he asked finally.

'No,' Marie replied, feeling her cheeks grow hot. She felt like a child whose nanny had caught her applying her mother's lipstick and thinking it beautiful, then peering in the mirror to discover a looping, clownish grin. 'You think me a child. I assure you, I am not,' she said, trying not to sound petulant, which was difficult to achieve as she found herself stamping a foot on the mattress as she spoke.

He smiled. 'I don't think you're a child.' He briefly flashed his eyes towards her, then looked away again. 'You took so long in the bathroom, I thought you were scared, or you didn't want to come out. If I ever saw you in pain, or if I hurt you, I would die. I wanted you to wake me. I thought, "When she comes out of the bathroom, if she comes over here and wakes me up . . ." but then you went to bed.'

'I placed a blanket over you!'

He nodded. 'And I could smell your perfume as you leaned over me and I thought I might perish from excitement. But you are not a girlfriend to me; you are not even just my bride. You are Marie, the only person I have loved, or will ever love. I will never touch you unless you ask me to.'

'Oh,' she said. 'You could have made that a dash clearer!'

He smiled again. 'I see that now. I am sorry.'

'I promise you, I am not nervous. Well, I am, but in the best way.'

'Me too,' Ben replied.

Marie felt everything change then. It was after three in the morning and she had expected to cry herself to sleep; instead, it would happen now. Very well then.

In years to come she'd look back on the moment before it happened as a stolen interval of sweetness and joy that few others in her life would rival. They sat, she in the bed, he in the armchair, anticipating what would occur next. Time felt as though it had slowed down, but happily. She found herself in no rush; now she knew what would happen tonight, she felt a wonderful exasperation to get there, but also a contentedness to tease it out. Through his glances and smiles and silences, he seemed to share her feelings, though one could never truly know what went on inside another's head. She hoped for his sake and believed he felt the same. She wanted him to feel the joy she felt; everyone deserved to know that once in their life. In the months to come and with the events that were to follow, she'd remember this moment of innocence, when her only concern was the timing of lovemaking, and wish herself back there.

'I think I will use the bathroom,' Marie said. 'Briefly this time,' she added. Inside, she checked her hair and lipstick and, when she emerged, she found him sleeping in the armchair again. Her temper rose – he was sleeping *again*? – and then her anger lowered once more when she saw his half-smile.

She removed her slippers and crept over to him. His smile grew slightly. She removed the blanket from him and still he kept his eyes closed but he was making the smallest flinching blink, giving himself away. She raised a shaking hand – what had come over her? – and undid the first button of his shirt. He swallowed, eyes remaining shut, still pretending to sleep. She undid a second button, then a third, slipping the black discs between her fingers. She loosened another button more and spread the shirt open, revealing the skin of his chest, skin she'd seen before, but only in its boyish form. Now it possessed hair; she'd never expected that. Though she hadn't imagined smooth skin either. She'd possessed no expectation either way, which she now realised was strange to have never envisioned, among her other daydreams of him, but there it was. The hair delighted and fascinated her, displaying proof he was a man. She stared at the skin, then glanced up to find him watching her, eyes now open, his face wearing a look she'd never seen. She must have missed him opening them for he'd been watching her some time, it seemed, and she watched him back, then returned to her task, removing his shirt, then his shoes, his socks, his trousers.

He didn't touch her or reach out for her, just watched her, helping her in her project where required, lifting an arm here, raising his hips there. At one point as she leaned over him her face brushed his and she believed she felt his lips press gently against her cheek. But when she turned to look at him his face remained still; perhaps she had imagined it.

Finally, the job was done, and she stepped back to see. He sat before her in the armchair, wearing nothing while she herself remained fully clothed. She studied each piece of him. He stayed in the chair, watching her, the look on his face extraordinary.

She knew he desired her now, but she felt apprehensive about rushing in. She didn't want to proceed through this event wrongly, to squander it with haste or cheapen it with a clichéd word or ill-timed joke. Though, as she would soon come to understand, some things in life one simply didn't get wrong, no matter the nerves. The truly right things happened easily.

She recalled that he would only touch her if she asked him to, so she honoured that now. 'Will you touch me?' she said. He nodded gently and did so. No further words were spoken; none were needed. He stood and slid her robe away from her shoulders, then lifted her nightgown over her head. He continued with her underclothes, and when he'd finished undressing her, she saw him glance at her body, crimson flushing his cheeks. Her beautiful Ben, he was all hers now – probably always had been. This person she'd swum with, played hide-and-seek with, now pressed himself against her. The body was the same shape, had the same proportions, the same curve of the ear, but every little thing was also different. The arms were the same, but leaner and more muscular; now these arms were holding her, in a wanting way.

He placed one hand on her shoulder, brushing the top of her breast, the other on her hip, glancing her bottom, as though touching those places fully would have been too much straight away, as though they would have made her turn into wisps of air. But then he did touch her directly on those places, softly, but with a man's grip, and she found she did not disintegrate, but instead became fire, yielding to him and finding herself exhaling and her hips and legs moving forward. Her lips grew dry, which shocked her, such a cliché, but the state had arisen so naturally from her body, with no art in it, so she licked them. It was her turn to touch him then, and she did so with a glancing touch of her own, across his legs. She then left her hand between them, to feel the hardness there, and he made a groan so soft and intense at the same time, so urgent and hot that it would forever define desire for her.

The scene comprised such a mixture of sweetness and want. The heat between her legs had grown to such a level it now caused her pain. Suddenly starving for something she'd never known before, she needed him to lie on top of her. He acquiesced and eased himself down. It hurt, in the best way; she found herself placing a hand at the back of his head, grasping his hair between her fingers, tugging and forcing the strands and pulling him closer, though they were already kissing. She wrapped one leg around him, to bring him deeper, the pain exquisite and fading. He groaned again at her movements.

'I love you,' he said.

'I you,' she replied.

Unnecessary words, but they made her softly weep anyway. As he began moving inside her, she felt like a vandal, blooming and wanton, slatternly and full. Everything in the room became buxom, the wardrobe lascivious, the bookshelf brown and fecund; every shape became voluptuous to her. The half-moon out the window turned round and glowing. She felt the little death then, staring at the ceiling, filled with sweetness and searing fire.

She looked over and realised he had been waiting for her, holding himself back, and she loved him even more for that. Now she wanted him to feel the same exquisite demise, and she pulled him towards her again with her leg wrapped, to encourage him to do as he pleased, and he did so, moving with more force and abandon now, which almost made her die again. Then it overwhelmed him too; he could hold out no more, and he collapsed his face into her neck. Once he'd caught his breath, he tenderly eased her leg back down. She looked over and found him utterly spent, wasted. This meant as much to him as it had to her; this had devoured him too.

He didn't love her because she'd converted to Judaism for him. He had loved her before time; it was written in the stars, and on his gravestone. But taking on his faith meant they could be together in flesh, it meant their bodies could join, where it was merely their souls joining before. They never made it down to breakfast. They missed the next day's luncheon as well. As they lay down once more and he pressed his lips to hers, she decided if she had her way, she'd resign from the rest of life and instead spend her time like this, just doing this, forever.

26
THE PRODIGAL SON

Lwów, November 1920

Almost two years had passed since Helena had last seen Dominik Karski. The Great War had ended, and the Austrian Empire had dissolved. Poland had entered into new wars, first with the Ukraine, then the Soviets. She speculated, and hoped, that Dominik had simply been conscripted into the new Polish army to fight these other wars, and that his lack of communication stemmed from the dismal state of the Polish post and not because one of the cannonballs he'd spoken of had finally caught up with him. She'd kept the flower he'd sent her, cursing herself for hanging onto this trinket for two years, given to her by a man she knew but briefly, whose regard for her seemed to stem solely from her ability to care for him during a vomiting spell. Still, she checked each day's newspaper for information from the various chaotic fronts, trying to glean any details she could, for both herself and Mr Karski. The reports said little, except to poke fun at the Russians, who seemed embroiled in government chaos. They had deposed the Tsar and his family in 1917, and now ordinary people, tailors and lawyers, were running the country.

Mr Karski began asking every day where his son was. 'When the war finishes, Dominik will go to medical school,' Mr Karski told her. Helena nodded kindly; he told her the same news every day.

He would tell her of the two universities they would have to choose between, one in Lwów, one in Krakow. One taught better organic chemistry, while the other had better laboratories and cadavers. People gossiped that the one in Lwów had come close to developing a vaccine for typhoid. Mr Karski would debate their relative merits for his son and Helena would nod and smile, as she did every day, noting how his condition seemed to be getting worse, how he rarely recognised a customer anymore, how he'd retreated into a nether world. Sometimes he'd call her Irena, the name of his dead wife. Sometimes he'd speak of his son as though he were still a small boy, wanting to repair a train set that had broken, looking for spare parts. Helena hoped if Dominik was alive, he would arrive back sometime before the father he knew had completely vanished.

Helena explained the situation as best she could to Mr Karski, and he waited every day by the counter, looking for his son, watching the door as the soldiers walked past, returning from this front or that.

Then one Tuesday, on a chilly November morning, without warning and for no apparent reason, Dominik came home.

He embraced his father for a long time, then nodded Helena a hello. She couldn't make out his feelings towards her, she could only tell he'd grown thinner, hollows enveloping his cheeks. She completed her tasks for the day, tidied what needed to be tidied, then excused herself, wanting to give father and son their privacy after years apart. She found herself crying on the journey home at his indifferent greeting to her, the tears turning to ice and stinging on her cheeks on the nasty, wind-blasted day. She cursed herself for weeping. Her pining and regard were entirely of her making; she'd done this all to herself. He had been gone nineteen months without word – what had she expected? A swooning, romantic reunion of flowers and declarations? She should have been content he'd even remembered her name.

She made herself rye soup on the stovetop in her third-storey bedsit and watched from her window as a thunderstorm began outside, the wood of the rafters and sills creaking from the pressure. A purple flash of lightning cracked across the sky like a vein and seconds later the thunder cracked so loud she had to clutch her ears. A leak began in the roof, dripping down onto her bed and making a puddle on the sheets. She grabbed a pot and placed it there. She had never felt so lonely. Then there was a knock on her door, and he was standing there.

She watched him for a moment, unsure of what to say. 'You're not celebrating with your countrymen?' she asked him finally. The sounds of riotous hijinks had echoed through the tenement since the afternoon, soldiers filled the streets dancing, drinking, kissing women. They were celebrating some treaty signing – she could not tell what exactly – and the locals had joined in, shaking hands and slapping backs at the glorious victory.

She stared at him. Should she invite him in? He was there, wasn't he?

'Can I come in?' he asked. She nodded, realising the head movement was all she could manage as her mouth had stopped working. She commanded it to wake up.

He walked inside and removed his coat. The brass buttons on the cuff made a chinking sound as he placed it on the coat rack. He removed his boots and left them at the door, and sat down in her one chair. She viewed his woollen socks; it was a funny sight to see him without shoes on. He'd existed only in her imagination for almost two years and now he sat in her apartment, his legs stretched out from her small chair, one leg straight, the other bent to the side. He'd taken her only seat, so she sat on the bed, next to the puddle.

'Would you like soup?' she said.

'Can I kiss you?' he said back.

For the first time since he'd arrived, he looked at her properly and their eyes met. She wanted to ask him, *Shall we not go to dinner first? Aren't we supposed to go on a date, and get to know each other?* Or, more likely, *Are you sure you are not mistaken?* But she stayed quiet, because she knew he wasn't mistaken, and she wasn't one of those people who lost their nerve or liked to sabotage every good and great thing that decided to come their way. He had come to her apartment of his own volition. He didn't appear drunk. If he wanted to kiss her because she reminded him of his dead mother or a nursemaid, she didn't care. No one got to choose who she loved, only her.

'Yes,' she said.

He stood, quickly, and walked to her. She stood to meet him, recalling as she did that no one had ever kissed her before, and she might have liked to ask for lessons, but now was not the time. He held her elbows gently and pressed his lips to hers. The sensation felt warm and lovely, and she knew instantly that she didn't need lessons, she knew what to do. She answered the kiss with her own, and pushed her tongue forward into his mouth. He groaned softly; she was pleased. She might have felt lucky at this point that he was showing her such attention, but she didn't stop to think such things: she was enjoying herself too much. When he began unbuttoning his shirt, she helped him and removed her own too. If her big lumpy body upset him, he didn't show it.

She'd seen his body before but not like this; everything was different now. That time when she'd cared for him, she'd been the one to move his arms and legs about, to gently tip his head from side to side to comb his hair. Now he moved himself. His body also looked different now, thinner than last time. His collarbones stabbed outwards and his ribs showed under the skin, the shadows of them darkening each time he inhaled.

*

Afterwards, she realised she'd forgotten the soup. When she checked it, she found it was not burned, but it had simmered down to a paste. She spread it onto two thick pieces of rye bread, which she'd also spread with a little butter she'd saved. They ate them in her bed as the storm continued outside. It might have been the most delightful meal of her life.

She worked in the pharmacy the next day. He said nothing to her; he spent the morning carrying stock around, chopping firewood and moving some furniture from the back room that was taking up space. Each time he came to the front area where they served the customers and prepared the tinctures, Helena looked at him, but he didn't meet her eye, concentrating instead on his tasks.

She spent a few hours in desperate sadness, then in the afternoon she resigned herself to the idea that it had been a one-time thing. Perhaps he regretted it and wanted to forget what had happened. She shrugged and settled into an acceptance of it, grateful for the time she'd had. No one could ever rob that memory from her now, no matter what happened in her life after this point. The taste, smell and sound of that evening would stay with her, carefully wrapped in a little parcel in her mind: his skin, the scent of rain, the roll of thunder. Even if her brain went the way of Mr Karski's and one day she could no longer make new memories, she'd always have this one, just as Mr Karski quite often retreated into reveries of his dead wife and his young son.

But she needn't have worried about treasuring a single memory, for that evening she received a knock on her door once more, and he was there. He arrived at eight o'clock exactly. She would have laughed at his precision if her mind had not been preoccupied with other things. If possible, this time was even better than the last.

Her complete lack of expectation that he'd find her in any way desirable, delicate or pretty meant she felt no compulsion to contort her figure into the shapes and angles from which it could best be admired. Mr Karski owned a set of Viennese ladies' periodicals, at least ten years old, which he left on the counter for his customers to peruse while they waited for their tonics to be prepared. The well-worn magazines spoke of better times, before war gutted the city, and between the commercials for soap flakes and brassieres, articles detailing how to entice male attention often appeared. Helena had read these in earnest and knew the way to garner men's affection was to arch one's back at all times. This drew in the stomach and presented the bosom outwards. According to the magazines, bending one leg and standing contrapposto like Michelangelo's *David* also displayed the figure in the kindest light to be gazed upon. But when she tried arching her own back in front of the mirror, she found it didn't draw in her stomach in the anticipated way. Her flat, thick belly stayed where it always did, the same width as her hips. Standing contrapposto only made her knee ache. So with Dominik she performed neither of these contortions. Instead she focused her energy on enjoying herself and deriving pleasure from the other body beside her. If her lack of posing disgusted him, he didn't show it, and by attempting to conceal nothing, she seemed paradoxically to please him more. If anything, her total unguarded dedication to her own pleasure seemed to increase his own desire, as if seeing the effect his body had on her own made him feel even manlier than if she'd lain there silently and struck a dainty pose.

He came to her bedsit every night thereafter. Always precisely at eight o'clock; he was never late once. Usually they lay together straight after he walked through the door, then again before bed and once again in the morning. Afterwards, she would watch him sleeping, the only time his face would relax. The creases and contortions would vanish; his brow would unfurrow. She flattered herself he came to her to chase away whatever demons gripped him. If she was going to hell for this, she didn't care; she was happy to help pack her bags for the trip and pay her own way. On the twenty-third of December, they held each other in bed in the early evening, before he rose and began to dress. 'Are you going?' she asked.

'Yes.' She felt sad and unsteady. This was disrupting their routine, but she nodded to herself, trying to accept it. Perhaps their time together had come to an end, as she always expected it would. But then he held out his hand and told her to dress too. 'You're coming with me.' She sat up, unsure, and didn't move. He laughed and found her clothes, which they had thrown on the floor earlier. He helped her into her underwear, blouse, skirt. Then he found her woollen stockings and kneeled before her. He guided her leg into one of them, then the other, pushing each stocking up her leg and under her skirt in silence, then drawing the skirt up so he could clip the stockings into the belt. They had seen each other naked, in every position and angle, but these movements, him putting his hands under her skirt, seemed somehow more erotic than the undressing.

He finished dressing her and led her out the door. He took her ice skating on the frozen pond behind the railway station. The city was starving, but people refused to forget Christmas. A man had erected a little wooden stall from which he hired out a few pairs of skates. She didn't want the time to end and she revelled in every sensation: the crisp feeling of her skate blades as they carved and crunched the ice, the feeling of his hand in hers as they stopped to rest. It was the first time he'd taken her anywhere, and she thought if it was the only time he ever did so, she would die happy.

The next day, Christmas Eve, they closed the pharmacy at four o'clock in the afternoon. They sang carols and walked to church at midnight. Afterwards Helena farewelled the men and wished them happy holidays, but as she reached the door Dominik caught up with her and asked her to stay: there was a blizzard outside. Mr Karski agreed heartily – she should stay there for the winter, in fact! It was a waste to travel back to her bedsit each day, and besides, they had plenty of room.

She looked at him and searched his face for his true intention; perhaps he had knowledge of her liaison with his son. But he stared at her with the same blank smile that seemed to pervade his face more and more these days. She and Dominik had taken over most operations of the pharmacy. He'd shown himself to be as competent a chemist as his father. Dominik knew all the recipes, for aspirin and all the balms, he poured the ingredients and mixed the tinctures, his hands moving quickly, his fingers flipping the lids off bottles. He guessed measurements with exactitude like his father did; he'd place a little mound of cocaine on the scale and look away before the arms had balanced, already knowing he'd made a gram. But one thing differed between Mr Karski and his son. While both operated the pharmacy with dexterity and proficiency, only one seemed to enjoy it. Mr Karski mixed every potion like it was the first time he'd done it, marvelling at the powders as they dissolved and transformed. Dominik, on the other hand, performed every task with a dead look on his face. Instead of watching with joy while the crystals formed, he'd turn to the window and stare at nothing. Helena put it down to youth. His father must have drilled Dominik in potions and pharmacy since childhood; she did not blame him for his jadedness. He would rediscover his love for chemistry one day; she could help him do this. She stayed in their house above the pharmacy that day and never slept in the bedsit again, returning only once to pick up her clothes and the two books her father had given her before he died.

That winter passed in a hundred days of happiness. In February, Lieutenant Karski received word from his regiment. The war with Ukraine was long over, but the war with the Soviets went on. A grey pallor of dread crossed his face as he read the telegram, and they spent the night lying awake, not speaking, unsure of what to say. 'I don't know if I'll make it this time,' he said finally, into the darkness. In the morning, he dressed and was gone. Helena cried for a week.

She waited for a letter from him but received nothing. A few weeks later, stomach pains and nausea gripped her, followed by vomiting. She'd eaten nothing out of the ordinary and considered whether one of the new potions they developed had made her sick. She consulted the *Merck Manual of Diagnosis and Therapy*, which Mr Karski kept in his library, and almost vomited again when she climbed the ladder to fetch the book from the high shelf. The manual contained information on poisoning, cancers, rheumatisms, fevers and every malady known to man, except the one that afflicted her. To diagnose this condition, she needed not a textbook but to cast her memory back to the hundreds of women in her village who had suffered this ailment before. Helena touched her stomach, realising a little life was growing there. She felt astonished. Not that she should feel so surprised given the way she'd carried on with the pharmacist's son, but she'd never experienced any regularity in her menstrual cycle and had in fact only experienced her monthly days once or twice a year since they had started. The same hormonal disruption had caused her to grow small darkish hairs across her top lip and down the sides of her face since puberty, and she'd always taken this to mean that there was something wrong with her, that her chances of conceiving a child remained non-existent. The human growing inside her now must have come from some miracle.

A few days later she sat smiling to herself when a local woman, Mrs Janko, entered and requested a tonic. As Mr Karski prepared the bottle on the other side of the room, the woman struck up a conversation with Helena at the register. 'You've fallen into tremendous luck here, haven't you?' the woman said. She observed Helena intently.

Helena nodded. 'Oh, yes,' she replied, forcing a smile.

The woman glared. 'You've ingratiated yourself with this old family – you, a bumpkin from nowhere.'

Helena swallowed and shook her head. 'No, madam,' she said. 'That's not it.'

The woman smiled tightly at her. 'It doesn't matter anyway. You don't need to deny any of it, for the luck you think has swung your way will prove itself otherwise sooner or later. Dominik Karski isn't right in the head.' She paused and stroked the fox fur around her neck. She seemed to wait for Helena to say something, but she didn't, so the woman continued. 'He had some breakdown on the Russian front – not in this skirmish, mind you, in the conflict from two wars back. The Great War. They tried to hush it up, but people found out. They've only taken him back now because the new conflict has overcome them. They will take anyone at this point, no matter how mad. War has sent him crazy.' The woman put on her gloves. 'If I were you, I would leave this place and go somewhere else. There are plenty of hotels and offices that would give a good sturdy girl like you the same sort of cleaning work.' Mr Karski returned with her tonic and the woman smiled tightly and left.

Helena shook from her mind the times when Dominik had joked about having no friends anymore, or when he'd spoken with such bitterness of the army that it had scared her. She chased away the moments she'd caught him staring into space, his face fixed in anguish, when she couldn't reach him or coax him back, until he'd snapped from the trance himself. She dismissed the time Mr Karski had grabbed her, in a moment of lucidity, looked her in the eye and warned her away from his son, the old man telling her that Dominik had changed since the wars started and now scared him sometimes. That he drank all the time, and then a darkness would come, and bad things happened.

What no one comprehended, when they warned Helena about Dominik, about his terrors and army scandals, was that these were the things that Helena loved most. This man who seemed so well stitched together, who showed such precision and punctuality, who showed up at her door at eight o'clock to the second, who had sent her a flower from the battlefield, and then disappeared without word – the idea that he harboured a shady side, some wickedness that might leap out one day, excited her. She never knew where she stood with him, and she hated to admit it, but this evoked an intense passion within her that she found difficult to suppress. She longed to see this darkness, to have it escape from his buttoned exterior, taking her by surprise. She was aware that she might get herself killed for it, but she would go to her death willingly, wrapped in ecstasy.

27

THE BEST CHEMIST
IN THE WORLD

By March 1921, Helena's pregnancy began to show, and she feared what Mr Karski would say when he discovered her condition. But then one day, when the sun blazed through the pharmacy windows, he held her belly himself and exclaimed, 'We shall have a brother for Dominik!' With wet eyes he showed her a box of Dominik's baby things they'd kept, handing her playsuits and train sets. He kept calling her Irena, and so after that she removed the name badge Dominik had made for her, so as not to confuse him. She loved feeling the baby kick inside her – truly the strangest sensation – and she smiled through a misted gaze at how her own father would have loved to meet his grandchild. She spent her days thinking of names, collecting little things for the baby. She knitted a pair of booties and a cardigan, both from yellow wool.

Women either complained of their pregnancies, of backaches and weight gain, or did not speak of them at all, as though it would be a sin to mention this bodily process. But Helena found everything, even the uncomfortable parts, to be a source of joy. At one point a large vein rippled to the surface of her vulva, then disappeared. She examined it with a mirror and marvelled. Her face swelled and her breasts grew venous and heavy, her nipples enlarged. A tremendous weight bore down on her pelvis. She felt full of life;

a ripe cantaloupe. She had worried at first that she might feel shame and agony at the judging stares of people for bringing a bastard child into the world. But as her belly grew and the child continued to move inside her, happiness overcame her and she found she could not care less.

The new Polish government travelled to Riga and signed an uneasy treaty with the lawyers and teachers who now ran Russia, finally ending the war with the Soviets. Yet the entire summer then passed with not a word from Dominik, and autumn arrived. Poland was now truly a free country for the first time since 1795, and a republic. She trained her eyes on the doorway, waiting for him to walk in, ready to show him the belly that carried his child. Still, Dominik did not appear. Her feelings alternated between agitation and fury. Where was he? He possessed no reason to be absent; each day some soldier or other would return and walk through the doors of the buildings and houses around them, welcomed into the relieved arms of weeping mothers and friends, but their doorway remained empty. Some days she would quietly plead with him, trying to send him a message through the ether: *Please come home. I have something to show you.*

Helena continued to work in the pharmacy, staying behind the counter. She wore a long heavy dress of wool, which made her sweat each day in the summer heat but which covered her well; most customers either didn't notice or didn't care, and if they gossiped about it outside, Helena never heard it. They still thought of her as Mr Karski's maid and she heard one woman praising Mr Karski for taking her in. Mr Karski nodded and smiled. He remembered nothing new at all now.

One night he knocked on Helena's bedroom door and asked to be let in. 'I won't touch you in your delicate condition, Irenka,' he said through the door, adding a k to the name to denote affection. 'It's only a cuddle I want.' She fastened a lock to the door after that and fobbed him off as best she could, both touched and horrified. She complained of loose bowels, stomach complaints, lung infections, anything to keep him away.

At thirty-five weeks, she delivered some aspirin to a blacksmith who lived on the edge of the city. She would have preferred not to go, but Mr Karski would be unable to make it there and back without forgetting the purpose of his mission, so it was decided there was little option but for Helena to undertake the journey.

'I won't be long,' she said to him.

She walked to the blacksmith's feeling a little unwell, and with a back that had ached all day; she would be relieved to return home to put her feet up. Arriving at the address, she found no one there. Spotting a barn, she walked towards the door, calling out to alert anyone who might be there to her presence. As she reached the door, she felt a pain tear across her abdomen, forcing her to double over to cushion it. She tried to walk further but found she couldn't. A white-hot pain began in her lower back and abdomen too, then shot down her leg. She cradled her belly and heard herself gasp. She would be going nowhere.

She called out for help, but no one came. She had walked across a little bridge to get there and the place suddenly felt like the remotest location on earth. She looked around. A pair of pliers sat on a crucible, the tool head glowing orange, still warm from smith's work. Its owner must have departed mid-job, setting down his tools for some reason. He had left the forge burning, and the heat that emanated from it made her sweat, or perhaps the pain in her belly, stark enough to nauseate her, had done this.

Another pain shot through her and she cowered. It was too soon, surely, for the baby to come. She felt a great wetness whoosh out from between her legs. Very well, her waters had broken, she would be meeting her child that day, and likely in that blacksmith's barn.

She took a moment to reflect on the sensation of what she now understood was labour. She had broken her arm once, falling off a fence on their farm. Her father had set it with a stick and bound it with torn pieces of cloth. The pain of the injury had made her head burst. This was not like that. This was like her arm being broken over and again, that head-bursting pain, happening every two minutes. And it was not her arm breaking, but something deep inside her, a pounding with a battering ram on her bowels, over and again, like a butcher tenderising a piece of already bruised flesh. With each thumping contraction, the muscles of her thrashed abdomen grew wearier and she feared she had not the stamina left to endure another. She found herself unable to focus on anything, unable to speak or hear, screaming silently into the earth. She located a piece of straw on the ground and stared at it; even that hurt after a while so then she stared at nothing. A slippery definition, pain: think on it for too long and it went away. What was it exactly? A stinging, a burning? When asked to describe their pain in the pharmacy, people invariably struggled. Helena attempted to define it now. Pain meant the inability to enjoy the current moment, and the desire for it to end. Pain of the heart, pain of the muscle, pain of the head: they were all the same, wanting the present moment to end. Happiness, on the other hand, was the opposite: the desire for the present to go on forever.

Her own mother had died giving birth to her and now she had the privilege of knowing why. She tipped her hat to every person in the history of human existence who had managed this feat. She thought back to all the women she'd seen in the village where she grew up, those who'd given birth who were patted on the head by husbands and priests, the way one pats a cow. How men had laughed and stayed well away, waiting in the kitchen or around the fire as their women bellowed and spat in a hidden room out the back.

She smirked at the fact that more than half the population would never know this sensation. She now joined a secret club of the torn flesh; in childbirth, women walked into a forest of pain. Her brain rocked with a hot, dizzying nausea as her lower abdomen cramped and spasmed.

A black substance fell from between Helena's legs onto the floor. She stared at it and swallowed. She knew from women in her village that this tar-like matter comprised a baby's first bowel movement and should not occur while the baby still lay inside the womb. It signalled that the infant had entered a state of distress.

She placed her hand between her legs and felt a long, slimed protrusion, shaped like a snake. She frowned, not understanding what she felt, and located the compact mirror she kept in her handbag. She squatted and stared at the reflection between her legs. She loved the beautiful textbooks Mr Karski kept in his little library at the back of the pharmacy, and she'd flipped through them whenever she found a spare moment, marvelling at the illustrations of the human body, the heart, the lungs, the arteries. It amazed her that all of this lay inside her, under her skin.

She recalled one text now that had particularly bewitched her, *A Sett of Anatomical Tables* by William Smellie. The doctor from Scotland had sketched illustrations of obstetric conditions, which she'd marvelled over, especially in the recent months of her own pregnancy. But her emotion at that moment was not set to marvelling; in fact her blood ran cold as she recalled one illustration in particular, that of umbilical cord prolapse. Was this what was occurring within her own body now? Yes. The snake she'd felt was the umbilical cord, the baby's lifeline. From the Scotsman's description she knew the cord provided the baby with oxygen before it entered the world, and the cord's unexpected journey outwards meant the baby was now squashing its lifeline between itself and the birth canal, and cutting off its own air supply.

The baby was suffocating.

She called out for help again, this time screaming. To her surprise, someone answered her call. A boy of about twelve poked his head around the doorway and peered inside.

'Help me!' she cried out again. He hurried over to her. 'Where is the blacksmith?'

'I am his apprentice,' the boy replied. 'Mr Lipinski walked to the apothecary to fetch the aspirin.'

'But I've brought it to him!' Helena held out the little bottle she'd brought. A miscommunication had occurred somewhere. The blacksmith would be almost to the pharmacy by now. 'You must find him,' she said. 'No, better. Fetch the apothecary for me, Mr Karski. Do you know him?'

The boy nodded. 'Are you all right?'

'I'm having a baby,' she said. 'Mr Karski will know what to do.' The boy stared at her, horror and fascination on his face. His rounded cheeks and hands indicated an age closer to ten; eight, even. Her uterus contracted then, and she sucked in a sharp breath and doubled over.

The boy looked scared. 'I will go,' he said. 'I know a short way there.' He walked to the door and peered outside.

'Wait,' she said. He turned back to her. 'Tell Mr Karski to bring his medical bag. Do not come back without the bag. You may have to carry it. Mr Karski is forgetful, he may not want to come with you.' She stared at the floor and thought. 'Tell him Irena is having her baby.'

'Yes, Mrs Irena,' the boy said. He smiled and turned for the door.

She returned to feeling her abdomen and her uterus contracted once more. The baby had been kicking her, every ten seconds or so, again and again. But now, she realised, she hadn't felt a kick for a minute. She waited another minute; the baby didn't kick at all.

She placed her hands between her legs in a panic. She could feel the top of the baby's head. It was absurd that the child's nose and mouth were so close but shielded from her. The child suffocated while it lay millimetres from air. She guessed she had about sixty seconds before the baby gave up, before the cells that required oxygen for every movement and chemical reaction stopped working. She bore down and pushed, feeling like her eyes might pop from her head with the exertion.

Her abdominal muscles spasmed and she considered the mechanics of human labour. She'd looked at the numbers, the physics, and found they didn't add up. The skull and shoulders of a baby were wider than a human pelvis, especially a small, young one like hers. Of all the mammal births in the animal kingdom, the human one was the most violent. Bones needed to bend and muscle needed to tear to make room. To bring forth life, one had to die a little.

From the angle of the baby's head she wondered if perhaps it faced the wrong way. She knew from her reading that the baby's face needed to point the other way to enable its exit from the birth canal. Was it stuck? She pushed and pushed; the baby didn't move. She looked to the doorway frantically, willing Mr Karski to arrive – where was he? Perhaps the child hadn't even made it to the pharmacy to fetch him.

A minute passed. She pushed again in fury, not caring if she split herself in two. She reached down to feel for any movement but found nothing. She waited again, crying and begging. *Surely not. Come on, darling.* She felt no kicks, no ripples. She waited another ten seconds, then twenty. She sensed the baby slipping away, and she raged and screamed with ragged breath. She prayed to whoever might be listening. She conjured every god and devil she could think of and announced her willingness to bargain with any or all of them. She called out to the demon Lamashtu, the goddess of Mesopotamia who menaced women during childbirth, the lady-monster who possessed a lion's head, the teeth of an ass, a body covered in hair. She saw the malevolent woman, seated on her thorn-covered throne, cradling a snake in one hand and nursing a pig at her breast, smiling wildly. She screamed at the demon every curse word she knew, insulting her, tormenting her. She struck a deal with her: *Let my baby live, and I will spend my life keeping it safe.*

Then she forgot the gods and devils and, wiping her eyes, spoke to the child instead. 'Little one, if you can hear me, please hang on. I will get you out. If you are still in there, please show me. My brave child, my miracle, I am sorry to have failed you so. If you are in there, please fight.'

She recalled the people who came into the pharmacy, the ones who lived, the ones who died. Some people fought, some people gave in. She couldn't begrudge this child for not fighting; it was so little. She didn't blame it for going, if it wanted to go.

She gasped and waited another minute in silence, each second feeling like an hour, the only sound the crackling of the flames in the forge behind her. Finally, she cried out. It had been too long. The baby had to be gone.

She heard herself howl, the primal shriek of a destroyed soul. She sank into a desperate sadness. She ordered herself to be calm: babies died in childbirth every day; she was not exceptional. She stared into the fire left by the smith, wondering what would happen now. She'd somehow have to birth the dead baby. Could she walk back to the pharmacy where Mr Karski might help her? She staggered to her feet, towards the door, and felt her abdomen flinch. She ignored it at first but it happened again. It was not a flinch, but a kick.

She waited for another and felt it, then three was enough, and she allowed herself the tiniest of smiles, then grit her teeth and growled. The child appeared to have upheld its end of the bargain; she'd now uphold hers. She moved to the bench and looked for a tool – something, anything she could use. She located a small blade that the smith likely used for trimming leather and walked unsteadily to the forge, where she held the sharp edge over the amber coals.

She placed a leather strap between her teeth. She allowed herself a millisecond to appreciate the horror of what she was about to do, then she took the blade, inhaled and drew a line with it down. She reached past it into the space she'd made, and poked her finger around, grasping liquid and slippery bulk, searching, wincing. She hooked her nail under a tiny triangle-shaped protuberance that she hoped signalled the apex of the foetal shoulder bone. *Yes.* She dug her nail down, waited for the rising contraction, screamed for it to hurry, then she pulled.

She took the knife and nicked a bigger tear. More space could be made. She dug the knife in, screeching, and the tear grew bigger. The baby kicked. She pulled again, and again, and finally the child's head was released. She waited for the rising moment, then pulled the child again. The shoulders now appeared. Again. A torrent gushed from her and with it, the baby.

A girl. She picked her up.

The baby's eyes remained closed and she didn't cry. A lily-white pallor graced her skin; her limbs hung limp by her side. Helena had taken too long. She slapped the child gently on the face and chest. 'Please, my love.' She rubbed the baby's sternum. Still nothing. She placed her mouth over the baby's mouth and nose and sucked, drawing the mucus away. She spat the fluid free, then repeated this. The child flinched. *Yes.* She rubbed the child again. *Go on.* A faint cry rose upwards. She rubbed the sternum again, pinched the baby's legs.

She recalled a beautiful sound she'd heard late one summer, climbing in the forest above her village. The insects and birds had come out for evening song. One bird sang a little melody that had echoed and pleased her ears above anything else. She'd paused there for minutes, listening, despite her feet getting wet from a creek she hadn't even realised she was standing in. She also loved the sound of rain, especially at night lying in her bed. The beaten thatched roof of the farmhouse in which she and her papa had lived had made the loveliest pattering as the rain hit it. Those beauteous noises of birdsong and rain were now as ugly as nails down a chalkboard compared to what she now heard: the celestial sound of her tiny daughter screeching like a demented banshee, mad and alive.

Helena looked down at the baby. The baby looked up at her and blinked. Two pools of jade stared at her from between moistened eyelashes; her eyes were just like Helena's.

Helena was ruined for the world now. Although blood, white pasty mucus, and more black meconium covered the baby in streaks and smears, the slimy creature appeared more beautiful to her than anything her eyes had ever had the luck to look upon. She apologised in advance to every human she would encounter ever after, for no one and nothing could come above the creature she cradled in her arms. She wiped the baby clean as best she could with the folds of her skirt and rested her on her chest. Pink skin and blonde hair emerged. The baby relaxed and her mouth went from open and screaming to a rosebud. Helena recalled the oath she'd made in the middle of it all, that deal with the devil to always protect this child. She already knew she'd keep the bargain, at the expense of everything else.

'Irena, what have you done?' She looked up to see the pharmacist in the doorway. The boy stood next to him, carrying the medicine bag. The boy's mouth hung agape, so wide it looked painful.

'There's something wrong with him,' the boy said, motioning to Mr Karski. He didn't seem to know where to look: at the bloodied and sweating Helena now cradling a newborn baby in her arms, or the demented Mr Karski ranting and mumbling in the doorway.

'I tried to come sooner, but he kept stopping and forgetting. Every time we moved forward a bit, he wanted to go back to the pharmacy. He only kept walking when I told him "Irena's having the baby". We walked back to the pharmacy five times.'

Helena shut her eyes slowly and then opened them again. Great drops of sweat fell from her forehead and doused her face, and she shook with exhaustion. 'You executed your mission perfectly, Artur. You have saved my life and the baby's. Stand tall, son – today you are a man.' The boy lifted his head. Helena smiled at them both.

Mr Karski took the bag and examined her. 'What a mess, Irenka,' he said, peering between her legs.

'Can you repair it?' she asked, not really caring about the answer.

'I can try,' he said. He looked at the baby, and he kissed Helena's forehead. 'My magnificent Irenka, my champion.'

Helena wiped away a tear.

'Come here,' he said to the boy, who maintained a stupefied look on his face, staring at the little baby and Helena. But then he nodded and became Mr Karski's assistant, holding the tools and catgut, and passing them when asked. Mr Karski applied neat stitches – nothing fancy, he was no surgeon, but they achieved the required task.

'What shall we call her, Irenka?' he said.

Helena already knew the answer. 'Marie,' she said.

'Maria?'

'Not Maria. Marie.'

'Ah. After Skłodowska, yes?' Mr Karski said, referring to the Polish woman who had won not one but two Nobel prizes. 'Or Madame Curie, as she's now called. Perfect.'

'Yes, after her,' Helena said. 'The best chemist in the world.'

28
DOMINIK'S NEW ASSISTANT

Krakow, July 1939

Dominik retrieved the patient record of Daniel Blumfeld and visited the tenement building listed as his address. He knocked on the door of a second-floor apartment but there was no answer. Paint peeled from the door.

He approached a woman hanging stockings along a line that hung across the courtyard. 'They're gone,' she told him, nodding towards the Blumfelds' door.

'Where did they go?'

'Dead,' she told him. She retrieved another stocking from her basket. Water dripped from the hosiery onto the concrete. She hadn't rinsed them properly and a line of soap dashed itself across one leg, glistening when the sun struck it.

'The boy and his mother? Both dead?'

She shrugged. 'Of course.'

'What did they die of?'

'Not sure. Wasn't here.' She wiped a soapy hand on her apron.

Dominik pressed her further – when did they die, who knew them, where did they take the bodies? – but the woman knew nothing. 'We weren't friends,' she said, as if that answered everything.

He knocked on more doors searching for information. Few people answered and those that did told him little. 'She wasn't liked.

I'm sad she's dead, of course,' was one woman's reply. She then shut her door softly but swiftly in Dominik's face.

He knocked on one more door and received no answer, but then realised he knew the owner. The name plate on the apartment read Wojtyła: this was the surname of Marie's friend Lolek, the librarian who also served as an acolyte at Dominik's church. He recalled Marie mentioning Lolek lived in this tenement. The studious and polite young man wasn't home, but Dominik knew where he'd be. He walked to the library.

'What happened to your neighbours, Lolek?' he asked the young man. 'The mother and the young boy.'

Lolek was restacking shelves with returned books. The stacks smelled of ink and vellum, and some other mustiness he couldn't place. 'Greetings, Dominik, how goes it?' Lolek always called him Dominik, never Dr Karski, even though Dominik was by far his elder and senior, and Lolek was only nineteen. It never came out as impertinent though, only avuncular; the librarian was an old man in a young man's body. 'Ruth died, two days ago. Very sad,' Lolek said. He placed a book on a high shelf, standing on his toes to reach.

'And the boy, Daniel Blumfeld?'

'Dead too.' Lolek swallowed as he said it and looked away.

Dominik squinted at him. 'What did they die of?'

'I believed Ruth took ill with a fever on Wednesday and by Friday she'd slipped away.'

'A fever – was it pneumonia?'

'I couldn't say.'

Dominik grew frustrated. Lolek was usually happy to speak at length on any topic. 'The son, Daniel. He had pneumonia too?'

Lolek shrugged. 'I don't know.'

Dominik left Lolek to his books and returned to his office to use his telephone. He winced at the news he'd need to tell Rachel Rosen now; he hadn't expected this. A fever surprised no one – Ruth, that bird-like creature, didn't take care of herself, and the neighbours cared nothing for her, either. He accepted her death as regrettable but understandable; it may simply have been a matter of time. But the boy . . . he had fought so hard to survive earlier.

He telephoned Rabbi Katz to ask where mother and son might be held awaiting burial, or when the funeral might be. The elder hadn't heard the news, but offered to make some calls of his own. He sounded excited to hear from Dominik, still glowing from the glorious wedding celebration, then demurred at the abrupt change in tone. The rabbi rang him back an hour later. 'She's not been buried,' he said. This wasn't kosher, but then, 'She was not much in the community.' Dominik thanked him, then telephoned the other hospitals in the city to ask if they held her. He needn't have bothered, for the hospital she lay in was his own.

'She's here, Dominik,' Matron Skorupska told him, 'in our morgue.' Ruth Landau had lain in his own hospital the whole time, brought in two days ago.

Dominik went to the morgue and removed from the cold chest the body of the tiny woman who'd pressed the tin charm into his hand. There was no sign of Daniel Blumfeld, though. 'Perhaps they took him somewhere else,' the matron offered. She was likely right. He instructed her to telephone the other hospitals again, to double-check the child had not appeared anywhere else. In the meantime, he'd take the opportunity to find out what had killed the mother, to ascertain if his old friend streptococcus was to blame.

It was a Sunday. Johnny wasn't working, and Dominik wouldn't ask him to come in for this. He would perform the autopsy alone; it would take longer, but he'd done it before. Ruth was small and would be easy to roll over, though it was always nicer to have a second pair of eyes, someone to talk to. When two bodies inhabited a room, but only one soul, an unwelcome mood could set in. Still, it couldn't be helped in the current situation, so he set to work, laying her body out on the slab, positioning her legs and gently placing down her cold head. Her limbs felt chilled and unyielding; although rigor mortis had already passed, she still felt stiff due to the refrigeration.

'Dominik, your daughter is here to see you,' the matron said, appearing in the doorway. He felt startled; he hadn't been expecting this. He put down the blade he'd been holding to the cadaver. 'She's returned from her honeymoon.' The matron smiled.

Dominik left the morgue and found Marie in the hallway. She wore the same cream suit she'd departed the wedding reception in, and she looked well. 'Hello, Papa.'

'How was it?' he asked.

She nodded and smiled by way of reply. 'For you,' she said, handing him a box of smoked cheese. 'From Zakopane.'

Dominik expressed his thanks and his wish to consume it soon. He opened the box and discovered six pieces of smoked highland cheese inside, moulded into the shape of sheep. He realised he'd be eating them on his own – Marie lived with her husband now – so it might take him some time.

'What are you doing here?' she asked, explaining that she had been to the house and, finding it empty, came here, for where else would he be on a Sunday?

Dominik told her about the deceased woman and how he wanted to determine the cause of death. He didn't mention that her son, Daniel Blumfeld, was likely Ben's cousin.

'May I assist you?' Marie asked suddenly.

Dominik stared at his daughter. 'Autopsies make for grim sights, Marie. Go and enjoy your husband.'

'I can handle it. Please. I'd like to help.'

Dominik protested some more but could find no justifiable reason not to allow her presence. Even having someone to pass him the tools would benefit the process. He showed her into the morgue.

She went quiet when she saw the corpse laid out on the slab; he might have heard her gasp. 'You don't have to, Marie,' he said at the sight of her green face.

'I'm fine.' She seemed to force herself forward, towards the body. He watched her eyes as they ran over the blue-grey flesh, the stiffened limbs, the blood pooled under the elbows and knees. He recalled the first time he had seen a cadaver as a student, the horror that had gripped him. That chemical smell, mixed with the reek of old flesh. But the disgust had soon turned to fascination and he'd felt enchantment at seeing the body, a de-animated human being, the ghost departed but the flesh remaining. He recalled his ecstasy at reading *De Sedibus et Causis Morborum per Anatomen Indagatis*, Morgagni's masterpiece on the autopsy. Still watching Marie, he saw she was her parent's daughter. Beyond her revulsion at seeing a decomposing body, she also had the same covetous look in her eyes, the need to know how it had died. She still placed a hand to her nose self-consciously, looking embarrassed and defeated at the action.

'No more horrid smell exists to the human nose than ageing meat and animal waste,' Dominik said. 'It stirs something primal in us – we want to get away from it because we don't want death to touch us, to capture us too. Do you know what sensory adaptation is?' Marie shook her head. 'Men who strip animal carcasses at the abattoir, women who gut fish at the market, the tanners and sewer men, do you know how they carry out their jobs every day, smelling odours so heinous they could be dredged up from hell itself? Eventually, we grow accustomed to fish guts, to animal refuse, to bodily waste. In fact, all we need is fifteen minutes. That's the time it takes for the cells in our nasal cavity to adapt. Dogs don't possess the same ability to acclimate, to forget. That's why they can follow a scent for hours; days, even. But we lose the ability to smell in fifteen minutes – bad if we needed to track someone, but great for this purpose.' He pointed to the body. 'Give yourself a quarter hour, and you won't be able to smell it anymore.'

Marie nodded and lowered her hand from her nose. She looked at the cadaver. 'She's not very old. How did she die?'

'We're here to find that out,' Dominik said. 'I think pneumonia.'

'Bacterial pneumonia?'

Dominik didn't smile outwardly but did so on the inside. 'Yes.' On instinct he continued the conversation, the way he would with an intern, a half-lesson. 'Causes?'

'Bacterial infection,' Marie replied, taking the cue. 'Staphylococcus, streptococcus.'

'How shall we ascertain cause of death? Where would streptococcus appear?'

'In the blood, the tissues?'

'Yes.' He swelled with pride. He raised his knife, then lowered it. 'I'm going to make an incision here.' He blushed, wary, aware for the first time that he was standing with his daughter in front of a naked corpse, breasts and genitals exposed, which he was about to cut open.

If Marie was embarrassed, though, she didn't show it. 'Between the fourth and fifth rib?' she asked.

'Yes. To retrieve lung tissue.' He positioned the scalpel and made the incision. As he did Marie moved silently next to him, and once he'd retrieved the piece of lung, she held out her hand. He put the scalpel in it; she returned it to the tray. She helped him prepare the sample, then stood by him as he placed it under the microscope.

'What do you see?' she asked in a politely urgent tone. Dominik made inquiries of a similar tenor himself from time to time.

'Nothing, I'm afraid,' he replied. 'No streptococcus.' He grimaced and scratched his head, disappointed. He'd felt sure the same bug that had once infected the son had now killed the mother.

He returned to first principles. 'She had a fever before she died.' He watched his daughter. 'What causes fever?'

'Infection?'

Yes, infection was the likeliest cause, the supreme culprit for elevating the body's core temperature above the healthy range, heating cells and tissue and causing irreparable damage when untreated. But there were other causes of fever, and he felt disappointed she hadn't offered more. A good clinician assumed nothing; they had the most common diagnosis in their mind, of course, but also ruled nothing out.

'Also tissue disease, inflammation of blood vessels, blood clots in the deep vein, a cancer, malaria,' she added.

He stared at her. Malaria was unlikely, but technically it was an infection.

'Malaria is unlikely, of course, unless this woman was recently in Africa, or a jungle in southern Asia,' she said.

Dominik swallowed and adjusted his glasses, impressed. 'How shall we decide?' he asked. 'How shall we narrow down the cause?'

'I don't know.' The look on her face was an honest one. 'Do we examine the organs, one by one, to find the source where the pathogen began?'

'That will require us to make a large incision and remove the organs one at a time – weigh them, examine them. Are you prepared for this?'

'I am,' she replied.

They got to work. Dominik opened Ruth Landau up and removed the heart, lungs, liver, digestive system. Marie didn't retch or vomit, but assisted him to weigh and study them all. Frustration bubbled as he examined them, for he found no source of the malady, no liver that had failed, no heart that had stopped from muscle damage, but something entirely different – and perplexing. '*Everything* has failed,' he said out loud. 'She didn't stand a chance.' Marie waited for him to continue. 'There is not one organ particularly inflamed; *everything* is larger than it should be. The entire body is inflamed.'

'Sepsis,' Marie said.

Dominik nodded, forgetting for a moment that she was his child, not yet eighteen years old, with no medical training. He forgot all of this, as if addressing a colleague. 'But where did it start? We've examined the vital organs. All are inflamed, but none show any particular point of origin. The heart, lungs, liver, digestive tract – they've all fallen victim to shutdown, but the infection didn't start there. It seems it didn't start anywhere.'

It was truly a mystery. He felt tantalised and frustrated, upset it was not pneumonia as he'd predicted, but still keen to find out the truth. He ran his eyes over the skin that remained, the limbs, the armpits, looking for a laceration or an abrasion; perhaps infection had entered the body that way. He examined the toes and the fingers, the neck, and found nothing, not a scratch. He grimaced.

'We have not checked everywhere,' Marie said.

He looked up. 'The brain. Yes, of course. Meningitis is rare, but possible.' He moved to locate a saw.

'Not the brain,' Marie called after him. 'We could look there, but may I suggest somewhere else first?'

'Where?' Dominik asked, squinting.

'The reproductive organs. Perhaps the infection started there.'

He tipped his head. 'I would check the brain.'

Marie shrugged. 'The uterus might be easier.'

Dominik grimaced, still wanting to check the cranium, then realised that his daughter in fact made a good point. They removed those organs and examined them. Beginning in the uterus, then moving to the fallopian tubes, the endometrium and into the peritoneal cavity, they discovered organs blemished with exudate, the hallmark of infection. Dominik stared at his daughter with pride and awe. 'Well done.'

Marie's face filled with unbridled joy then suddenly fell to a scowl. 'What is that?' she asked, pointing to the uterine wall where thin, jagged indents lay in lines across the organ.

Dominik studied them. 'Scratches,' he replied. 'Someone – or something – has scraped the womb clean.' He stared at the uterine wall for some moments and felt a deep pity for the woman for suffering death this way. He imagined Ruth Landau's last days, her desperate attendance at some dubious clinic at the back of someone's house. Had she engaged with some new fling who had treated her as badly as the last, or had she submitted to the caresses of some sweaty and indolent partner for food and money, only to find he abandoned her when she conceived his child? He looked at Marie and wondered if she would demur from the sight. She seemed not to, viewing the discovery with a physician's eye. He felt enormously proud of her, acknowledging what he'd long suspected and now accepted: she was exceptional. How had she failed that entrance exam?

But he also hoped she finally understood: this was the reason women needed to get married.

29
YOU'VE DONE IT NOW

Dominik returned to Lolek Wojtyła. 'Did Ruth Landau have a man friend?'

Lolek shrugged as he stamped books behind the borrowing counter. 'I wouldn't know.'

The tone was unusual; was it defensive? For a moment Dominik considered he might be looking at the man in question. 'Were *you* her man friend?'

'No,' Lolek replied, with a look of blank honesty.

Dominik believed him. 'I imagine she fell pregnant and removed the pregnancy,' he said. 'She had someone perform a procedure on her, or she may have even done it herself. Whoever it was, they used dirty instruments, and she died as a result.'

Lolek looked as if he might cry. 'My heart breaks hearing such things.'

Dominik watched his face, racked with anguish, and apologised for bringing it up. 'I only tell you because you knew her, and I inquired as a favour to someone else. I must ask you again, do you know what happened to the boy? Due to the way Ruth died, he couldn't have had the same infection as his mother, you see? His mother couldn't have passed on this type of illness.'

'The boy died. I am sorry,' Lolek said, looking away. He collected another stack of books from the counter and began stamping their inside covers.

Dominik realised he was conversing with a man to whom lying did not come naturally. He seemed unversed with the custom. Dominik spoke softly. 'Anything is helpful – even if I could find the child's grave. Was there a funeral, do you know? I'd like to pass information on to someone, even if it's bad news. To tell them I made the proper inquiries, made every effort to find him.'

'I don't know, Dominik. I'm sorry.'

'I went to your building. I asked around. It seems Ruth was not liked.'

'I liked her.'

'Others didn't.' Dominik studied the young man's face. Lolek's bones ran wide but fine across his cheeks, a Polish face, with a delicate pointed nose springing out from the middle of it; he possessed a slightness. A grown man, but a handsome one. Funny that the voice that came out of him always sounded so deep, a strong, dark bass. He sounded like Dracula might if the vampire were a fresh-faced acolyte from Krakow.

'They didn't like her keeping the company she did. She had a new friend, yes.'

'A new friend? Was he Daniel's father?'

He shook his head. 'I've only seen him the past few months.'

'Do you know who Daniel's father is?'

'He's dead now.'

'I am asking after the young boy on behalf of his family, relatives of his father. I will be sad to tell them he died, but at least then they will know.' Dominik realised he might need to reveal more than he first thought to get his way. 'They spurned him before, which they regret, and would like to make amends.'

'You are speaking of your daughter's new mother-in-law?' Lolek asked, looking directly at Dominik.

'Yes.' Dominik sniffed at the assertion; the librarian knew more about it than he'd first thought.

'She's too late. The boy's community rejected him. They may have taken him back in time, but the bigger problem is what's coming. An orphan would not have stood a chance. It's for the best that he's gone.'

Dominik bowed his head.

'You're saddened by the news?' Lolek asked.

'There's no room for sentiment in my position,' he said, waving his hand and trying to appear casual. Then he found the pretence too much and bowed his head again. The death of a child never came without wretchedness and grief, and this child . . . well. 'Yes. I am saddened,' he admitted. 'I liked that little boy.' The young man touched Dominik's arm. Dominik wondered how he'd break such news to Rachel Rosen.

'I am sorry,' Lolek said. 'I did not know he meant that much to you.' Dominik thanked Lolek and went to leave. As he reached the door, Lolek asked, 'Do you ever visit Podgórze?'

Dominik grimaced, confused at the change of subject. 'Rarely.'

'Next time you visit, on the way back to the station is St Marta's. A magnificent cherry tree grows out front – you must view it. At midday, to see it at its best.' Dominik stared at Lolek and watched the young man slowly nod. Dominik straightened, ascertained the sweet librarian was trying to tell him something, and made a plan to visit the cherry tree.

Dominik travelled to Podgórze the next day. St Marta's was an orphanage run by a local order. He sought directions at the station and arrived in time to view the cherry tree at midday. It was pretty but not as spectacular as Lolek had made out. Perhaps Dominik was a harsher judge of cherry trees; he'd seen a few in his time. Midday was also the time when the children of the orphanage played outside. The boys and girls ran circles round the tree, picked its fruit and skipped under it as the nuns, one old, one young, tutted and clucked. Among the children he saw one child whose eyes, two shining bluebirds, he'd seen before.

The younger nun summoned the children to her in a warm, honeyed, singsong voice. 'Irena, Paweł, Weronika,' she called as the children ran to her. 'Inside now. It's dinnertime. Krystian, time to come inside.'

The boy she'd called Krystian dropped his rope and ran to her, which seemed strange, for Dominik knew the boy's name was not Krystian, but Daniel. The last time Dominik had seen him, sandy-coloured locks had graced his crown in longish strands, and two forelocks, curled and arranged in front of his ears, had framed his face, reaching down almost to his shoulders. His head now contained only tufts; someone had shaved his hair almost back to the skull, leaving only a soft downy fuzz that covered his head evenly, like a duckling's.

As Krystian returned to retrieve his rope, he had no choice but to look in Dominik's direction. Dominik ducked behind his automobile by the road. He was too far away for the boy to see him clearly enough to recognise him, but Daniel had done so well answering to Krystian that Dominik didn't want to do anything that might jeopardise the good work of concealment the child had already managed. As he crouched at the front wheel of his car, clutching the hub cap, Dominik performed an act he executed so rarely he'd almost forgotten how. He smiled.

At the end of July, the hospital board met to decide on the new Chief of Medicine. When Dominik walked in and announced his intention to run, Dr Igor Wolanski came so close to having a stroke that Dominik could claim later he actually saw the blood clot moving up the man's neck, under his skin. But Dr Wolanski kept it together. A brief interruption followed as Dominik's illustrious colleague made an official protest that Dr Karski had withdrawn from the race for Chief of Medicine months ago and therefore could not make a presentation, but this protest was denied. One of the board members asserted that Dominik had reinstated his application the previous day, which was plenty of time according to hospital by-laws, and the floor was opened for both men to deliver their presentations.

Dr Wolanski went first, making a colourful and compelling exhibition of his intention to ban thirty per cent of the city's inhabitants – in other words, all the Jewish people of Krakow – from attending the hospital, as well as all the gypsies, if any ever had the intention of admitting themselves to the hospital for treatment. He included a truncated version of his now-famous slide presentation, 'My Travels in Germany', dimming the lights to show the board his photographs. He also produced a dubious graph to support his position, showing how infection rates would drop under his Aryans-only policy, and how resources currently spent on treating such plague-ridden people would now be diverted to worthier patients. He completed his speech by saying success three times – 'Success! Success! Success!' – a random piece of theatre to nicely round off an already histrionic display.

The board thanked Dr Wolanski and invited Dominik to state his case.

Dominik's presentation did not contain the sparkle or theatre of Dr Wolanski's. He produced no charts or slides or repetitious chants. Instead he calmly walked to the front of the room and, without an introduction, reminded the board that by banning thirty per cent of the city's patients, they would also reduce the hospital's income by thirty per cent. Some of the patients they would turn away included many of the wealthiest families in the city, not to mention a few of the board members. As for infection rates, Dominik also mentioned a medicine he was developing that could kill bacterial infection: an antibiotic, it was called, which he would happily patent in the hospital's name. Bacterial infections like staph, strep and pneumonia infected fifty per cent of the Polish population each year – fifty per cent of the world, in fact. In essence, if the hospital was in possession of this new drug, they could be selling a dose to every second person that walked through the door. They could also manufacture and sell it to every hospital in the country if they liked.

Dr Gruener, smoking a cigar at the back of the room, announced that his father had contacts at IG Farben who'd said they would happily manufacture the antibiotic once developed. The hospital might expect to earn a billion zloty. If, however, they favoured Dr Wolanski's approach, Dominik was more than happy to take his discovery somewhere else and the hospital could, rather than increase its earnings a thousandfold, proceed to reduce them by thirty per cent.

The board took a respectable amount of time to consider – two minutes or so – then thanked Dr Wolanski for his colourful and passionate presentation and named Dominik Chief of Medicine.

Afterwards, Johnny insisted that they celebrate, producing a bottle of champagne from somewhere and pouring Dominik half a glass, assuring him he did not have to drink it; it was more just to mark the glorious occasion. Dominik accepted the drink politely and took a sip, then excused himself and stole away to his office as soon as he could. He did not tell anyone about his ascendancy to the new role; he did not notify the professor, nor did he tell Marie. It was not modesty that compelled him to remain so secretive. He did not want to inflame the situation. His instincts were validated when he received a visit from Dr Wolanski in his office soon after.

'You've done it now, Dominik,' his incensed colleague said. 'I warned you to withdraw from the running. You agreed to do so, and I thought we had a deal.' It would not have surprised Dominik to witness steam spouting from the man's ears, and he had both hands balled into meaty fists.

Dominik winced and waited for his colleague to hit him. 'Get it over with, Dr Wolanski, if you propose to beat me.'

'Ha. You expect me to react with mere violence? I'm afraid I intend something far more dangerous. You agreed to revoke your application for hospital chief, and in return, I consented not to telephone my friend in Lwów. Now that you have reneged on your side of the bargain, I feel delighted to follow suit. I will call my friend as soon as I leave your presence. I don't know what I'm going to find out about you, but can I tell you, the thought excites me! From the way you've been acting, I sense I'm about to discover something grotesque, horrid and, for me, wonderful. Try to enjoy your post as Chief of Medicine while it lasts – I doubt you will hold the position for long. Who knows, after I've completed my investigations, you might cease to practise medicine at all.'

Before Dominik could say anything, Dr Wolanski departed.

Dominik sat in his chair and stared at the wall. He tried to distract himself with a patient report on his desk and found he could not read the words. He finally switched off the light and sat in darkness. He would have to leave his office eventually, but for now he would stay there, hidden from everyone. Dominik had covered his tracks in Lwów, but some loose ends remained that could never be tied. He would have to hope that Dr Wolanski was bluffing about the friend, or that he was too lazy to really check things out. Dominik would have to depend on the idiocy of the person investigating him if his past was to remain in darkness. Perhaps so long as only a stupid person investigated him, he would be all right.

30
LET'S PLAY CATCH

The week after the autopsy, Marie went to the university and asked to see Mr Strawiński. She waited in the reception area of the admissions office for forty minutes before a secretary showed her through. Marie had a speech prepared, which she delivered as soon as she walked in the door; she didn't know how much time she would have.

'Sir, allow me to retake the examination. For admission to medicine. I will seek tutoring; I will ask my father, Dr Karski, to help me prepare. I must have studied the wrong areas last time, for I possess the aptitude. My father will steer me in the right direction. I will make an excellent student and won't let you down.' She recalled the feeling she'd had as she assisted her father with the autopsy. The glory that had flowed through her; how she could feel her eyes getting beadier as they'd inspected the tissue, formed a hypothesis, made a diagnosis. *This is how I will live my life*, she'd thought.

Mr Strawiński put aside the crossword he'd been working on and screwed the cap back on his fountain pen. 'Please leave before you embarrass yourself further,' he said. 'You failed the exam.'

'I know. But my father will tutor me. Let me take it again.' She felt these assurances should suffice; after all, Strawiński himself had called Dominik the cleverest man in the city.

Mr Strawiński scratched his chin and sighed. 'I had hoped to spare you any embarrassment, but I see I must be more explicit. I thought this would be the easy solution for you, Miss Karska, or should I say, *Mrs Rosen,* but you don't seem to comprehend. Please listen carefully. You will never study medicine, or any other course, at this university.'

Marie examined the man's face. A crumb of indeterminate origin rested in his moustache, from cake maybe. Spittle or some other moistness seemed to be making it cling to his bristles. Marie considered telling him, but in the end said nothing, instead watching the crumb as it moved up and down as the man continued to speak, waiting to see if it fell of its own volition.

'I don't say this to be mean, Mrs Rosen. I say this to be fair. Even though we have places left next semester for Jews, do you think I would give you a place to study to be a *doctor*,' he said, sneering at the word, 'and deprive a man of a place, when he would do the job twice as well?'

Marie recognised the argument; she had heard similar words exit her father's mouth. 'I don't know. Yes, I suppose.'

'And what happens when you have children? You are married now. Will you work then? Will you leave the children at home to look after themselves? Or perhaps you will bring them to work with you?' He laughed cruelly. 'Carry them on your back while you treat patients? No, you will not. You will leave the profession to raise the little ones, as you should – babies need mothers. Even if you do not have children, if you are barren, what patient will see a *lady* doctor?' He hooted uproariously. 'What person would trust a woman to know the library of knowledge and have the skill required to diagnose a disease, understand anatomy and physiology, prepare a treatment? These are difficult items, requiring some greatness of mind, would you not agree?'

'I agree,' Marie replied. 'But I believe I possess a greatness of mind.' She looked down.

Mr Strawiński smiled with a patronising grin and spoke softly. 'Of course you do. Your father has told you this, and he sees you through a daddy's eyes. But in the real world, you are a woman, and even if you think you possess some intelligence, others do not. No one will trust you! No one will submit to be treated by you. You will never work fully in the profession the way a man can. And then it will be my fault, the soft-headed person who wasted a study place at university meant for a future doctor, to allow a *woman* to be trained instead.'

Marie stared at the ground meekly, shaking her head.

He spoke more softly now, as though trying to comfort her. 'I suggest you take your failure for the gift that it is. You are a young woman who has forgotten her place, or perhaps you never knew it to start with. The world is not here to serve your fantasies and desires. You present value to the world in certain areas; in others none. I say again, you must learn your place, and the sooner the better.' He leaned in. 'Women don't have the intelligence of men. It's just the way you're built. Don't try to force something that doesn't come naturally, dear. You'll only wear yourself out.' He threw his hands up, as though his final sentence brought a resounding conclusion to his argument.

Marie looked out the window. Rain had begun to fall, a summer thunderstorm. Fat drops began spattering the glass and a glorious perfume of fresh water entered the room through a window that had been left open. Mr Strawiński stood up from his desk and pulled it shut and the smell left the room.

'I hope for all our sakes I'm as stupid as you say,' she said.

He sat back down and smiled at her. 'I'm sorry, I don't follow.'

'I hope I am as thick as two planks of birch wood, because if I'm not, if I'm as clever as I think I am, I have the potential to make a small difference in this world, to make someone's life a little better, and you would deny me the opportunity to do that. How many people have already suffered unnecessarily when a woman could have helped them? How many have already died? What losses we delivered to the ledgers of human endeavour when we decided the most useful thing about these people was what lay between their legs.'

Marie turned back to the window to watch the rain, but not before she caught a glimpse of the university admissions officer's face, which was fixed in a look of shock. The crumb had come loose at some point and his moustache now lay bare. After several seconds, he addressed Marie in a stern tone. 'Let this lie, girly. You have a good excuse with the failed exam. I'm sure your father has accepted it, and others will too. Leave it now, or you may come to regret it.'

Marie moved to leave. As she reached the door, she paused and turned back to Mr Strawiński. 'Your father has cancer, yes?'

He smiled. '*Had* cancer. He is cured now.'

'How wonderful. How was he cured?'

'Papa received radiation therapy, administered at the hospital where your father works.' He grinned, self-satisfied.

'Were you aware that the radiation treatment that saved your father's life was invented by a woman?'

'Oh, I don't know about that,' he said, shifting in his seat uncomfortably.

'It was. Invented by Marie Curie. Deemed so important a discovery that she was given the Nobel prize.' She leaned in. 'Your father would be dead now if that woman had not been allowed to study. Good day.'

The man stared at her and said nothing, and Marie left the office. She passed a woman in the stairwell on her way out; she recognised her from before.

'Hello, Secretary Sadka,' Marie said. 'Nice to see you again.' She made to keep walking, but the woman took Marie's arm and guided her down to the landing and into a hallway.

She seemed to look left and right, as though checking that no one else was coming, then she spoke. 'You scored thirty-eight in the chemistry exam,' the woman told Marie. She glanced up the stairwell and pulled her further to the side.

Marie nodded her thanks. 'I didn't know my score. Thirty-eight out of what, may I ask?'

'Thirty-eight out of forty,' she replied.

Marie raised her eyebrows. 'Not good enough to pass though, it would seem. I guess the examination requires a perfect score?'

The secretary laughed. 'Thirty-eight is high. The average mark for that paper is twenty-two out of forty.'

'I was told I failed.'

'Yes.' The woman touched Marie's arm, then hurried up the stairs.

The words were meant to comfort Marie, surely. Instead they delivered to her a sinking feeling of such despair that she felt herself unable to leave that dusty corner of the corridor for half an hour.

Later that day, Marie carried groceries back to Ben's apartment, now her apartment too, and her home. She had moved in after returning from their honeymoon and had spent the time since becoming acquainted with her new husband. She now knew how he cleaned his teeth, what he looked like when reading the paper, how he turned over in bed. She had been shown those private places and invited to those unguarded moments for days now. He'd introduced her to the delicious beige foods of Judaism, as he'd promised to do. Kugel was her favourite – that glorious noodle pie! She smiled at the thought as she made her way home. She had shopped at the markets in the square and now walked down Grodzka Street, towards Kazimierz. Twilight lingered. It was August, and honey-suckle from the park wafted under her nostrils as she walked.

She smiled and made a detour towards the park that lined the edge of Old Town to smell more of it.

She had not long left the main road when she became aware that someone was following her. Their footsteps clicked on the cobblestones about ten metres behind her. She told herself at first that she was imagining it, that the individual was merely going about their business, but when she quickened her pace, the person increased theirs too, and soon almost caught up to her. Marie could feel her heart beating and her breath quickened. She crossed the road to see if that would deter the person; it did not. They moved to the other side of the lane with her and continued to walk faster. Marie wondered if she should scream, but she glanced over her shoulder and relaxed. 'Oh. Hello, Tobias.'

It was the younger brother of Jozef Kowalski, the young man she had avoided dancing with at the highland fling for young people. Tobias was fourteen years old, if she recalled correctly, and she had known him almost all his life. 'How are you?' she asked.

The boy made no reply but grinned at Marie strangely.

'Can I help you with something?' she said.

The boy just continued smirking in silence. 'Want to play catch?' he said finally.

Marie studied him. He stared at her with an unnerving gaze, wild and undisciplined, and he swayed a little. She wondered if he'd been drinking. 'No, thank you,' she said. 'I must get home.' She decided against walking into the park despite the lovely evening; she would walk back to the main road instead. She turned to do so, strolling back past the youth, only to find a car blocking her path. The car's owner turned the headlights on, momentarily blinding her. Once her eyes had adjusted, she discovered the car belonged to Jozef. He sat inside, glaring at her through the windscreen.

The younger brother was behind her again. 'Let's play catch,' he insisted.

'I don't want to play,' Marie said. She heard a creak in her voice.

'Too bad. These are the rules. You start running while I count to ten. Then I try to catch you. If I do, I get to beat you with this.' He held up a piece of wood about a metre long. At one end, someone had hammered a long nail only halfway in, so it stuck out from the pole at a right angle.

Marie felt like laughing at the outrageousness of it but found herself instead picturing the stick being swung at her and the nail digging into her skin, piercing her thigh, her back, her face. Surely there was some mistake. 'Tobias, you cannot be serious. We are neighbours,' she said in a pleading voice.

'Not anymore,' he replied. 'You are a dirty Jew now.' The boy's eyes danced.

Marie's throat went dry. She peered at her surroundings. They stood in a laneway overlooked by the backs of buildings – no houses, only offices, all closed for the day. There were no doors she could run inside and beg for assistance and no one around; the street was deserted. Screaming would not help. She peered past the boy with the stick and looked instead to his brother, Jozef, who stayed seated in the car. Would he help her? He had fancied her once, desired her – perhaps she could appeal to some softness in him. But to her horror, she saw a glare not softer than his little brother's, but something harder. While Tobias wanted a bit of violence, the older one possessed real hurt in his gaze. She had spurned him at the dance, disrespecting him in front of his family and friends, and now she would pay.

She could not run back to Grodzka Street; the car was in the way. 'Shall we start?' Tobias said, swinging his timber weapon. She turned to the park. She had no choice – she started running. The boy yelped with excitement behind her. 'One, two, three . . .'

Marie threw her groceries down and moved her legs as fast as she could away from him. The engine of Jozef's coupé roared to life behind her. The boy reached ten. 'Time's up. Here I come!'

Marie looked ahead. Her only hope was to lose them in the shrubs and trees of the park. Tobias quickened his step, gaining on Marie. She winced and urged her legs to go faster, her lungs burning with the effort. Her legs felt like lead. She heard the boy's breath behind her, young and excited, like a panting bulldog. He caught up to her and tapped her ankle with his weapon, trying to trip her. She stumbled slightly but regained her balance and kept running.

He caught up to her again, angrier now. He swung the stick and it connected with her hip, piercing the thin material of her summer dress and tearing a hole in it, and taking a piece of her flesh with it, too. Marie cried out in pain. The boy shouted in victory. 'Got you!' he celebrated, as though he'd kicked a goal on the soccer field.

She felt horrified: a boy so young, reacting without guilt or shame at having torn a piece of flesh from a human being. She cried for her own pain but also for his innocence gone. She reached the edge of the park and ran towards some bushes, hoping to hide in them, but he caught her again. This time, he swung his stick lower and it hit her on the knee, the nail gouging another piece of flesh as she tripped and fell to the ground. The boy pounced on her, straddling her back. She moved her arms to grab him or scratch him but the angle did not allow it. She tried to wriggle free, but he was too heavy; he weighed far more than her even at fourteen. She could scarcely believe it when she sensed him raising the stick over her head to bring it down once more. She folded her hands over the back of her head and braced for the impact.

'Enough, Tobias,' the older brother said.

The younger brother whimpered. 'No fair, I caught her,' he complained, as though he'd been treated unjustly in a card game.

Marie sighed with relief as the boy got up off her back. She stood up. Dirt and grass covered the front of her. 'Thank you,' she said to Jozef.

'Look at you,' the older brother said, contempt in his voice. 'Pig.'

Marie flinched at the words, so sharp and horrid and clichéd. She had heard other people called such things and the violence of the words had shocked her then, but to be labelled thus herself felt almost ludicrous.

'You disgust me,' he added in a sanctimonious tone. He pointed to her bloodied hip, where her dress had torn. Her underpants had torn also, and her soft flesh exposed itself to the park. He concluded with one final moniker. 'Slut,' he taunted.

Marie flinched again, this time far more deeply. The racial epithet had rung hollow, shocking though it was, but now she could confirm the real reason for her attack. He hated her because she had spurned him. In the space of months, she had been called 'Jew', 'slut' and 'bitch', three words she had never been called in the seventeen years prior. She mourned the little pieces of her those words had torn away. She contemplated what crime she had committed to garner such descriptions: she was the same person as before – what had changed? That was it. She had grown up, become a woman, and now she would pay.

'Thank you for putting a stop to this, Jozef,' she said, hoping to appeal to his nobler nature.

He shrugged. 'You're nothing now. I wouldn't have you for all the gold in Poland. Just wait until the Germans get here.'

It would take a long time before the memory of the rabid look in the boy's eyes left her. Marie ran through the park; the brothers did not follow her. She circled back and re-entered Grodzka Street, further up the road. She ran to the closest house she knew.

Her father opened the door to her and led her into the living room. She told him what had happened as he sat her down to dress her wounds. She waited for him to comfort her, to say he would go to Kowalski's door to give him a piece of his mind, or to the police to press charges. Instead he only shook his head.

'Well, Papa, what should we do?' she asked.

'I wish you had never married that boy, Marie. You've brought this on yourself.'

'This had nothing to do with my new religion, Papa! It was all Jozef Kowalski's wounded pride.'

'Do you expect everyone to feel as happy about your conversion to Judaism as you do?'

Marie heard herself gasp and narrowed her eyes at him. 'I thought you would be upset that your daughter has been treated so.'

'What possessed you to make life hard for yourself?' he replied. 'The world is cruel enough and now you have made it crueller. Do you expect me to celebrate what you've done?'

'Don't you think we should at least go to the police?'

He had cleaned the wound at her hip and now moved on to her knee. The gash had not closed properly and blood still oozed. 'What will the police do? You're a Jewish woman walking alone through a Catholic park. What were you thinking? You should have just danced with the boy, Marie. None of this would have happened. I say this in a loving way.'

Marie cleared her throat. 'He said to me, "Just wait until the Germans get here."'

She thought she saw her father shudder. 'He's not wrong. Do you understand now how much you've put your life in danger?'

Marie's face fell into a look of grief and shock. 'I thought you would protect me.'

'How can I when you deliberately throw yourself into harm's way? You have such little comprehension of how people think of you now you have left the sphere you grew up in. You have married, but you remain a child.'

'Did you know I passed the entrance exam?' she said, ignoring him.

'I beg your pardon?'

She told him of visiting the admissions office, what the secretary had told her. 'I expect you think I'm lying,' Marie said, 'or you'll say the secretary told me that to spare my feelings, that I didn't really ace that exam.'

Dominik sighed. 'On the contrary. I believe every word.' A peculiar look overcame him. He appeared lost in his own thoughts for a time, then he seemed to swell with pride. 'I have no doubt that man faked your exam results.'

Marie beamed, delighted at the unexpected reaction from him. 'What can we do about it?'

'Do? There's nothing we can do,' he replied. 'We must accept it. I am pleased that you are finally learning how the world works, daughter.' He spoke in a jesting tone, but his voice was dark and possessed a bitterness she rarely heard in him. The tone seemed not directed at her, but some other force. 'I hope now you will finally start listening to me,' he said. 'Marrying a Jewish man, applying to university – I did not counsel against these bold and reckless actions for my own amusement. I did it to protect you, Marie. Do you see that now?'

She swallowed; a rage gripped her. 'I see it.' She inhaled. 'You say these things not to protect me, but to stifle me! You suffocate me! What good is protecting me against the world if I have to live in it? You have damaged me.'

Dominik shook his head. 'You are acting like a child again.'

Marie scoffed. 'If I am, it's because you made me this way. I have you to thank for what I am.' She stood from the chair and snatched the cloth from him; she would finish bandaging the wound herself. She fetched her coat and went to leave, then stopped and turned back to him. 'How old was I when I was christened?'

Dominik shrugged. 'I beg your pardon? I don't know.'

'Yes, you do,' she replied. She folded her coat over her arm. 'You were there, you told me yourself. You remembered the priest, you said, the prayers spoken – you told me the whole story. Assured me it was a Catholic ceremony, not a Jewish one. Or do you not recall telling me about this?'

'I remember telling you. What of it?' he said, though his face already betrayed that he knew.

'How old was I?' she asked again.

'Four months, I suppose,' he said quietly.

Marie glared at him. 'You told me that when you first met me, I was already one year old.'

He stared at her and swallowed. The gesture shocked her; her father had never looked so uncomfortable.

'How could you remember my christening, which occurred when I was four months, if you only first met me when I was one?'

'I can explain—'

She scoffed at him triumphantly and left the house. Any hope of a reconciliation was now gone. She had discovered his curious largesse in the records office, his suspicious donations to every charity in town, and now she had caught him in a lie to her face. This signalled the final straw. Her mother had not simply left, as she'd always been told. Something else had happened, and her father knew what.

Previously she had hesitated; she had felt wary and guilty about delving further into her father's private life and history. No longer. He had proved himself unworthy of the respect she gave him. She placed her scruples aside; she would investigate him directly now, and she would find her mother.

31

THE TRAIN TIMETABLE
TO LWÓW

Now that she'd finished school, Marie possessed a great deal of
free time. She made perfunctory meals for her husband in the evenings, which he laughed at and offered to cook himself the next
time, but what else was she to do? She was bored keeping house,
the drudgery of it, scrubbing toilets and washing clothes, hanging
a shirt to dry only to find a stain and having to repeat the process, of sweeping food particles from the floor, only to find more
the next day. With each push of the broom into a dusty corner,
each pairing and folding of socks, she felt herself growing stupider. Ben was at work all day, supervising a summer camp, so
now Dominik would reap the spoils of her boredom. Her father
should not have antagonised her so; now any pretence of protecting his feelings was gone. She turned her energies to investigating
him and finding her mother, and her father could go to hell for all
she cared.

She went to the hospital on the pretext that she was waiting for
him. She knew he was not there, that he was at a conference that
morning, but Nurse Emilia let her wait in his office, telling her how
beautiful she'd appeared at the wedding and expressing a wish to
see photographs soon. Marie promised to bring her some next time.
She retrieved a novella from her satchel and pretended to read, but

as soon as the nurse closed the door, she put it back and began looking through her father's office.

Marie spent an hour searching his things. She read many documents: the autopsy report for Mrs Blumfeld, declaring death by septic fever, and his research on bactericide. Despite the gruesome display of the autopsy, she'd been thrilled to work under her father, to assist him, and she felt fascinated to read the report and her father's diligent notes. But her anger brewed inside her like a tempest, and while she allowed a nod of begrudging respect to his excellence as a physician, she continued in her quest to find something untoward. After an hour, she'd found nothing, however, and had begun to grow despondent, when she was surprised by the sound of a man's voice.

'Oh, I do apologise,' he said.

She turned to see an overweight man in a white coat entering her father's office; he'd come in without knocking. Marie threw some of her father's papers down guiltily, hoping the man hadn't seen. He had a tall and muscular frame that had now grown soft, like an athlete who'd run to fat, and a handsome face that had begun to sag.

'I am Dr Karski's daughter. He sent me to find a paper for him,' she lied, hoping that the man hadn't seen much. But then she studied his face and noticed a similar look of panic in him, though not as well concealed as her own. He didn't offer up his name, but his coat read *Dr Igor P Wolanski*: a colleague of her father's whom, from the faces Dominik had made on the occasions he'd referred to him, she sensed he didn't like.

'I simply came in here to find a patient document,' Dr Wolanski replied. 'We share some patients, you know, Dominik and I; it happens sometimes.' Marie had to smile. He was not as good a liar as she, though he possessed the air of someone who lied often. There was an insincerity to him, and with his buffoonish mannerisms, he wore his emotions on his face plainly.

'Are you friends with my father?' she asked, to see his reaction.

'Wonderful friends,' he said quickly. 'Your father is an excellent physician.'

Marie almost laughed at the disingenuousness in his voice. She wondered what this man wanted from her father. 'You probably spend more time with him than I do,' she said, watching his face.

'I daresay I do – we are buddies. But sometimes he does the strangest things. Did you know he had applied for the position of hospital chief?'

Marie nodded softly. She had not known this, but saw no point in saying so. She waited to see what came next.

'I convinced him to pull out of the race – it would involve far too much work for his abilities, you see, and I care about his wellbeing. He agreed to withdraw his application, but then turned up at the meeting and made a submission. The board awarded him the position. A stupid decision.' He shook his head.

Marie had no idea what the man spoke of – applications and hospital chiefs – and she had no interest in the minutiae of clinical politics. But she knew from the way the man spoke that he had not sought her father's withdrawal from this position out of concern for his wellbeing. She considered how to use this situation to her advantage. The man clearly stood in this office for no good reason; she had caught him red-handed. What might tempt this oaf to divulge more information than he should? What poison seduced him most? Did he like women? Men? Money? Power?

She watched his nervous face, his blinking. His white physician's coat bore his name in rich, sloping letters that took up half the pocket. Curlicues furnished the letters to the extent that one had to squint to make out the words. A seamstress, or perhaps his poor wife, must have spent hours hand-sewing those ridiculous letters onto the fabric with gold thread. Her father's own doctor's coat hosted his name written in black, in block letters. *Dominik Karski*, it read: no middle initial, no title, no calligraphy.

Prestige. Unearned advancement. That's what he wanted. She realised he must have competed for this Chief of Medicine position also, and her father had defeated him, striking a blow to his ego. He had not entered her father's office to retrieve a patient file. He had another motive; she needed to find out what. This man potentially represented not an opponent to her, but an ally. She would get to him with flattery.

'My father speaks very highly of you,' she said. His face lit up. There was no scepticism on his part at the compliment; he accepted it readily. This man was susceptible to sycophancy. 'In fact, many of the doctors and staff here speak of their respect for you.'

'Glad to hear my efforts are being recognised.' He beamed at her, a grin better suited to a young boy who'd learned to tie his shoe-laces, thinking he performed a great feat, when everyone else in the class had learned the skill three years ago.

'Perhaps you are right about him not being suited for the chief's position,' she continued, 'perhaps you would have been a better choice. My father has seemed out of sorts lately. I speak not from malice, but a place of concern. I worry for his wellbeing only. As I'm sure you do.'

'Absolutely,' the doctor replied.

'My father is so secretive, you see. He never tells me anything. I wish I could know more about him, so I could help him. I find my father is quite the enigma.' Marie watched for his reaction.

'Your father is not the man he says he is.'

Marie stiffened. 'Indeed.'

'I too say this only out of concern.'

'Of course.' She smiled at him, encouraging him to continue.

'He tells everyone he is from the north, for example. He's not from the north,' the doctor said, grinning.

Marie scratched her head and turned away, hoping he couldn't see her discomfort. Marie had met but a few people from the north of the country and had always accepted without question her father's claim of being from there.

'Where is he from, then?'

'Your father is from Lwów,' he stated plainly.

Marie blinked. 'Why do you say that?'

'I lived in Lwów, for a time. Russians have lived there, Cossacks, many tribes. I made some telephone calls, found out what I could. Your father worked in a pharmacy there, as a young man. Did you know? It was owned by his father. Your grandfather, I suppose. The pharmacy was called Karski's, in the centre of town. Did very well, I'm told, until the old man died.'

Marie kept her actions casual, shuffling a laboratory document on the table and doing her best to contain her excitement at encountering these gargantuan revelations about her father. A pharmacy, a grandfather! The words flummoxed and bedevilled her, and a feeling of crackling exhilaration flowed through her, like a dry spark of lightning without any rain. *Lwów.*

'Lwów, you say?' She'd heard of it but had never visited. Her father had taken her north, south and west, but never east. She pictured the map of Poland in her mind. Lwów was one of the last great cities before the map fell off into the Russian abyss.

'I had hoped to find out more about him. Unfortunately, all my friend knew when I telephoned was that he worked in a pharmacy there, and a possible last known address.'

Marie nodded. She did not blame Dr Wolanski; one could only learn so much from a telephone call. But while her father's colleague seemed satisfied with what he could discover over the phone, Marie knew she would not stop at that. As she bade the odd doctor farewell, she began picturing the train timetable to Lwów in her head.

32

A CIRCUS THAT SHOCKS SATAN HIMSELF

The department of defence put out a call for every man between fourteen and sixty in the city to meet in the town hall at seven o'clock on Saturday August 26, 1939.

The stifling air of a hot summer evening wafted down the baking cobblestones as Dominik and Lolek walked to the hall. It seemed a holiday time, and some men even entered the building in vacation clothes – cotton shirts and sun hats. Dominik wore his work suit; he had worked the weekend shift until five o' clock, then attended the vigil mass at six, walking to the hall from St Peter & Paul's afterwards. Father Wiktor had informed everyone during his homily that it was their duty as Poles to attend the town hall; if they didn't, he said smiling, they'd go go straight to hell.

Lolek had performed his acolyte's duties at the service and Dominik had waited for him to change out of his vestments so they could walk to the hall together. Men already filled the room by the time they arrived; it seemed as though every man from the streets around Dominik's house had shown up. No one seemed sure exactly what they were doing there. Dominik looked over and saw Johnny, who was already walking towards him.

'How goes it, Domek?' he said with a broad smile. 'We've saved a place for you on one of the good chairs, the ones with the cushions.

The others will stab your behind, they're like torture instruments.' He pointed to a group of chairs at the back of the room.

Dominik found himself desperate not to sit near anyone he knew, but the offer had been made, so he and Lolek joined the group. At least he would be sitting up the back, out of sight. A man in a military uniform called for attention, and everyone took their seats.

'My name is Major Tadeusz Marenski,' he said. He tipped his hat to the crowd. 'Germany and Russia have made a pact to divide up Poland. They won't admit it, but we know they have.' Mutters rippled through the crowd. Dominik had heard the same reports: Mr Molotov and Mr Ribbentrop had met earlier in the week. He imagined the two old enemies carving up Poland between them over a meal of bratwurst and borscht, Germany claiming the west, of which Krakow was the jewel, and Russia taking the east.

'What are we going to do about it?' someone called from the crowd.

More mutters rose up. Dominik felt a black anxiety settle inside him; he did not want to be there. He leaned across his chair and spoke to Lolek. 'What is this meeting about? Do you think we can leave soon?' He glanced at his watch, trying to appear casual. 'I have bacteria I'd like to check on.'

Lolek shrugged. 'I think we might be here a while, Dominik.'

Dominik looked around the crowd. Some of the older men wore their uniforms from the Soviet War of 1919. These threadbare clothes looked absurd, with riding jodhpurs instead of trousers; they had been made for a cavalry war, not one with tanks. A maudlin dustiness seemed to violate the clothes – and their owners. Dominik looked away, feeling pity for them.

The major addressed the crowd again. 'We'd like every man, sixteen to forty-five, to report for training. We have officers at the front of this room, reservists, who will sign you up. You will be given a uniform and instruction. Compulsory training will take place this Tuesday at the fields along Kolna Road. All must report at eight o'clock.'

A frenzy of discussion exploded.

'Are we not being too rash?' Dominik said to Johnny. He attempted a light-hearted chuckle but couldn't quite manage it, coming out with more of a choke. 'If we begin to arm, will it not encourage an attack? Should we not keep our heads down, go about our business? Anyway, we are but doctors and farmers – what do we know of war? Shouldn't the army step in?'

'What army?' Johnny replied.

Dominik swallowed and realised the implication. *They* were the army, the doctors and the farmers. Krakow's own men would be defending the town.

A young man from the row in front had already stood up. He moved to the front to sign up for the training.

'Who else will come forward to defend Poland?' Major Marenski asked the crowd.

A man in a blue shirt stood up. 'I will!'

'Me too,' said another, moving to the front.

Soon, choruses of 'I will' and 'Yes, me' and 'Long live Poland' echoed about the room. Almost every man in the hall had risen to their feet and begun lining up. Dominik had no choice but to follow. He joined one of the lines, with Johnny standing behind him.

'Do we all need to register, or can we just leave?' Dominik asked him.

'We can't leave,' Johnny replied, chuckling. 'Everyone's already seen us.'

Dread came over him, like a cloud. The humidity of the day had combined with the sweat of the men inside, creating a sweltering environment with no relief. A foul breath emanated from the man in front of them, and he lifted his arm to expose a sweaty armpit. Dominik was no stranger to body odour, but today he smelled every drop of his fellow man, every unwashed groin, every day-old breath.

Marek Nowakowski, a young intern from the hospital, stood behind Johnny in the line. 'Will the Germans invade, Johnny?' he asked.

'Yes, young man,' Johnny replied, lighting a cigarette. 'Didn't you hear? Hitler thinks we're vermin.' He turned to Dominik. 'Do we have any great fighters here?'

Dominik shrugged. 'Paweł Kamiński had a fight with his harvester,' he replied. 'Lost his arm.' Johnny raised an eyebrow and exhaled smoke out the side of his mouth.

'Poland has excellent pilots,' Marek remarked.

'True!' Johnny said. 'Too bad we don't have any planes.'

Another man in line, the one in the blue shirt, turned and joined their conversation. 'The English will come, and the French,' he said.

'We don't need their help,' Marek declared.

'We do,' Dominik said.

The men nodded and didn't reply. It was the reaction Dominik expected to such a comment. He garnered great respect from the town as a physician, he saved lives and destroyed illnesses, but when it came to swinging a bayonet, no one looked to him for guidance.

As the meeting broke up, people gravitated towards the shepherds from the highlands who'd come down from their flocks, to ask them for advice about how to fight. In truth, osteoarthritis burdened every shoulder, knee and hip of those gnarled men, and few knew which end of a rifle was the working one. Dominik had treated many of them for ruptured cruciate ligaments, haemorrhoids from overexertion, chilblains from sleeping in freezing paddocks and the many other chronic afflictions borne from a life spent in manual labour. These men stood in far worse shape than Dominik and most of the other men of the professional classes, who worked behind a desk and took exercise for leisure, not their livelihood.

Still, for the sheer size of them, no comparison existed in that hall. This suited Dominik just fine. He desired no such attention.

They reached the front of the line. The major greeted them.

'Where will you send us?' Johnny asked Marenski, shaking his hand.

'You will defend the town, and perform other duties,' he replied.

'Will there be reinforcements?' Dominik asked.

'Of course,' the military man scoffed. 'Definitely.' Though he didn't say from where.

It was Dominik's turn. A bespectacled man dressed in uniform sat behind a table. He smiled at Dominik and asked him his name.

'Karski, Dominik. Doctor,' he said.

'Middle name?'

Dominik adjusted his glasses. 'It's Henryk. I am a surgeon, sir. Perhaps I would serve the commonwealth better that way?'

'That's one less man on the front line' was the bespectacled soldier's reply.

'Of course. But I have extensive experience with infection. In the field, your biggest problem is not the bullet wound but the microbes that make it their home. You may have read my paper on this topic?'

The bespectacled man looked at him. 'I have not. Have you served in the army before?'

'I have.' Dominik spoke in a low voice and gazed at the floor. He dreaded the questions that would be asked next, what information he'd have to turn over.

'Where did you serve, Mr Karski?'

Dominik sighed. 'I fought in the Battle of Lemberg, on the Polish side.'

'Good. And did you serve in the Great War, Dr Karski?'

Dominik hesitated, looking around.

'Doctor, sir?'

'Sorry, what was the question?'

'Where did you serve in the Great War?'

Dominik looked towards the door, then spoke. 'I fought for Austria–Hungary.' He cleared his throat. 'Polish Auxiliary Corps. I fought in Russia, Italy, Battle of Łowczówek.'

Major Marenski moved closer. 'You fought at Łowczówek? I did too!' he said, smiling. 'Which division?'

'Fifth Battalion.' Dominik closed his eyes. He had no idea what this man knew.

'Ah. I served in the First. What is your name?'

Dominik didn't answer; he didn't need to. The bespectacled military clerk did it for him. 'This is Dominik Karski, sir.'

The older soldier turned slowly to Dominik and, seeing the expression on his face, Dominik's heart sank. 'You are Dominik Karski? They called you the Butcher of Lwów. Is this you?'

'I'm sure there are many men called Dominik Karski in Poland.' Dominik shrugged. 'I'm certain several served in the army.'

'True. But there's only one Dominik Karski who won the Vertuti Militari. Is this you, sir?'

He had no choice but to confirm it, for it was true. 'Yes.'

Major Marenski laughed. 'See here, Corporal,' he said to the clerk, 'we stand before a legend.' The man looked at Dominik admiringly.

'That was a long time ago,' Dominik said.

The major had already moved to the front of the room. 'Attention, everyone!' he called out. 'Who has heard of the Vertuti Militari?'

The crowd turned to him, a few men nodding; others shrugged.

He smiled broadly. 'It's a military honour. It's as significant as the Order of the Red Banner, or the Iron Cross, but more prestigious because it's Polish. The Vertuti Militari is rare too, given only for extraordinary acts of bravery. I only know of a handful of these medals given for the entire eastern front during the whole of the

Great War. One of those men? His actions caused the fall of Russia. Have no fear, gentleman, your city is safe, for this Vertuti Militari stands among you.'

A wave of excitement rippled through the crowd. Everyone looked around to mark their candidate for the man who might be the saviour of the city. Many turned their heads to the highland farmers, now assembled in a group at the side of the room. A giant shepherd, perhaps seven foot tall and half as wide, received most of the attention from the crowd. He shook his head. 'Not me,' he said with a laugh.

The major laughed too. 'You all look the wrong way, men. The one you seek is right here in front of you. Behold, Major Dominik Karski, the Vertuti Militari.'

Mutters and gasps coursed through the hall. Dominik swallowed as a cheer went up and applause followed. People threw their hands out for Dominik to shake.

'Dr Karski, we had no idea!' Marek the intern said. 'Mr Hitler had better watch out!'

'I wish you hadn't said anything,' he said to the major. He looked out the window and wanted to defenestrate himself. Questions came his way.

'So what should we do, Dr Karski?' Marek asked.

'Yes, how will we defeat the Germans?' the man in the blue shirt said.

The major stepped in, to Dominik's relief. 'Enough of that now, give the man a break. All volunteers are to report for training, Tuesday at eight.'

Dominik headed for the way out, his heart thumping. Johnny caught him as he reached the door. 'You sly fox, Domek. You kept that quiet.'

'Yes, well.' Dominik couldn't look Johnny in the eye. Johnny smiled at him and Dominik said nothing.

'I always knew you were hiding something,' Johnny said. Dominik swallowed again. 'Poland couldn't be in better hands,' he added.

Dominik quickly made his exit. That night he fixed himself a simple dinner. One good thing about Marie being gone was that he no longer had to maintain appearances. He still did everything as before, in case some neighbour knocked on the door for medical advice, but now at least he could let his mind wander. He finished his supper, washed the dishes and put them away and retired to his bedroom. He sat at his desk and pored over the books *The Three Kingdoms of Poland*, the *Annals of Military History*, and every military record he'd found in the library. He read them all, not sleeping but reading, until his eyes felt gritty and numb, and it hurt to close them, even to blink. He read of every battle Dominik Karski fought in, every exploit of the Fifth Battalion, every action that he was supposed to have contributed to.

In the morning, Dominik sought out Lolek at his apartment. Lolek showed him to the kitchen. 'Would you like some tea? Or coffee, maybe? You look terrible.'

'No, thank you,' Dominik replied.

Lolek filled the kettle anyway. 'What is it that you want, Dominik?'

'False papers. Two sets. One for me, one for Marie. To get us out of Poland.'

Lolek put down the kettle and laughed. 'May I ask why?'

'You already know. War is coming. I can't protect my daughter anymore. I want us to leave.'

'Where do you want to go?'

'Anywhere you like.' Dominik shrugged. 'Not Europe. Somewhere far away.' He gave a nod. 'The furthest place from here you could imagine.'

'You want me to organise fake passports for you?' Lolek said. 'What makes you think I know how to do this?' He prepared two coffees in the Turkish style and gave one to Dominik.

Dominik sipped the bitter substance and winced.

'Would you like some sugar?' Lolek offered him the bowl.

Dominik shook his head. 'I never have sugar.'

'This does not surprise me.' Lolek served two spoons' worth into his own cup.

'Did you put that Jewish boy in a Catholic orphanage?'

Lolek put down his cup. His sweet face looked pained.

'Relax, son. I'm not here to turn you in. I want to employ your services. All this time I thought you were a choirboy. Now I see you are a rebel.' Lolek's old-soul face took on a different shape then; a knowing look danced across it, as though he'd conversed with Jesus and Beelzebub and felt intimidated by neither. 'You put that boy in the orphanage. You must know things – people.'

Lolek nodded. 'I do know someone who could probably help you. But I warn you, he is unscrupulous.'

'Unscrupulous is exactly what I'm looking for.'

'It will cost a lot of money.' Lolek's voice rose in warning.

'That won't be a problem.'

'What of Ben?' he asked, sipping his coffee. 'Will he go with you?'

Dominik looked out the window. Ben was a lovely man. But a third person would only slow them down. 'My priority is my daughter's safety. I can't worry about anyone else, I'm sorry. Two passports only.'

'Marie will never leave without her husband, you know.'

'She will. When I order her to.'

'She is not a child anymore, Dominik.'

'Indeed. But I will prevail upon the young man. I'll explain to him that it's safer for Marie this way. Ben will agree, and together we'll convince her to leave without him.'

'I suppose he won't be able to argue with that.'

Dominik drained his coffee cup and stood to leave.

'I admit I helped put Daniel Blumfeld in the orphanage,' Lolek said. 'I changed his name.' Dominik turned back to look at him. The young man collected the coffee cups and stood to wash them in the sink. The soap scent wafted towards Dominik from a breeze through the open window. It was the same soap Dominik had used in another lifetime, an old-fashioned scent. 'His mother made me promise to look after him. I put him in a Catholic home because he's in danger. It's not his own people that I fear. It's who's coming next.'

Dominik nodded.

Lolek turned to face him and leaned on the sink. 'Interesting language, German. Do you speak it?'

'Yes.'

'How would you translate *vernichtung*?'

Dominik scratched his head. 'Vernichtung . . . it means destruction, or annihilation.'

'Very good. Tell me, how would you translate this: *die Vernichtung der jüdischen Rasse in Europa.*'

Dominik swallowed. The translation came to him, yet he stammered as the words left his mouth. 'The annihilation of the Jewish race in Europe.'

'Hitler addressed his parliament in January of this year,' Lolek said. 'That's exactly what he said to his ministers and politicians. Did you know this?'

Dominik shook his head.

'Most people don't. It wasn't in the Polish newspapers. I have the luxury of reading Hitler's speeches in his mother tongue, however, for we get German-language periodicals at the library. You have to smile at the word choice, *annihilation*. For such an orderly people, the Germans do love their Gothic excess.'

Dominik sat back down. 'Why wasn't it in the papers?'

'Because nobody wants to believe it might happen.'

Dominik searched for a rationalisation. 'Perhaps with good reason. That man is a dimwit and a demagogue. He can wax lyrical all he wants about annihilating a people, but he has not the wherewithal to actually carry it out.'

'But I think on some level you already know this to be possible. Why were you so opposed to Marie becoming Jewish, marrying a Jewish man?'

Dominik shrugged. 'Because her life would always fare worse. She would enjoy acceptance by neither culture.'

'Yes,' Lolek replied, 'but you saw a darker reason too. I agree with you about Hitler's inadequacy for carrying out *vernichtung*. Ineptness seems to define him, if you ask me. He shouts well, but plans badly. But he has the most efficient bureaucracy in the world under him, and they all want to impress him. And this is what scares me. They will find a way to carry out his wishes. People are shaking their heads in the street, Jews and Catholics alike, saying it won't happen, surely not. They think when Hitler gets here, he's going to ban our Jews from the swimming pools, make them wear the Star of David, take their civil service jobs and the like, the same harassment our brothers in the faith have suffered for centuries. He will do all that. And then war will create a vortex where anything goes. Their animal instincts will break forth from their uniformed restraints. It will be a pornographic display.' Lolek stepped away from the sink to dry his hands, then he turned to Dominik. 'Mark my words. When the Germans get here, they will enact *vernichtung*. When it comes to our Jewish people, the Germans will put on a circus to shock Satan himself.'

Dominik watched the young man's face, which did not change.

'An interesting work, the Talmud,' Lolek said then, his face finally brightening. 'I recall one quote I enjoyed; forgive me if I paraphrase: *Do not be daunted by the enormity of the world's grief.*

320

Do justly now. Love and show mercy, now. You are not obligated to complete the work, but neither are you free to abandon it.' He tossed the tea towel he'd been using to wipe the cups onto his shoulder. 'If you can spare getting your daughter's husband out as well, I beg you to do it.'

The words haunted Dominik as he walked home. The sun shone softly and warmed his shoulders, so different to the sweltering conditions of yesterday. He walked through Kazimierz, the neighbourhood of his own daughter, of his daughter's husband. He said good morning to Rabbi Katz; the old man shook his hand. Once home he telephoned Lolek and told him to add a third passport to his order, for his son-in-law.

33
GREATER LOVE HATH
NO MAN

On Tuesday, Dominik went to the sports field where he and four hundred other Krakow civilians were to receive instruction on how to fight a war. He joined his assigned group and a soldier called Sergeant Maczko gave them uniforms and showed them how to pack a rucksack and load a gun. When it came to the gun loading, Sergeant Maczko held up his rifle and began pointing out its parts: the barrel, the trigger, the chamber. He went to load it, but then said, 'Wait. Major Karski, would you do the honours?'

Everyone turned to Dominik. He bristled at the military title. He had told them to call him Doctor, as usual – even Dominik would do – but no one had listened, insisting on calling him Major, the soldierly label that sounded ridiculous attached to his name. Their particular group numbered around twenty; he knew all of them and they knew him. He'd treated seven of them for infections, and one for a bowel obstruction. He'd sutured the heads, arms and legs of a least five of them, and delivered four of their wives' babies, as far as he could remember. The last man in the group he didn't technically know as a patient, though he had put stitches in his head: that man was Johnny.

The twenty Krakow locals all looked at Dominik and waited. He could feel Johnny smiling at him encouragingly. 'I've not loaded a rifle in twenty years,' Dominik said to the young sergeant. 'I've never even seen a gun like that before.' He motioned to the long arm, which lay comfortably in the young officer's elbow as he nursed it like a baby.

'Don't worry, Major Karski, sir,' the sergeant replied in a reassuring tone. 'This rifle is almost exactly the same as your service rifles in the Great War! It is only a touch shorter – you won't even notice the difference.' The young soldier laughed, and others joined in. Sergeant Maczko stood tall and slight, like a beanpole, and when God gave out chins, he seemed to have blessed the young soldier with none, giving him a gormless look. Considering he held a weapon in his hand, the young man's seeming foolishness served to terrify Dominik even more than if he'd been a strapping fascist ordering everyone around.

Everyone looked at Dominik again. He felt the weight of expectation from every pair of eyes, especially from every citizen of Krakow who now knew of his military prowess. If he embarrassed himself this morning, news of his failure would spread through the sports field, the hospital, the city, before the day ended.

He had no choice but to take the rifle and attempt to load it. He'd read of this particular rifle, the standard Polish army service gun, modelled on a German one with similar parts, including the directions on how to load it and how to shoot it. He'd even given himself a little exam on it at about two that morning, though he'd never actually held a gun in his hand. Holding one now, the weight of it shocked him; it felt heavier and clunkier than he'd imagined. Sergeant Maczko offered him five rounds of ammunition. Dominik opened the magazine at the top of the rifle and placed the bullets in the slots, quietly double-checking they were facing the right way. Once finished, he closed the magazine and turned the bolt to load the first round into the chamber. 'Magazines', 'bolts', 'rounds' – words that had never entered his head until last night. He drew in a breath and turned to the officer, ready to be laughed at for doing something wrong.

'Very good, Major Karski, sir. Like you loaded a rifle only yesterday.' The beanpole sergeant smiled at him and took the rifle.

'Thank you,' Dominik replied, trying not to exhale too loudly and let his relief show.

'Care to take a shot?' the young officer asked then, pointing towards a target that stood at the other end of the field, perhaps a hundred yards away.

Dominik shook his head. 'Not necessary, thank you.'

'Yes, please, sir. Show us how it's done.' Dominik looked at the young man's smiling face and the beaming faces of his patients and colleagues and wanted to run away. He took back the rifle. They'd laid a wooden square low to the grass for the shooter to fire from.

Holding the rifle, Dominik lay his torso on the wood. The grass beneath the rest of him felt wet with the morning dew and the moisture soaked two circles into his knees. He stared at the target in the distance and lined up the rifle, tucking the butt into the section of chest next to his right armpit, as he had read to do, and laying the barrel on the wooden square.

The group of men went quiet. Dominik looked at the grass ahead of him and watched a patch of wildflowers sway in the morning breeze. He shifted the rifle slightly; the wind, slight though it was, would move the bullet. He trained his eyes on the head of the target in the distance. The men had whispered that morning they would be shooting at paintings of Hitler, but the Polish army would have needed confidence and organisation to put up such pictures. Instead, they'd placed hurriedly assembled outlines of a human figure, only a tracing of the head and shoulders.

What retribution would come his way if he was to miss this shot? They would find him out, that was what. What harm would Marie suffer, what would happen to his patients? He would lose his house, his assets. Prison would be a luxury; he would likely be lynched. The missed shot would reveal him to the world. With one more deep breath, he lined the rifle up and pulled the trigger.

The bullet exited the barrel and shot into the field. A thunderous crack rang out and the butt of the rifle smacked back into his body with flesh-bruising recoil, the force of it almost knocking him off the square; no manual had told him about that part. He had to stifle a gasp at the violence of it, hoping no one noticed. No one was looking at him. Everyone was watching the target, one hundred metres away, as the bullet sped towards it. It took a split second to get there, which felt like an eternity to Dominik. When it finally came to a stop, Dominik could barely look, but when he did, he saw the bullet had hit the board on which the target lay. He couldn't tell where exactly from that distance, but he could confirm the bullet had at least connected with the board; it hadn't veered off into the wild fields behind.

The crowd of men responded with polite applause and the amused surprise of seeing Dominik in a different light – the polite, reticent doctor now utilising a tool built for ripping through flesh, the thing that usually, in his other life, he repaired.

'You may go again, sir,' Sergeant Maczko said.

Dominik stood and offered him the rifle. 'One is enough for me. I should give someone else a turn.'

'Nonsense,' the young man said. 'We have plenty of rounds for everybody.' He waved towards a crate of ammunition to his left.

Dominik wanted to sigh. 'How many rounds should I shoot, then?'

'Empty the magazine, sir,' the sergeant said, a broad, encouraging smile blessing his face.

Dominik inhaled and tried not to appear nervous. The first shot had hit the board, but repeating that feat, not once but another four times, seemed nigh on impossible.

He lay back down on the wooden square and flicked the bolt to load the next round into the chamber. The officer shushed the crowd as he lined up the rifle, adjusting the position of the butt slightly to accommodate the recoil; he'd sat it a little too much towards the armpit last time. He pulled the trigger and the bullet exploded from the barrel. The metal shell that surrounded the bullet flicked free from the chamber, escaping out the side of the rifle and glinting in the sunlight as it spun outwards, coming to rest on the grass beside him. He hadn't expected that; it must have happened on the previous shot, too. Again, none of the manuals had mentioned this part.

He loaded the chamber once more with the bolt, not rushing but not delaying either. He felt accustomed to it now. All the variables of wind, recoil and force had shown themselves and there was nothing more to correct or amend so he might as well get on with it. He fired the rifle again, then a further two times, loading and shooting in quick succession.

Another round of polite applause emanated from the crowd once he'd finished. They reacted less enthusiastically than before, seeming shocked at the speed with which he cocked, shot, reloaded, again and again, without flinching. To him it was his usual reversion to the automatic mode. Once he felt he'd mastered something, he moved forward without wasting a second on the superfluous tasks of hesitation or thinking. To the other men, it probably seemed something colder, a ferocious man who'd concealed his errant behaviours behind a facade of health care now reverting to his natural state of violence. He wondered which judgement he preferred them to make; probably for the purposes of this exercise, the latter. It bode well for them to think of him as a killer.

'Shall we check the board?' Sergeant Maczko asked the men. Before Dominik could argue, the group set off down the field to examine the target.

Dominik had no choice but to follow them. As he did, he replayed the shots in his mind, making an estimation of how close he might have come to hitting the target. Johnny fell back to walk alongside him, saying nothing, as though in quiet solidarity. Dominik hoped he'd at least come close; the young officer had commanded him to hit the head and he'd aimed for it, but somewhere inside the line of the body would be a respectable result that no one could criticise him for.

Up ahead, some of the men gasped and pointed, and as they came to a stop at the target Dominik saw why. He had hit the target's neck five times. He felt a little disappointed not to have hit the head, but then Sergeant Maczko bent down and spread a tape measure across the bullet holes.

'My goodness!' he exclaimed. 'All the shots are within sixty millimetres of each other!'

'I am out of practice. I did not hit the head.'

'Yes, but the way they are all so close together, that's even more important! You hit the same mark again and again. Those are the shots of a marksman.'

Dominik felt his back being patted and his arms slapped by the men around him as cheers and laughter rose up from the group.

'Well done, sir!' Sergeant Maczko remarked, clapping his hands. The others joined in the applause. 'That's why they call you the Butcher of Lwów.' That wasn't why, but Dominik said nothing. Johnny winked at him and Dominik had to turn away.

He nodded to the group. He hadn't disgraced himself. After lifting the rifle and feeling its weight and bulk, he'd realised the key to operating it would come down to calm and focus. The calm he possessed in spades; he was known for not breaking a sweat, ever; he could stitch an aorta between the patient's heartbeats. His own heart pumped religiously at a resting rate of forty-two beats per minute, slow enough for him to squeeze the trigger of the rifle between beats, allowing for a stillness and hold that reduced disturbance in the bullet's trajectory to a negligible amount. The second item, focus, meant focus of the mind and the eyes, with the latter being the most important. To hit a target, you had to look at it. As simple as this sounded, it was true, and difficult for most people. He'd noticed from early in his life that he possessed excellent eyesight, above that of his peers. Of all those gifted with aim, a pair of hawk's eyes united them.

Dominik wished he could have removed his eyeglasses to take the shots. He wore them for ornamentation and camouflage, and they contained only plain glass, magnifying nothing, concealing everything – just another layer to confuse and occlude the truth for those who possessed the energy or inclination to ever raise a suspicion. No one ever did, which meant either the fake spectacles did the job, or he himself did such a good job with his other concealments that he never needed to wear glasses in the first place. He'd worn them so long, however, that to remove them now would draw attention. Had he taken them off this morning, though, he might have hit the target's head.

As the morning went on, each man had a turn with the rifle. Many knew their way around a gun, particularly the cattle and sheep farmers, but no one's shots were as close together as Dominik's. Johnny came closest; his shots all hit the target's head and neck, but not close together. As he'd promised to shout each man in the group a beer for every bullet he managed to shoot without maiming himself or others, his performance was met with much cheering and hollering. As the day wore on with none matching Dominik's feat, his name and reputation grew. At lunch, provided by the army, talk of his performance spread through the larger group. Dozens approached him as he ate his meal in the hastily constructed mess tent; they shook his hand and asked about his time in the Great War. Dominik replied patiently and politely to their inquiries, claiming he'd had some lucky shots. After lunch, he could see the men in his group regarding him differently, stealing looks at him. When the day ended, the men came up to him with pleading eyes.

'What are we going to do, Dr Karski?' they asked. They meant about the war that was coming. One of the group, the one he'd relieved of his bowel obstruction, related the odds they faced, claiming that the German army totalled about four million men. Poland had a million on a good day. Adolf Hitler had built two thousand new tanks, while Poland had two hundred, mostly tiny, machines.

Dominik gazed at the men and shuddered at the responsibility his new-found fame as a sharpshooter had brought him. The men looked to him as some sort of leader. He needed to discourage their expectations. He reassured the men that those statistics came from gossip; such lopsidedness in military matching wouldn't occur. But then Sergeant Maczko joined the group and, with the same hopeful look in his eye, assured Dominik of the truth. 'I've heard generals talking,' he said to the men, 'and they outnumber us four to one. Their tanks outnumber ours ten to one. They will slaughter us.'

Dominik scowled at the young man, first for his indiscretion in revealing misgivings about the armed forces to recruits; second, and more importantly, for dragging him further into the discussion, inducing the men to turn to Dominik even more for help. He wanted no part of this. He looked into the group of faces, his patients and colleagues, men he'd cared for and repaired, and whose children he'd delivered. As soon as Lolek's unscrupulous friend had secured the fake passports, he'd leave the country. He would never have to experience this mismatch of power between brave, young Poland and mighty, war-thirsty Germany. He would never feel the havoc wreaked, or see the river of blood that would run through Old Town, as thick as the Vistula. But these men would and, as he gazed upon their pitiable, terrified faces, he realised he needed to compose some words to reassure or at least placate them.

'Try not to worry,' he began. 'The Germans are mean and organised, yes, but we are at home. They only have their reputation on the line; they defend pride and a dream. We defend women and children, and we'll defend them to the death.' He attempted a smile, satisfied that he'd spoken enough rousing words to comfort and cheer them, and began walking to his automobile, which he'd parked in the lot behind the sports field.

Then someone grabbed his arm. 'So you are saying we will all die?' Sergeant Maczko asked. He'd caught up to him, with several others following. The young soldier's face wore a look of bald fear. Dominik observed the others who had joined him; they wore similar expressions. A group of grown men simultaneously contemplating the end of their lives. Dominik would leave Poland soon, he reminded himself.

'Yes, we will all die,' he said.

'What can we do?' another man asked. The faces all looked to him again, hopeful and terrified.

Dominik realised with disappointment that he needed to say more. He composed some more phrases and spoke them. 'There is nothing to do except fight back,' he said. 'Not because we will win – we won't. But we must fight, because we are defending our homes, protecting our people, and we have no other choice. There will always be darkness in this world, no matter what we do. But there will also always be light. The game is to always keep slightly more light than dark, to tip the balance towards it. So we will stay and fight, even though we may lose. And the world will be that little bit brighter because of what we did. No one grand will remember our names, no one outside Poland will know how we acted. But we will know. And our families will know. The people that really matter will know. They'll know that when it came down to it, we didn't run. We picked up a weapon, we stood in the tank's path, and we said no.'

He had reached the end of his words. The men nodded solemnly and said nothing more. Johnny smiled through misted eyes, and Dominik tipped his head in anguish. Not only had he made a speech, he believed what he'd said. He continued walking to his car, wishing he'd kept his mouth shut.

Johnny visited Dominik the next morning. Dominik showed him inside and boiled water for tea. He prepared a plate of poppy seed cake, Johnny's preferred choice from Dominik's repertoire of sweets, and studied his friend's face. 'There's something different about you,' he said.

'I'm not hungover,' Johnny replied. 'I haven't had a drink in a month.'

'I'm pleased for you, Johnny,' Dominik said. 'You look well.' He spoke the truth; Johnny had never appeared better. He'd filled out some and he smiled more, too – not the maniacal joking grins he'd had permanently plastered on his face before, but softer, quieter smiles that reached his eyes too, expressions of genuine contentment.

'It's a dreadful state of affairs, all right,' Johnny said. 'I blame you, of course.'

Dominik scowled. 'What did I do?'

Johnny smiled, another genuine one. 'When I began here in Krakow, I was a lost man. I didn't want to go on living. But then you invited me to your house and showed me your splendid home and family. It filled me with warmth, and I felt alive for the first time in months. I saw your lovely daughter and your wholesome home, and I remembered what it had been like, with my family. It made me feel sad, but in the best way, for I saw that other people in other houses also had the happiness I'd once possessed. I could have it again. So I blame you for all of this, Domek. If I hadn't smelled that buttery sausage, eaten those lovely sweet jams of yours, I would still have my lips wrapped around a bottle. If it weren't for you and your house reeking with such goddamned felicity, I'd probably be dead by now.'

Johnny looked at Dominik with earnest eyes, an expression so pleasant and hopeful it startled him. For an absurd moment, he considered confessing to Johnny, telling him everything. How nice it would be to show himself to someone, just once. But then he turned his gaze away and busied himself with preparing the tea things, hoping the moment would pass, which it soon did. He sighed with relief. He saw how foolish it would have been to reveal himself, and thanked God he'd had the sense to hold his ridiculous tongue.

He felt doubly glad when he discovered that Johnny had news of his own. 'My father has found me a war job, old chap,' he said. 'Looks like I won't be fighting with you here. I'm to travel up north. It's a desk job – I'll be taking notes for some fat old general. I'm terribly sad to be missing all the fun.'

The kettle boiled. 'Oh.' Dominik poured the hot water, and tried in vain to think of something more to say. Finally he sighed, reminding himself that he was pleased for his friend, happy he'd be removed from danger. 'Taking notes, you say? Do they know you can't use a typewriter? Perhaps take Matron Skorupska with you. She likes doing your paperwork.'

'Already asked her,' Johnny shot back, smiling. 'She's packing her bags now.'

Dominik almost smiled himself, then he scratched his head. 'Wait. Which side shall you fight for?'

Johnny seemed to read his mind. 'The Nazis will have to do without my sharpshooting. I shall be fighting for Poland. My father is a raving Hitlerite, yes, but a Pole first. He only likes the Nazis when they stay in their own country. I look forward to boring you with numerous letters about my adventures.'

Dominik nodded. 'When do you leave?'

'A fortnight or so. September fourteenth.'

The conversation continued, about where exactly in the north Johnny was going, about how long they thought the war would go on for. Dominik found himself nodding but not really listening, trying to appear happy for his friend and not letting him see how lonely he already felt. He wondered if this was the last time he would ever see him; it probably was. Finally, when the teapot was empty and the cake was eaten, it was time for Johnny to depart. He drained his cup and stood; there was no reason left for him to stay. He collected his coat and Dominik showed him out.

Johnny reached the door, but stopped and stood there.

'Did you forget something?' Dominik asked.

Johnny nodded. 'I'm going to give you a hug, old chap.'

'Oh. No, thank you,' Dominik replied, as politely but forcefully as possible.

'It's not an offer,' Johnny said, 'it's a demand. I am going to die, and so are you. Well, perhaps I won't, now I'm working for Colonel Fatso, four hundred kilometres behind the front lines. But you will almost definitely bite it. Hitler will set up shop in Krakow, you watch. Such a pretty town, he won't be able to help himself.'

He leaned in and, before Dominik could protest further, they were embracing. 'Take care of yourself, my friend,' Johnny said into his ear. 'Try not to die, actually. If you can manage it.'

Dominik swallowed and commanded his voice not to break. 'I will do my best. The same to you.'

The hug ended, and Johnny disappeared, walking into the sun.

Lolek telephoned Dominik that evening, sounding panicked. 'I can only get two passports.'

Dominik listened to him breathing down the line and tried to comprehend the words. He'd opened a window in the heat and the sound of a fierce discussion now rose up from the street below. Men and women were digging up dirt in the little patch of park behind the house to make a bomb shelter; the council had begun ordering people to do so. Two of the men were arguing because one wanted to dig wider, the other deeper. An anxious back and forth ensued, until one of the women told them to be quiet and do both. 'I don't understand,' Dominik replied. 'I have the money for three passports.'

'Yes, but the man who works at the British embassy, the one who has been securing the false documents, has run off. Someone reported him and now no one can find him. He'd already given my contact two blank passports, but that's it. Two is all we can get.'

Dominik did not know what to say.

'What do you want to do? Whose names shall my man put in the passports? Will it be Marie and Ben leaving, or Marie and you? Dominik? Are you there?'

'I truly don't know, Lolek.'

Lolek sighed down the telephone line. 'Would you like to know what I think?'

'Not particularly.'

'Give the passports to your daughter and son-in-law. It's the right thing to do.'

'I don't want to.'

'I know you don't.'

The digging continued outside his window. It had rained the night before and the smell of upturned soil and wet grass, rank and green, now wafted into the room. He felt the heart attack symptoms that had afflicted him a few weeks earlier returning.

'You don't understand, Lolek. A parent's duty is to protect their child. How can I do that if I'm not with her?'

'And what harm will come to her if she is made to live beside you always, an extension of you, not her own person? If you keep her a child?'

334

He recalled his daughter, with the mind of a grown woman at eight years old. He could not believe he was contemplating this. For almost eighteen years he had lived for her only. Now he was simply expected to destroy all that, to throw her into the path of every danger he had been shielding her from?

'You have done a wonderful job,' Lolek said. 'You have raised a strong and intelligent woman, full of kindness and principles. And now you must let her go. People must be free to lead their own lives, Dominik. The greatest protection you can bestow on her is to allow her to stand on her own two feet. Let her make her own mistakes. Otherwise you will shorten her stature; she will walk through life tethered to the ground, when she could stride so tall.'

Dominik grimaced. 'I need to get out of this place too, you know. I can't explain why.'

'Is it more necessary that you leave ahead of Ben, a Jewish man, whose life is at risk?'

Dominik inhaled. In war's mayhem, people would seek out difference and strike it down to save themselves. By staying, he would be discovered. His secret was too dark, too strange. He would be killed. 'Of course Ben is more at risk,' he replied brightly. 'He shall have the second passport. Please make them out to Marie and my son-in-law.' Strangely, he felt his shoulders relax once he'd said it. It was decided now; he would die, and with that came liberty.

Lolek sighed. 'Oh, Dominik. You do a good and noble thing. Thank you.'

'You're welcome,' he said. The line went quiet. 'I feel as though you might be composing some sort of speech, Lolek. Please don't quote God at me.'

'I promise I won't. But if you will permit me a small indulgence, I will paraphrase his son.'

Dominik sighed. 'Very well.'

'Greater love hath no man than he who lays down his life for another. Bless you, Dominik.'

It was only after he'd hung up that he realised. As soon as the illicit passports arrived, Marie and Ben would take the next train out of the city. By that time, Dominik would have already reported to his regiment. Their paths would not cross. He would never see his daughter again.

34
THE PHOTOGRAPH

While Dominik attended the sports field with the other military-aged men of Krakow, Marie waited for Ben to leave for work. She then packed a suitcase and left him a note, before boarding the nine o'clock train to Lwów. Her husband would shout and curse when he found out she'd left, and then he'd shrug, knowing by now what his wife was like. She'd be back before long, in any case. Determination gripped her.

The train took eight hours, running due east. She passed the time in agitated reverie, trying to read a pulpy novel someone had left on the seat beside her, but finding herself unable to focus. She settled for staring out the window and shifting in her seat, and was thankful to finally arrive in Lwów, after what seemed like double the time. As the train pulled into the main station and she alighted, a sight on the opposite platform disturbed her: people rushing to board another train set for departure from the city. People always hurried to catch a train, but it was the number of them that caught her eye: hundreds, possibly thousands of people scurrying forward at once to board this locomotive. She figured it seated maybe six hundred, so there were far more people trying to get on than it had room for. They were dressed in travelling clothes, and held numerous suitcases under their arms. The sight alarmed her immensely. Why did so many hurry to leave the city; what news had they heard? She did not feel inclined to hang around to find out, and she vowed to make her time in Lwów as brief as possible.

She exited the station to discover a city even damper than Krakow. A warm mist hung in the air as she walked down the road to the town centre, making her top lip, her neck, everything, feel moist. Marie held two addresses in her hand, both given to her by Dr Wolanski. The first was the address of the pharmacy where her father had worked, the second a house Dominik may have lived in.

She walked to the pharmacy first, going straight there from the train station, cradling a map of Lwów in one hand. When she arrived, an apothecary indeed stood on the site, but it did not bear the name Karski. Instead, it was called the Golden Bear. She walked inside and asked the shophand if he knew about Karski's pharmacy. The young man shook his head and offered to ask his boss. He disappeared out the back and returned with an older man. She repeated her inquiry to him: was this the apothecary once called Karski's? It was, he said, but he did not know those people. He seemed to study Marie; she caught him looking at her and he tore his gaze away quickly. 'What is your name, Miss?' he asked.

'Marie Rosen,' she said. 'Mrs.'

'I see.' He appeared to study her again. Then a customer entered, asking for a cough tonic, and the man dismissed her. 'I don't know anything about the Karskis,' he said, then wished her good day.

Marie stepped out of the shop and grimaced as the blazing afternoon sun hit her eyes. She tipped her hat down to shade her face, her fingers sweating in her gloves. She felt lethargic and deflated; the pharmacy had been her best option. She still had the other address to try, though it was a tenuous thread to follow, far weaker than the first. Visiting an apartment block and asking random people if they knew of someone who had lived in the city almost two decades earlier? Aware she likely proceeded on a fool's errand, she unfolded her map and headed to the apartment block.

She followed the map and arrived at a decrepit courtyard. A tenement building surrounded it on all sides. The entire apartment block possessed a decaying air, with a sorrowful fawn paint peeling off the double-brick walls, and faded iron latticework leaning along its balconies. Perhaps a former inhabitant had possessed a green thumb, or perhaps it was a current resident who'd died. Either way, the person who'd looked after the greenery had neglected their post, as the plants sat snarled and desiccated in cracked pots, reduced to dry sticks and dust.

She began with apartment 1A, knocking on the door. A child answered.

'Good day, may I speak to one of your parents?' Marie said. The girl of about five stared at her. She turned and shouted down the hall in a language Marie faintly recognised but didn't understand. Marie spoke Polish, French, German and now some Yiddish; whatever tongue the child spoke, it was not on that list.

A woman came to the door, speaking in the same language as the girl. Marie could tell from the woman's pose, intonation and the few similarities to her own language that she said something like 'Yes, what do you want?'

Marie spoke slowly, in Polish. 'Do . . . you . . . know . . . Dominik Karski?'

The woman stared at her blankly and Marie decided she had not understood her. She was about to attempt sign language when the woman replied.

'Please, come inside!' the woman said in accented Polish. Marie's heart leapt. She showed Marie to the kitchen and made her sit. She poured Marie a vodka and one for herself, chinked her glass with Marie's and sat. Marie didn't want to appear rude, so she downed the vodka, fire burning in her throat. She felt light-headed and nauseous. The woman offered her cake next, some sort of raisin loaf, which Marie accepted gladly, if for nothing more than to soak up the alcohol that now sloshed in her stomach. The telephone rang and the woman excused herself.

The little girl held a doll, which she introduced to Marie, speaking in the same mildly familiar Slavic babble that Marie supposed was Ukrainian, the second language spoken in that city, and a distant relative of her own mother tongue. The vodka coursed through Marie; she felt a pleasant warmth as she sank back on the chair, listening to the woman speak on the telephone, hearing mostly a cacophony of sounds, but understanding a word here and there. She allowed herself to anticipate what the woman might say about her father.

The woman hung up the telephone and returned to the kitchen. 'Now. Please tell me the name once more,' she said to Marie.

'Dominik Karski,' Marie repeated.

The woman shook her head. 'Never heard of him.'

Marie at first considered this to be a joke, but no, she was assured that the woman had no knowledge whatsoever of her father. Marie thanked her and tried to excuse herself from the apartment, saying she had an appointment, and was finally permitted to leave once she had accepted another shot of vodka, eaten more cake and helped stage a wedding between the little girl's doll and a teddy bear. Stepping out of the apartment into the sweaty summer air, she felt a little woozy.

Marie knocked on 1B and received a similar reception from another young family who demanded with joy that she come inside. Marie learned her lesson, accepting only one shot of vodka this time, drinking it slowly, while trying to ascertain as quickly as possible, without seeming rude, if the family knew Dominik Karski. They had never heard of him either. She knocked on the doors of the rest of the first floor, 1C through to 1G, and received the same reception within the two doors that opened: young Ukrainians with vodka, cake, never-ending smiles and absolutely no knowledge of Dominik Karski.

In 2B she experienced a minor victory, a woman who spoke native Polish. She invited Marie inside and, after the requisite vodka was politely proffered and reluctantly but dutifully consumed, she told Marie a little history of the building. Marie grew excited and asked if she knew Dominik Karski. The woman shook her head. She'd never heard that name, but had only moved in five years ago.

Marie slumped, disappointed, but at least now she knew what to look for: someone older who'd lived in the tenement for many years, since the Great War at least. She thanked the woman and continued knocking. The rest of the second floor either weren't home or delivered the same result as before. She reached the third and final floor, burping, and realised she was drunk. She walked along the verandah and reminded herself not to topple over it. Only two apartments here even answered her knocking, both with the same result. No Dominik Karski.

Marie drew conclusions about the stupidity of her mission. What else did her plan involve – knocking on every door in Lwów? Her father's dim-witted colleague, Dr Wolanski, had furnished her with an address for a pharmacy and a tenement building. That was the length and depth of his guidance. She'd travelled eight hours by train on the dubious clues of this cunning and pompous man. No one knew of Dominik Karski in that building; he had likely never lived there or anywhere in the vicinity. All Marie would return to Krakow with was an enlarged liver.

She checked her watch. Her drunken state made her vision exceedingly blurry. After peering at it through just one eye, she managed to ascertain that the hands read a quarter past seven. A night train was departing at eight, which would return her to Krakow in the early hours. If she hurried, she'd make it. Earlier, as she'd knocked on the door of one of the tenant families, she'd found them packing their belongings, stuffing clothes into suitcases, but also candlesticks and photographs, as though they were leaving for some time. It had reminded her uncomfortably of the scene she'd witnessed at the station earlier. Would she encounter a similar scene tonight when she arrived at the station? Would a conductor bar her from boarding an already full train, trapping her in this place of hot mist and rats?

She decided not to wait to find out. As she reached the bottom of the stairs, a woman called to her from the courtyard. 'Wait!' Marie turned to find the woman from 2B walking towards her. 'I thought you were gone already,' the woman said, smiling. 'I'm glad you're still here. I know someone who might assist you with your inquiry, but she is away today. She will return tomorrow morning.'

'Thank you, but my train departs tonight. It is impossible for me to see her. I must leave now.' She started to walk away.

'Shame,' the woman from 2B replied. 'Mrs Bronowska tells many stories from the old days. She's lived here thirty years.'

Marie stopped and checked her watch; the hands now read twenty minutes past seven. She imagined the lines of people already forming on the platform. If she wanted to stand even a chance of boarding, she needed to leave now. 'Tell me, please. Why were so many people at the station earlier, rushing to board the train?'

'They want to leave the city,' the woman from 2B said. 'They think war is coming.'

Marie swallowed. 'When? Tomorrow?'

'Maybe. Perhaps a week from now, perhaps two. This city is a sitting duck. It will receive an attack from both sides. Between them, they will raze it.'

Marie felt like laughing in her drunken state. 'Why don't you leave?'

The woman smiled. 'I don't believe them. Besides, hell will freeze over before I pack up my apartment. I hate moving.'

Marie walked back into the courtyard. The smell of onion and potato wafted under her nose and she could hear pots and pans clanging; the Ukrainians were preparing their suppers. The vodka imbibing seemed to have continued also; she could hear singing too. A child laughed and another cried. She looked up through the courtyard to the sky: the evening sun shone softly through the clothes that hung between the buildings. 'Very well, I shall return tomorrow.' Marie sighed.

The woman smiled. 'Come at ten. She will be back then.'

She spent the night in a hotel two blocks away. The concierge accepted her payment and asked no questions, nor for her identity documents. Marie had expected to encounter some sort of harassment, as a young woman travelling alone, definitively drunk, even though she wore a wedding ring. But the man at the counter had taken her money happily. When he gave her the key to her room, she saw that the rack hosted the keys for almost every other room in the place. She might be the only guest – tourism in Lwów didn't enjoy high demand that night. She checked into her room, wondering what consequences awaited her for staying another day in the sitting-duck city.

The next morning, woolly-headed from yesterday's vodka consumption, she took breakfast in the hotel's dining room – she was the only diner, bar one other – and walked back to the tenement. She knocked on the door of 2C at ten am sharp and received no answer. She waited fifteen minutes and knocked again. Still no answer. She wondered what time the next train to Krakow departed. She knocked on the door of 2B. 'You said your neighbour would be back by now,' she said when the woman answered.

The woman stuck out her head and peered at the closed door, as if by staring at it, it might open. It didn't. She turned back to Marie and shrugged. 'Perhaps she is not coming back today.'

343

Marie widened her eyes. 'But you said she'd be here! I booked a hotel room, stayed here overnight purely to see her.'

The woman from 2B pushed out her chest and gave Marie a defiant look. 'I'm sorry,' she said, 'but what do you want me to do about it?' Marie observed that the woman wore the same dress as yesterday – not completely unusual, for it was just a house dress, but her hair also looked unkempt, as though she hadn't brushed it. Had Marie taken advice from a mad person, someone not in control of their faculties? She was in the midst of cursing herself for these crimes when the woman spoke again. 'Ah, here she is now,' she said, pointing down at the landing. An old woman of perhaps seventy climbed the stairs with a suitcase. She puffed and wheezed. 'That's Mrs Bronowska.'

Marie rushed to her. 'May I help?' she said, gesturing at the suitcase.

The woman nodded, her face flushing red. 'Thank you,' she said through strained breaths. Marie took the suitcase and helped her up the final steps.

'Weronika, this young lady wants a word with you,' the woman from 2B said as they approached.

'What about?' Mrs Bronowska asked, shooting a look at Marie.

'Oh. Nothing really,' Marie replied, laughing nervously and waving her hand, trying to appear casual. 'I wanted information on a person who used to live here. Perhaps you knew them.'

Mrs Bronowska walked on and stopped at her apartment door. 'What person?'

'Dominik Karski,' Marie replied.

Mrs Bronowska turned. 'Who's asking? Why do you want to know about him?'

'I'm his daughter,' Marie replied.

Mrs Bronowska squinted and said nothing. She straightened her back and ran her eyes across Marie's face, then up and down her body. Finally her face relaxed. 'Yes, you are.'

344

Marie's heart thumped so hard in her chest she swore the old woman would hear it. 'You knew my father?'

Mrs Bronowska smiled. 'Come inside.'

The old woman showed Marie into the kitchen. As they walked down the hall, Marie stole glances into the other rooms. A simple, old-fashioned apartment presented itself, scrubbed meticulously clean. Portraits on a mantlepiece displayed the apartment's inhabitant in various poses: standing next to a horse, dressed in riding clothes, wearing her Sunday best holding a baby, posing next to a motorcar, in front of a church in a wedding dress. Mrs Bronowska opened a kitchen cupboard and looked forlorn. 'I'm so sorry,' she said, sighing, 'I've run out of vodka. Will you accept tea?'

Marie exhaled with relief and felt like hugging her. 'A shame. But no matter, tea will be lovely, thank you.' She helped her prepare it, then carried a tray to the small kitchen table, where they sat.

'I used to look after you when you were a baby,' Mrs Bronowska said.

Marie, who'd been sipping her tea, barely restrained herself from spitting it back into the cup. 'You did?'

'You lived upstairs in 3C. I met your father many times. He worked at the pharmacy when he returned from the front.'

So much new information assaulted Marie at once, she knew not which to process first. 'Karski's Pharmacy?'

Mrs Bronowska sipped her tea. 'The apothecary about two or three kilometres from here. Yes, Karski's. Your grandfather owned it.'

Mrs Bronowska took a shortbread from a little plate, then offered the plate to Marie. Marie could only refuse by shaking her head; she'd lost her appetite. Mrs Bronowska clearly felt no similar effect on her own hunger. She bit into the biscuit and chewed cheerfully. 'I am starved after my journey. I was visiting my son and his family in Żółkiew. Lovely town, but it rains too much there. Have you ever been?'

'No,' Marie said, hoping she didn't sound abrupt. 'Mr Karski, my grandfather, was a pharmacist. And my father, Dominik Karski?'

'He assisted your grandfather. Was going to become a doctor. But then he was conscripted into the military. He was a lieutenant, then a major. Quite dashing in his uniform, he was.'

Marie stifled a smile. Overwhelmed as she was, she remained in command of her senses enough to address this point. 'You are being kind, Mrs Bronowska. The idea of my father looking dashing in anything does stretch the bounds of possibility.'

'I assure you, he looked handsome in his regimentals. In his civilian clothes too.'

'Perhaps he had the charm of youth when you knew him.'

Mrs Bronowska took another biscuit and leaned back in her chair. 'Perhaps.' She took on a professorial air, pointing her biscuit to the sky, as though appraising some grand item of philosophy. 'So, your mother took you to Krakow, is that what you said? That's where you both live now?'

'My mother?' Marie sat up. It was the first time anyone had mentioned her. 'I live in Krakow; my mother does not. She may have done once, but my mother's not there now. She left when I was a baby. That's why I'm here. I'm trying to find her.'

'That doesn't sound like Helena,' Mrs Bronowska replied. Marie shivered at the sound of her mother's name. 'I wouldn't think she'd leave you. She doted on you. I don't consider myself a sentimental person, and that is my unsentimental assessment. You were everything to her.'

Marie looked through the window. The morning sunlight fell through the lace curtains. 'She did leave me,' she said. 'But perhaps not on purpose. Maybe something happened to her.' She thought of her father back in Krakow. She wondered if Dr Wolanski had let slip to Papa about the conversation they'd had. 'Perhaps my father had something to do with it.'

Mrs Bronowska laughed. 'Your father? You mean Dominik Karski?'

'Yes,' Marie replied.

'I suppose it's possible in a hypothetical sense,' Mrs Bronowska said. 'He was a military man. He distinguished himself with violence. And I did see him shout, more than once. Though not at Helena, and not at you. But that's a merely theoretical supposition, based on his character. When it comes to the practicalities, how could he involve himself in such a thing? He died before you and your mother left Lwów.'

Marie took her turn to laugh. 'My father is alive. He lives in Krakow. You must be mistaken.'

Mrs Bronowska put down her biscuit. 'Dominik Karski lived briefly in the apartment upstairs with you and your mother. After he returned from fighting in the Great War, then the Ukrainian wars, then the Soviet wars, he caught influenza. He died on the floor of that apartment, about three metres above where we sit right now. I am not mistaken; I saw his body being carried away. I know where they buried him.'

35
THE NORTHERN CEMETERY

The cemetery was a fifteen-minute walk from the tenement building. Marie weaved her way through the Lwów streets, still reeling. The old woman had to be mistaken; she'd search the graveyard and return, assuring her of her error. Arriving at the site, Marie entered at the north-western corner. The graveyard stretched over a single city block and she estimated that about three hundred graves lay inside. Some stones possessed ornate carvings, and there were old family crypts from empires long departed with doors and stairs, their roofs blessed with angels and marble pots for hosting flowers. Others were more simple, just headstones of thin granite.

She traipsed the rows in a methodical fashion, reading each gravestone twice. Towards the back, they changed from neat modern plots to more decrepit stones with moss growing over their tops. Giant birch trees grew everywhere, their roots disturbing and displacing the stones. Many were knocked over or cracked, seemingly forgotten, and she half expected a hand to reach up through the ground and grab her. Reaching the end, she found no gravestone that bore the name Dominik Karski. She sighed and shook her head. She'd expected this result; still, she felt strangely disappointed not to find his name there. She checked again to make doubly sure, this time beginning in the middle row, marking the starting place with a white stone, then branching out in the opposite direction from before, to view each gravestone with fresh eyes. She completed a circuit of the grounds and encountered the same result: no stone with the name Dominik Karski.

So the old woman had made a mistake. Of course she had.

She sighed, agitated, and proceeded to the exit. At the gate she encountered a middle-aged man pushing a wheelbarrow. He doffed his cap to her and greeted her good day in Polish.

'Do you work here?' she asked, realising as soon as she spoke how obvious this was.

'Yes, miss,' he replied. He lifted a shovel from the wheelbarrow and began digging into the earth.

Marie smiled at the curious profession, how the man cradled death and decay every day. As he dug those graves, did questions to the universe run through his head? Did he ask why, what the point of it all was, why we are born just to die again? If such thoughts did burden him, they did not affect the swift execution of his task. The hole he'd been digging had grown half a metre in width just while she'd been standing there. Marie pointed to the plot. 'Who are you digging this grave for?'

'Not sure yet,' he said. 'They just told me to dig a few.'

Marie grimaced. 'I'm looking for a grave I was told was here, but I can't find it.'

'What name?' the gravedigger asked.

'Dominik Karski,' she said.

He didn't stop shovelling when he gave his answer. 'Western corner. Fourth row from the top. Four – no, five across.'

Marie thanked him and made for the western corner of the graveyard, shaking her head. She prided herself on her attentive-ness and she'd checked each grave twice and not seen her father's name. Arriving at the fourth row, she walked along it slowly. The headstone of the fourth grave stated that a woman lay beneath it,

Helga Branczowa, who had died in 1915. Marie moved to the next grave and heard herself gasp. She cursed herself for not having made note of it before. The headstone didn't contain the name Dominik Karski. It bore no name at all.

It displayed dates of birth and death, announcing the grave's occupant to have been born September 15, 1894, and to have died November 7, 1922. The first date was certainly her father's date of birth; they marked every September 15 with a small cake, a minuscule amount of ceremony that Marie still had to cajole and plead with him to have. The second date obviously could not mark her father's death, despite what it said, for her father was very much alive. But this date of her papa's supposed demise was in fact not the strangest element of this gravestone. Above these dates, where the person's name should lie, there lay no words, but several gouges and scratches in the granite, as though someone had removed the name with a hammer and chisel.

Marie returned to the gate and found the gravedigger. By now he'd dug half a metre down and stood in the hole, shaping and widening the sides to fit a coffin. 'Why is the name missing from that grave?' she asked, peering down into the hole to speak to him.

'Someone chipped the name off,' he replied.

'Do you know why?' Marie said. 'Was it a grave robber?'

He shook his head. 'Not saying that doesn't happen. Any mother or father whose child was foolish enough to bury them with jewellery has long been dug up. There might have been eighty gold teeth in this hectare, all gone. Someone even dug up a stinking fur coat once and wore it out of here. But whoever destroyed that stone didn't disturb what lay under it. The ground remained flat and the grass had grown over when I found it.'

'You're sure the stone once read, "Dominik Karski"?'

He stopped digging and rested an arm on his shovel. 'I'm sure. I dug that grave myself.' Marie's mind swirled as the gravedigger kept talking. She nodded and smiled politely at him, not taking in

his words, remaining stuck on the previous ones. 'I couldn't understand it. He was a war hero, did you know? Why would anyone do
that to one of our champions? But then his funeral was strange, too.'

'Strange, how?' Marie said.

'Only two people there. A young woman and a baby. Two
people, for a Vertuti Militari. Very sad.'

Marie thanked him and returned to town. There were fewer
people in the streets now. Those who remained moved quickly,
collecting repaired coats, purchasing luggage. Marie observed them
but continued on her mission. She arrived at the tenement and
ascended the stairs to Mrs Bronowska's, puffing and sweating as she
entered. 'I saw the grave. Someone had chiselled off the name. Did
you do this?' she asked the old woman.

Mrs Bronowska laughed. 'Not that I recall. I didn't know such
a thing had occurred. But you believe me now, your father is dead.'

'But he's *not* dead. I saw him four days ago. He has worked at a
hospital in Krakow for fifteen years. A thousand people could assure
you of his being very much alive.' She had an idea. 'Do you have any
photographs of him?'

'I don't think so,' Mrs Bronowska replied.

Marie's heart sank; this would have solved the issue once and for
all. A photograph, even from twenty years ago, would have shown
her father's face.

Mrs Bronowska looked apologetic, then she smiled. 'I do have
a photo of your mother, however,' she said in a conciliatory tone.
'At least, I think I do. Shall I see if I can find it?'

Marie turned to her and tried not to gasp. 'I'd like to see that,'
she said. Her heart was suddenly racing.

Mrs Bronowska disappeared down the hall into one of the bedrooms. 'The funniest thing,' she called out to Marie, 'I found it in
your mother's oven. I went up there after she'd left with you. She vanished one day without telling anyone where she was going. Anyway,

after she'd gone, the landlord asked me if I wanted anything that was left in the apartment, before he threw it away. I think he just wanted me to clean the place out, so he didn't have to carry everything down the stairs. There wasn't much left when I arrived, but I found a photograph in the oven. She'd tried to burn it, but the flames must have died before they could finish the job, and most of the picture remained. Yes! Here it is.' Her voice grew louder as she walked back up the hall. 'And how lovely! I'd forgotten. It is a photograph of her, and you too.'

Marie felt her heart thump in her chest again. Mrs Bronowska handed Marie the picture. Flames had singed the left corners of the small sepia photograph, but they hadn't encroached on the picture's subjects. A mother and baby posed for a photograph in some kind of studio. Neither person smiled; the photographer would likely have ordered them to sit still for the long exposure. As she searched the baby's face, a child of less than one year old, Marie gasped, recognising her own nose, ears, eyes. She'd never seen a photograph of herself so young. But the shock of this was nothing compared to seeing her mother's face for the first time.

Now she could fill in the features that had existed as a blank in her head all these years. She could add eyes, a nose, a mouth to the figure in that memory she'd treasured for so long. She studied the face and felt instant recognition. Of course that was her mother. That memory, which had seemed so out of reach before now, materialised in her mind and merged with the face in the photograph to become whole. It was a face she'd always known.

She looked at her mother's hair in the picture – she'd seen that hair before too. The monochrome image comprised only variations of brown and white, but she could tell her mother had blonde hair. She'd tied it in a braid for the photograph and arranged it down her left shoulder. Marie had seen this hair before, its exact shade and thickness – she'd found it in a box, hidden below the floorboards of her father's bedroom.

36
THE BUTCHER
OF LWÓW

Lwów, August 1922

Baby Marie was already eleven months old and hadn't met her father yet. Dominik hadn't returned home from the front, despite the Ukrainian war having ended over a year ago. Neither Helena nor Mr Karski had received a single letter, not one clue as to where Dominik might be. But fighting with the Soviets continued in the east and parts of Ukraine; that was where he must be.

Helena still worked in the pharmacy for Mr Karski. She'd look after the ledger while the baby slept and go out the back to feed her when required. Each day Mr Karski drifted further into that condition Dr Alzheimer had described in his paper a decade earlier. He still believed Helena to be his wife. He had tried to arrange for a wet nurse upon Marie's birth, but none could be found; the city was still technically at war. 'I asked Mrs Biała, but she said she doesn't do it anymore. She looked at me as though I was crazy, Irenka,' he said to Helena, a look of indignation on his face.

Helena discovered Mrs Biała had most certainly been a wet nurse, but was now in her late fifties. She had nursed Dominik twenty-eight years ago. Helena didn't mind giving the child her own milk, even though it marked a person as poor. The baby went to her breast greedily and happily, and Helena would sit in the rocking chair, letting Marie suckle while she closed her eyes and leaned back with a smile.

One crisp September morning, two well-dressed men came to the pharmacy and offered to buy it from Mr Karski. 'We are offering you a very fair price in these uncertain times,' the taller one said. Mr Karski thanked them kindly but assured them he had no desire to sell.

Helena wiped a bench nearby and tried to listen. She recognised the taller man; he owned two apothecaries on the other side of the city. She wanted to say something, but she knew how improper it would look for the girl everyone supposed was the cleaning woman to intervene in a business matter. She looked over to Mr Karski to gauge the level of discomfort on his face. The meeting remained civil, for now.

One of the men leaned in. 'We know you are unwell,' he said to Mr Karski. 'You are losing customers and, if the news of your condition came out, you would lose more still.' The man offered Mr Karski a satisfied grin. The colour drained from Mr Karski's face. Helena stifled a gasp. How had they found out? 'Be reasonable, old man. You have done well, made piles of money. Now it's time to retire before you kill someone. We are giving you a grand opportunity here, to leave with your reputation intact.'

Mr Karski stepped back and reached out his hand, gripping the bench behind him. Helena walked into the back room, waited thirty seconds and then returned. 'Mr Karski, there's a coal delivery in the laneway. The man wants to speak to you,' she said.

The men believed her and collected their coats. 'We will return on Friday,' the taller one said. The shorter one stared at the floor; he'd said nothing the whole meeting. Helena recalled that he was the pharmacist at one of the tall man's apothecaries.

The two men left, and Mr Karski followed Helena into the laneway. It didn't matter that there was no coal delivery there, and no man who wanted to speak to Mr Karski, because by the time they arrived outside he'd forgotten the purpose of his visit there anyway.

They went back inside, and Mr Karski had already forgotten the visit of the two men, too, though a general feeling of discomfort and anxiety afflicted him for the rest of the day. It was upsetting to witness, and Helena's efforts to calm him were unsuccessful. He'd let out a scream at random moments or smash a beaker into the sink after minutes of quiet. Helena felt only pity, seeing him trapped in a prison of darkness and confusion. What a sickness this was, the menace of lost memories, for what were people if not the sum of their experiences? They were animals.

The price the men had offered Mr Karski for his pharmacy was indecent – it did not even cover the cost of the stock sitting on the shelves. What choice did he have? If he refused, the men would reveal his condition. He might be driven from town. Guiltily, Helena felt more concerned for herself and her daughter. She had not drawn a wage for herself in several months; there hadn't seemed any point. If Mr Karski lost the business, Helena and Marie would starve unless she found another job. But who would hire her and allow her to bring a baby to work, like Mr Karski did? She silently begged for Dominik to show up.

The men returned on Friday and Mr Karski did not remember their reason for coming. They expressed their desire to purchase the pharmacy again, for the same dastardly price. Mr Karski looked panicked and they presented the same threat of exposing him to everyone if he didn't comply. This time, Helena intervened.

'Mr Karski, beg pardon, but is your son, Dominik Karski, not about to take over the business when he returns from the front?'

Mr Karski mercifully took his cue. 'My son, Dominik, will be taking over this pharmacy. He is very bright and as soon as he returns from war, he will run this shop.'

The men both looked surprised; they hadn't considered this. The taller one sneered at Helena, and they left, promising to be back soon.

She wrote a frantic letter to Dominik and sent it to his last known location, hoping it would reach him, although she'd received no reply to others she had sent. He was their only hope now. The letter was never answered, and it didn't matter, for Mr Karski died two weeks later.

Helena found him in his bedroom, still in his pyjamas. He was stone-cold; she'd been downstairs in the pharmacy for two hours before she went to check on him. He often took a nap in the mornings or didn't come down exactly at nine am, so she hadn't been worried. But when a customer came in and asked for a cough syrup that required preparation by mixing, Helena was forced to fetch him. She looked at his grey face and closed his eyes. He was definitely dead. She supposed it had been a heart attack. She sat on the edge of the bed and wept softly, wiping her tears with a shaky hand. This gentle man, who had taken her in and educated her. Her loneliness had overwhelmed her after her own father died, and Mr Karski had soothed that torrent. She wept for his kind heart, his terrified looks when the dementia had overcome him, the confusion and sadness that had ripped through him each day at sundown. Feeling pathetic, she wept for herself too. Was every person she ever loved destined to leave her?

She forced herself to find composure. She told the customer wanting the medicine they had run out and he left. She locked the front door behind him and placed the closed sign in the window. She needed to act quickly. She returned to Mr Karski's bedroom and found money in a cigar box in his dresser. She went to the safe – she knew the combination, she'd watched him do it, ashamedly standing by the doorway without his knowledge – and she emptied it of the pharmacy's money, hiding it in her suitcase.

The two men returned that afternoon, inquiring after Mr Karski's welfare in a way that made Helena shiver. She had no choice but to tell them he was deceased. She silently pleaded for Dominik to walk through the door. He didn't.

The two men declared the pharmacy abandoned and Dominik missing in action, presumed dead, and took possession of it without paying a mark. Helena returned to her old tenement building and secured an apartment that had become vacant. It cost almost twice the rent of her old bedsit, but she had no choice. She had a baby now; she could not live on the street. In her bag, guiltily but gratefully, she carried the money from the safe and the cigar box and her little portion of savings.

A man from the church found her the next day, asking what she wanted to do with Mr Karski's body. Helena blinked at him as he explained, standing in her tiny kitchen, turning the brim of his hat in his hands. As no one else had come forward, she had to pay for the funeral, otherwise Mr Karski would go into an unmarked grave. She agreed mournfully to pay; she could not allow that. She paid for a plot, a coffin and the burial service; it cost more than half her money. The funeral was on Saturday, and by Monday the tall man and his short companion had taken over the pharmacy and renamed it the Golden Bear, like their other businesses across town.

She offered her services to the Golden Bear. She made a compelling argument: she knew the place well, had controlled the prescription records for over a year, knew the customers, the stockists, the orders. In truth she had also mixed medicines out the back, titrated dosages, refined chemicals, distilled alcohols. She could recite the periodic table backwards; she could make aspirin with her eyes closed. Her skills lay on par with those of any young man with a degree in chemistry. She kept this to herself, offering to work merely as a pharmacist's assistant.

Even this was too much for them. The shorter man laughed at her. 'I don't think so, girly. We do need a chambermaid, however.'

'What is the pay?' Helena asked.

'Four marks per week.'

Helena scoffed quietly. 'Mr Karski paid me eight. As his cleaner.'

'Times have changed.' The man shrugged. 'Few jobs exist, and everyone wants them. I can pay whatever I want, and someone would still agree to do it.'

'But four marks will only cover my rent. How will I eat, clothe my baby?'

He held up his hands in exasperation. 'Combined with your husband's wage, you will have enough.' Helena thanked him politely and left. She wrote yet another letter to Dominik telling him what had happened. It did not surprise her when she received no reply.

At that point she finally accepted that Dominik would not be coming back. He had been gone for two years without a word. She must have sent him fifty letters in that time, receiving no answer when announcing the birth of his child, the death of his father, the loss of the family business. He was gone.

And so she had to laugh when, without warning and for no good reason, he appeared a few weeks later at her apartment, waking her at dawn with a dull knock on the door. He stood in her decrepit studio, looking even thinner than before. His neck seemed slender as a stovepipe as he turned his head to look around, the tendons protruding from the sides like reeds. A vein throbbed in the centre of his forehead as he looked at her, pushing a Y shape through his taut and powdery skin. He wore an odd mishmash of civilian and army clothes; his military service coat with its chevrons and epaulettes covered his torso, but regular black trousers encased his legs, as though he'd lost half his uniform somewhere. Heavy woollen army socks covered his feet inside civilian leather shoes, the thick material bunching out at the ankles. He looked clownish and menacing. Still, she embraced him desperately. She tried to kiss him; he turned his cheek. The coldness added to her worry but she did not dwell on it. There would be time to fix these things.

'Where have you been?' she asked sweetly.

He blinked slowly. Was he drunk? 'What happened to the pharmacy?' he said. 'Why did you not save it?'

She explained to him breathlessly what had happened, that she'd had no choice.

He nodded and looked out the window. Marie woke in her crib and began screaming. 'That's the baby, I suppose.'

Helena smiled; she couldn't believe she'd almost forgotten. 'Your daughter.' She collected Marie and offered her to Dominik. He hesitated, then took the bundle. He looked at the baby's face.

'My daughter. Marie,' he said. He must have received some of her letters, then.

Helena felt awash with happiness. He was home. Everything would be all right now. She asked him what he'd do for work now the army had discharged him. He batted the question away by throwing their only chair against the wall.

She felt herself jump. The chair lay in pieces, a splintered leg leaning against the wall. If in future she required a definition for momentary madness brought on by despair, she would recall his face in that moment. He stood there grimacing. She wondered if she should leave with Marie. She measured the steps to the door, and found he'd be close enough to grab her as she walked past. Previously, she had expressed some juvenile wish to see this violence, and she admitted to herself with shame that it still aroused her a little. But now she had Marie, and she did not possess this fantasy anymore, only one in which her daughter enjoyed a long and healthy life, away from a father who might kill them both.

Helena tried to reason with him calmly, explaining about his father's estate. The pharmacy was gone, but surely Dominik could return there and tell the men who he was. They could go to the police or charge them in court, surely, for Dominik was Mr Karski's heir and the men had taken the pharmacy under false pretences. She gently implored Dominik to fight.

He looked at her coldly. He didn't want to work in a pharmacy. He didn't want to do anything.

That was not the point, Helena tried to tell him softly, to make him see.

They needed money; they needed a livelihood for their daughter. This didn't seem to register. Every night Dominik would leave them in the early evening, neglecting to say where he was going. He would return in the early hours, stinking of vodka.

One day a soldier came looking for him. 'Major Karski didn't attend the ceremony yesterday,' he told Helena. Dominik had mentioned nothing about this. She said as much. Also, 'He's not a major, he's a lieutenant.'

'He's been promoted,' the man replied. 'He's a major now. The ceremony was to present him with his medal. He's been awarded the Virtuti Militari, Golden Cross.'

When Dominik finally returned home, reeking of vodka and sporting a purple bruise above his eye, she told him about the promotion and the medal, and passed on the man's message that he needed to attend the military office to collect it. Dominik merely gave a bitter laugh and went out again. He then went missing for four days, leaving no word, returning as drunk as she'd ever seen him, slurring and stumbling and relieving himself in the corner of the apartment.

She wouldn't stand for this. Days and weeks of gentle pleading and encouragement gave way to anger. She didn't care if he lashed out at her for her excesses, she was too tired and too poor. They would be dead soon anyway if Dominik didn't pull himself together. She shouted at him as she scrubbed his urine from the floor. 'You need employment, you need to collect your medal, what's wrong with you?' She shouted the words so loudly she surprised herself. Dominik jumped in his chair a little. He stood and walked to the window. Helena caught a whiff of the stale alcohol on him as he passed her; he stank worse than the urine she was scrubbing away, a nasty, hot smell of sweaty bar fights and vomit. She retched. He stared out of the glass and she watched his bony shoulders rising and falling as he breathed, the nodules of his spine protruding through his shirt like a line of pebbles.

He turned from the window and looked at Helena. 'I'll tell you why I don't want that medal.'

Helena stopped scrubbing the floor. She sat up on her haunches.

'It was 1918. The Great War had just ended, as you know. When the Armistice was called, we returned home with a shrug. Ukrainians had stormed Lwów, claiming it for themselves, wanting to take it from Poland. Another war had broken out.

'By the time I reached home on the twenty-first of November, the Poles had regained control of the city. I found myself a ranking officer in the newly formed Polish army. The men who had been fighting came to me and asked me to give them forty-eight hours, to "clean up the city". Shops had been broken into during the fighting. They wanted to collect the money and goods that had been left, to get to them before the retreating Ukrainians did.'

'They wanted to go looting,' Helena said.

He nodded. 'Yes. But the goods would have been taken anyway. If someone was going to have them, I wanted it to be Polish men. I wanted the men who had experienced the Great War to enjoy a little pleasure for a change, a few moments of glee. There was a boy in my unit who had lived down the road from me. He had been so keen to join up that he'd said he was sixteen when in fact he was twelve. I saw his head torn off by a cannonball. I also saw the man who had been my chemistry teacher trampled to death by horses. In the morning, when we came to bury his body, we found his face eaten away by rats, his cheek chewed off, revealing his teeth and jawbone underneath, so he looked as though he was grinning through the side of his face. After making it through such things,

I saw no harm in looking the other way while the soldiers collected a few fur coats and jewels.

'I was unaware, however, that as Austria had retreated during the Great War, they had broken open the Polish prisons. The criminals who'd been released had now joined the Polish army, volunteering to fight against the Ukrainians. These bandits were now leading the mission to relieve the city's stores of their goods. Some of those store owners fought back.'

Helena felt her eyes mist over and a strangled cry escaped the back of her throat. She knew of the event he spoke of. A gusting wind howled outside; night began to fall. She lit a lamp and yellow light bloomed throughout the room. Marie played on the floor with her ball. A sweet, rank odour rose from her; she needed changing.

Dominik did not acknowledge the smell. He just stared into space, forming the next words to say. 'I came down to watch. I found I had misjudged the situation. Jews defending their shops against Polish looters came across as anti-Polish. A group of men claiming to represent the Jews of the city declared themselves neutral in the conflict. But we were told the Jews had attacked Poles with axes. Many believed this. And the worst parts of humanity came out.

'I saw one soldier swinging a Jewish baby, perhaps four weeks old, by the leg. He threatened to bash the infant against a tree unless its mother turned over all the house's gold. Other men made a group of Orthodox Jews get on all fours and scrub the footpath with toothbrushes. A soldier tried to cut a rabbi's forelocks away, and when the rabbi resisted he shot him, before relieving the corpse of his gold teeth. I turned a corner to find boys chasing a young Jewish woman, about my age, with sticks. The girl looked up and saw me in the crowd. She gave a tentative smile – so strange in that situation – and then she spoke to me.'

Helena breathed out. 'What did she say?'

He lit a cigarette, hand shaking. 'She said, "Dominik."'

Helena gasped.

'I looked again. I knew her. Her name was Mila. She lived two blocks from me growing up. I had known her for twenty years. Her parents owned a general store where I would go after school. Mila worked behind the counter and would sneak boiled sweets into my pocket while her father wasn't looking. I think she secretly loved me. She always smiled at me, a big, warm grin. "Keep your chin up, Dominik!" she used to say. She always looked so happy. But on that day, she looked to me and mouthed "help".'

'What did you do?'

'I looked at her, and I turned away.'

'Why?' Helena cried. 'Why did you not help her?'

He ignored her question. 'I will never forget the look in her eye when I turned back to her. Once she saw I would not help, she lost all hope. She stopped struggling. The men tore her clothes off. Now she wore only her girdle and suspenders, a stocking covering only one leg. So strange to see her not wearing clothes. She had always looked so put together, so refined, but now she looked like an animal, with her hair out of place, her white flesh on display, the hairs on her legs showing, her toenails curling into the dirt road.

'What happened to her?'

'She went to heaven.'

Helena would later recall how the phrase forced her to clutch her mouth and convulse. 'Why did you not put a stop to it?'

Dominik sucked on his cigarette and exhaled, his hand trembling. He stared at a crack in the wall. 'You don't understand. You weren't there. I had already promised them. I thought we could get peace this way. I was right. Morale is a flimsy thing,' he said. 'Once it cracks, it crumbles. The fight went out of the Ukrainians after that. The Poles retook the city and won the war. After that day, I was forever known as the Butcher of Lwów. I hated the title – what had I done? I had not killed anyone. Why was I the butcher?'

'You were the butcher because you were the leader. And you stood by while your own people were raped and murdered.'

He blinked. 'I won battles in the Great War. But I will always be remembered for this.'

She realised now he had already supervised the atrocity when she'd met him. While she had been learning to make aspirin, he had been supervising the rapes and bashing murders of his fellow citizens.

He continued. 'Now we have dispatched the Russians too, and we have a glorious new nation. Everyone is being rewarded for their past deeds that helped bring forth our republic. All the men in our unit have received a handsome commendation for their actions on the eastern front. These nice Polish men have given me the Vertuti Militari for my actions on the battlefield. They think I'm a hero.' He blinked, a giant, fearful flinch. The statement hung there long enough for Helena to imagine him confronting that scene, considering whether to take a stand against men rabid with war. His look and his crumpled posture said he questioned this too. 'There is a Jewish saying,' he said. '*Whoever saves a single life is considered to have saved the whole world.* How lovely that would have been, to save her life.'

'But you did not.'

He coughed. 'No.'

'I pretended not to know her,' he said softly, his voice breaking. He inhaled and seemed to fold into his clothes, becoming a little bundle. He slipped off his chair and onto the floor, curling into a ball. As she walked over, he was cowering and whimpering, a pile of clothes and hair, some fingernails and teeth – that was all that was left; the soul was gone. She left him there.

Marie cried. Helena picked her up; Dominik flinched. She carried the baby to the bed and sat down. She needed to, for she knew she would faint otherwise.

37

DIGNITY

Dominik asked Helena to come to bed, but she refused. He took a blanket from the mattress and laid it on the floor, then went to sleep. During the night, she heard him whimpering, but she didn't comfort him. After midnight, he left the apartment. He disappeared for hours, then a neighbour knocked on the door in the early morning and said he was outside. Helena felt happy for him to stay there.

She came down at midday. It had been raining all morning, with cold, sleet-like shards tapping on the windows and roof. He lay unconscious in the laneway behind the tenement, the icy rain-water dropping on his face. He looked a pathetic sight, a shivering, bedraggled bone bag lying on the footpath behind a rubbish bin. When she touched him, his cheeks felt icy and rigid, like wet stones. She managed to muster some pity, rubbing his brow softly and trying to wake him, to help him to his feet.

'Leave me here,' he muttered, finally rousing. She ignored him and helped him upstairs to the bed. His forehead was burning. Helena spoke to the woman in the apartment next door, a widow called Mrs Bronowska. 'My husband has a fever. Do you have any aspirin?'

'Of course not,' said the woman. 'And if I did, I would keep it for myself.' She stepped away from Helena. 'Don't come near me with your flu.'

Helena scowled at the accusation, but when she returned to the apartment and saw Dominik's sweating pallor, she realised with horror that the woman had made the correct diagnosis.

It had arrived in Poland in 1918, had gone away for a time, and now it was back. Dominik had influenza. By the evening, he was running a fever of forty degrees Celsius.

'You can't die,' Helena told him. 'You have a baby.'

He tipped his head up, sweating and puffing, and pointed to Marie. 'Sometimes it's better to die.'

'I'd rather you didn't,' Helena pleaded with him. 'You will kill three people. You are the only one of us who stands any chance of earning a proper wage. We will run out of money. If you die, we will all die.' She heard the panic in her voice and sat up straight, changing tack. 'Let's go somewhere else!' she tried. 'We'll move to another city, where no one knows you. What about Krakow? Your father always spoke of it. We can start again.'

He grabbed Helena's arm and she gasped at the strength of his grip. 'I will die so she can live.' He motioned to Marie, who gurgled in the corner. Helen looked at the baby, then back at him. 'I must pay for my crimes. I give my life to make up for what I've done. This is my gift to her. I return one soul to the balance, so that she may live. Let me die, then forget me. Go on with your lives, and never mention me again.'

She had left the window open a crack to help cool him down; now the rain, growing heavier, came in at a slanting angle and fell on their rug, dampening it. The mat would soon start to smell, so she walked to the window to shut it. She returned to Dominik's bedside, ready to plead with him some more. Instead she found him dead, his blue eyes still open, staring at the ceiling.

She recalled how the life had gone from his eyes not just then, but some years ago.

*

The graveyard that held Mr Karski was full. She buried Dominik instead in a newer cemetery in the northern part of the city. The plot and the coffin together cost her two-thirds of the money she had left. She cried every day for two weeks and nervously waited out the incubation period, expecting to come down with influenza herself, but she didn't. Marie remained unaffected, too.

A fortnight was all she could allow herself to mourn; they needed food. She set her sights on finding a job. She visited a pharmacy on the other side of the city, travelling for an hour with Marie on three trams. She dressed in her best clothes and brought some examples of medicines she'd made herself. She found the pharmacist in a quiet moment and explained herself. 'For the past four years, I have worked at Karski's Apothecary as the assistant to Mr Karski,' she declared. 'I controlled the prescriptions ledger, I prepared and administered pharmaceutical preparations, I looked after the inventory. I know how to store medicinal ingredients properly. I can do it all,' she said.

The pharmacist raised a monocle to his left eye and stared at her. He stood behind a thick marble counter far more opulent than Mr Karski's, but the bottles of medicines behind him were less organised and covered with dust. 'I'm afraid I don't believe you,' he said.

'But I—' She tried to explain further, but he held up his hand to stop her.

'I'm talking now. Are you asking me to accept that Mr Karski allowed you to prepare medicines? If so, I should be very concerned.'

'I didn't mean—'

He interrupted again. 'You have no degree, no qualifications whatsoever, yes?'

Helena swallowed. 'Yes.'

'Yet you took it upon yourself to prepare and administer medications to unsuspecting people, whom you could have killed.'

'It wasn't like that. I helped many people.'

'Leave here before I telephone the police.'

She gulped back a sob. 'Please. I'll do anything. I don't need to work as your assistant. I can sweep your floors, clean the latrine, anything. I'm almost out of money. I have a baby.' She pointed outside to Marie, who sat on a bench, playing with her ball. She hadn't wanted to draw attention to her, she hadn't wanted him to know she had a child, but now it might help. Perhaps pity could secure her employment.

He peered out the window and looked at the baby. He turned to Helena. 'Where is the child's father?'

'He died,' Helena told him. 'He was a soldier.'

The pharmacist smiled. 'There, you see. All will be well. Go down to the veterans' bureau – they will help. You are entitled to the war widow's pension.'

Helena bowed her head. 'I'm not a war widow. We were never married.'

He stared at her with a look that Helena could only describe as contempt. 'The child is a bastard?'

'Please, sir, what are we going to do? How are we going to afford to live, to eat?'

He laughed cruelly. 'You should have thought of that before you lay with that soldier, girl. Now you have rendered yourself useless and produced another mouth to feed. Do you expect me to pay for your mistakes?' He seemed to savour each word, speaking slower than before, as though it was a speech he'd been waiting to say. 'Too bad the soldier who you claim impregnated you is not still alive. He was eligible for study money, did you know? Philanthropic organisations are giving out scholarships for returned servicemen to get degrees. All you have to do is write to them. You might have profited that way, if he was willing to accept the child as his.'

Helena wiped a tear. 'But he is dead. What should I do, then?'

His face passed through a series of expressions: pity, then disbelief and finally derision, as though a loose girl with a bastard child had duped him into talking to her. As Helena began to really cry now, big desperate tears rolling down her face, he spoke curtly. Any hint of civility was gone, but at least he was still speaking to her. 'Go to the street on the south corner of the market square. Do you know it?'

Helena nodded, feeling confused.

'There are three or four bars in that area. Returned soldiers go there. Ask around for the best one.' He gave a quick, unsure glance at Marie, then nodded. 'Now get out of my store.'

Helena went down to the market square the following day, carrying Marie in her arms. The clock had only struck three in the afternoon, but the bars overflowed with men, most dressed in military uniform, all in various states of drunkenness. The sounds of laughter and carousing assaulted her ears, and the smell of vodka emanated from the tables and carpets, the rough medicinal sharpness hitting her nostrils, as did the fruitiness of vomit.

A never-ending party was taking place, it seemed, in opposition to the haggard scenes of hunger and worry she'd witnessed in the rest of the city. Men of varying shapes and sizes sat around, fat and thin, handsome and ugly. Women congregated in small pockets by the doors and entranceways, watching them. One man opened a bottle of vodka, wrapping his mouth around its opening and gulping. He spit some liquid onto those around him, who laughed and shoved him. A woman wearing a purple dress, her lips painted red, walked over to him and struck up a conversation. She whispered something in his ear and he put his arm around her waist and led her away to some place Helena couldn't see. Marie began to cry, and the men looked over at the sound. Helena rocked the baby and walked away. She had seen enough; she understood what the pharmacist meant.

She returned to the tenement and knocked on the door to Mrs Bronowska's. The woman had once offered to mind Marie, for a fee. Helena had thanked her but declined politely and the woman had walked off in a huff, seeming offended. 'Do you have a dress I could borrow?' she asked when Mrs Bronowska opened her door. 'A nice one?'

Mrs Bronowska's face lit up. 'This way.' She led Helena down the hall and showed her to her bedroom, where she opened her wardrobe and peered at its contents. Six or seven old-fashioned dresses hung on a rail; two coats, both thinned and worn, one with buttons missing, hung next to them. A moth escaped from the inside, flapping its dusty wings in Mrs Bronowska's face. The woman batted it away, cursing. She studied Helena's body, running her eyes up and down, and stroked her chin as though appraising a scientific specimen. 'This will fit you,' she said in a satisfied tone, taking one of the dresses from the rail and presenting it to Helena.

Helena slid it from the hanger. The dress felt dusty. It went in at the waist and needed a corset underneath to hold it up. 'It looks thirty years old.'

Mrs Bronowska looked insulted. 'You want to attract a man, yes?' she demanded. Helena nodded tentatively. 'Men care nothing for fashion. Clever collars and the newest lace trim – men don't notice. How your chest looks, that's the only thing they care about.' She placed her hands on her hips.

Helena scratched her head. 'I think I need a corset to wear underneath. To give it some shape?'

Mrs Bronowska shook her head. 'Not necessary. Young women don't wear corsets these days! How old-fashioned.' Helena wanted to laugh. 'What will you do about your face? Do you have any lipstick?'

Helena said no.

Mrs Bronowska frowned. 'The other women will be wearing it. I can give you some.' She also gave Helena a coat and a hat to wear. She tried to give her shoes too, but Helena's feet were far too big to fit into any of her pairs. Mrs Bronowska shook her head with certainty. 'Don't matter. Men don't look at shoes,' she said, nodding.

Helena collected the items and thanked her.

'You're welcome!' Mrs Bronowska said. 'Shall we say one mark?'

Helena turned to her with surprise. 'I thought I was borrowing them. I shall bring them back.'

'That's my price for borrowing,' Mrs Bronowska said, crossing her arms. 'Let's say one mark fifty, and I'll mind the little one, too.'

Helena handed over the money and passed her the baby. It was the first time she'd left the house without Marie. As she walked away the baby started crying and reaching out for her; Helena had to wipe away a tear and force herself to leave.

Upstairs, Helena heated water on the stove, then bathed with a cloth, careful not to let the steam from the water cause the lipstick from Mrs Bronowska to run. She'd not let Helena take the lipstick with her, only applied one coat and then replaced the tube in its drawer by her dresser. Helena dried herself, put on talc and changed into the clothes. She possessed no mirror but tried her best to see her reflection in the apartment window. The dress seemed lumpy around her hips, though perhaps she saw only the distortion from the window glass.

She walked to the market square. The bars remained open and seemed even fuller than earlier. Helena walked inside the first one. As she appeared in the doorway, the men looked up from their conversations, then back down again. She found a spare stool at the bar and sat. A man stood behind the counter, serving drinks. He rushed back and forth across the bar, bringing bottles of vodka to the tables. Men stood three-deep at the counter, hollering at him to serve them next. As he wiped a line of sweat from his brow, Helena motioned to him that she wanted to order a drink, but he ignored her, serving another two men.

'Men buy the drinks,' a man next to her said. He wore a lieutenant's uniform and had a handsome face. 'Women aren't even supposed to be in here.'

Helena apologised. 'I see. Thank you.' She stared at him expectantly, smiling. But he did not offer to buy her a drink. He ordered two for himself, paid and walked off with them.

Men constantly brushed up against her back as they tried to move past; they'd established some sort of informal thoroughfare behind her so that every time someone wanted to access the bar, they jostled her this way and that as they passed. Two hours went by and no one offered to buy Helena a drink. Finally, she gave up and returned home. She explained what had happened to Mrs Bronowska, who urged her to go again the following night. 'The baby is fine. We had a lovely time,' she said. 'You will have better luck tomorrow. You must try harder! You have been with men before, yes?' She laughed. 'After all, that baby came from somewhere! So use your charm, smile and invite conversation. Make a man think he will feel good if he spends time with you.' Helena sighed.

The following evening she visited the bar she'd gone to the first time and found the situation in fact worse than before. Today was Sunday and not even a quarter of the men populated the room. She sat by the bar and looked around. The same barman from the day before approached her and asked her what she'd like. 'I thought women couldn't order drinks?' she said.

He shrugged. 'They can tonight. Do you want one or not?'

She ordered an apricot vodka. 'I saw you here last night,' a woman's voice said as Helena sipped her drink. She turned. The woman wore a green silk dress in the new style, and wore her hair arrestingly short; the hairdresser had cropped it close to her neck. Helena's hair still reached her waist and she wore it plaited down her back. 'You're looking for a husband, yes?'

Helena bristled and turned away. 'That's none of your business.'

The woman laughed and lit a cigarette from a silver case. 'Steady. I'm not the enemy. I'm making conversation.' Helena shrugged. The green-dress woman drew on her cigarette, blowing the smoke away from Helena.

Helena sighed. 'Help me. I need to marry – I have a daughter. I can't find work and we'll starve without money.'

The woman laughed. 'Boy, is that what you say to the men? I bet they line up for you.'

Helena went to leave but the woman grabbed her arm, and she sat back down. 'Take some free advice. Look around. Not at the men, but the women. They're all here for the same reason. How old is your daughter?'

'Fourteen months.'

'Don't ever tell a man about her.'

Helena scoffed. 'He will find out eventually. How can I not tell him?'

The woman stubbed out her cigarette in a tin ashtray. 'None of the women in this room have babies or children. They are your competition, understand? No man will choose you – a woman who is not a virgin, who has another mouth to feed at home – over one of these better-looking ladies.'

Helena gazed at the floor.

'I say this to be kind. There are too many women for all the men left, both in this bar, and in Poland. The war killed a quarter of the young men and the flu finished another quarter. Despite the funny old dress you're wearing, you don't look stupid. I believe you can add up those numbers, yes? There's only half the young men there used to be, but the same number of women. That's two

374

women for every man. Don't take it personally, but you're not much to look at. Very well, these men won't marry you. Never mind, you can still get a thing or two. A man might ask you to go into the alley with him, for example. You look him in the eye and tell him your price. Five marks for a suck, ten for full service. But get the money up front.'

Helena almost slipped off her bar stool. The gramophone's needle got stuck in a groove, repeating the same bar over and again. The barman cursed and went to fix it, ripping the record from the player. Helena felt nauseous. She imagined herself performing those acts with strangers. The money. Ten marks would almost pay an entire month's rent and she could earn it in an hour? She thought of Marie at home, her green eyes shining as Mrs Bronowska placed spoonfuls of porridge in her mouth, as she played with her wooden ball, as they sang songs together. She looked at the woman again. She was a fierce beauty, her blonde hair shining in the electric light of the bar. She carried herself with grace, willowy and lithe. Helena felt like a dumpy child next to her.

She looked around the bar again, noticing the less elegant women, the ones who looked more like her. They painted their mouths bigger and more reddish; they had their slips showing. Two streams of women, one for marrying, the other for paying. Helena reflected then on that strange, subtle quality humans called dignity. She could never lower herself like that. She told the woman as much.

The woman lifted her hands in surrender. 'Only trying to help,' she said. 'Enjoy your evening.' She stood and walked away. Helena watched her go, the green silk of her dress swishing across her behind and glimmering in the light.

A few minutes passed and Helena sat alone. A man approached her, one of the barmen. He wiped the bar in front of her and whispered. 'I'll meet you in the alley in ten minutes,' he said, not looking up from the bar. Helena scowled at him. 'Valentina, in the green dress?' he continued. 'She told me you would show me a thing or two.'

Helena looked across the room at the woman she'd spoken to. She winked at Helena as though she'd done her a favour. 'Get your coat and meet me out there,' he said. 'I want everything. I'll pay three marks.'

Helena sat there defiant for several minutes. Her heart sank slowly and she ordered another glass of vodka. She tipped the vodka into her mouth; the liquid sent a ball of heat into both cheeks, then burned her throat as it went down. She left the bar. The next day she returned to the Golden Bear pharmacy and accepted the job to clean their floors.

38

THE SHRINKING BABY

The pharmacist, who she'd learned was called Mr Panczow, smiled as she entered. 'Of course you can clean these floors, my dear. The pay is three marks per week.'

Helena stared at him. 'You said four marks.'

'That was before. Now it's three.'

Helena swallowed. Rent on the tenement was three marks per week. 'I can't survive on three marks.'

He smiled. 'I had another woman in here yesterday looking for work. If you don't take this job, she'll have it.' He gave a self-satisfied shrug and crossed his arms. She considered walking out, just to never have to see him again. 'If you work well, I will add a fourth mark.'

She began work the next day, leaving Marie with Mrs Bronowska. She agreed to pay the old woman one mark per week to watch the child, though she didn't know where she'd get this money from once her savings ran out; she'd have to rely on Mr Panczow's promise of the bonus mark. She arrived early and scrubbed the pharmacy, washing the benchtops with lime, cleaning and polishing all the glasses. She cleaned the windows, dusted the shelves. She didn't enjoy watching Mr Panczow work the way she had her old employer. Mr Karski had loved chemistry and he'd concocted every potion with the same wonder, working with precise movements. Mr Panczow was a businessman first. When one customer came in complaining of a cough, he gave them laudanum, charging almost double what Mr Karski had charged, and encouraged them to purchase several other chest ointments and respiratory tinctures that Helena knew to be useless. He checked and criticised her work, too. 'You should use a silk cloth for polishing those glasses,' he said one time.

'I couldn't find any silk cloths. Cotton does the same job,' she said. It was the truth.

He grabbed her arm and squeezed it; the roughness of his grip shocked her. 'Use a silk cloth, or feel free to leave. You think you know everything, but you are not the expert – I am. You know nothing. I have others who want your job.'

Helena looked away, feeling terrified. His grip left a mark on her arm that started out red, then went purple, black and finally faded to yellow. She winced as she lifted Marie for a week afterwards.

'There's dust on this sill!' he said the next day, pointing to the window. 'Do you expect me to serve customers in this pigsty? Stupid girl.' Helena walked over to the sill and examined it. No dust lay anywhere on the wooden frame, except for a single piece of lint that seemed to have been retrieved from a pocket and placed there. Helena cleaned it away and apologised. 'Don't you understand how important hygiene is in a pharmacy?' he said. 'But then you don't understand much, do you?'

She avoided him when she could. The following day, as she cleaned out the storeroom on his orders, she bent over and felt his hands squeeze her hips. She'd jumped in fright and shrieked. 'Relax, stupid girl,' he said darkly. 'Get out of the way. I need something in here.' He'd gripped her bottom and shoved her to the side, fetched a bottle and left.

At the end of her first week, she waited by the door as the pharmacy closed. He remained with his head in his accounting book. 'Is there something you want?' he said finally.

She cleared her throat. 'I'd like to collect my wages.'

He scoffed and moved to the register. He fetched a handful of notes, counted them and threw some down onto the counter.

Helena picked them up. 'Three marks?'

'That was the agreed amount.' He leaned back against the counter.

'You said if I did well, I'd get four.'

'If you say so.'

'Did I not do well?'

'You were adequate.' He shrugged. 'I had to help you with many things.'

This was a lie; Helena knew she'd kept every surface clean enough to eat off, she'd reorganised the stock and polished the windows.

She listed these things to Mr Panczow and he smiled. 'Maybe doing well means different things to you and me.' He did something then that made Helena wince: he exposed the top row of his teeth and used them to bite his bottom lip. The girlish gesture terrified Helena.

'I don't follow, sir,' she said, hoping for some mistake on her part.

'I think you do, or else you are a bigger simpleton than I thought. If you want to keep this job, I advise you to understand what doing well means.'

Helena pocketed the three marks and left.

The next week she worked each day, avoiding Mr Panczow where possible. She'd just enough in savings, plus her meagre earnings, to pay her rent and buy food, and to pay Mrs Bronowska to watch Marie, for perhaps another three weeks.

The following Monday, Mr Panczow touched her breast as she leaned over to ladle soup into his bowl. Helena tried to pretend she hadn't noticed, even though he'd squeezed hard enough that she'd flinched and spilled some of the soup on the tablecloth.

'Stupid girl,' he said, pointing at the spill.

'I'm sorry,' she said. She wet a cloth and dabbed the table.

'That will leave a stain. I shall have to take the amount from your wages to replace it.'

She moved the dishes to the side table and removed the cloth. 'It won't stain, I'll see to it now.' She rushed to the laundry at the back of the building and plunged the tablecloth into the sink, soaping the stain and running it up and down the washboard. The spot consisted of grease and vegetable stock and she knew it would come out easily with the laundry soap. Still, she scrubbed as though her life depended on it. She wanted no trace of the stain to remain; she'd give him no opportunity to reduce her pay.

'Shhh, calm yourself,' his voice purred as he appeared behind her in the laundry. She kept scrubbing and ignored him. He placed his hand between her legs. She froze. She implored herself to keep scrubbing but her hands wouldn't. 'Don't you see?' he whispered into her ear. 'You make trouble for yourself where none's needed. This could all go away. We could be good to each other. Other men wouldn't want you, but I could make you feel good. And I will give you five marks per week.'

'What about Mrs Panczow?' she asked, hoping the mention of his wife would provoke him to desist.

'Don't worry about her. She's visiting her mother in Lublin.'

She felt a stiffness press into her and heard his breath grow faster, as though the thought of his wife being away made things even more wonderful. She snatched the tablecloth from the laundry tub. 'Excuse me,' she said, 'I must hang this out to dry.' He didn't move. Helena pulled the tablecloth around and the sopping bundle began to drip onto his trousers and boots. He jumped out of the way and she escaped.

From then on, she only entered the back areas when Mr Panczow was occupied with a customer. Whenever it was just the two of them in the pharmacy, she stayed towards the front of the shop, by the windows, cleaning and organising the glasses and tools in full view of the street. She could rely on his tight-fistedness to help her avoid his advances. He'd never relinquish an opportunity to sell a potion to a customer, so she used these moments when he was most occupied, with an especially gullible old heiress or a wealthy young hypochondriac, to undertake her most dangerous missions to the places where he could best trap her – the back of the storage pantry, and the darkened laundry with its single doorway. She managed to go three weeks without another incident.

Then her money ran out. One Thursday, she collected her pay of three marks at the end of the day and travelled home. She arrived at the apartment to find the landlord's agent standing on her doorstep to collect the rent. She paid him the three marks, realising only then it was the only money she had, not just in her purse, but in the whole world. Every last mark she had was gone.

A week later, she dressed Marie one morning and shuddered. The green pullover that normally ran tight around the baby's middle now hung loose. The same jumper that had a month ago been growing too snug was now too big for Marie. Helena stared at the clothes and heard herself whimper. She felt her eyes moisten with tears and panic. Children were supposed to grow out of their clothes – clothes were not supposed to get too big for them. There was no food in the house; they had been subsisting on scraps from the priest's at the presbytery on the corner but they only doled them out on Sundays and today was Friday, so she lifted her dress and pressed the child to her breast. The child's mouth gaped open eagerly, desperately; she found the nipple and sucked. Helena observed with horror that a patch of hair was missing from the back of Marie's head. After twenty seconds or so, the baby looked up at Helena with wide eyes, accusingly, and began to cry. Helena looked down to ascertain the problem and gasped when she discovered the cause. Her milk had dried up.

Helena had always suspected she would love being a mother, but she'd never known quite how much. She wondered if all mothers felt the same – likely so – but she had to say her baby was special. Marie was a gorgeous playful child who garnered compliments wherever she went. She was above all cheeky; if you told her not to touch something, she would go right ahead, looking at you the whole time. When she had first given birth to Marie, Helena noted how becoming a parent had rendered her vulnerable: she loved something so much that her life would become pointless if it was taken away. She found her heart bursting with love and fear in equal parts that something would happen to this bundle, this heavenly creature. She understood now why her father had looked at her in such a way, the heart pain he'd felt. To have a child was to live in constant joy and constant terror, to rejoice for every minute they lay in your arms, mewling and snuffling sweetly, to sigh with horror in the same breath, at how awful it would be to lose this. Helena looked down at the baby now and felt the unique torture and shame of knowing she was starving the only person on the earth she cared about. She ran downstairs to beg for help, knocking on Mrs Bronowska's door.

The woman glared at her when she answered. 'You haven't paid me in two weeks for minding the baby,' she said. It was true. Helena promised to pay her soon and begged her for some food for Marie. Mrs Bronowska gave her a potato. 'It's all I have. The child has rickets, too,' she added, pointing at Marie accusingly. Helena closed her eyes and realised the woman was likely correct. She imagined her perfect daughter's brittle bones snapping like twigs and decided that in her whole life she had never felt more wretched.

The next day Helena went to work at the pharmacy with a new resolve. She'd had to beg Mrs Bronowska to watch Marie again.

The older woman eyed her with suspicion when she proposed it, and initially refused. Helena closed her eyes and swore she would get the money.

She cleaned the benchtops before opening as usual, drew back the curtains and replenished the bottles and jars. When the time for lunch arrived, she served Mr Panczow his meal in the upstairs apartment and, as he sat down to eat, she touched his arm.

He looked at her hand resting on his elbow.

'You will pay me ten marks a week,' Helena told him.

He swallowed; a look of excitement danced across his face. 'Six.'

Helena shook her head. 'Nine.' She reached down and put her hand on his thigh. She could feel the hardness already forming. She shuddered. Some of the beef soup had spilled on his shirt, forming a brown stain. He wore some cheap cologne he must have doused himself in; she'd smelled the same scent on far younger men, and it made him seamier, more desperate.

'Lie down,' he said.

'The money first,' she said. He nodded and disappeared to the other room. She heard the safe clicking open; he never normally opened it with her around. She crept to the door and tried to see the numbers he entered to open it, but before she could, he turned and she quickly averted her eyes. He gave her the nine marks, which she placed in her pocket. She went to lie down on the floor, but he stopped her. 'No, the table.' He turned her around, pushed her torso onto the dining table and lifted her skirt. She flinched on instinct, her arms and legs seizing up, her body saying, *No, wait, what's happening?* while her mind knew the agreement she'd made and forged ahead.

As he entered her, she assumed the role of a scientist and evaluated her own insignificance in the universe. In the scope of all human experience, all time, all stardust, she was but a speck of nothing – a blip – and her own discomfort and shame in that moment added little to the memory of the cosmos. She reminded herself of the nine marks in her pocket, of how this would never remove the smell of his cologne as he thrusted inside her; it wouldn't diminish the odour of his soupy breath on her neck, which would stay with her forever, but it would put food in her daughter's belly. From that day forward, the smell of beef soup would always make her retch.

With her scientist's eye she noted how curious it was that this act went from the pinnacle of human love and connection to a trough of gnawing shame with a different person. She felt no physical pain – he remained reasonably gentle for the duration of the act – and as his breathing grew even faster, his thrusts more urgent, she began to wonder with horror when she'd last had a period. She made a mental count of days and found she couldn't remember the date of the last one, but it must have been three weeks or more. With her erratic cycle, she couldn't know if her body had already produced an egg for fertilisation this month or if it was about to. Before she could finish her thought, however, Mr Panczow withdrew and climaxed onto the back of her skirt. She felt grateful for this small consideration. He had performed it for his own benefit, but she'd profit from the act as well.

'Clean yourself up and get back to work,' he said, patting her on the head. 'Don't think you can shirk your other duties now.'

The lunchtime congress became part of the daily routine. At first Helena dreaded it, checking the clock every few minutes and feeling anguished to find the minute hand had moved forward, inching ever closer to midday. But Mr Panczow continued to pay her the nine marks per week, and the sight on Marie's and Mrs Bronowska's faces when she brought home mutton, butter and sugar helped to ease her horror. She was even able to increase Mrs Bronowska's wage for looking after Marie.

Mr Panczow started making further gestures; he gave her two marks to buy a new dress (she found one for half a mark and pocketed the rest), and gave her extra food to take home 'for the little one'. Helena originally felt tenderness towards him for these actions, but soon realised he extracted payment for them also. For every bonus mark he gave her, he'd grab her breast as she reached for a bottle from the shelf; for the pieces of beef, he'd reach under her skirts as she polished the beakers and rummage around for as long as he felt like. She never had a moment where she felt left in peace and she spent her work hours flinching, wincing and looking over her shoulder.

39

VIRTUTI MILITARI

They had just finished their lunchtime coitus. Helena was lying on the floor with her skirt up to her waist, Mr Panczow on top of her, when a tallish woman dressed in a fur coat and red leather gloves walked into the kitchen. Helena recognised his wife from a photograph he displayed in a silver frame in his office and motioned for Mr Panczow to move. He looked irritated, not understanding, until the woman herself greeted her husband. 'Good day, Henryk.' She stepped past them to walk further into the kitchen.

Mr Panczow seemed to visibly shrivel at the sound of his wife's voice. Helena had never seen him move so fast as he sprang upwards and re-buttoned his trousers, as though moving speedily at this juncture could cloud her eyes to the true nature of the situation.

'My dear Karolina, I thought you were at your mother's for another week,' he said in an absurdly formal tone, hurriedly putting his shoes on.

'Evidently,' his wife replied. 'I came home early. Mama and I quarrelled.'

'Darling, this is not what it looks like,' he said. Helena had stood up from the floor by now and moved to the doorway. 'This woman, she seduced me. She's a witch.' He pointed at Helena. Helena laughed at the preposterous remark.

Mrs Panczow removed her leather gloves slowly, pulling at each finger one at a time. 'I know that,' she said. 'She lured you in.'

Helena spluttered with disbelief. 'That's not it, Mrs Panczow.'

But the woman wore a determined look on her face as she turned to Helena. 'I know you,' she said. 'You cleaned floors for the old pharmacist who worked here. He put a child in you. Everyone said you were a sorceress, making potions, mixing medicines. Now I have seen it with my own eyes. You are a conjurer and a whore.'

'No, madam, I must protest.'

'Look at you. You are a witch. Leave before I tell everyone!'

Helena fetched her coat and ran from the pharmacy. It was Wednesday and she hadn't received her wages since the previous Thursday, but it would be an exercise in futility trying to recover that money now. She returned home.

The next day she went to find new work. She started at the west side of town, asking to be a housekeeper, explaining her experience. She tried the Goldfinch Hotel first, approaching the manager and providing her credentials. 'Yes, I know you,' he said with a sneer. 'The Panczows are valued customers of ours. Please leave.'

She tried another hotel around the corner and received the same response, only this time, before the man asked her to leave, he called her a stealing whore. She laughed at the outrageousness of it; surely Mrs Panczow hadn't spoken to everyone. But at the next place she asked at, a barber's, where she offered to sweep up hair for three marks a week, they called her a whore, and also a witch, and escorted her out. She tried what felt like every business in Lwów to find work. Most places weren't hiring, and the rest were friends of Mrs Panczow's.

After three weeks, her money ran out. She went to another church twenty blocks from the apartment and begged for kitchen scraps; on Mondays and Thursdays they gave out potato skins, sometimes bones and gristle, or stale bread. She gave everything she received to Marie. By the fourth week she caught sight of her reflection in a window and gasped. She'd stopped eating and now bore the signs of that endeavour. She figured she must have lost a third of her body weight, her ribs poking through her skin. She could make out the shape of her pelvis when standing and her bones stabbed through her bottom when she sat down, making all chairs uncomfortable.

Famine had swept through the region. Every bird and rat had vanished, and she had heard reports that people were killing each other in the countryside and then eating the corpses. She knew the fate that awaited her; she'd read too many of Mr Karski's books not to. Having reduced her fat mass to less than ten per cent, she didn't need to worry about her menstrual cycle. Her body was now burning muscle to function. Once those stores had depleted enough, she'd contract an infection – whatever was going around, any would do – and her organs would shut down. If she died, Marie would die too.

But before they could reach that point, the baby herself fell ill. Helena returned home from an afternoon scavenging for kitchen scraps when she made the discovery. She'd left Marie with Mrs Bronowska for an hour, begging the old woman to take her while she went out, promising to bring back food for everyone. After she'd collected the baby she put her down for a nap, and returned an hour later to find Marie lying back in her crib, barely moving, her arms hanging limp by her sides. She was awake but hadn't cried; normally upon waking she screamed like a madman for Helena to pick her up. Instead she lay still in her bed and stared into space. At first Helena wondered if an insect had bitten her and she looked around but could see none. Both cheeks flushed crimson and she breathed slowly, grunting with the effort. Helena pressed her hand to Marie's forehead and gasped. A raging heat transferred itself from her little head to Helena's palm.

She told herself to remain calm. She wet a cloth with cold water and placed it on Marie's head. Marie didn't move the cloth, even though under normal circumstances she'd have swiped the object away in irritation. She seemed to lack the energy or care to do so, and this scared Helena more than the fever. She undressed the child and placed wet cloths under her arms to bring the fever down. She did this for two hours, wetting the cloths again every time they warmed up. She recalled the feverish stupor of the baron she'd administered aspirin to that very first week she had worked for Mr Karski. The fever had sent that grown man into a netherworld and she knew its effect on a small child would be far worse. Babies couldn't regulate their thermostats the way adults could, and a fever left untreated would cause irreparable damage to the blood vessels, organs and brain.

She removed the wet cloth from Marie's forehead only to find the skin underneath hotter than before. She wanted to weep. She ran downstairs and knocked on Mrs Bronowska's door to beg her to watch Marie while she went to fetch help. Her neighbour's footsteps shuffled up the hall, slower than usual. When she opened the door, Helena gasped.

'I feel like I'm on fire,' Mrs Bronowska said to Helena. Great rings of red circled her nose and eyes, and her cheeks flushed almost as red as Marie's.

'You have influenza,' Helena said. 'Go back to bed. I'll find help.' Helena stepped backwards, keen not to let Mrs Bronowska's breath fall on her. She knew what Marie had now and where she had likely contracted it. If Helena caught it as well, they'd all die. She washed her hands with carbolic soap and ran the soap around her mouth. Marie had probably given her influenza already, but it couldn't hurt to wash. She told Marie she'd be back as soon as she could and, as she left the apartment once more, she reached the doorway and heard Marie not cry, but speak.

'Mama,' she said.

Helena sighed. Had she heard her correctly? Yes, she was sure of it. The baby had never spoken before. Helena wiped a tear and walked back to the crib.

'That's me,' she said to her daughter. 'I promise I'll come back.' She begged God not to let Marie die while she was gone. If she did, Helena would collect Marie's little body and throw them both out their third-storey window.

She ran to the Golden Bear pharmacy and banged on the back door. When she heard Mr Panczow inside call out 'Go away!' she banged again. Finally he opened the door. The look on his face was a mixture of shock and delight. 'Helena,' he said. 'My wife is here.'

'Good,' Helena replied. 'I want to speak to her too.'

She moved past Mr Panczow into the pharmacy and walked towards the storage cupboard for the acids. He caught up to her and grabbed her arm. 'What do you think you are doing?'

Mrs Panczow came down the stairs and shrieked in horror. 'Get that whore out of here!'

'I don't have time to discuss this,' Helena said. 'My daughter has influenza and she'll die if I don't give her aspirin. I will take a sufficient amount, then I will leave.'

'You'll do no such thing!' Mrs Panczow cried.

'You would let my baby die, madam? If I don't give her aspirin, that'll happen. I'll pay,' she added. She had no money; she didn't know why she said that.

'I don't care about your bastard child,' Mrs Panczow said. 'One less urchin.'

Helena went to slap her, but Mr Panczow stepped in front of his wife. 'Careful, my darling,' he said. 'She said her baby has influenza. She likely has it as well. I say we let her take what she wants and leave before she infects us too.'

Helena offered Mr Panczow a grim smile of thanks at the gesture.

Mrs Panczow said nothing, so Helena went to the store cupboard and collected a syringe and five vials of aspirin already made up, leaving one in case a customer needed it in the morning. She walked past them to the back door and out into the night air, sprinting back to the tenement. She leapt over the cobblestones, ducking and weaving around the people walking down the laneways, holding onto the glass vials with a careful grip, hoping against hope that Marie remained alive: the difference between life and death for a baby with a fever could be minutes. She willed her legs to move faster. She hadn't eaten in two days and she felt like she might faint; burning white dots speckled her vision like stars.

She arrived at the tenement at last and ran up the stairs, wondering if she was about to have a heart attack. Reaching her floor, she ran inside the apartment; Marie made no sound. She raced to the crib. Marie's eyes were closed.

Helena heard herself whimper as she placed her ear to the baby's mouth and prayed. The faintest little whoosh of breath escaped. She picked Marie up and attempted to rouse her, rubbing her chest and pinching her legs and sitting her up on her lap. She drew a child's dose of aspirin into the syringe and injected it into Marie's mouth. She placed more wet cloths on Marie's forehead and rocked her gently on her knee. She let twenty minutes pass, then she touched the baby's head. It felt only as warm as her hand. She let out a cry of thanks. She walked downstairs and gave Mrs Bronowska one of the vials of aspirin, instructing her to take a spoonful every four hours. She returned upstairs and went to sleep, holding the baby in her arms.

She'd reduced the fever and Marie remained alive for now. But a high temperature was only one symptom of influenza. There were many others, and there was no cure. Marie's lungs filled with fluid and she developed an ugly hacking cough that brought tears to

Helena's eyes. Even worse was the sound of her rasped breathing, her effort to draw in every breath. Helena boiled water and placed a towel over Marie's head to give her lungs a steam bath, making her inhale the hot, moist air to break up the phlegm. Marie resisted; she cried and tried to push the towel away, but Helena apologised and told her it was necessary. It broke her heart to see her daughter in pain. She removed the towel and saw her little face, red and stained with tears. She hated herself.

She slept sitting up for ten nights in a row, her back against the cold brick wall, holding Marie to her chest and patting her body, listening to her wheeze and struggle, praying for her to make it until morning. Helena's spine curved and ached as she held the baby upright; her neck spasmed, but she refused to let Marie lie flat, lest she begin choking on the mucus that ravaged her lungs. Helena hallucinated from the tiredness, seeing spots and clowns in the apartment and a dancing bear that had once come to their village, whose handler had whipped and teased him to make him dance. On the eleventh day, after ten days of terror, Marie finally fell asleep on her own, breathing clearly, and Helena was able to put her down in her crib. Afterwards, Helena lay on her bed in a stupor, arms splayed outwards.

After a few hours of restless sleep, she woke and looked around the squalid apartment. A pot, two blankets, some clothes, one photograph and some kitchen scraps stared back at her: these were her only possessions. They lived on bones and gristle from the church, potato skins and whatever they could collect from begging. Marie wore no shoes because she owned none; she'd grown out of the other ones and Helena couldn't afford to buy her more. Helena checked Marie in her crib, then sat on the floor and wept.

It would always be like this.

The next twenty years of Marie's life stretched out before Helena. Even if they survived the famine and Helena found work, it would be as a laundress, cleaner or chambermaid; she possessed no qualifications to do anything else. No woman did. She would work fourteen hours a day, seven days per week, making only enough to cover rent and food. She'd procure used shoes and clothes for Marie by begging at the convents. If Marie survived to school age, she could attend until she was six or eight years old, but girls didn't receive education after that. Marie would start working at nine at the latest, perhaps joining Helena in the laundry, and Helena would try to keep Marie away from the prying eyes and hands of unscrupulous men. With any luck, Marie would charm and marry a man at sixteen or seventeen, a factory worker or a bell boy. He wouldn't possess wealth but hopefully some kindness. She'd have her first child before eighteen, with six or seven more before she was thirty.

Helena recalled the promise she'd made when giving birth to Marie, to spend her life protecting her. She'd break this vow every day.

She fell into another aching and agitated sleep that night, gaining no rest despite having been awake night and day for almost two weeks. She woke at dawn. Something that had occurred to her some weeks back now came into focus. Before it had seemed like an idle joke. She found a pen and paper from when she used to write to Dominik on the front and wrote a letter to the university in Krakow, the one Mr Karski had spoken of. She addressed it to their admissions department. She made perfunctory salutations and introductory remarks, then got straight to the point.

My name is Major Dominik Karski, she wrote. *Winner of the Vertuti Militari. I wish to study medicine at your university.*

40

THE EASIEST SACRIFICE

A reply arrived three weeks later. She'd taken Marie to line up for food scraps at the church – they always got more when the baby accompanied her – and had collected what gristle and bones they could until it started to rain. As Helena couldn't risk Marie falling ill again, they'd returned home. On the way back upstairs, she'd absent-mindedly checked her letterbox. A creamy white envelope lay inside, the crest of the university embossed on its right corner.

Helena lifted it from the letterbox in disbelief. She'd written the words in a fit of agitation, as an angry joke more than anything else, and had never expected a reply. She returned upstairs and put Marie down on the floor, rolling her the little wooden ball to play with, which Marie tried to catch between her fingers. Helena placed the bones in the pot and added water and potato skins to make a broth. As she stirred, she opened the envelope and read. The letter offered a full scholarship to study medicine at the university, the course Mr Karski had intended for his son, the one he'd told Helena about during his happy, demented ravings each day at sundown. The grant came with full board and a living stipend.

The offer astounded her. She smiled with surprise and delight, then remembered it was not for her, Helena Kolikov, the unskilled, dirt-poor mother of a bastard child; it was for Major Dominik

Karski, the Vertuti Militari recipient and war hero, a man she had buried in a graveyard in the northern corner of the city.

She heard the sound of a fist pounding on her front door. She found Mr Dubrowski, the agent for the landlord, standing there. He wore a stern look on his face. 'You are three weeks in arrears on your rent.'

'I can pay you tomorrow,' she lied. Marie gurgled behind her on the floor, still trying to catch the wooden ball in her hands. Helena stepped aside so Mr Dubrowski could see Marie, hoping that her cuteness and spirit might woo him into showing mercy.

He looked down at the baby, then back at Helena. 'Payment in full by the end of the day. I will return at six. I have a new family ready to move in. Pay me then, or I will personally throw you out into the street.' He made a swinging motion with both arms, as though demonstrating how he intended to carry out the act.

Helena stared at the letter from the Krakow University, then at Marie. She had no way to procure nine marks by six o'clock. She collected their belongings – their clothes, a few books and their singular cooking pot – and placed them in her suitcase, the same one she had brought from the country when she first arrived in Lwów. They would go to Krakow; they had nothing to lose. She expected the people at the university would ridicule her and kick her out, but perhaps before they did so, she could keep the ruse going for a day or two, long enough to collect the first monthly stipend cheque and wrangle some food or even living quarters for a time. Once discovered, she would try to find work as a housekeeper again; maybe she would have better luck in this new city, where people didn't call her a whore.

Marie wouldn't settle, so Helena read to her from a book of fairy-tales she'd found in a rubbish bin. As she read one story in particular, Marie looked up at her and smiled, her green eyes open and awake. Helena felt such joy at this response, the first evidence of happiness the child had shown in weeks, that she read the same fairytale again, then again. She reached the end for the fourth time, then told her daughter several important things about where they were going and why. She then instructed Marie: 'From now on, call me Papa.'

Her hands shook as she fetched Dominik's clothes from the wardrobe and put them on. She cut off her waist-length hair, chopping the plaited bundle that was tied with a ribbon at the nape of her neck, and smoothing down what remained with some grease from the stove. She placed the plait in a box to keep; she didn't know why. Finally, she placed Dominik's glasses over her eyes. She didn't need to wear glasses herself, and she knew she would develop a headache from staring into these lenses that had been fashioned to treat myopia. She gathered up Marie and her suitcase.

As they were leaving the apartment, she recalled that among the meagre belongings she had placed in the bag, she had enclosed a photograph of herself and Marie, the only one she possessed. Mr Karski had paid for them to have their picture taken together a few weeks before he died, proudly claiming that he wanted a portrait of his two beautiful girls. She retrieved the image and ran her hand over it. They had posed for it in a photographic studio a few blocks from the pharmacy, Marie sitting on her lap. The sweetness of the image struck her; it hailed from a time of innocence and joy. But it would pose a liability to them now if it remained in her possession, so Helena threw it into the smouldering embers of the stove before exiting the apartment for good.

As she walked to the train station carrying Marie in one arm and their suitcase in the other, she used the journey to gauge people's reactions to her manner of dress. An old woman squinted at her and a little boy pointed. She gasped and walked faster; she would need to improve. When she arrived at the train station, she checked her reflection in a bathroom mirror. What she saw discouraged her less than she'd expected. Her eyebrows marched across her face like two caterpillars; she had never plucked them into arches like women did these days and instead had left them in their natural state, thick and unruly. Her jawbone protruded more than most women's. She possessed a modicum of masculinity in her natural features. She made use of the dark hairs that grew across her top lip and down the sides of her face, which had always embarrassed her. The hairs by no means formed a beard, but if she took to them with a blunt razor, she could shape them into something like stubble.

They boarded the train to Krakow. The fare cost two marks, but Helena had none, so she hid in the vestibule while the conductor made his rounds. A man in a silk shirt reading a newspaper offered her some bread and sausage; Helena took it gratefully, sharing it between herself and Marie. For the next ten hours, as the train followed a line directly west, passing through towns she had heard of but never seen – Rzeszów, Dębica, Tarnów – she spent the time not looking out the window but staring into the carriage, watching every man who walked past, who sat in a nearby seat, who lit a cigarette by her window. She studied how they walked, how they stood, how they got on and off a train, how they spoke to the conductor. She compared this with her own movements and the movements of any women who crossed her path. The men walked with their shoulders pushed back, whereas women seemed more likely to hunch politely. Men coughed and blew their noses loudly; women covered their mouths when eating and performed ablutions daintily. Men splayed their knees out when seated and leaned on the furniture, while women reduced their limbs to as small a package as possible and sat perfectly still.

This was not true of all specimens of each sex, of course: certain women walked with a grand confidence and lazed on chairs, while some men excused themselves quietly after sneezing and kept to themselves. But for the purposes of her exercise, which was to categorise a credible set of behaviours she could later appropriate to pass herself off as a man, one general truth availed itself to her about the differences between men and women. While women took up as little space as they could in the world, men took up as much.

She had once met a woman who lived as a man, so she knew it could be done. It was a tradition in the faraway place her father had come from. Women with no male siblings or heirs who found themselves in possession of a family farm could apply to the village council to run the business themselves, to herd the sheep and goats, to grow the crops. Once granted permission, they would transform themselves into a man and live as one thereafter. It was easier that way – people trusted a man to run the business more than they trusted a woman – and so that's how it went. One of these men had visited her father once, on their farm. The sight had fascinated Helena as a twelve-year-old. It was only after the man had left that her father told her. That night, lying in bed, Helena had stared at the ceiling and tried to detect signs of womanhood in the burly individual who had stood in their farmhouse, who had helped chop wood with her father, who had herded their goats from one pen to another with detached efficiency. She had seen a woman nowhere, not in the man's movements, not in his speech. He had possessed a man's face, a man's jaw, a man's hair, and he had walked and talked as a man did, and she had not considered for a second that he had been anything other than an old farmer from the mountains. Finally, after many hours lying awake, Helena had realised how the person had deceived her.

People only saw what they wanted to see.

People didn't see what they were not looking for. Helena had not been looking for a woman masquerading as a man – why would she? The farmer from her father's hometown had walked like a man, dressed like a man, talked like a man, *was* a man.

Helena would pursue the same principles.

The train pulled up to Krakow station and she asked for directions to the university. She walked through the medieval city gates carrying their suitcase with one hand and Marie with the other, and arrived in the middle of the most beautiful city she had ever seen. Grand old buildings standing four and five storeys high surrounded a giant square on all four sides. An undercover market stood in the middle, where sellers and customers entered and exited carrying spices and fabrics. Marie wriggled to get down and they walked slowly to a fountain, Marie clasping Helena's finger. She placed one hand in the water and squealed with delight at its coldness.

Helena entered the university dressed as a man, and at the admissions office, in the deepest voice she could muster, announced her name to be Major Dominik Karski. The secretary gasped. Helena swallowed and prepared to be found out, but the secretary made the noise not at her, but her companion.

'She's so *dear*,' she gushed, peering sweetly at Marie, who responded appropriately with a smile as though she had been trained. 'May I?' She indicated that she wanted to hold Marie. Helena handed her over. The woman cooed and gurgled and spoke to Marie in a made-up language. Marie seemed to view her with polite bemusement, smiling a half-smile and offering her the handkerchief she had been clasping since they boarded the train from Lwów, as some sort of trade. 'Where is her mother?' the secretary asked.

'She passed away,' Helena replied, speaking as deeply as she could.

The secretary clasped a hand to her heart and sighed. 'What a tragedy. You poor man.' She looked at Helena, dressed as Dominik, with a mixture of grief and desire. Helena gazed at the floor and tried to contain her excitement; the woman accepted her as male. 'Will this little one be staying with you in your room, then?'

'Oh, I think yes,' Helena replied, realising she had not thought of this part. She had not even thought they would get as far as they already had. 'Will that be a problem? We have not looked for alternative accommodation.'

'It will be fine,' the secretary replied. 'We've never had a baby in the halls of residence, but if anyone has a problem, they will have to cross me.' She placed her hands on her hips, pretending to appear tough, and smiled widely. She showed them to their room, still cooing and gurgling at Marie and grinning with admiration at Dominik – that was, Helena dressed as Dominik – for the length of the journey from the admissions office, across the green, to the halls of residence.

Studies would begin the following week. The woman from the admissions office presented Helena with food vouchers that she could redeem at the buttery in the halls of residence for meals. The first instalment of her student stipend would not arrive until the first of the month, another week away. The woman from the admissions office had prostrated herself with apologies about this, but Helena did not care in the slightest: they had somewhere to stay and food to eat for a week, which far exceeded their previous situation.

With no other source of food, 'Dominik' and his daughter ate at the buttery for breakfast, lunch and supper. The place served mainly grey boiled beef and carrots steamed to the consistency of wet newspaper, but both tasted as rich and luxurious as roasted duck to Helena. At first she worried that someone would notice their seemingly constant dedication to the hall's culinary delights and grow suspicious. Few other students used the food hall. Term had not yet begun, so she guessed many students had not arrived at the university. Most days, she and Marie found themselves eating alone in the cavernous hall lined with wooden tables. One cook in particular, a plump woman of about fifty, would nod every time they entered and watch them as they ate. After three days she came up to them and Helena braced for her cover to be blown.

'What's her name?' The cook pointed at the baby, who was eating a bowl of potato soup. Marie had insisted on operating the spoon herself and had deposited soup across the table, the chair and her own person, all the while looking pleased with herself as though she had performed the job with the daintiness of a princess.

'Marie,' Helena, as Dominik, said.

The cook smiled. 'Where is her mother?'

Helena told the same story as before: mother dead, father widowed.

The cook stared at them both in horror and pity. She lifted her apron and gently wiped the soup from Marie's face. 'There's a good girl. You are very clever, eating on your own, helping your papa.' She laughed and cleaned the soup from the table.

Marie shook her head and said, 'Mama,' and continued eating her soup. Helena froze and waited for the cook to deduce the truth.

The cook paused and put her hand over her mouth. 'The poor darling,' she whispered to Helena. 'She misses her mama.'

Helena exhaled and could not believe her luck – even more so with what came next.

'Who will look after her while you study?'

'I had not thought of that yet,' Helena-as-Dominik replied. This was the truth. She had not contemplated anything past benefiting from free room and board for a week. She had not expected to keep up the ruse this long, to the point where she would actually study medicine at this hallowed institution; the thought was too ludicrous. She had not unpacked their suitcase, instead keeping it ready for a quick getaway when some chambermaid or staff member discovered them. 'I suppose she will come with me to lectures,' Helena-as-Dominik said.

'Nonsense. You need to pour all your focus into learning. A young man cannot be expected to study and look after a child. How ludicrous. I will do it!' the cook said. 'Please let it be me! I am only filling in for a friend this week – I don't normally work here. My working days are over. I am usually at home, a short walk from here. I could take Marie in, look after her while you study.'

'Oh, but I could not pay you much.'

'I do not expect much.' She rubbed Marie's cheek and made a cooing noise. She had stopped looking at Helena at all, directing all her attention to Marie, dabbing soup from her mouth, adjusting her chair so Marie sat closer to the table, praising her when she deposited a spoonful in her mouth and only spilled half the contents on the table, instead of all. Marie smiled and accepted the attention and praise happily. She took after her father in that respect; her real father, Major Karski, when not dumbfounded by grief, terror and darkness, had loved to have his back rubbed, his hair stroked, to receive pleasure openly. Helena had always smiled at this.

When they returned to their room, Helena sat Marie on the bed and held her shoulders. 'You must call me Papa now,' she told her. Marie looked at her curiously. Helena wondered how much she understood. She was sixteen months old now; what did she make of the person before her, dressed as a man, with a man's haircut?

Marie looked out the window and pointed at a finch perched on the branch of a birch tree. 'Bird,' she said. Helena swivelled Marie's little shoulders back to face her and pointed at her chest.

'Papa,' Helena said again, louder this time.

'Mama,' Marie said, equally loud. Helena walked to her new desk and sat, turning her back to the child. 'Mama, Mama,' Marie said. Helena ignored her daughter and pretended to write something on some paper the university had given her for her lectures.

'Mama,' Marie said again. This time Helena heard a strain in her voice as her daughter began to scream. 'Mama!'

Helena turned to her and snapped. 'Not Mama! I am *Papa* now.' Marie began to cry, sobbing large wet tears that rolled down her face onto her little neck. Helena winced. She wanted to go to her but she turned back to the desk and closed her eyes, trying to ignore the sobs coming from the bed.

'Mama, Mama, Mama,' her daughter cried, repeating the word over and over until eventually the individual words blurred and became one continuous one, 'Mamamamamamamamamamamama.' Her voice sounded lugubrious and thick with tears. Helena gritted her teeth and did not turn around, her heart breaking. After a minute or two, she heard Marie slump over onto the bed, lying down now with emotional exhaustion. She stopped speaking, and Helena wondered if perhaps she had cried herself to sleep. She was about to turn around when Marie spoke once more.

'Papa?' she said.

Helena's chest swelled with love and guilt. She turned around and embraced her daughter. Over the next days, the baby slipped up a few times, calling for her with 'Mama', but mostly absent-mindedly when she wanted to show her something in excitement: some ducks in a pond, a stick on the ground. Helena dished out the same punishment each time, ignoring her and depriving her of attention until she corrected herself. After a few days she never called her Mama again.

The speed with which Marie had learned the lie both astounded and saddened her. Her daughter's intelligence pleased her, especially her ability to follow this fundamental rule, but she had robbed some great innocence from her daughter.

By the time Marie reached two and then three years old, Helena knew her daughter had no obvious memory of what had occurred. She never referenced it or even alluded to it, never called her Mama by accident when distracted. Instead something else replaced these direct slips of the tongue, a general sort of unease that seemed always to sit inside the little girl. She would wake screaming in the night. When Dominik inquired after the nature of the nightmare, Marie could never explain what she had seen. She claimed repeatedly that there was a monster in the wardrobe, and when her father showed her the cupboard's contents and revealed nothing lived there but clothes, she would nod and not believe him.

In his first year of medical school, Dominik Karski achieved a rank of fifth in a class of one hundred and twenty students. In years two, three, four and five, he placed first.

By the end of the first year, in her actions, her words, her thoughts, Helena *was* Dominik Karski. She'd never thought of herself as being much of what the world defined as 'woman', anyway. It surprised her what went into creating femininity – the painted face, the coiffed hair, the bright clothes; it was a costume too.

She dabbled in early preparations of synthetic testosterone, adding calcium and phosphorous to her jawline. But as the men of the area possessed round, wide faces anyway, and her own strong jaw naturally ran square, Helena already met them halfway in this marker of manliness. And after a while she stopped taking the hormone, after reading of its propensity to encourage cancer. She wore a back brace always – for her scoliosis, she told people. In truth, her spine ran straight as an arrow, but the contraption bound her already small breasts and enhanced the barrel chest she naturally possessed. But with all her efforts to add maleness to her frame, she could have saved her energy.

In sixteen years, she'd had no real close calls. She could count the times on one hand that someone had looked at her strangely, and even if those people had some suspicion, they never expressed it aloud. The idea that Dr Karski was a woman wasn't ludicrous, because it didn't cross people's minds at all. People only saw what they wanted to see, and when they looked at Dominik Karski, they wanted to see a man who would save their lives, who cured their diseases, who donated handsomely to their church. Helena recalled the promise she had made to her daughter when she gave birth to her. She would always sacrifice herself for her daughter. She served the time easily; she regretted nothing. Living as a man for sixteen years had been a minuscule price to pay to spend each wonderful day of those years in the company of her daughter.

41

THE SECRETS HER FATHER KEPT

Lwów, August 31, 1939

Marie telephoned her father from the public box at the train station. 'I am in Lwów,' she told him, saying nothing more. She waited for him to reply, but heard only the sound of his breathing. 'Papa, are you there?' It felt strange, using 'Papa', knowing what she did, but what else could she say? 'Papa' was all she knew.

'I am here,' he said finally.

'Explain yourself,' she said. Again, he said nothing.

Marie hardly knew where to start. She found herself spluttering out the words in angry sobs. 'All these years . . . you have known where my mother is . . .' She looked down at the photo of her mother, which she cradled in her hand. 'You have kept her from me.'

Dominik sighed down the telephone line. 'Please understand, everything I did was for you.'

'I want to see my mother,' Marie said.

'That's not possible,' he replied quickly.

Marie gritted her teeth. 'I return from Lwów tonight. I will come to your house. If you are not there, prepared to explain everything, I will tell everyone your secret. I will tell the priest, your friend Dr Wolanski at the hospital, the newspaper—'

He interrupted her. 'Please don't do that, Marie. You will only put yourself in more danger.'

Marie sobbed desperate, angry tears. He seemed to listen to her crying and said nothing more.

'Be there,' she said, and hung up the telephone. She walked to her train. Where she had worried yesterday about the concerning crowd sizes and being able to board, she saw now she had been mistaken, not in her observation of people wanting to leave the city, but in the destination they might head towards. Those people clamouring yesterday had been wishing to board trains to the south-east, to friendlier countries like Romania or Bulgaria, or to the countryside. No one was stupid enough to be heading west, to Warsaw or Krakow, towards which the Germans were striding. In the end, she boarded her west-bound train with ease, finding the platform deserted and the carriage half-empty. The only people who joined her were nervous workers going as far as the neighbouring towns, or people rushing back to surrounding villages to be reunited with family, looking deranged with worry, biting their nails and gripping the armrests until their knuckles turned white. Marie gave these people only cursory glances, then turned back to her own concerns, staring out the window as the locomotive pulled out from the station. A sea of tenements and cracked buildings rushed by.

Her father wasn't a Stalinist agent or a devil worshipper, as she'd imagined when she'd first broken into his bedroom. He concealed a secret far worse than that. Anger boiled inside her; she felt like smashing the seat in front and screaming. She could scarcely believe what she had learned, the face that had stared back at her in the photograph. Now she went back over every conversation they'd had that summer and saw everything differently. When her father had told Marie she couldn't marry Ben, it came not from anger or bigotry, but a genuine knowledge of what being different did to a life. When he'd counselled her on the unlikelihood of women studying at university, it came not from an opinion of backwardness and prejudice, but from experience. Marie felt dismayed to realise she now knew a little of how the world worked. Women were excluded from the places they wanted to join.

She recalled something Mrs Bronowska had told her before she left, stuffing another biscuit in her mouth as she said it. 'Last time I saw you, you were such a skinny baby. Everyone was, the whole city was starving. But your mother was by far the skinniest. A walking skeleton. She gave you every scrap of food – she always went without. She let that man at the Golden Bear do horrible things to her to keep you alive.'

Marie reflected on how her father had no friends. She had teased him about it, but now she knew why. He could only preserve the lie if he never let anyone get too close. She realised now why he locked his door. Not to conceal the physical reality from her, but something far more primal. He locked it to seal himself away from a world where he existed in falsehood, to steal some moments for himself. He could only ever relax behind a locked door. He couldn't share his real self with anyone, not even his daughter. How lonely it must have been, always answering to someone else's name.

As the train stopped at Rzeszów, Marie realised she had been sitting there, staring into space, for four hours. She felt wetness on her cheeks; she'd been crying and hadn't noticed. The anger had long seeped from her and now all she felt was sadness. She wept the rest of the journey home.

She arrived back in Krakow and went straight to her father's house, letting herself in.

He wasn't there.

She walked through every room, calling his name. She checked his wardrobe, after breaking into his bedroom once more. It didn't matter now, but she found herself taking the lock apart gently, not so he wouldn't find out, but to take care of his things, to disturb these objects as little as possible. Once inside, she found some clothes missing. She gently sifted through his drawers, then replaced things as neatly as before. Both back braces were gone. She returned to the sunroom and sat in his armchair in the fading light, staring at the wall. She waited an hour, knowing it was futile, and finally left.

She walked back to Kazimierz. On the way there she ran into Dr Wolanski walking down Grodzka Street. He bounded over to her. 'How was your trip to Lwów, young lady?' he asked. 'What did you find?' His face contorted with glee and anticipation, and he seemed to bounce with excitement.

This was the moment; her father would now pay for his crimes. She arranged the words in her head and opened her mouth to speak. 'I found nothing,' she said.

Dr Wolanski slumped and he looked flummoxed with disappointment. 'Tell me if you ever do find anything,' he said.

She farewelled him and walked on, past the church where Father Wiktor would be preparing for mass. As indiscreet a man as they came: no one went to confession unless to tell him sins they wanted the town to know. Here was another chance to reveal her father. But she did not enter to speak to him; instead she kept walking. She now knew, of the secrets her father kept, she would never tell anyone.

Krakow, September 1, 1939

Marie received a knock at her door the next morning. She opened it to find Lolek standing there and she invited him in. Lolek stepped inside but remained in the hallway, holding the front door open with his hand. He shook his head. 'I won't stay. Here are two passports, one for you, one for Ben. You must leave Krakow today.' Despite the comical words that were leaving his mouth, he wore a serious expression. 'You're going to Australia. It's a country in the Southern Hemisphere. Heard of it?'

Marie looked down. In his hands lay two pieces of paper, written in a language she couldn't read but recognised as English. 'Australia, yes. I know it.' She stared at him. 'My friend. What's going on?'

'War is here. Your father wants you out of Poland. This is your way out.'

Marie's mind whirred. 'Where is he? I need to see him.' She moved into the living room, to call her father.

Lolek didn't follow her in. 'You can't telephone him,' he called. 'He's joined his battalion.'

Marie walked back to him. 'But I must speak with him!' Her voice strained; she felt desperate and wretched. She did not wish to reveal him now; all she wanted was to see him. Lolek said nothing. She exhaled. 'What does he expect? That I'll pack a suitcase and leave the country without saying goodbye?'

Lolek's face remained solemn. 'Yes, that exactly. And I urge you to leave now. Germany has invaded. It may already be too late.' A crashing sound rose up from the courtyard. Lolek jumped and looked skywards, thinking it a bomb dropping, but Marie recognised the sound: a cat had upended a rubbish bin.

Marie shook her head. 'We've been listening to the radio. It says Poland has been achieving one victory after the other, that the Germans have not penetrated our borders. For goodness sake, the hejnał is still playing in the square, every hour.'

'The radio is lying,' he said plainly. 'They don't want a panic. Did you hear the crash towards the square this morning?'

Marie shrugged. 'The wireless reported an explosion in the bakery. A fire from an electricity fault.'

'Another lie. That wasn't some little bread shop blaze. The Germans made a direct hit on the Sisters of Mercy building in Warszawska Street.'

Marie shuddered. 'My God.' That was her convent school. She listened in horror as he told her the rest, shaking her head, not wanting to believe it. 'The Germans have also bombed the airstrip just outside of town, taking out one of the only planes guarding Krakow. The first captain of the local air force is already dead, shot down in a dogfight this morning about a kilometre from here. They've also blown up the army buildings along Rakowicka Street, and they have bombed the railway station. Trains are still running, but not for long. It will take their planes a few hours to fly to Germany, refuel and come back. That is why you must leave now. There might not be a train station by the end of today.'

Marie felt her head spinning; she needed to sit down. 'I won't do it.' She gestured towards the documents. 'Thank you for going to this trouble, but I won't leave Poland.' She heard the strident note rising in her voice.

'If you won't do it for yourself, do it for Ben,' Lolek said. 'Jewish people may have no future in Poland.'

Marie stared at him.

He leaned towards her. 'Your death is a possibility, but his is a certainty. You can pass as a gentile – he won't. It's that simple. Make your father happy by removing yourself from danger, and make yourself happy by removing your husband. This is your chance to save Ben's life.'

She swallowed. Mrs Kranz, their next-door neighbour, arrived home from the market, carrying enough tins of beef to last her several weeks. She greeted Marie good day and craned her neck to listen to the conversation. Marie nodded to her politely and waited for her to walk inside. 'But my father. He's not coming with us?'

'It's just you two, on your own. Your father is going to stay and fight.'

She could not fathom it. 'I need to speak to my father,' she whispered.

Lolek shrugged. 'You will write to him.'

'Ben will take some convincing. He won't leave easily.'

'He will, because you'll tell him he's doing it to save your life. Rather than the other way around.' Lolek handed her the passports. 'Australia is a colony of the British Empire. They speak English there. A very strange language. A ludicrous concoction of Norman French, German, Gaelic, Celtic, Viking. A mess of spelling variations, containing no logic. Do you speak any?'

'*How do you do, Mickey Mouse? May I have one Coca-Cola?*' she said in her best English. She smiled proudly.

Lolek raised an eyebrow. 'It's a start. Try to learn more, in case someone stops you.'

Marie scowled. 'Who will stop us?'

He touched her arm. 'Take the train to Lwów. Cross into Romania – they like Polish people there. Journey overland to Greece or Italy, then by boat to Port Said. You will find passage to Australia there.' He took an envelope from his coat and gave it to her. She went to open it, but he held her hand. 'Open it later.' She nodded and looked down at the envelope. 'By the way. Happy birthday, Marie.'

She looked up. 'I'm sorry?'

'Today is the first of September. It's your birthday, yes?'

'Oh.' In the chaos of the morning she had neglected to even notice. 'Yes. I turn eighteen today.'

'My regards.' He touched her shoulder and smiled warmly.

'Will I ever see you again, Lolek?'

'I think no.' His face fell. 'But you will always be here, in my heart. Be not afraid. I feel you will survive what's coming. Goodbye, Marie.'

In the end, Ben took no convincing at all. Marie showed him the travel documents and told him how preposterous the scheme sounded. He agreed with her, then told her they would leave Poland at once. Marie shook her head and laughed at him; how could he agree to such a plan so easily? Ben shrugged and explained plainly. 'Your father visited me yesterday, while you were gone. He made me promise that if ever he asked me to leave the city with you, I had to agree, no questions asked. He told me he would only ask me to do this if he thought your life was in danger.'

Ben did insist on telephoning his mother first. Marie listened as he told her the news. She heard Rachel Rosen gasp down the telephone line and pause. She considered for a moment that her mother-in-law would tell her son not to go.

'You must go to Australia,' Ben's mother said finally. 'You have responsibilities now, to your wife.'

Ben agreed, but asked, 'Could you come with us?'

'I have some business to tie up first,' she said brightly. 'Afterwards, I'll be right behind you.' The reply unsettled Marie; she wondered how truthful Rachel was being.

'I love you, Mama,' Ben said into the telephone.

They packed their suitcases quickly and walked to the train station. They visited Dominik's house on the way, at Marie's insistence. It wasn't that she didn't trust Lolek when he said Dominik had already left, but rather that, if by some fluke of luck or change of plan he was there, she wanted to check, just in case. As it was, they found the house empty. The lights were off, but Marie still went inside and looked in every room. Then time was running out to catch the day's only departure east so she reluctantly descended the stairs and joined Ben outside.

On the way, they passed Mrs Nowak, Marie's old neighbour, stacking her sandbags out the front of her house as usual. She nodded a greeting to Marie as she passed; perhaps tonight her barricade would come in useful. The woman had been claiming for three years that Germany would invade and everyone had called her crazy. Now, as people scurried about with shovels and buckets of water, frantically digging trenches and sewing name labels into

413

their children's clothing to identify them in the event their little bodies became bomb-charred, Mrs Nowak looked like the only sane person in town.

Marie could feel sweat on the back of her neck as they crossed the market square. The cafes and bars lay empty. A mood had settled upon its inhabitants – a stiffness and weariness had overcome everyone. The very buildings themselves stood brittle and empty, as though bracing for impact. The few people who remained looked right and left, running their eyes over others in the square, including Marie and Ben. They discussed the morning's events nervously, with devastated faces. The wind blew like a hot breath; late summer had brought forth a cloudless day, clear but hazy, a baking heat. The sun sat low in the sky, seared red; everyone pointed and remarked on it. Marie would remember forever the sight of the sun on September 1, 1939, a bloodied orb that squatted over Krakow.

They left the square and walked up Warszawska Street. Marie stared at what had become of the Sisters of Mercy building: a crater now took up residence where her convent school once stood. The classroom where she'd taken mathematics was now a pile of bricks and rubble. The force of the bomb had blown out all the glass from the windows; only rectangular shells of concrete remained, and a dozen gaping holes had appeared in the facade, looking like a group of disembodied mouths, all screaming at once. She found Sister Paulina weeping out the front. The nuns had all survived the blast, she told Marie, a small gift from God. She hoped the Lord's generosity would continue in the days to come. She wished Marie good luck and pressed her to hurry if she wanted to catch a train.

They arrived at the railway station and Marie understood what she meant. Mayhem greeted them. Marie had stood in that very place barely a day earlier; now the landscape had transformed.

Where a polite brick building had once stood, piles of rubble and twisted metal had taken its place. The Germans had bombed the entrance so they had to climb over hills of broken tiles and debris to enter. Astonishingly, the trains still ran; the Germans had largely missed the tracks, with only the station house suffering a direct hit. People rushed back and forth, hauling suitcases and children, boarding trains and shouting. Ben hurried to what remained of the ticket office and purchased two fares to Lwów. Marie could only imagine what they would find there now. If they made it that far, they would then change trains and make their way down to Bucharest.

As Ben retrieved twenty zloty to pay for their tickets, Marie shuddered at how much money they would need for their journey. With train trips across multiple countries, it might take weeks to cross Europe. Then they would need to purchase passage to Australia, a six-week journey by ship. The man selling the tickets advised them that the train east would depart in five minutes; they had no time to do anything but board it.

They found a compartment with empty seats and sat down. Ben busied himself looking at a map of Galicia Lolek had given them. It was a tourist's atlas for a driving holiday, containing illustrations of scenic interest points. Marie mentioned to Ben about the cash they would need. Ben swallowed. They quietly looked through their purses and coats to gather up every coin and note they could find. They counted up their money: a little over four hundred zloty. They might survive a month in Poland on that amount. Marie stared out the window in despair. 'How could we have been so stupid?'

They discussed what to do. They could return to Krakow and close their bank accounts. But it was Friday afternoon. The banks would be shut by the time they returned to the city and wouldn't open again until Monday. If they opened again at all.

Marie stiffened. 'The envelope!' She'd forgotten about it. She dug it from her bag and opened it. She had to stop herself from gasping. Inside lay a brick-shaped wad of money in a currency she'd never seen before. She turned towards the window to conceal it from the compartment's other inhabitants and removed one of the notes to read its inscription. She recognised enough words to see it came from the Bank of England, the denomination twenty. She replaced the note in the envelope and flicked the money with her thumb to calculate the total. She counted one hundred notes, and the same again when she counted a second time. The little envelope held £2000. Marie blinked. It was enough money to live off in Poland for five, maybe ten years.

'Where did Lolek get this money from?' Ben asked in a whisper. She was about to reply but then found she didn't need to. The money came not from Lolek, but her father. One might receive £2000 from the sale of an apartment in the richest corner of Main Square.

Marie dropped her head onto Ben's shoulder, turned her nose to his chest and sobbed quietly. He stroked her hair and wiped her eyes.

Her taste for exposing her father had long evaporated. The last thing she wanted was to denounce her parent. All she wanted now was to see him, to talk. So much remained to say. 'What if I never see him again?' she asked Ben, between gentle sobs.

Her husband said nothing for a time, then finally answered, 'You will.'

No matter how much she wished differently, the train continued on its course east, away from Krakow. It held a different group of passengers than it was likely used to. Marie had peered into each compartment as they'd walked along the corridor that ran down the carriage's side to find empty seats. Usually at this time of year, excited children and their work-wearied parents would have filled a train such as this, the passengers setting off for pleasure by the lake shores, for hiking and summer sports. But no one was travelling on holiday; instead all the occupants were residents of the towns and cities east of Krakow, frantically trying to outrun the Germans. No one was dressed in holiday clothes, no one wore a linen suit or a striped sundress and sandals. They clothed themselves for the workday, in grey flannel suits and viscose dresses, felt hats, leather shoes. People had readied themselves for what was to come; they just wanted the next thing to happen now. They'd raged and toiled over the last year, living proudly in denial; now they accepted what would arrive and grew impatient for it to properly start – for the Germans to reach their towns. Some had been through this before, and they scarcely believed it could happen again so soon – here came another fight. Once again Poland would not be the star of the show, not even a competitor, instead forced to host a contest between uninvited guests.

Two men who sat in the corner of their compartment possessed the clear look of highland shepherds, off to join some rural regiment or post. They both wore their hair long enough to necessitate tucking it behind their ears; the army barber had not got to them in time. They appeared awkward out of their traditional clothes; one kept adjusting the shoulders of his military uniform. They both grasped their army-issued rifles like they'd never held them before. One held his gun upright like a shepherd's crook. They spoke softly to each other about their herds; this was a most inconvenient time to be donning a uniform, and an apprentice not twelve years old seemed to be watching their sheep for them. They'd broken with a thousand-year tradition to come down from the mountain before the proper time, to collect their uniforms and take up arms. Their faces looked forlorn as they studied their rifles with awe and fear. Who knew what fate awaited when the Third Reich reached their farmhouses.

The train stopped at Wieliczka and more people got on. A woman walked down the corridor and entered their compartment, standing by the seat across from them. 'May I sit here?' she asked.

Marie nodded, shifting her bag to the floor, then resumed staring out the window. The yellow fields of oats rushed by, ready for harvest. Someone would need to harvest them soon or else they would spoil. She glanced at the woman again. Something about her voice unnerved Marie. The woman wore a boxy, unfashionable dress and looked uncomfortable wearing it. She kept her hair short, in a man's style. She wore lipstick, but it ran a little crooked around her mouth, like a child had put it there. The dress hung limp across a strong flat frame. The woman kept adjusting it like it was something she was unused to wearing. She fidgeted with the armholes, moving them down and up again, and tugged at the neckline several times. Tan lines betrayed that these were not clothes she usually wore; darker skin graced her neck, while that on her chest was white.

What had once existed as a fuzzy and imprecise thought in Marie's brain now came into stinging focus. She had recently seen her mother for the first time in a photograph, and now she looked upon the flesh-and-blood version in this train carriage.

'Are you travelling to Australia?' the woman asked. Marie forced herself to nod, and almost didn't manage the feat. The muscles in her neck felt too stiff to function. 'When you get there, consider the Melbourne university. They have an excellent school of medicine. They accept female students.'

Marie stared at her and said nothing.

'My name is Helena Kolikov,' the woman said.

'Marie Rosen,' Marie said. They shook hands. Marie knew the hands well. They were long and fine-boned. She'd always thought her father had excellent hands, delicate and dexterous. Now for the first time she saw how beautiful they were too, attached to the female body. They possessed a length and a size slightly larger than her own hands, but still delicate. 'Refined' seemed the best way to describe them.

Helena held out her hand to Ben. 'Helena Kolikov.'

Ben stared at her, then kissed her hand, in the Polish way of a younger man greeting a woman his senior. 'Benjamin Rosen.' His voice croaked in shocked awe.

Marie peered around the compartment to see if anyone was watching them, if anyone suspected that something monumental was occurring, but everyone seemed caught up in their own affairs. No one paid any attention to Marie and Ben, or the woman sitting opposite them.

'Do you know the story of the Glass Mountain?' Marie asked.

Helena nodded. 'It's a fairytale. I used to read it to my daughter when she was small. It was her favourite.'

There were so many things Marie wanted to say, she did not know where to start, or how much time she had to say them. She brushed her hair from her face and chewed her lip. She found herself scowling, unable to speak. But she didn't need to, for the woman did.

'You look sad – why?' Helena said to her.

'I didn't say farewell to my father. We're going away and I was unable to see him before we left. I wanted to tell him many things.'

Helena nodded. 'What did you want to tell him?'

Marie felt tears on her cheeks. 'I never told him how much I admired him. I wanted to be a doctor, always. I never told him why but it was because I wanted to be like him. I thought this for years and never said it. All this time, I didn't realise what he'd endured—' She heard her voice breaking and shook her head. 'I never told him how much I loved him.'

Helena looked at her and spoke in a soft voice. 'He knew.'

Marie heard herself sob. She commanded herself to calm down; she did not want to draw attention to herself, to make people look over. 'May I ask a question?' She didn't wait for a reply before speaking again. 'My father came home every night at six o'clock and prepared my dinner. Even when I was seventeen and could take care of myself. He washed my clothes, darned my socks, possessed an obsession with my nutrition. Why did he do it?'

Helena shook her head. 'I can only talk of my own madness when my child was born. She was a bundle of beauty, such as I had never known. I almost lost her when giving birth. My world changed after that point; everything was for her then.' She shrugged. 'Perhaps he always wanted you to know he was there. In case you needed anything. Perhaps his life meant nothing without you being safe and happy.'

Marie looked out the window.

'Do you know what I love most about my daughter?' Helena said. 'Her resilience. She'd never give up. It is the mark of true intelligence. I always did well at my studies, but from early on I discovered my daughter was smarter than me. It was the greatest joy of my life to know this. From the moment she was born, there was no cell that mattered to me outside her own skin. Stupid, really. For a long time, I thought the best way to protect her was to keep her close. I know now that the best thing is to set her free and watch her fly. I also wanted to keep her near me for selfish reasons. I wanted to be with her every day. You see, she's brought my life such joy.' She swallowed and cleared her throat, and didn't speak for a long time. 'May you one day know the same joy,' she added.

Marie turned back to Helena and took a deep breath. She recalled the memory she had cherished for as long as she could remember, of her mother reading to her. 'My mother said something to me the last time I saw her. It haunts me still and I wish to God I could remember what she said. I've been trying to remember for sixteen years.'

Helena coughed. 'You likely give it more importance, more gravitas than it deserves. I mentioned the madness of parents. It was likely a poor and rushed speech that has calcified in your mind. But I'm guessing she might've said something like: "You mean more to me than the sun rising. I don't want to exist on an earth without you in it. I live for you only. I will spend my life making you safe. I must go now, but I will always be with you. From now on, call me Papa." Something foolish like that.'

Marie did everything she could to hold back her sobs. She spoke in a low voice. 'I always thought my mother abandoned me.'

'She did not. She's always been here.' Helena smiled broadly.

Marie fought back more tears. A guard wandered through the carriage and announced the next station.

'I shall alight here,' Helena said.

Marie shook her head, feeling desperate. 'Could you not stay a while longer?'

'With regret, I must leave. Before I do, I shall say happy birthday.' She whispered. 'I have some gifts for you back at the house, a hat and some books you might like, but I did not bring them, for I did not want to burden you with carrying them on your journey. Forgive me.'

Marie laughed through her tears. 'You are forgiven.'

'I have brought one small gift, however, which I shall leave for you.' She turned to Ben. 'Go, young man,' she said to him. 'Make generations. Give Dominik some grandchildren.' She winked.

He blushed and nodded. 'Goodbye, Helena. Thank you.'

'Goodbye, Marie,' she said. She reached across and squeezed her daughter's hand.

'Goodbye,' Marie replied, choking on her tears.

As Helena walked past the two shepherds, she touched one on the shoulder. 'God bless you,' she said to them both. 'Poland thanks you for your service.'

'Thank you, Aunty,' the closest one said, employing the term of respect for a female elder. They turned back to their rifles.

The train screeched gently to a halt at the station. They watched as Helena exited the carriage and walked to the other side of the platform to wait for the next train back to Krakow. The train pulled away.

Marie sobbed, realising she might never see Helena again, but then she turned around and their eyes met. Her mother watched her and didn't break her gaze until the train had travelled so far that it tore the sight away.

Marie finally looked away long after her mother had vanished from view. She buried her head into Ben's chest.

'Look, Marie,' Ben said. She lifted her head. Ben pointed to the seat opposite, where her mother had sat. A small jewellery box of faded maroon lay on the seat. Marie snatched it up; the velvet cover felt cool in her hands. She didn't need to open it. She knew what lay inside.

ACKNOWLEDGEMENTS

To Zbigniew Borzdynski. You read this book several times and provided exemplary suggestions. The Polish have a reputation for showing extraordinary hospitality to strangers. You displayed this, and I am forever grateful. *Dziękuję bardzo*.

To Irena Borzdynska. Thank you for suggesting many of the Polish names that now feature in these pages and for patiently teaching me Polish over many weeks and months.

Thank you to Monika Dzierba, my first Polish teacher, and thank you to the students of the Polish Language School 4 Today in Melbourne for sharing many wonderful evenings learning this beautifully challenging language.

To Meital Miselevich, thank you for reading this book and providing invaluable feedback, including checking the Talmud in its original Hebrew.

To Henry Buch. You escorted me around the Jewish Holocaust Centre in Elsternwick. Hearing your story has stuck with me ever since. Thank you for sharing.

Thank you, Beverley Cousins, for shaping and tightening this novel. I could not have felt more delighted when reading your suggestions.

To Amanda Martin. Thank you for sharpening every page, steering my voice, and going to extraordinary lengths to include everything I wanted to say. To Penelope Goodes, thanks for doing a brilliant job checking up on a complex time in history.

As always, thank you to Jeanne Ryckmans for championing my work and providing invaluable guidance.

To Madeline Burns and Charlotte Laurence, thanks for reading this book and showing your enthusiasm and encouragement, and Lucy McGinley for once again making killer suggestions to sharpen the story. Thanks Dominic Givney and Jane Givney for bringing realism to the medical scenes and truth to the opening chapter, and to Eloise Givney for providing thoughtful feedback on the issues raised in this book. And to all three of you for keeping me and Fin company at some crucial moments. To David Givney, thanks for calling me every week and continuing to encourage my career.

To Margaret and Laurie O'Donnell, thanks for welcoming me into your home and caring so beautifully for your grandson. You helped me to complete the edit on this book.

To Finley, I tried within these pages to capture the feeling of bearing a child and fell gloriously short: no words can replicate this love.

And to my husband, David, thank you for coming with me to Poland, for reading this book countless times and with unfailing energy, for providing invaluable feedback, and for being by my side as I wrote the first line and the last.

JANE IN LOVE
Rachel Givney

At age twenty-eight, Jane Austen should be seeking a suitable husband, but all she wants to do is write. She is forced to take extreme measures in her quest to find true love – which lands her in the most extraordinary of circumstances.

Magically, she finds herself in modern-day England, where horseless steel carriages line the streets and people wear very little clothing. She forms a new best friend in fading film star Sofia Wentworth, and a genuine love interest in Sofia's brother Fred, who has the audacity to be handsome, clever and kind-hearted.

She is also delighted to discover that she is now a famous writer, a published author of six novels and beloved around the globe. But as Jane's romance with Fred blossoms, her presence in the literary world starts to waver. She must find a way to stop herself disappearing from history before it's too late.

A modern-day reimagining of the life of one of the world's most celebrated writers, this wonderfully witty romantic comedy offers a new side to Jane's story, which sees her having to choose between true love in the present and her career as a writer in the past.

'Artfully written and engaging, *Jane in Love* is a lively
effusion of wit and humour.'
Graeme Simsion

'*Jane in Love* is pure romp with the playful spirit of fanfic. Rachel Givney is a screenwriter with a highly developed understanding of plot structure and narrative drive, and there are some hilarious scenes as Jane comes to terms with electricity, internet technology, and flush toilets.'
The Age